John Rolfe of Virginia

James H. Tormey

Published in the United States by
Beckham Publications Group, Inc.
PO Box 4066, Silver Spring, MD 20914
ISBN: 0-931761-35-2
10987654321

John Rolfe of Virginia

James Tormey

THE **Beckham**
PUBLICATIONS GROUP, INC.
Silver Spring

PREFACE

It has been said that Captain John Smith saved the Virginia colony. A more accurate statement might be that he kept Virginia alive during the "starving time" of 1608-1609. It was John Rolfe, however, who saved Virginia. His development of Virginia tobacco gave the colony economic stability—eliminating the need for gold and other treasures that were never found. Rolfe's marriage to Pocahontas brought the Powhatan War to an end and ushered in a period of growth for the colony. While many books have been written about Pocahontas, none has viewed events through the eyes of Rolfe. He was, above all, a man who had come across the Atlantic to stay—a man with that incredibly optimistic and brave group of settlers who planted the seeds of a new nation in a land of great promise.

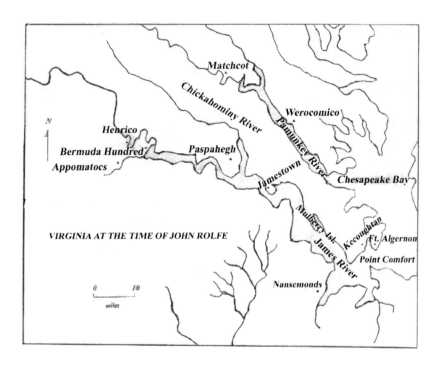

Matchcot

Chickahominy River

Werocomico

Pamunkey River

Henrico

Bermuda Hundred
Appomatocs

Paspahegh

Jamestown

Chesapeake Bay

VIRGINIA AT THE TIME OF JOHN ROLFE

Mulberry Isl.

Kecoughtan

Ft. Algernon

James River

Point Comfort

Nansemonds

0   10
miles

N

January 1, 1622

My Dear Son Thomas,

I pray that this letter finds you well and that God will bring you his richest blessing in the year ahead. It pains me that we should be separated, first because of the joy I would have in your company and second because, although you are but six years of age, you are not here in Virginia with me to learn first hand the story of your heritage. But England is the best place, both for your education and your health, until you are old enough to make the journey here.

Unfortunately, I am far from well. The Almighty brought me through a maze of dangers and hardships to the present day. Now, however, I am in the grip of a fever that rarely leaves me. Having seen the effects of sickness on my friends and neighbors here in Virginia, I find it only prudent to have drawn my last will and testament. With that act accomplished, I undertake to relate my Virginia experience including the story of your mother Pocahontas and myself.

You are unique among Englishmen. There is none other having an English father and a mother who was an Indian princess. I would call her Rebecca, her Christian name, but the world has known her as Pocahontas and so I expect she shall remain to the world. That she should be taken from you and me is the saddest part of this story. But I thank God that she survives in you.

If it is not God's will that you and I should meet again in this life, I urge you not to fail to come to Virginia when you reach manhood. Not because your great uncle Opechancanough, now king of the Powhatans, has said the son of Pocahontas should be the king of Virginia. That is just a ruse by which that old fox would see our lands returned to Indian control. You should come because England is being reborn here. It is a difficult birth and not yet accomplished but gives promise of passing the best of our English heritage to men and women not encumbered by an aristocracy.

There is danger here, of course. One of the purposes of giving you this relation of my experience is to alert you to those dangers. But I am confident that you, being of the lineage of Powhatan and Pocahontas, besides having my example of what can be accomplished here, will not shrink from the opportunity.

Until we meet again, whether on earth or in heaven, I leave you in the care of my brother Henry. He may find portions of this account to be beyond your comprehension at this time and will keep them for you. I likewise entrust you both to the care and keeping of the merciful God who watches over us all.

Your most devoted and affectionate father,

John Rolfe

~1~

I had never thought that our new life would be jeopardized by a storm. Storms could do great damage to a farmer's crops, as I well knew from my life in Norfolk before the voyage. But I had no real experience of the sea and I had regarded time aboard ship as a period that might be uncomfortable but would surely end with us successfully reaching Virginia. After all, the captain of our ship, the *Seaventure,* was Christopher Newport, one of the great sailors of our time, who had taken the original Virginia expedition to Jamestown and had made two successful crossings since to re-supply them.

My mind was more filled with thoughts of my wife Sarah who accompanied me than of any storm. Sarah had not wanted to go to Virginia. We had a comfortable life on the large farm that our family had owned for generations. My father had died and I was, at twenty-four, the eldest son. Why exchange that for the hardship of carving a farm out of what she thought of as a wilderness in Virginia? Besides, she was with child and the uncertainty of giving birth in a place unknown to her was not reassuring.

To Sarah's everlasting credit, she had never expressed any sort of doubt or reservation about our venture after we sailed from Plymouth. She had entreated me earnestly on the night before our departure to remain in England but once aboard the *Seaventure* she was as committed as any adventurer in the fleet. Though she was silent, I was aware of what had been her reservations and they occupied my mind a great deal. I suppose that I rationalized that our child would not be born until well after the completion of our crossing which at the most would take sixty days from our departure in June.

Partly out of consideration for Sarah's health I had subscribed to the mess of Admiral Sir George Somers. Sharing the table of the admiral afforded better fare that would not have to be prepared along with the food of the other passengers. We were thereby introduced to Master and Mistress Horton who also shared in the Admiral's mess. Though older than us, I being twenty-four at the time, we had in common his interest in farming. She was sympathetic to Sarah who was beginning a new life far from England.

If I had been asked what concerned me most besides the welfare of my wife as we began our adventure I suppose I would have answered the threat of Spanish opposition to an English colony. Surely the leaders of the Virginia Company in London had taken this into consideration for our fleet consisted of no less than eight vessels and the *Seaventure* was even towing a pinnace behind us. Also reassuring was the presence on board of Sir Thomas Gates, the new governor of the colony. He was a seasoned soldier who had recently served with His Majesty's army in the Netherlands.

A lesser concern was the threat that the native population of Virginia might rise up against us. I thought, however, that the same soldiers in the fleet who would protect us against possible Spanish opposition would also protect us from the Indians. Moreover, attempts to win over the Indians were proving successful. Were there not two Indian boys, Namontack and Machumps, aboard our ship who were returning from a visit to England? Surely these lads would harm no one.

How difficult it is in this life to judge which tides will befriend us and which will sweep us away. As we approached the end, or what I believed to be the end, of our sea voyage my earlier misgivings about Sarah's health and happiness were largely behind me. Concerns for the Spanish or for Indians were likewise receding. Our only concern for the sea seemed to be the need to endure a few more days of discomfort from our cramped accommodations aboard ship. Or so I thought.

Captain Newport and Sir George Somers were accustomed to discussing the progress of the voyage at table. Although both men were seafarers, they made an interesting contrast: Newport had a weathered appearance while Somers had the look of a courtier. The rest of us were naturally most attentive because, although the wind and weather had been favorable, we were becoming impatient to reach Virginia. From the conversation we understood that their intention was to sail south until reaching the 27th degree of latitude after which our course would be changed to sail in a northwesterly direction to Virginia.

As it happened, we reached our southern limit on July 23rd, a Sunday. After the Church service that had been conducted by Reverend Bucke on deck in the warm sunshine, Sir George Somers announced to those assembled that we would be changing our course and that we should reach the coast of Virginia within seven or eight days. The passengers greeted this news with cheers and applause that seemed to please Sir George. Orders were then given to change course and the sailors climbed to the rigging to adjust the sails.

The customary cannon shot from the *Seaventure* to announce our change was even greeted by cheers on this occasion as we all anticipated beginning the last phase of our ocean voyage. Sir Thomas Gates, designated to be our governor, observed these actions. Somers and Newport were, after all, responsible for transporting us to Virginia. Sarah and I felt drawn to Sir Thomas. Sarah remarked that he resembled her father while I believed his benign appearance belied great reserves of strength.

In the changing of course we sailed close to several ships in our fleet. The others could be seen in the distance changing their course to parallel ours. The *Diamond* and the *Falcon* were close enough for us to hail. There was much waving, with passengers crowding the rail trying to shout to friends aboard another ship. It seemed more like a holiday outing than a journey almost two months old.

We awoke the following morning to a howling wind. There had been no sound like it during all the time we had been at sea. I dressed and made my way on deck where I found that, in addition to the wind, we were sailing in darkness although the sun should have made its way over the horizon long before. Thick clouds filled the sky such that I could not see more than half way up the mainmast. Without the faintest indication of

3

where the sun stood in the sky I found I had no sense of direction. From our course change of the previous day I knew the sun should have been on my right but, though I looked carefully, I could not find it.

I returned to find Sarah and advise her to wear a cloak because it had begun to rain. When we made our way on deck en route to the captain's cabin I noticed that the wind had increased; it was fairly shrieking. We made our way across the deck as quickly as we could to the shelter of the cabin where coffee and toast were waiting for us. The Hortons did not appear that morning and the only person we saw in the cabin other than the steward was Captain Newport who entered briefly. Seeing us, he warned that we were in for some "heavy weather" and that we should remain below decks.

If we needed more than the warning from Captain Newport to convince us that the storm was severe then the return to the passenger cabin provided it. In my efforts to help my wife back across the deck I had little opportunity to look about; our attention was taken with the effort to move into the gusting wind. I did notice, however, that there was little sail in use. I did not envy the sailors who had taken the sail in with such a wind.

If anything, it was darker than it had been earlier. A person could see very little, even on the open deck. And it was difficult to hear anything but the shrieking, howling wind that masked any sound but the occasional shout of an officer. But there was no sign of panic. I had grown quite confident in the ability of the crew of the *Seaventure*, a feeling that I believe was shared by all the passengers. The thing for us to do was to find shelter from the elements. Isn't that what we did back on the farm when a sudden storm arose?

A short while after we had returned to the passenger cabin, an officer entered and walked to the center of the cabin. He was dripping wet and stood there with the water running from his clothes onto the floor where it would run this way and that, depending upon the motion of the ship. "The captain has given orders that all passengers should remain below decks. Anyone who goes above could easily be swept overboard and there would be little chance to save him. And be careful as you move around below. There are more injuries from falls on shipboard than for any other cause. Do you have any questions?"

"What about food?" asked a woman.

"Food will be distributed at noon as usual. But there will be no cooking fire. I think you understand why."

"How long will this storm last?" asked the woman's husband.

"That I cannot say. We are in a warmer clime where the storms are more severe than in England. You should not be alarmed if I tell you that we are in for a rough ride. We must keep our bow headed into the wind so we are not hit broadside by a wave. It will mean some pitching about but that is better than having our deck under water."

With these cheerless words, the officer excused himself and left us. There was a silence. People were gathered together but they really had little to say. A young member of our group of passengers decided to fill the void with his crying but was hushed by his mother who took him back to his berth. I could not help thinking of the contrast between our buoyant mood yesterday when we stood on deck in the sunshine and today as we huddled below knowing that the wind and waves were tearing at our ship, intent upon our destruction. There was little we could do but pray.

Throughout that entire day the wind howled like some great mindless creature. I would listen for some reduction in its intensity which would invariably be followed by a return to its high pitched wailing or even an increase in sound as if to make up for any preceding lull. I came to realize that listening expectantly was foolish; that I would tire myself needlessly. We had all endured storms that lasted a day and on into the night. Why should it be different on the ocean?

Almost immediately after I had made this resolution, the wind seemed to grow quieter; it was no longer shrieking. Our violent motions seemed to subside somewhat. Emboldened by this change I decided I would go on deck to try to see what was happening. Halfway through the passageway to the deck I met Master Swift, the ship's navigator. Not all the storms in the world could dampen his good humor. "Good day to you, Master Rolfe. Out for a stroll on deck, are you?"

As I started to respond, the ship rolled so that I fell sideways against the bulkhead. Swift reached out to keep me from falling down the steps behind me. The howling wind returned in all its fury as if it wanted to have a voice in our conversation, indeed it almost drowned out my feeble reply. "I wished to see how we were faring."

"Take a peek if you must but I would not advise staying on deck long. Unless, that is, you want Mistress Rolfe to arrive in Virginia a widow. We have had to cut loose the pinnace we were towing."

Chastened, I climbed the few remaining steps to the deck. Whereas before it had been raining, it now seemed to be coming down in sheets. If I had not had my hands on the rail, the water coursing over the deck would have swept my feet out from under me. Adding to the unreality were great patches of foam on the crest of waves that hurtled by. The irregular motion of the ship jerked the yards and rigging so severely that I wondered why they did not give way. I heeded the advice of Master Swift and retreated carefully to the passenger cabin.

Later in the afternoon, Reverend Bucke decided to gather the passengers together for prayers. Hardly half of them could drag themselves from their bunks to gather around him. The rest were sick from the violent motions that they had suffered that day. Sarah excused herself, saying she could not go. She urged me to, however, and I joined the rather pitiful group kneeling on the cabin floor around Reverend Bucke. He was a devout man and the prayers he read over us could not have been more sincerely hoped for than they were by that miserable, half sick group of seafarers. I shall never forget seeing him standing there in the gloom with a passenger standing by him with a candlestick to light the pages of the prayer book. Though we could hardly hear him for the sound of wave and wind we were comforted that the Almighty would hear the petitions of our minister.

Realizing that the faithful who had gathered around him were being jostled by the constant movement of the ship and that, at best, only a few could hear his words, Reverend Bucke dismissed them with a blessing. Ending their devotions with "Thanks be to God," they moved slowly back toward their berths.

It is hard to say which was worse, the noise or the motion to which we were subjected. I have been in Lincoln Cathedral near the choir when their voices, along with the entire congregation's, were raised in song. Above the sounds of the full-throated multitude could be heard the soaring treble of the boys choir. In the same way, the sounds of the storm seemed to cover the complete spectrum of noise, making it difficult to think much less to speak and be heard. The noise was so deafening that you could no longer even hear a child crying, nor any other voice except one shouting directly in your ear.

The motions of the *Seaventure* were as unpredictable as they were violent. We were literally being tossed about by the waves; and, when we were suspended by some gigantic surge, we did not know whether we would continue to arc upward, roll over sideways, or even tumble forwards. I had heard that one of the most desperate contortions to which a ship might be subjected was pitchpoling when a ship would literally somersault with its stern thrown forward over its bow. Such a motion seemed no challenge to those waves. If it should happen we would certainly be dismasted and probably be damaged by the shifting of ballast.

I think that even the bravest of us must have been gripped with fear. Living in Norfolk, I had heard seamen tell of desperate conditions at sea and I had even made a few short voyages myself during which the weather was unfavorable. I never dreamed that the wind and waves could combine to give the impression of absolute fury, uncontrollable rage. Under these conditions, rest was not possible. We could only grip each other or some part of the ship and hold on, praying for quiet and safety.

As the storm continued into the second day we were beset with a new danger. Whereas before the threat was from the water from above, it now occurred that we were also endangered by water from below. The ship was leaking, and leaking badly. That there should have been some leakage in a new ship whose planks had not yet swollen to the maximum would not have been a surprise. But the leakage was major, rising four our five feet above the ballast below us. The terrible stresses on the hull had parted seams in several places.

This discovery had been the cause of a great stir among the members of the *Seaventure's* crew. Men passing through our cabin, en route to the space below us, carried cordage with which to stop leaks. There was commotion, but it was purposeful commotion, as they went below to inspect along the waterline. It was a fearsome thought that we might sink or be ripped asunder and this added another layer of terror to the concerns of the passengers. At least the crewmen were doing something while we could do little more than watch them coming and going.

Soon, however, we were to be saved from inactivity. Our Governor himself came into the passenger cabin to issue instructions. Sir Thomas had the physique and voice of a man used to giving orders. "I don't have to tell you the situation is serious. Because of the leaks all of us must man pumps or buckets. I want you to assemble in three groups to work in three parts of the ship: one hour on, one hour off. Everyone must take part including the women."

At last we had something to do. We did not have to be coerced. Our bodies were finally becoming accustomed to the violent motions of the ship. In fact, those motions might even have been lessened somewhat by the amount of water taken on below.

In a short time we had been gathered into our groups and ours had moved forward in to the forecastle of the *Seaventure*. There my wife and I became part of a line that passed buckets of water from below to men on a staircase. At the next level the water was thrown over the side; all in all a laborious process to pass a small amount of water back to the sea. But we could not rely on the pumps alone even though they were manned vigorously by some of the stronger men aboard.

I was taking the bucket passed to me by my wife and passing it to a gentleman on my left, Henry Paine. We spoke little and for this I was grateful. There was no use expending energy on speech when it was so difficult to make oneself heard

~2~

A great stillness came over our ship when we grounded. It appeared that the *Seaventure* had not only drawn up onto the bottom but had become wedged between rocks so that we were held stationary without the slightest movement. Almost simultaneously the storm seemed to have passed over us so that the waters were quiet. I was aware, however, of the damage that water could do to a ship which was aground on a rocky shore. It was with relief then that I heard Captain Newport announce that we must quickly abandon ship to avoid the possibility of being shifted by a rising tide or an onshore wind.

The ship's boats were immediately lowered over the side and filled with passengers to be rowed to shore. After seeing Sarah to one of the boats, I joined a group of men to bring food and baggage from below. Once again we formed lines, only now we were no longer passing buckets of water in a contest we could not win. It is amazing how much easier it is to work when you can see progress, as we did when the pile of our belongings grew on the deck. In little over an hour we had brought up most of what could be salvaged and began sending some supplies along with passengers to the shore. I was among the last passengers to leave the *Seaventure*. To be able to leave it at all seemed a great reprieve. It was only hours earlier that we had believed it would be our common grave.

Once ashore, we faced the task of moving our supplies away from the water. That first day we carried them no farther than the line of palmetto trees where we believed they would be safe from the ocean tides. During this time Sir Thomas Gates and Captain Yeardley seemed to be everywhere, directing and encouraging us as we stumbled toward safety and rest. The last sound in my memory was hearing Yeardley report to the Governor that he had posted sentinels around our group. By then we had moved to a grove of cedar trees beyond the palmettos. My wife was already asleep when I lay down beside her at the foot of a cedar tree.

"John, wake up," said Sarah as she shook my shoulder. When she saw my eyes were open she went on, "They are calling your name."

I stretched and stood up. From the sun in the sky I judged it was midmorning. The difference in our surroundings from those of the preceding days was astonishing. During the storm everything had seemed gray or black and had a nightmarish quality whereas we were now surrounded by land and water of the most brilliant colors. The sky had been washed clear of every cloud and mirrored the blue of the ocean. The sands of the beach were white or gold and reached inland to trees having a canopy of rich green. The sight of it was as refreshing as food or drink. With the thought of food came the realization of how hungry I was. I walked quickly to the nearest group of men where food was being distributed from the stores that had been saved from the ship.

The roll had been called to see anyone of the company was missing. Our deliverance from the storm had indeed been miraculous. How the sailors who had tended the ship had kept from being swept overboard was a mystery. Every one of our one hundred fifty passengers and crew had been rescued, including even the ship's dog and the few remaining swine. How ironic that those pigs should survive the terrible storm only to be rowed ashore where they would soon be slaughtered for our food.

Because Governor Gates was a military man, the formation of an encampment was almost second nature to him. The soldiers were assigned as sentinels and to patrol further into the island while the passengers were given more routine housekeeping tasks. Meanwhile the sailors were returning to the *Seaventure* to salvage whatever might be of value.

This story would no doubt have had a different ending were it not for the rescue of our carpentry tools from the ship. I did

14

not know what lay ahead but I did know that with axes, saws and hammers we could make shelter for ourselves on that island. Our group began the construction of huts. The women took a particular interest in the construction of what was to be our homes for the indefinite future. Here they would be conserving our few belongings, mending and washing clothes, and preparing meals from what the island had to offer.

One of the groups of men had been sent in a search for food. Although we still had some stores from the ship, including a few swine, we had no idea how long we would be on the island. From the first the most rewarding effort was from fishing. Several inlets or bays protected from surf were located where fish could be caught easily including bonito, bass, and snapper.

This island or group of islands was named Bermuda, a name that had earlier caused great uneasiness among the seamen who thought it to be inhabited by evil spirits. The evil spirits turned out to be wild hogs. They were so abundant we could hear their high-pitched squeals from our camp. It would seem there had to be inhabitants on these islands but we saw no sign of them.

We were divided into small groups or messes for the purpose of preparing food. We were once again invited to join the Admiral's mess. "We have precious little of our stores left, Master Rolfe," said Captain Newport, "but we have John Powell who will do his best with what we have."

"We are grateful for all our blessings," I replied, "and John is not the least of them."

I could say that with all truth. Powell was a natural cook. He had already found some berries that he intended to use for adding flavor in the preparation of meat.

"I don't know whom we can thank for the hogs," said Captain Newport, "but they were probably from a Spanish ship that came aground here."

"I wonder why they did not colonize these islands?" asked Captain Yeardley, one of the company commanders.

"Probably because of the treacherous shoals."

Once again I marveled that we had been blown towards Bermuda by the fiercest winds imaginable and yet had not been destroyed on the shoals. As Sarah and I retired to our shelter we counted the small blessings we enjoyed in addition to life itself. We had eaten, we were dry for the first time in days, and we were on firm land. I must admit, however, that I still felt as if I were on a swaying ship, a condition that did not leave me for several more days.

The search for food continued and was successful from the outset. Besides the fish that were so abundant, it was discovered that some of the islands were home to birds that could easily be caught. These creatures had no fear of us and could be attracted by calling out to them. They even provided us with eggs that were as good as those from any chicken.

In addition to the fish and fowl we soon added the wild hogs to our menu. This first came about when an enterprising sailor who was sleeping near the pen where our pigs were kept discovered that a boar was entering the pen at night. He managed to tie a rope to the leg of the intruder so that in the morning we had increased the inventory of livestock. This process was repeated and the clever sailor was treated as somewhat of a hero. It was soon discovered, however, that the ship's dog, a nondescript creature called Matey, could run down the hogs in the forest. Grabbing his quarry by the ear, he would hold it fast until the animal could be secured by ropes.

With ample supplies of fish and pork available, the Governor decided that some of this flesh should be preserved for future needs. He directed that salt should be derived from the boiling of seawater. Two men were assigned to tending a fire under a large pot used for this purpose. I wondered if there had ever been a shipwrecked group our size that had found such plenteous supplies of food available.

Within a few weeks, we were reasonably well established and our leaders, assured that we could survive, began to focus on how to bring about our rescue.

"In a small boat," said Captain Newport, "making five or six knots, I should say some of us could reach Virginia in seven or eight days."

"You mean one of our ship's boats?" replied Sir George Somers.

"Yes, using one of the longboats. But it should be reinforced to make it more seaworthy."

"And the plan would be for them to reach Virginia and return with other ships to rescue us?"

"Yes."

"It is a long shot. But it might work," said Sir George. "It would require a good navigator. Virginia is at a height of thirty-seven degrees latitude. To sail south of that is to risk grounding on the outer banks."

"We could send either James Swift or his mate, Henry Ravens."

"I would leave that decision to you, Captain Newport, but from what I have seen of James Swift, I believe we should keep him with us. We are likely to need him if we have to fashion boats and make our own way from here."

"Then Ravens it is. I have already sounded out both men. Either of them would be willing to go."

Sir George Somers could leave nautical decisions to Captain Newport with confidence. His many years at sea had left their mark on Newport, not the least of which was his hook that he wore in place of an arm lost while a privateer. It gave him a slightly menacing look.

So it was decided that the first try at escape would be by means of a small boat. Planks from the *Seaventure* were used to cover a portion of the sturdiest of the longboats and sails were fashioned to make what the sailors referred to as a sloop rig. Henry Ravens, accompanied by Thomas Whittington and six others were selected from volunteers to make the journey and they departed with the blessing of Reverend Bucke and our entire company on August 28, 1609.

Sir George Somers and Governor Gates did not wish to be dependent on the success of Ravens's mission for our rescue. There were too many uncertainties to take that risk. Because they had a shipwright, Richard Frubbisher, as well as carpenters equipped with tools it would be feasible to construct a larger vessel than the longboat used by Ravens.

Sir George and Frubbisher spent several days in planning. They could not hope to build a ship the size of the *Seaventure* but enough timber could be salvaged from our ship that could be augmented by local cedars in the construction of a seaworthy pinnace. Sir George had already located an area for the worksite where there was deep enough water nearby to launch the hull when complete.

Thirty-five men were chosen to work on the pinnace. Gentlemen volunteered to work as they had while fighting the storm on the *Seaventure*. I was not chosen at first but when I told Frubbisher that we had a carpenter shop and sawpit on our farm in Norfolk he said he would welcome my help. Frubbisher himself supervised the construction of blocks to support the keel while one of his assistants took a work party to cut and bring in the tree that had been selected for the keel. Rather than dragging it to the boatyard they rolled it to water and floated it most of the way. One of the men suffered a bruised foot from being too near the log as it was being rolled. Frubbisher was irate over this and insisted the men had to be more careful. "There's a hundred ways you can cripple a man building a ship, particularly when you move big pieces. If you want to work for me, keep your eyes open and watch out for the other man you work with." It was a worthwhile caution; we had no physician on the island and could ill afford injuries.

Sarah and I made the acquaintance of a gentleman living nearby whose name was William Strachey. He spent some hours with us as we waited out an August rainstorm. He was older than I but I was comfortable in his company. He was not nearly the age of the Governor or Sir George Somers, both old enough to be my father. Strachey was an educated man. A keen observer of the world around him; not just events but people and their interactions. He told us that he kept a journal and questioned me on my part in the boatyard activities.

Strachey admired Sir George Somers and Captain Newport who had brought us through the great storm safely. I asked him if he had overheard conversation between them on the probable outcome of Henry Ravens' passage to Virginia.

"Given reasonable weather, they agree it depends upon Ravens' ability to find the capes that are the entrance to Chesapeake Bay. Once within the Bay, he should have little difficulty finding his way up the river to Jamestown."

"God be with Henry Ravens," I said.

After Strachey had left Sarah and I fell silent. It was a comfortable silence; and, since we had managed to keep dry, we were pleased with our shelter. As a farmer, my natural inclination was to regard rain as a blessing. Presently she spoke about the child who was coming and wondered if it would be born on Bermuda. I put my arm around her to hold her close. God had watched over us thus far on our journey. I prayed he would continue to do so.

~3~

Richard Frubbisher could not have asked for better masters to work for than Governor Gates and Sir George Somers. They were supportive, giving him every reasonable resource at their disposal; they were even tempered, neither quick to find fault nor over generous with praise; and they set the example with their own willingness to work for the benefit of our whole company, never demanding privilege for themselves at the expense of others. With the free hand he was given, Frubbisher seemed almost to delight in finding ways to transfer his experience and skill to the problems of construction while shipwrecked. Very soon he learned the capabilities of the carpenters and men he had working for him and was using them to best advantage. Work at the boatyard continued until late in the day and Frubbisher spent the evenings after supper huddled with one or another carpenter to discuss the next day's work.

Because of the limitations of the wood at his disposal he decided he could not make the stempost of the pinnance from a single piece. The curvature of the stempost, a piece defining the bow of the vessel, was too great. He resolved to make it from two pieces which he would splice together, using some of the few spikes he had recovered from the *Seaventure* for this purpose. When the stempost and the corresponding sternpost were in place we were able to visualize how the pinnace would eventually appear, although they only were the backbone of the vessel. The transom at the stern that was fashioned from planks off the *Seaventure* also helped to define the ship. In the meantime, work was proceeding on the individual ribs with the carpenters laying them out from patterns given to them by Frubbisher. When Frubbisher discovered I had a head for figures he asked me to check his calculations for the size of the ribs, saying there was no time to be wasted in errors. I found no errors in his numbers that were merely proportions based upon the size of the keel.

We likewise did not have the ability to make the ribs from a single piece since the curvature was so great. Our shipwright said we were not to be concerned, that even in England he would have fashioned ribs from a floor piece and two nearly vertical pieces called futtocks. The floor pieces were to be placed over the keel while the planking of the hull would be connected to the futtocks. Much of the shaping of these pieces was done with axes and adzes which required considerable time and patience. Frubbisher urged his carpenters to lay out the designs quickly so he could employ as many men as possible in the process of shaping.

With this labor, the ongoing search for food, and the further exploration of the islands we occupied ourselves to the fullest. I did not see how there could have been any cause for complaint, especially since our leaders were so obviously devoted to our survival and rescue. Perhaps the root of the discord that followed originated from our ability to survive in relative ease. Some of the sailors who had been to Virginia with Captain Newport began to speak disparagingly of that place. I was seldom in the company of the sailors but there were several employed in our boatyard and they would occasionally make knowing remarks about how grim indeed we would find Virginia after the ease with which we had found food in Bermuda. I suppose I have an optimistic temperament because I put no store by these remarks. In retrospect, I see that they were not directed toward me but rather at some individuals they were attempting to influence.

Perhaps the most insidious idea planted in the heads of the gullible was the concept that because we were no longer crew or passengers of the *Seaventure* we were no longer subject to the authority of our leaders. This argument was intended to appeal to the ignorant that felt they were always under constraints from which they wanted to free themselves. It ignored the fact that we needed leaders in order to survive and that we could not possibly have chosen more able and conscientious men to be our leaders.

So the cancer spread from grumbling to covert efforts to recruit adherents and finally an outbreak of rebellion. By then there was a group of six men, led by one John Want, who schemed that they should be allowed to proceed to one of the other islands where they might support themselves without the discipline of our leaders and the requirement to participate further in the Virginia venture. When their mutiny came to light they were brought before Governor Gates who heard their pious assertions of their rights and demands to be set free to live apart from our company.

"Which of you men will speak for the group?" asked the Governor.

"With your permission, sir, I will," said John Want.

"Is that agreeable to the rest of you?"

There was a general nodding of heads from the five men.

"Speak up then. This is a very grave matter."

There was a chorus of "Yes, Governor."

"You are charged with plotting to overthrow the authority invested in me by royal charter. What do you say to this charge?"

"Begging your pardon, sir, but we were not planning to overthrow anything. We only want to go our way in peace. All of us men signed up to go to Virginia. But we have not been brought to Virginia and so the bargain has been broken."

"You are en route to Virginia. At some future date everyone in this group will set foot on Virginia. You were never promised that you would reach Virginia in a certain number of days. Would you have it that if we did not reach that place in sixty days then you were free to go elsewhere? Or seventy days? Or eighty?"

"We plan no harm to anyone. We just ask the freedom to go to another one of these islands where we can live in peace."

"What you are proposing is still mutiny. Since there are only six of you it would probably not cause us to fail but if you had conspired successfully it would have been another matter. With thirty it might be a threat to our survival."

Want had no response.

"You could be subjected to harsh penalties but I have it in mind to grant you your wish. You will be taken this very day to another island. All six of you. Since you wanted no more to do with us we wish no more to do with you."

The six murmured and look at one another in astonishment. They had not expected this.

"You will allow us a share of the stores, won't you, Governor?"

"You would like to have it both ways, wouldn't you, John Want? The stores are for the survival of our company. You have rejected us and shall have none of the stores."

I thought it was a remarkably benign punishment. The Governor could have had them flogged before exiling them from us. The mutineers knew this and accepted their banishment without murmur. It was, after all, what they had said they wanted. I felt that the Governor had handled the matter wisely. No surgeon could have removed a growth from a body more quickly than he removed these men from our presence. He knew the value of swift punishment where the violators would be separated from the group where they might otherwise foment trouble. They were given a few minutes to gather their possessions before being taken to a boat. By acting without harshness he gave no further arguments to the seamen who believed they owed no further allegiance now that they were on shore. In retrospect I found it puzzling that this disturbance should have begun among the seamen. One would have thought that they were accustomed to discipline based on the need for everyone to cooperate for mutual safety.

Also disturbing to me was the divided nature in the character of John Want. Outwardly a religious man, he was frequently at prayer and could quote the scriptures. Our minister, The Reverend Bucke, thought he was a member of some sect, however, because although outwardly religious he had to be urged to attend our services. I was disturbed by these failings in men who should have been steadfast and others shared my unease. We were never quite as comfortable in the

23

unity of our company as we had been and were on the lookout for signs of disaffection wherever they might arise.

In October it was no longer possible to deny that my wife was with child. Mistress Horton during this time proved herself to be a kind friend. I shall never forget the sight of Mistress Horton, an agreeably stout woman of perhaps forty years, fussing over Sarah to make her more comfortable. She would even send her maid, Elizabeth Perkins, to call upon us and offer assistance with any work, particularly the laundering of clothes. Elizabeth was a cheerful and attractive young woman who turned the heads of many of the unattached men of our company. We noticed, however, that her favorite was the Admiral's cook, Thomas Powell. He would often appear at our modest shelter at the time that Elizabeth was there, usually on the pretext of bringing Sarah an offering of soup or some other nourishment for my wife. Before my supply of tobacco ran out, I would offer him a pipe and he would have an excuse to visit with us while we smoked. He was an imaginative cook, surprising us with the dishes he prepared such as soup prepared from a turtle captured by the men.

Mistress Eason, the wife of another passenger was also with child. This too was a comfort to my wife since that good woman already had small children and eased my wife's mind on the subject of childbirth, assuring her that in our location and company there would be no difficulty. Besides, we might soon be rescued she said and the children could then be born in Virginia. She went on much about names, saying that if they had daughters they of course be named Virginia and James if they were boys. During this time I received much good-natured joking from men at the boatyard. James Swift wanted to know if I planned to populate the colony single-handed to which I replied that I would require considerable help and I expected him to do his part.

In the meantime, the banished party of six mutineers under the leadership of John Want was not faring so well. Within two weeks of their departure, an emissary appeared from their island appealing to the Governor that they might return. They had numerous reasons for discontent, chief of which was their realization that they had been unable to persuade sufficient adherents to their cause. Their small numbers affected their ability to accomplish much whether it was gathering of food, providing a comfortable camp, or fashioning means for escape from Bermuda. In his wisdom the Governor had granted them none of the company's tools so all they had was the odd knife or hatchet that belonged to an individual. Naturally the messenger did not dwell on these considerations; rather a case was made for their profound regrets that they had separated themselves from their fellows and how much they wished to return where they might make their contribution to the welfare of all. These first messages were delivered to Captain Yeardley rather than the Governor. Yeardley denied the request without even hearing the agent who brought the supplications.

This doleful scenario was repeated almost weekly until John Want appeared himself to ask the Governor's pardon. To the various reasons that had been offered previously was added religious references to the prodigal son and other Biblical personages who had gone astray but through God's mercy had found their way to redemption. Surely Governor Gates could find it in his heart to forgive. Few members of the company were present for this or the other visits representing the banished group but it was common knowledge they had occurred and what had been said. It was obvious that John Want had lost any sense of righteousness or justification for his previous arguments. He was allowed to see Governor Gates and his entreaties included pledges of steadfastness and unselfish labor in the common cause. Sensing the extent of the man's remorse and his sincerity, the Governor relented and permitted the six chastened men to return to our company. The mutiny was apparently resolved but I suspected there were still troubles ahead in dealing with some of the men.

Although John Want and his confederates gave the appearance of being humbled by their experience I wondered what really was in their minds. I believe they took care not to draw attention to themselves but the basic cause of their dissatisfaction probably remained: they saw no point in going to Virginia when Bermuda afforded easier ways to feed themselves. In this regard I believe the primary source of discontent continued to be the seamen. They were the only ones who had been to Virginia and knew the conditions there. Occasionally I would overhear a remark about how the Indians of Virginia would not allow them to work freely as they did in Bermuda. Whether this was idle grumbling or an attempt to draw the hearer into a conspiracy I did not know. I confess I did not know what I could do about the situation myself and tried to drive the suspicions from my mind.

In the light of hindsight I would say that Captain Newport probably contributed to the problems that the Governor had with the sailors. While he may have been one of the ablest sailors of his time he did not exercise a restraining influence on his crew. In fact he made things more difficult for the Governor by seeking preference for the seamen. He sought to have the easiest duties assigned to them and seemed to overlook either their deficiencies or their excesses. There was never any discord among our leaders; it was just an apparent inability on the part of Newport to expect the same level of conduct from his men that was expected from the passengers. While this could have been understandable aboard ship it was hardly justifiable under our circumstances.

All during October beacon fires had been lit and tended during the night to assist a navigator from Virginia who was approaching our island. This was a reasonable time in which to expect rescue. In addition, all of us, whether we admitted it or not, had made a practice of scanning the horizon for the sails of a ship. At first we reminded ourselves that a watched pot never boils. Then we justified ourselves by counting the weeks needed for Ravens to reach Virginia, a ship to be dispatched, and the return journey to be made.

By the end of October we were beginning to have doubts. Had Ravens encountered another storm? Had they been dismasted by a sudden squall? We knew from our experience of the storm that no longboat could have survived in those seas. What if they met hostile Indians upon reaching land? The men of even a small Indian village could probably overwhelm the eight men we had dispatched to Virginia. We realized there were a multitude of unfavorable outcomes to the passage by Ravens.

There were also problems possible within the colony. Suppose many of the other ships of our fleet had been disabled. Was there a ship available to come to our rescue? Were they facing problems of a more serious nature that precluded their coming at once? One could become dizzy considering all the possibilities. But as time progressed and we were well past the middle of November it seemed more likely that the first requirement for our rescue had not occurred that Ravens had not reached Virginia. It was time to rest our hopes on other possibilities.

Help was not coming.

~4~

If help were not coming, our situation was more difficult. We could not expect to transport our entire company in the pinnace that was under construction. Sir George Somers had the common sense to propose a solution: we should build a second vessel. He had conferred with Richard Frubbisher who grudgingly admitted that he could spare two of our four carpenters. Frubbisher was a careful and cautious man who was taking every pain to build the best pinnace possible in his improvised boatyard and he loathed the thought of giving up two of his carpenters.

"Frubbisher has seen the light," said Sir George in our mess. "I explained that we could not arrive in Virginia with only half our company. It would cause us too many problems. Who would we leave in charge? Our best chance for success is to keep everyone together."

Governor Gates was hugely relieved. He had been troubled by the same concerns but our transportation was primarily the responsibility of Sir George. "I suppose we could transport ninety or perhaps a hundred in the pinnace but not much more."

"We need an additional worksite but it's not practical to transport workmen to another island daily. Give me a workforce of twenty men, along with the two carpenters, and we will set up camp on the other island."

"I will give you every support."

"Thank you. Now, because the work on the first boat is going along well and we do not want to delay departure, I suggest the second boat be of a simpler construction. In fact, it will have to be because we are limited in what we could take from the *Seaventure*."

The creation of a second camp occupied our thoughts for several days even if we were not directly involved. We were going to see less of Sir George but he still came to our island to confer with Governor Gates. At the suggestion of Reverend Bucke the first pinnace was to be named *Deliverance* and the second *Patience*.

I was somewhat amused at the name *Patience* because there was no patience shown by Sir George in its construction. He regarded it as a challenge to finish as soon as possible, preferably before the *Deliverance*. Frubbisher, in the meantime, was spurred to greater efforts. The sound of chopping and hammering rung out from his boatyard throughout the day and sometimes at night when men would work by the light of torches.

On November 26, 1609, Elizabeth Perkins was married to Thomas Powell. Mistress Horton had at first opposed their marriage while we were shipwrecked, feeling herself responsible for Elizabeth. Then, as she realized we would not likely be otherwise for the foreseeable future, she relented. No mother exercised more care for her daughter's wedding than Eleanor Horton did for her maid. There was much sewing to be done to provide a proper gown. In one respect the wedding was simpler. No guest list was required as all our company was witness to the vows administered by Reverend Bucke.

In mid-December we had a great hailstorm. Everyone took shelter immediately. At first we were relieved to be protected from the hail but then we became concerned because of the fragility of our simple shelters. In the meantime, there were great squeals issuing from the hog pens where our captured swine were directly exposed to the hail. Normally they would have found shelter in the brush and they were in a panic that resulted in one pen being overrun by frantic hogs. At about the same time the storm subsided and a hue and cry went up from our hunters who set the dog Matey after the fleeing creatures. When I reported what had happened to Sarah she showed a wry amusement.

"Don't you see the humor in this, John?"

"No; perhaps you should explain it to me."

"Certainly not, trying to explain humor can be a great bore."

"Why should that deter you? The whole conversation is about boars." My remark caused her to smile even more. "It took a week for those men to capture these hogs, not to mention the effort of Matey. To them this is a tragedy."

"Try to look at it from the perspective of the hogs, dear."

"Never. Once a farmer begins to see things from the hog's, or the cow's, or the chicken's perspective, he is doomed."

"I shall have to remember that if I am to be a good farmer's wife."

The season of Christmas was upon us. The Reverend Bucke, who had served so capably in the offices of the church, cheered us with the good news of the birth of our Savior. At the same time he cautioned us that our present trials were but a test of our faith and that we must never lose hope. I wondered if the Governor had encouraged him inasmuch as the Governor always seemed to seek the positive ever since the onset of the great storm and our shipwreck. I do know that governor Gates ordered another great feast similar to that held for the wedding of Thomas Powell.

In the evening of February 1, Sarah felt pains and told me that I should fetch Mistress Horton because she was beginning labor. Within a few moments that good lady and Mistress Eason as well were at her side, comforting her and making preparations for the birth of our baby. Although banished from the shelter I hovered nearby, knowing I was powerless to assist, but ready if they should call on me. Long after the encampment was dark a feeble light shone through the thin walls of our shelter where a new life was struggling to enter the world. Shortly after dawn I heard a tiny wail and a few minutes later was provided my first glimpse of a baby girl. I was no judge of newborns but she seemed to me to be the tiniest, and yet the most perfect, of creatures. During my vigil I had tried to calculate and had ended by guessing that the child had arrived at least a month early.

With the safe delivery of the baby I felt that a great burden had been lifted from us. "Why should you have been so concerned John?" my wife chided. "You have been present at the birth of many a calf and lamb."

"Those experiences did nothing to reduce my anxiety."

"Have you thought of a name for our daughter?"

"I would like to name her after you."

"I thank you for the thought but I have a better suggestion. Let us call her Bermuda."

"That is certainly a beautiful name. But is it a Christian one?"

"To me it is as Christian as the names given to some of our Protestant friends in Norfolk, names like Patience or Charity."

"Then I shall see Richard Bucke to arrange for baptism."

I had grown to like Bucke who seemed to have an endless reserve of energy. While on shipboard I had come to admire his ability as a preacher.

And so, on February 11, Reverend Bucke officiated at the christening of Bermuda Rolfe. Mistress Horton was her godmother while Captain Newport and William Strachey were the child's godfathers.

From the first we were concerned for the infant who appeared frail in addition to being quite small. We realized this particularly after the birth of Mistress Eason's child, a boy, in mid-March. We thought the boy showed himself to be healthier which added to our concern. I can say however, that Bermuda did not suffer from lack of care; her mother and godmother fussed over her continually.

The tensions and undercurrents that existed among our company grew to the extent that they would have been noticeable to anyone. The basic issue, it seemed, was a challenge to the authority of the Governor. Why this should have been I do not know because no person could have exercised authority in a fairer and more openhanded way. We could not have been better organized for harvesting food from the abundant supply in Bermuda. Nor was anyone oppressed in the building of the two pinnaces. I believe, in fact, that there was an evil spirit abroad among us simply desiring to have his way no matter what the cost.

~5~

There was a somber atmosphere about the camp on the night of March 14th. Usually, in the evening there would be singing and sometimes the sailors would dance after the evening meal. But that evening was quiet; only a few men gathered near their shelters to speak in lowered voices. Early on the following morning there was a loud sound of arguing, followed by shouts that awakened me.

I got up and walked toward the end of the camp from which the shouting came, expecting to find some sort of calamity. The shouting had not ceased. Several members of the guard trotted past me on their way toward a group clustered around the front of a shelter. When the soldiers approached the group Thomas Godby stepped forward, "They have gone into the woods. The sergeant of the guard has gone after them but he will need help."

The sergeant's reinforcements paused a moment to look at a man lying on the ground and then moved into the woods. At that moment I arrived and asked what had happened. "There was a fight," said Godby. "Edward Samuell was saying that Robert Waters were trying to steal his knife. Well, I guess he did steal it because before we hardly knew what was happening Waters had picked up a shovel that he used to hit Samuell. He hit Samuell full force on the side of the head just below the ear. It was a mighty blow. I don't see how any man could survive it." I looked down on Samuell. There was a small amount of blood on the ground beside his head "Is he still breathing?" I asked.

A man kneeling next to Samuell replied without looking up. "I don't think so. But his heart is beating." Someone came and put a blanket around Samuell to ward off the chill. It was a futile gesture; in a few minutes his pulse was gone.

I was unaware that Captain Yeardley, the company commander, had come up.

"Who did this?"

"Robert Waters," said Godby.

"Was he alone?"

"He did it himself, Captain; if that's what you mean. But he has run off with several of his friends."

"All right. We will find out who they are. Reverend Bucke and some of the women will lay out Samuell's body for burial. You remain here, Godby, and help them. The rest of you fall in for calling of the roll."

Besides Waters, there were seven others who had fled to the woods. They were not involved in the murder of Edward Samuell but they must have feared that they might have been implicated as mutineers. We learned later that almost all of Sir George Somer's men had fled to the woods that night, undoubtedly for the same reason. The tensions that we were aware of must have affected them even more strongly. We were now faced with a larger scale mutiny than had originally been contrived by John Want. There had to be among that group at least a few with strong powers of persuasion and the personal conviction that they should risk being mutineers rather than go to Virginia. Some of them, being sailors, had not invested in the Virginia Company. Others were indentured and were determined not to go.

I was surprised to hear that one of the Indian boys, Namontack, was missing at the roll call. Surprised because he was always cheerful, unlike most of the mutineers who were complainers and slow to do their share of the work. If Machumps had been missing it would have made more sense because he was surly and not well liked by most of us. Machumps seemed to be jealous of any attention given to his companion, Namontack. They were about as unalike as any two Indian boys could be.

After roll call we were told to go about our usual duties but to be sure to take our weapons with us to the worksite. Sir

George Somers had come over from his island to confer with Governor Gates. I was glad I did not bear their responsibility. What would the mutineers do? Would they attack us to get the weapons and tools that would be necessary for survival in Bermuda? Could they be persuaded to return? We had been on the island for over six months and our leaders knew the mutineers well enough to judge whom they would have to deal with. They also had to decide how our work parties would be reorganized since most of Sir George's men had joined the mutiny. Richard Frubbisher was called in to discuss who could be spared to go to the other island.

My wife was not as distracted by the mutiny as I would have expected. Perhaps this was because she had long been aware of the dissatisfaction within the camp. In this, she showed greater sensitivity than I. Her concern was more for our baby Bermuda who was not thriving. The infant did not sleep well which is common among small children; neither did she take much nourishment. We both realized that we had a sickly child and wondered how well she would fare on the sea passage which was still ahead of us. Mistress Horton was very solicitous and tried to reassure my wife. She was visiting her when I returned from the roll call.

"We are to return to the shipyard," I told the two women.

"Oh, go along then," replied Mistress Horton. "We will be fine here."

"Did they catch any of the mutineers?" asked my wife.

"No, the sergeant of the guard could not keep up with them. They are far away from us and in hiding by now."

"Won't the Governor pursue them?"

"Apparently not. I suspect he does not want an armed confrontation. If the mutineers do not want to fight perhaps he can deal with them."

As I trudged to the boatyard, I hoped that nothing I had said might cause alarm to either of the women. Mistress Horton was the more likely to be upset but as time passed in Bermuda she seemed to be calmer than before.

What made the mutineers dangerous was their unpredictability. I regarded them almost as irresponsible children with whom it was difficult to reason and there was no denying that they had inconvenienced us considerably. We had to reorganize our work parties and increase security. Men from our boatyard went over to Sir George Somer's group on the other island because most of those men had fled to the woods. There was a sense of uncertainty as to what the mutineers might do. Most of them were simple seamen but they had been swayed by a few who were capable of causing a great deal of trouble.

We needed no encouragement to carry our weapons with us and we guarded the worksites to give them no opportunity to damage the ships.

In late April the health of Bermuda Rolfe worsened. She was no longer able to keep her food and slept only fitfully. Although the child received all the attention that we could provide nothing seemed to help. I prayed almost constantly that God would help the infant and looked for signs of improvement, but there were none. All my life I had thought my prayers had been answered and was deeply troubled that this helpless baby should suffer so. I began to think that I was at fault, that I had brought these difficulties on my little family by insisting that we go to Virginia. Although I did not voice these concerns to my wife she seemed to sense them and tried to shield me from the effects of the baby's decline.

I had told her that I would be excused from work in order to assist her.

"You must go to work, John."

"Is there not something that I can do?"

"Nothing that I or Mistress Horton cannot do better. Your place is at the boatyard. Now go."

And so I went. But my mind was not on the work. All three of *Deliverance's* masts were now erected and men were attaching the shrouds that would hold them in place.

Sensing that my thoughts were elsewhere, Richard Frubbisher asked me to work on the measurement of sails. A careless worker on the shrouds could cause injury to himself or others. But with the sail makers I would merely take measurements needed to reduce some of the *Seaventure* sails to fit the smaller *Deliverance*. There would be enough canvas left over to outfit the *Patience* whose hull was now also in the water. I was so distracted that I have little memory of what I did to help.

In mid-afternoon a member of the guard came with the message that I should return to camp. He had no particulars but I knew that it probably concerned the baby. We trudged along in silence until reaching the shelters where I thanked him and he returned to his post. I saw only a few people as I walked through the camp. When they saw me they were silent, causing me to know more than I could from any words that the child had died. The news had spread very quickly through our company.

The Reverend Bucke was waiting at our shelter. "I am so sorry, John. Your daughter is with the angels now, where there is no sickness or crying."

I had no words to respond but nodded my head dumbly. Inside, my wife sat by the cradle I had fashioned for Bermuda. Mistress Horton, who was at her side, rose and touched me on the shoulder before leaving us. I sat by Sarah with my arm about her. Neither of us had words to express our grief. God had blessed us with this child and then had taken her away.

Nicholas Bennitt, one of our carpenters, made a tiny coffin for Bermuda Rolfe whom we buried in a grove of cedars overlooking the ocean. It was, and I am sure still is, a place of great beauty and serenity.

~6~

With the two ships nearly completed, the attentions of Governor Gates and Sir George Somers were focused on reconciling the mutineers. Sir George continued to treat with them alone because both the Governor and he felt it advantageous to do so. Nevertheless, I have it from William Strachey, who was in a position to observe the Governor, that both men were very much concerned. How would they be able to explain leaving over twenty men on an island when Virginia needed the skills of these men?

At first Sir George dealt with the mutineers through messengers. Then he arranged to meet their leaders to negotiate with them. By so doing, he appealed to the vanity of the leaders; much could be gained in this way at little cost. Sir George knew too that if he could persuade the leaders they could deliver the followers. First he convinced them that if they did not accompany us to Virginia they could be subject to punishment later as mutineers. Then he told them there was nothing in the way of supplies or assistance that he could provide to them. Finally he made the point that Governor Gates was willing to pardon them and they would not be subject to punishment for mutiny at a later date. Knowing Sir George, I expect that he conveyed all this in a manner that was sympathetic and without censure.

Richard Knowles and William Brian were among the first group of four men who returned. Although they had been among the men led by John Want in an earlier mutiny, I did not consider them to be conspicuous troublemakers. Word had been spread that they were to be treated in an evenhanded manner. Perhaps because there were no floggings as Sir George Somers

37

had told them, six more returned three days later and all but two had rejoined our company when we began loading our ships for departure. The two holdouts were Christopher Carter and Robert Waters who consequently were left on Bermuda. Waters had killed Edward Samuell and there had been no offer of pardon. Carter may have committed some offense which had never been reported. A final disturbing note was the mystery of the missing Indian boy Namontack. I, along with several others, believed that Matchump knew more about his disappearance than he ever disclosed.

As a memorial to our deliverance from the great storm Governor Gates directed the fashioning of a cross from large timbers salvaged from the *Seaventure*. A brief description of our shipwreck was inscribed on copper plates and affixed to the cross so that those who followed us to Bermuda someday might know the dates of our arrival, the names of our leaders and our gratitude to God for our salvation. None of us, even though we had passed nine months in Bermuda, had forgotten the magnitude of the storm. Nor could we help to realize after weeks of sailing in a nearly infinite sea how miraculous it was that we should be cast up on such a small island, that our ship should be held fast so that we could make our escape to land, and that we should be able to rescue not only most of our belongings but also the ship's timbers from which to fashion parts for the *Deliverance* and the *Patience*.

All of us on Bermuda had shared the experience of that storm. It was as if we had been initiated together into a society with special rites but could not understand what had happened to us. We did not talk much about it but we all felt that our lives had almost been taken from us, only to be given back again. We also had shared the experience of life on the island. At last, in early May of 1610 we began the necessary preparations for departure. Our stores were carried to the ships where there was a twenty-four hours a day guard to prevent any last minute mischief on the part of the mutineers. Thanks to the foresight of Governor Gates we had a good supply of salted meat and fish to take on our journey as well as live hogs from the seemingly inexhaustible population on Bermuda. None of us had increased our personal belongings during the time we were shipwrecked but we carefully prepared the articles we had for the journey ahead.

On May 10 we embarked on the *Deliverance*. The mood was not festive as it had been at our departure from Plymouth the preceding year but there was a good-natured atmosphere. It occurred to me that it was seldom that a group of passengers sailed on a ship that they had fashioned with their own hands. My wife was in good spirits even though we had paid a final visit earlier that morning to the gravesite of our daughter. "Look, John," she said, "There are the Easons with their little boy. I must speak to them." She moved across the deck toward Mistress Eason who held their six weeks old son. I was glad to see her taking interest. She had not truly been well since the death of Bermuda and I was worried about her.

Earlier in the morning, Captain Newport had gone out in a longboat to mark the channel for our departure. He set buoys as a guide for our safe passage through the reefs. Our sails were then set and the ships began to gain headway. It was a short lived breeze, however, and Captain Newport wasted no time in ordering that a longboat be launched for the purpose of towing us. Sir George Somers did the same aboard the *Patience*. It seemed an unusual way to begin a voyage but we could not wait for the wind; while drifting it would be too easy to move out of our marked channel.

Despite the efforts of Captain Newport to insure a safe passage through the shoals we were startled to hear a scraping noise beneath us. It could mean only one thing: we were scraping bottom. There was a groan from the passengers around me. They knew how serious this could be. Several shouts went up from seamen, intending to alert the captain who needed no alerting. Newport waved his arms to the longboat, signaling them to rest on their oars. As for myself, I could not have been more aware of our sliding onto rock if my own body had been dragged over it.

By then Captain Newport had moved to the bow of the *Deliverance* in order to make himself heard better by the men in the longboat. "Walsingham! Bring your boat to the stern."

By then Walsingham, who understood our predicament perfectly, was already rowing back toward us, his shout of "Aye, captain," floating over the water. Several seamen had removed the bridle that was used to tow us by the bow and were walking along the rail, passing the lines around the shrouds so that the towline could be attached at the stern. It was done in a manner of minutes and soon there was a strain on the towline. To our immense relief, we slid easily off the shoal.

I need hardly say that we moved with extreme caution until we were clear of the shoals. We preceded under tow, avoiding any white water and using the sounding lead most of the time to tell us if we were entering shallow water. Finally, toward the end of the second day we were free and were able to use a complete set of sails. This had to be modified soon because, although the *Patience* was quite seaworthy, she was not able to keep up with us.

On the evening of the second day I asked Sarah if she would like to accompany me on deck. The moon was already up and I felt a desire for fresh air. "No thank you, John," she replied. "I am rather tired."

"You are not seasick, I hope."

"Not at all. This ship is so similar to the *Seaventure* that I feel quite used to it already."

I found a place on deck where I could sit in comfort without being in the way of any of the crewmen. We had a following east wind which was carrying us briskly along. The nearly full moon was rising over the mizzenmast and a light from the *Patience* was visible slightly behind us. The sky seemed filled with stars. Could this be the same ocean which had done its best to destroy us the preceding July? It hardly seemed possible since the waves were actually pushing us gently toward Virginia. I felt a surge of well-being flow through my body. After considerable danger and hardship we were on our way toward a new life. It was a foolish comparison but I felt I knew a little of how the Israelites must have felt when they were about to enter into the promised land. We were approaching our promised land. We were rapidly putting the past behind us. In the future our energies would be devoted not merely to surviving but to building a better home for all of us. I cannot recall ever being so lifted by an emotion and I hoped that everyone in our company felt some of the elation that I felt.

I sat for several hours in what I believed to be a perfect awareness of myself, of the sea and sky around me, and to the Creator to whom I owed everything. I mention it because I have never again felt quite the way I did that night on the deck of the *Deliverance*. It was the feeling that I was in exactly the place I should be and doing exactly what I was expected to do; and that awareness filled me with an unspeakable joy. I am not sure that if I could recall such powerful feelings again that I would wish to do so. Presently, I overheard the officer of the deck relinquishing control of the ship to his relief. He informed him that he was to sail so as to keep the light from the *Patience* always in sight, but if for any reason he lost sight of her he was to notify Captain Newport immediately. It was time for me to go below.

A remnant of the feelings I experienced remained with me in the days to follow. I was freed from the concerns of survival and work on Bermuda to look forward to the future. I was naturally concerned about my wife who had been weakened by the strain of our child's sickness and death but hoped that a fresh start in Virginia would refresh both her spirit and her health. I had missed being away from farming and thought we should reach our destination early enough to plant crops for the growing season ahead. In my mind's eye I tried to visualize how the natives went about farming. I had been told that they planted several crops on the same plot of ground rather than separately as we do. Barely a week after our departure from Bermuda, however, my mind was diverted to signs of impending landfall. We saw numerous limbs of trees, reeds and grasses that indicated we were near the mouth of some great river or bay. Captain Newport directed soundings to be made that showed that we were in relatively shallow water.

Sarah and I were on deck on the evening of May 20th. Neither of us felt that we could sleep because of the excitement of nearing land. We were hoping at any moment to hear the lookout's cry from above us. "How can we expect him to see land, John, in such darkness?"

It was a reasonable question. "Not unless someone had a fire along the shore," I replied. "You notice how little sail we are carrying and soundings are made frequently. The captain is taking care not to go aground."

We were silent. Suddenly there was an excited murmuring and laughter from others standing on the deck. "That smell," someone cried. "It's like walking through a garden."

We breathed the most pleasant aroma possible. It was fresh and to me was like newly cut fields of grass. I took deep breaths. "I did not know that land could smell so sweet," I said.

"Surely we will see land tomorrow," said Sarah.

She was right. The following day brought us a view of the low lying coast which we followed northward until we came to the southern entrance to Chesapeake Bay. At this point the wind failed us and the outgoing tide was so strong that the current would have carried us backward if we had not put out an anchor. This was no great concern, however, because we knew we could advance on the following flood tide. But the wind returned before the tide and we sailed smartly across the southern portion of the Bay until we saw Point Comfort on which the Virginia Company had established a fort. Not knowing our identity, the men at the fort fired a warning canon. We promptly anchored and sent a longboat to identify ourselves and find out what had happened to the other ships with which we had left Plymouth the preceding year.

We had reached Virginia on May 20, 1610, after a journey of eleven months and three weeks.

~7~

Governor Gates sent Captain Yeardley in the longboat to Point Comfort to identify us and determine how we were to proceed. We watched expectantly from the deck as the boat approached the palisades of the fort built by earlier settlers. Surely they would be amazed at our arrival, we thought, since it had been almost a year that we had been missing. For our part, we wanted to know the fate of the other vessels that had sailed with us.

From being with him during the past year I knew George Yeardley to be an efficient man. He proved again to be so during this mission for within an hour we saw the longboat making its way back toward us. As it approached the ship I could see that it carried one more passenger than had gone to shore. He was seated in the stern and conversing animatedly with Captain Yeardley.

"That gentleman is George Percy," said James Swift.

"Dear me," said my wife. "What a homely creature. And so thin looking."

"He has lost weight since I last saw him," said Swift. "But he has never been much prettier, I am afraid."

I had heard of the Percy family who were of distinguished lineage and had great influence in England. After being welcomed on board by Governor Gates and Sir George Somers, he was escorted to the captain's cabin where they could confer. In the meanwhile the rest of us gathered about Captain Yeardley and questioned him about what he had learned.

"All the ships we left England with arrived here safely with the exception of the pinnace we were towing that we cut off during the great storm."

"What about Henry Ravens and the men we sent from Bermuda?"

"Never heard from."

"And the settlers at Jamestown?"

"They have had a terrible time to hear George Percy tell it. And he should know since he is the president of the council now.

"What about Captain John Smith?"

"He was injured and had to go back to England last year."

"Tell us more about Jamestown."

"There has been a great famine. They expected to trade with the Indians for food but the Indians hardly had enough for themselves. And the Indians have been hostile. Our settlers don't dare go outside the fort at Jamestown without fear of being shot by the savages. And there has been great sickness, fevers and the bloody flux. I could go on but it sounds as if conditions there are terrible and there have been many deaths."

"Surely someone could have planted their own food if the Indians would not trade."

"Don't you know what famine means?" Yeardley snapped. "Without rain nobody gets a crop, neither us nor the Indians."

"How are things at Point Comfort?"

"I was not there very long, but they did not look to be poorly. Captain Percy was upset about that. He said they have been starving at Jamestown while the men at Point Comfort have been living well from fishing. He was telling me all about it as we came back in the longboat. Percy would like to send the people from Jamestown down here to keep from starving."

"You would think Captain Percy would have learned sooner that there was food at Point Comfort," Sarah whispered to me.

"True," I nodded. I thought to myself that because Percy was president he probably felt obliged to make his headquarters at the settlement at Jamestown. But he certainly should have kept himself informed on conditions elsewhere. From the brief glimpse I had of him he did not strike me as the sort of man who makes a strong leader. But that was probably not fair; I should reserve judgment.

44

Presently our leaders emerged from the cabin. They then got into the longboat and departed for Point Comfort with George Percy. I heard Governor Gates tell Captain Newport that they would return within two or three hours; that he wished to take advantage of this opportunity to visit Point Comfort before going on to Jamestown.

Nearly all of the passengers were on deck as we watched the boat move toward the fort. In the minds of all of us, there was only one thought, that the situation at Jamestown was grim. I heard a woman crying softly and looked behind me to see Mistress Horton with her handkerchief to her face. Her maid Elizabeth stood nearby comforting her.

I would have liked to say some words of comfort; she had been so kind to us. Not knowing any more about our situation I said nothing but turned to Sarah.

"John," she said, "could we go below? I am not feeling well."

"Of course. I think you should rest now. We will learn more when the Governor returns."

Sir George Somers had continued to include us in the admiral's mess. For this he had not only my gratitude but also my regard for him as a gentleman. Therefore we were able to hear more from Captain Percy who had returned to the *Deliverance* with Governor Gates. During the meal he did not talk much about the conditions at Jamestown; no doubt they had been described earlier to Governor Gates. In our presence he was retelling some of the events since the fleet arrived from England the previous summer.

"John Smith was president at that time and he prided himself on all he had done to preserve the settlement at Jamestown. Ye Gods, the vanity of that man! You know that his father was a yeoman from Norfolk yet you would have thought Smith was to the manor born. We had to swallow our pride to accommodate that man; and, after all, it was our work, not his, that kept us going here."

"Smith was surprised to have six ships arrive and there were no instructions carried by either John Ratcliffe, Gabriel Archer, or John Martin regarding the leadership of the colony. I think that he was delighted because he was reluctant to surrender authority and did not have to in the absence of instructions. But he had to consider how to accommodate all these people since there were almost two hundred here already and an additional four hundred arrived. So he decided to send Francis West with a large party of settlers to the falls of the river to start a new settlement."

"Is Francis West the brother of Lord De La Warr?"

"Indeed. And like the other persons of quality in this colony, he was often at odds with John Smith. Smith came to the settlement site that West had chosen at the falls and criticized it. Then Smith had his accident."

"What accident?"

"Smith managed to ignite the powder bag he was carrying and he was only able to extinguish it by throwing himself in the river. But the damage was done. The flesh on his thigh was badly burned and all agreed that he should return to England. Hallelujah! We were overjoyed at the thought of losing the swaggering martinet."

"But he had brought you through the preceding winter safely, had he not?" asked Governor Gates.

George Percy looked at our governor and slowly nodded his head. Perhaps he thought he had misjudged his audience and overstated his criticisms of John Smith. At least I noticed that he refrained from further slurs on Smith's leadership.

"Was the site West chose at the falls a success?" asked the Governor.

"Well, yes and no. It had to be abandoned because of flooding. But it can be reoccupied or the settlement relocated. There was a site nearby that was preferred by John Smith. In the meantime we had men at other sites. John Martin took a group to Nansemond on the south side of the James and I sent a group of men to establish Fort Algernon on Point Comfort."

"I congratulate you on Fort Algernon. It is an excellent location and well defended. How far is it from the Nansemond site?"

"About ten miles upriver."

"That does not strike me as being as well located."

"Well, we have abandoned it. The natives there were particularly unfriendly."

"In what respect?"

"After all but a small detachment of our men returned to Jamestown the Indians overran our outpost. We later found the bodies of our men. Their mouths had been stuffed with bread."

"Stuffed with bread? Why should they do that?"

"One of our chief concerns with the natives has been to trade for food. Perhaps they felt we drove too hard a bargain."

"It sounds as if your ventures have not been very successful."

"You have not heard all. There is worse to come."

I glanced at Sarah. There was no need for her to hear this. Mistress Horton had not even joined us for supper and for that I was glad. I thought perhaps my wife should retire but when I looked at her inquiringly she shook her head. She would stay and listen.

"I consider the fate of John Ratcliffe to be one of the sorriest chapters in the history of this settlement. He took an expedition of fifty men to trade for food with Powhatan, the paramount chieftain in Virginia. You could call him their emperor because all of the villages for many miles send him tribute. Ratcliffe took his party in one of our pinnaces and made his way up the Pamunkey River to the site of Powhatan's village. Initially, I am told, all went well and I suppose that led Ratcliffe to relax his guard. But on the second day the negotiations broke down because it appeared that the Indians were not giving full measure of corn for the copper that Ratcliffe had agreed to trade. When our men tried to return to their ship they were ambushed. Remember, this was at Powhatan's village so he greatly outnumbered Ratcliffe's men. Poor Ratcliffe was captured and killed. Only sixteen of the fifty men escaped to return to Jamestown. Powhatan's men even tried to capture the ship but were unsuccessful."

There was silence at the table. We all waited for Governor Gates to say further if he chose. I glanced at his face and saw that the color had risen in his cheeks. I expected him to speak out in fury at the wretched report from George Percy but he spoke in a cold, controlled voice. "Do you mean to say, sir, that a force of fifty armed Englishmen allowed themselves to be surprised and nearly destroyed upon visiting an Indian village? Did they not take hostages against their safety or post a guard which could cover their movements to and from their ship?"

"They had the opportunity to take hostages but did not do so. Obviously, John Ratcliffe is not able to justify his actions to us but if he were here I would be extremely critical of him. From the report I must conclude that he was completely deceived by the apparently friendly Indians on the first day."

"And this chief Powhatan, isn't he the same man who accepted a crown from the English along with numerous gifts. Did he not send emissaries to England bearing pledges of friendship?"

"The same man, sire."

"Then how could he be capable of such treachery?"

"Because he is treacherous by nature. He saw an opportunity to do us grievous harm and he seized it. If your well-armed force were to approach his village today he would probably greet you with offers of friendship."

"And my response to that," said the Governor, "is that he must be treated as the enemy he is. Our dealings with him will be military operations. There is no reason we cannot be militarily successful in a territory occupied by natives armed only with bows and arrows. But we can speak more of that later. Is there more that I should be aware of?"

"Yes, and it is a matter that I consider most serious. It concerns Francis West who was sent on a trading mission as our food supplies became so diminished that we were near starvation. He was to go up the Chesapeake Bay to trade with Indians of other tribes. A major part of our difficulty here has been that food supplies of the local tribes have been scarce."

"Yes, we are aware of that."

Percy paused before he went on. It was obvious that he did not enjoy reporting on the misfortunes of the Virginia colony, particularly to a man like Gates who held leaders accountable for results. I was uncomfortable myself because what had begun as a simple relation of events was becoming a hearing with judgments that did not favor the Jamestown leadership.

"Yes, of course," continued Percy. "Well, West's mission to sail north and trade was moderately successful. He secured food but hardly enough to sustain the entire colony. Then, upon his return he stopped at Fort Algernon. While there, he conferred with the men at the fort and reached the conclusion that he did have ample food to sail back to England along with men from the fort. And he did this without reporting to me or explaining his actions in any way."

"My God, Percy," said the Governor. It was obvious that he was upset but he looked around the table and refrained from further comment. This forceful military man could hardly believe the loose arrangements that had prevailed at Jamestown. "Very strange," he said. "Very strange."

The tension had increased with the telling of Percy's story. Because I was not in a position of leadership I grew increasingly uncomfortable, feeling that perhaps my wife and I were inhibiting the serious discussion. I thought the time had come for us to excuse ourselves. We slipped away from that somber group gathered in the cabin of the *Deliverance*.

"What a blow," I said to Sarah. "It was quite reasonable for Governor Gates to expect that if the four hundred settlers from our fleet reached Virginia they would greatly increase the strength and vigor of the colony. As it happened, they all arrived but the colony has only been able to establish one outpost, starvation has thinned their ranks, Ratcliffe and his men were ambushed, and Francis West has deserted them to return to England."

"How could West do such a thing?"

"That is a mystery. Perhaps we will know someday. But there is nothing that the Governor can do about it now. He has to take account of what remains at Jamestown and then he must decide what to do."

We anchored that night near the Indian village of Kecoughtan. Earlier we had been able to glimpse about a dozen lodges along the shore about a mile from the fort. There appeared to be cleared areas that I expected were used for farming as well as forests which stretched upriver as far as the eye could see. Now that it was dark we could no longer distinguish the lodges but we could see the lights of several fires winking in the distance.

"Those very people could be our enemies," said Sarah. "How strange it seems to be sailing into a territory where the people are ready to turn on you in an instant. And yet we will go ashore soon and attempt to make a home here."

"I am sure that with men like Thomas Gates we will be safe." I regretted the words even as I said them. I was not at all sure and I had always tried to be honest with Sarah just as she was honest with me.

We remained on deck for several hours. Mostly we sat in silence commenting only on the land visible beyond the rail of the ship. Throughout the day the water had been especially calm compared to the chop we were accustomed to on the ocean. Although we spoke no more about what we had heard in the cabin, the conversation would not leave my mind. How strange it seemed to me that nothing seemed to be working. A great deal of the difficulty I expect had to do with the famine which affected everything the settlers tried to do. I remembered years of poor crops in Norfolk and I had heard my father speak of severe famine. There were years he said when people in our parish might have starved had it not been for the tithing barns kept by the church. But there were no tithing barns here. I was getting an introduction into the difficulty of starting a settlement from scratch.

Suddenly we felt the patter of raindrops that arrived with a sudden gust of wind from the south. As the wind continued seamen began to move about the deck securing lines and sails that could fly loose. I heard Master Swift call for the boatswain to launch a boat for setting a second anchor.

As we descended to our berths on the lower deck of the *Deliverance* we could see flashes of lightning. The ship began to roll as it was attacked by rows of waves that had been generated quickly by the strong winds. A loud thunderclap indicated that lightning had struck nearby. I silently prayed that our ship would not be hit. After coming this far we did not need a dismasted ship to contend with. Despite the sudden rolling and the noise, the passengers below deck were cheerful. Why not? The Lord had brought us through a three day storm in mid-ocean. We would ride out this welcome from the winds of Virginia.

~8~

Sleep did not come easily that night. Although the thunder had moved away from us, toward what I judged was the east, the fierce winds continued to howl and the waves, their companions in mischief, tossed us about till well past midnight. I felt some sense of security in the knowledge that we had a second anchor to hold us. But as the distraction of the storm began to subside my thoughts returned to the reports we had heard from Captain Percy earlier in the evening. The thought of famine was depressing and we would have to deal with it. I wondered how hard the settlers had tried to support themselves and how much food had they expected to receive in trade with the natives. Somehow, I reckoned, the Indian population that was not inconsiderable had managed over the years to sustain itself. It was obvious that we had not come to a desert. I had the faith and optimism of a farmer: men would plant and labor and God would give the increase.

The desertion of the colony by Francis West was another matter. And, of course he had not acted singly. He had sailed back to England with a pinnace filled with willing companions. It spoke to the lengths to which men would be driven by hunger but it also indicated the state of mind among the leaders at Jamestown. If Governor Gates and Sir George Somers had been weak-willed we would have perished in the storm off Bermuda. By their example and direction they had kept us bailing until the *Seaventure* came to rest on the rocks. I had confidence that their infusion of leadership here in Virginia would enable us to do what was humanly possible in order to survive and ultimately to prosper.

But the dreadful events related by Captain Percy the night before were driven from my mind when I emerged on deck the following morning. The winds were gone and had taken with them all the clouds so that the sky had a fresh and scrubbed look that permitted you to see clearly everything on the horizon. To the north lay the nearest land and the lodges of the native village, Kecoughtan. Captain Newport told us later that the people of Kecoughtan had greeted the first settlers in 1607 and treated them with great hospitality before they sailed upriver to Jamestown. I was able to see a few people moving along the shore in the morning light. The water was as smooth as glass. The only movement on it was from a few seagulls and a bird about the size of a gull that skimmed over the surface occasionally dipping his outsized beak into the water. The graceful movement of this creature was a delight to watch and attracted the attention of most of the passengers on deck. Beyond the water and the narrow shore was the forest of Virginia. Its May foliage was primarily the light green color that we were accustomed to seeing in England in the spring. I could tell that these were great trees and their root systems would doubtless carry them through years of famine. We could see the green of the forest extending upstream to the west; and to the south, at a distance of several miles, were more of the woodlands that surrounded the mouth of this great river.

As there was no wind to drive our two pinnaces upriver, Captain Newport and Sir George had determined to take advantage of the next flood tide to carry us. They had to wait, however, until the ebb tide was past. When it was determined that the outbound current had ceased the anchors were brought up and the longboats were used to tow us further toward midstream where the incoming currents would be stronger. Our mizzen sail that could take advantage of a breeze from any direction was raised but hung limply in the bright sunlight.

The evening meal was a subdued gathering. Governor Gates was quieter than usual and even though Sir George Somers tried to keep the conversation going he had little success. Sir George, after all, as a seafarer was satisfied that all was being done that could be to get us to our destination. Governor Gates had to deal with what would greet us when we finally arrived.

I continued to be aware of my subordinate status at these meals and refrained from entering into the conversation unless I was asked to. Because Mr. Horton and I were farmers we were questioned about the length of growing seasons and what seeds we might have brought with us. Fortunately, since most of our baggage survived the wreck of the *Seaventure* I had a goodly supply of seeds. I had used some for planting a small garden for Sir George while on Bermuda. Somehow my success in this very modest venture increased my importance in the eyes of our leaders who were quite rightly concerned about our ability to produce crops.

On the morning of the second day our destination came in sight. Jamestown lay on the north bank of the James River on a low lying island that hugged the shore so closely that it blended into the mainland. There was some marshland distinguishable on the downstream end of the island but it was primarily wooded. A timbered palisade extended for several hundred hundred yards paralleled the riverbank. There was an open gate in the palisade and near the gate a small wooden pier extended a short distance into the river. Surprisingly, a whisper of a breeze crept up on our stern when we were still a quarter of a mile from the pier, making it unnecessary for us to be towed. The two pinnaces of the settlers were nearby at anchor affording us the courtesy of tying up to the pier. The ability of the ships to come this close to shore was convenient and was one of the reasons this site had been chosen for the first settlement.

Despite the gloomy reports we had heard about conditions at Jamestown there was an air of expectation and excitement as we left the ship. I noted that Sir George Somers, who had transferred to our ship earlier that morning, gave way so that Governor Gates was the first to disembark, followed by Somers, Newport, and Yeardley. Captain Percy, who had preceded us upriver, met them and escorted them the short distance to the gate. Captain Yeardley, whom I had learned was careful to make a military appearance, arranged to have his column of soldiers follow next. This seemed sensible to impress both the settlers as well as any natives who might be watching from a distance. The gentlemen in our group of passengers followed in no particular order with my wife and I being a part of that group. Behind us were the tradesmen and laborers.

Contrasting with the group of people departing from the *Deliverance* who were soon followed by more from the *Patience* was the lack of human activity at the fort. I could see no one manning the walls or at any of the gun ports. There were cannon mounted on towers at the ends of the wall but no one to service them. Parts of the wall were in disrepair so that a few of the posts that were intended to be upright were leaning at odd angles. There were only three men with Captain Percy each of whom rivaled him for gauntness and, I was to learn later, were among the healthier individuals at Jamestown. Inside the fort, that was triangular in shape, was a collection of what I could only describe as huts, made of wood and mud, and roofed with what appeared to be tree bark. Some of these flimsy roofs had collapsed and parts of other huts were even more dilapidated. They had missing doors or collapsed walls. Some were damaged by fire but unrepaired.

There were several larger buildings paralleling the row of dwellings but closer to the center of the fort. I judged these to be the storehouse, guardroom, and residence of the president. Separate from them was the church that could be identified by its cross and crude bell tower. I was touched by the thought that settlers struggling so hard to make their way in a new place would devote so much energy to a church and asked myself if there was a reason that God had permitted his children to come to such a condition as existed in Jamestown in the spring of 1610.

As we entered the fort, people began to appear from the doorways of the huts. Governor Gates was standing in the clear space in the center of the triangle and Yeardley's guard was in formation behind him. Captain Percy made no effort to present the settlers to the Governor but waited patiently as they began to assemble around him. After what seemed to me to be an interminable length of time there were thirty or more of them. They were a pitiable lot, facing our group that numbered about a hundred and thirty with some crewmen left aboard our ships.

The Jamestown survivors seemed diminished not only by the size of our group but also by our comparative fitness. All of us were well fed but where their limbs were exposed we could see little flesh. Some would not have seemed human were it not for their hollow eyed expressions.

"Captain Percy," said Governor Gates, "how many settlers are here?"

"Sixty. But some are sick and others are yet to assemble."

"Would you have the bell rung to come to the church?"

"Of course."

The settlers behind Percy turned slowly and began to walk slowly toward the church. We followed them, careful not to exceed their pace. They moved into the church, where some crude benches had been constructed, and took places on the front rows. Out of consideration for their weakened condition, none of us sat until we saw they had all taken seats.

After Reverend Bucke offered a prayer, Governor Gates asked the assembly to listen as William Strachey read from portions of the new Charter of the Virginia Company that pertained to the leadership of the colony.

"The first charter of the Virginia Company, dated April 10, 1606, is rescinded, and is replaced by a second charter which changes the form of government of the colony. All rights and privileges of the Company pertaining under the first charter are retained but the offices of president and council are abolished in favor of a governor appointed by a new council located in London. Sir Thomas Gates is hereby named Governor with absolute authority to rule the colony."

There was no immediate reaction in the assembly to this announcement although it was a radical departure from the previous arrangement where the president depended on a local council for authority to manage the affairs at Jamestown. They watched in silence as President Percy handed his seal and documents of authority to his successor.

Governor Gates faced the assembly to speak. "You will be informed of several other changes in the charter including the right of individuals to own land. I also intend to have the laws of the colony written and a copy will be posted here in the church. Do you have any questions?"

A man, who appeared impossibly thin, rose to his feet. His sunken eyes bespoke the agony he had endured for many months. There was utter silence in the church as he spoke in a hoarse whisper, "Governor, I can only express the one thought that is in the mind of every person here in Jamestown – we are starving." He sank back onto his seat.

"Sir," replied the Governor, "If I may borrow your words, there is only one thought in the minds of all of us who are newly arrived – these people are starving. We would have been fools if we had not noticed your misery or callous knaves if we did not care. It is my intention to have the food we brought shared equally with you. I must say, however, that we have not come expecting to supply Jamestown with food and cannot expect to exist long on what we have brought. Our first business, therefore, will be to see what we can do to obtain food. If those efforts are not rewarded we shall use our two pinnaces and the two here at Jamestown to transport our entire company back to England."

There was a moment of silence followed by a loud shout from the assembly. There was applause; and, as I turned to look at my wife, I could see that she was smiling. I had not seen such her appear so happy in weeks. Everyone was clapping, including the new arrivals who had become quite uneasy after arriving at such a forlorn place. The cheering continued as Governor Gates left the church followed by Sir George Somers and Captain Percy.

~9~

The remainder of the day was given to removing our belongings from the *Deliverance* and preparing a place to stay within Jamestown. Captain Percy had evidently given thought to this because I saw him pointing out to Governor Gates and Captain Yeardley the houses that were for the use of the new arrivals. These were the best of the unoccupied dwellings. Shortly after, we were called together and Captain Yeardley designated our quarters; the Rolfes and the Hortons were to share a house along with Elizabeth, Mistress Horton's maid, and her husband Thomas Powell.

The house was one of a row that extended along the side of the triangular fort that was nearest the James River. Since there had been so much sickness in Jamestown, our first order of business was to clean the small building thoroughly. There were no clues as to who had been the previous occupants, only a crude bench near the fireplace, beds fashioned from saplings, and a broken broom made from rushes. There was a rancid odor about the place which we set about to remove by opening the shutters of the two windows and removing all the remnants of litter we could sweep away with the broom.

Robert Horton and I joined a group, escorted by soldiers, who left the fort to collect firewood.

"What do you think of Jamestown, Robert?" I asked.

"Not what I would call a castle."

"Surely you were not expecting a castle."

"No, and if I were I would have soon changed my mind. I've hardly seen one stone since I've been ashore."

"They say the first forts built in Ireland were shaped like this one," I ventured.

"I have never been to Ireland."

"Neither have I but I understand that the intent is to establish some protection against attack, even if only of wood."

"There is plenty of wood here."

"And so we have a wooden fort. How about land to farm?"

"Now that is something I know more about. I heard there was much land near Kecoughtan that is under cultivation. I wish we could have seen it, John."

"We will, I expect. But first I want to see what land is being farmed here."

We returned to the fort with our firewood. The women were busy cleaning out the house and had sent Powell to fetch water from the river. They planned to wash down the building as best they could before nightfall. They had found rat dung all around the fireplace, according to Elizabeth, and believed the creatures had been attracted by grease and small bones they had found. "Why couldn't they have carried that to the trash pit?" asked Sarah. "Or even to the river if they were too lazy to dig a new pit?"

Although it was far from being a castle, as Robert Horton had said, the fort was indeed a refuge. Its timber palisades gave protection from the arrows of the natives and to a lesser degree from the Spanish who might attempt to attack from the river. In plan, the fort was shaped like a triangle with its base on the river and two equal sides pointing inland. There was a circular turret at each corner and on each turret four or five cannon were mounted so that cannon fire could be directed either toward the river or inland. Captain Newport had told us on Bermuda that the cannon were regarded with great awe by the natives who were quite understandably terrified both by the noise and the wide pattern of destruction the cannon could produce.

"Aye, it is the cannon they fear the most," he had said. "They can abide a musket since it fires but a single shot and has no more power to pierce a shield than one of their arrows if fired from the bow of a skillful warrior. The first time they saw a cannon fired by Captain Smith in 1607 it blew down small trees and branches by the score. They fled to the woods although we had only done it for a demonstration. We could scarcely convince the Indians to come back."

I chanced to greet Captain Newport as I left the *Deliverance* and commented that the cannon must still be serving well because the fort remained intact.

"True, Master Rolfe. With a force of only sixty, and half of them sick, Captain Percy could not defend it without the cannon. But, you cannot take a cannon with you every time leave the fort. So instead of attacking the fort, the Indians just wait in the woods until they spy someone who has ventured out unarmed or alone. Every Indian man is a hunter, and..." His voice faded as he imitated a bowman drawing back his string. He looked particularly grim as he drew his hook, not a hand, back to his face.

In the evening, Thomas Powell returned from his duties as cook shaking his head. "You have never heard such stories as Captain Percy was telling the Governor over supper. I could not hear it all, but thank heaven for that. It was the sorriest, saddest tale you ever heard and it poured out of the man like a dirge. Once he got started the Governor did not try to stop him but let it all pour out. Sickness of every kind you can imagine: fever, hallucinating, and flu. Not just flu, but bloody flu. People dying out in the woods where the natives shot them; people dying who ran away to the natives and never came back; people whom he sent out on expeditions who died the same way like poor Captain Ratcliffe. But worst of all, they had no food. Think of all those healthy souls who left England with us last year. Scarce any of them left even to ask what happened. They could not get anything to grow and the Indians had nothing to trade. They ate all their stores. They ate all their animals, they captured rats and mice, and they ate anything that moved."

"Have mercy, Thomas, can't you see you are upsetting the mistress?" said Elizabeth.

"I beg your pardon ma'am." He hesitated and then went on. "But you might as well hear it from me since I heard Captain Percy with my own ears. It will be all over the camp tomorrow."

"Go on, Thomas," said Robert Horton.

"Well, I could hardly believe this, but Captain Percy said there was a man who ate his own wife."

59

There were groans from his listeners that expressed our dismay. How could someone be reduced to such an abomination?

"Surely you misheard him, Thomas." I asked in the silence.

"Lord, I wish that were so. But he went on and on about it. He told how the man had killed her and cut her in pieces to conceal the body. People got suspicious and they found what remained of her in his house. So Captain Percy tried him and the man confessed. Then they hanged him."

I did not sleep well that night. We were all tired, especially Sarah who had not complained but I knew was affected by excitement of our arrival and then the grimness of the survivors at Jamestown. She was not her usual self even though she did not complain and had tried to help the other women settle the tiny house.

The next morning we were summoned by the ringing of the bell to congregate before the church. Reverend Bucke led us in morning prayer after which every able bodied man was assigned to membership in one of three watches to be detailed for guard duty. I was assigned as a member of the watch that extended from eight in the morning until four in the afternoon. After showing us our posts, Captain Yeardley excused us until the hour we were to be posted, with the provision we were not to leave the confines of the fort and would come immediately if summoned by the bell.

After receiving these instructions I was notified that the Governor wished to see Robert Horton and me. We went directly to his quarters where he quickly informed us of his intention.

"I need the estimate that you gentlemen can provide of when food could be produced here. Captain Yeardley will furnish you an escort to reconnoiter the planting area outside the fort. Please respond by mid-afternoon. Do you have any questions?"

"Sir, we have been assigned guard duty on the day watch."

"Captain Yeardley will arrange for your relief."

"We would like to know where the existing fields may be found.

"Your escort will show you."

And so we ventured from the fort to view what remained of the fields of the company. We were told that there had been some plantings inside the fort but they were long since devoured by the starving occupants. In fact, some of the gardens had become gravesites owing to the reluctance of uneasy settlers to venture far outside the walls of the fort.

In addition to the soldiers in our escort there was an early settler named John Laydon. We had to proceed slowly, despite my impatience to respond to the Governor's orders, because, although Laydon was not an old man, in his weakened condition it would have been cruel to attempt a quicker pace. He must have had a sturdy constitution because he had come to Virginia with the original settlers in 1607. Not far from the fort he showed us where corn and peas had been planted the previous year.

"None of it amounted to much at any time," said Laydon. "I am a carpenter, not a farmer, but I planted some in order to eat. We tried planting in early spring but had no rain at all. Then we tried again in June but still had no rain. The only thing we got was a few peas from the first planting. We got none of the corn from either planting. It was all shriveled up before a single ear appeared."

The only trace of farming was a few spindly stalks, scarcely two feet high, which gave mute testimony to Laydon's words.

"How did they choose this area for planting?" asked Robert Horton.

"They looked for places that were easy to clear but they didn't want to be too far from the fort. We copied the Indians who plant around the cleared trees and stumps, not bothering with rows. We stayed away from pine trees that make the ground too sour. We would do better if we were off this island and on higher ground."

"Did you manure your gardens?"

"As long as we had chickens and pigs. But they are all gone now."

"Since you were here since 1607, what plant would you say gave you best results?"

"The corn. There was good growth in 1607 but we were too

61

busy doing other things to plant much. Most of our food came from Captain Smith's trade with the Indians. Then 1608 was a dry year and last year it seemed there was hardly any rain at all. We got a few vegetables from water we carried from the spring. Most of the water around here is brackish." He nodded in the direction of the nearby marshes.

We were standing in the middle of the area that had been planted by Jamestown settlers but no English farmer would recognize it as farmed land. In addition to the felled trees the stumps remained. That was understandable; it required years to remove stumps. Given rain and steady workers these fields could be tilled; and, God willing, there would be crops. I turned to Laydon and asked, "Have you done no planting this year?"

"Sir, there is no seed."

We reported back to the Governor, who asked if we had reached any conclusions regarding planting.

"I believe we have, sir," I replied, looking at Horton who nodded his head.

"Speak up, Master Horton." It was obvious that the Governor was not in a good mood.

"Yes, Sir Thomas," said Horton, commencing what was the longest speech I had ever heard from him. "We have been to their fields, seen their condition, and talked to one of the men who helped in the planting last year. The fields are poorly drained, surrounded by tidal marshes, and show no evidence of any manuring. Last year's planting produced nothing to speak of and they have no seed for this year. I don't think we can expect any increase except from the few seeds Master Rolfe and I have left from England."

This was greeted by silence from the Governor, Sir George Somers, Captain Newport, and Captain Percy. The Governor glared at Horton for a while longer and then turned his gaze on me. "I deduce that Master Horton's conclusion is not favorable for production of food supplies, particularly since we have barely two weeks of supplies on hand. Do you have anything to add, Master Rolfe?"

"Nothing, Sir Thomas."

"Could you produce crops from the seed you brought?"

inquired Sir George Somers.

"On a very limited scale, sir. Perhaps there is enough to support twenty persons; but only after a season for growing. I used much of my seed in Bermuda."

"Bermuda. Now that is ironic," said Somers. "Had we realized the conditions here we could have brought fish and ham. We could even have brought live hogs to replace those consumed. We did not appreciate the wealth of food on those islands."

"With two small boats, Sir George, we could scarcely have expected to re-supply the Virginia colony," murmured Captain Newport.

"What's done is done, gentlemen," said Governor Gates. Our task is to decide what is best under the circumstances. Are there more questions for Masters Horton or Rolfe?"

Hearing none, the Governor thanked us and we withdrew.

That evening we talked about our visit to the fields and meeting John Laydon. The women had met his wife Anne and asked us what kind of a man he was. What could we say, other than the fact that he was alive proved that he was a survivor? He was a sturdy sort, probably a good provider since his wife was also still living. Elizabeth seemed to set great store by the fact that Anne Laydon, like herself, had married after leaving England to come to Virginia.

"What's more she came as a lady's maid, like myself."

"How did she and her husband survive when so many others died?" asked my wife.

"Captain John Smith sent them to live at Kecoughtan the winter before last. She sets great store beside John Smith. She said he could get along with the Indians and that no sooner had he gone back to England than the trouble began. She said the Indians respected him even though he could be a rough sort of man."

It was strange how hardship could bring out the best or worst in people. I thought of how Governor Gates and Sir George Somers had brought us through our, shipwreck, mutinies, and travel without loss of a single person except for those due to misconduct. Sir George, in particular, seemed to be exhilarated by danger. Our Governor seemed more calm, but very resolute. I did not have the same feeling for Captain Newport, despite his kindness to Sarah and me. I just had a notion that he was detached from us; and, although he was a marvelous sailor, he did not seem as ready to undergo hardship with us. But perhaps I was unfair. He had not lost his hand sitting home by the fire. We had reached Virginia, as much due to his skill as anyone else's, and it was not right for me to sit in judgment, even if only in my own musings.

~10~

The following morning I was summoned to the Governor's quarters again. I wondered if he questioned what had been said the day before. If so, why wasn't Horton summoned also? I hurried through the clearing of the fort, not wishing to keep the Governor waiting. People were gathered about the door, probably waiting to speak if called upon but the guard told me to enter without waiting.

"Ah, Master Rolfe, there you are. William Strachey is indisposed today and unable to act as secretary. Would take his place for the time being?"

"Of course, Sir Thomas."

"Good, we are deliberating on the situation at Jamestown and the actions we should take. Please record the names of the persons present and those items that I instruct should be a matter of record."

The group that met the day before had been increased to include Captain Yeardley and the Reverend Bucke. Bucke acknowledged my presence with a friendly nod while Yeardley kept his attention focused on the Governor.

"I see we have three possibilities, gentlemen," said the Governor. "We can stay at Jamestown, remove to some other place in Virginia, or return to England."

"I believe there is a fourth possibility, Sir Thomas," said Sir George Somers.

"And what is that?"

"We might remove to Bermuda."

"I thought of that. It is a means of survival but I would not consider it practical. We would have to send a vessel to England to tell Lord De La Warr where we went. I believe it would complicate the situation for him. No, if we leave Virginia we must return to England."

"Consider, if you will, Sir Thomas," said Somers, "how we arrived after only a ten days sail from Bermuda. To return to England must require at least three or four times as long a journey."

"Gentlemen," spoke Captain Newport, "I must say that navigation to Virginia is not as difficult as returning to Bermuda."

"Why not?"

"If blown off course while en route to Virginia one can sail along the coast until finding the capes. In the wide ocean, reaching Bermuda with all four vessels might prove a problem."

"Surely not for a sailor as skilled as yourself, Captain Newport." Sir George Somer's easy smile took the edge off his comment.

"There is another consideration," added the Governor. "We had trouble with the men while in Bermuda. I believe we would have difficulty with these men if, after all our hardship, we find ourselves back in Bermuda."

"The presence of a plentiful food supply in Bermuda should make a powerful incentive," said Sir George.

"I grant you that," replied the Governor, "but after their bellies were full some of these men would question the command of the whole expedition. And, for all the Virginia Company in London knows, we would be another lost colony unless we send to England. It would be better to sail for England."

There was a silence. Finally, the Governor spoke again.

"I do not wish to appear heavy handed, Sir George. If I did not want counsel I would not have convened this group. A return to Bermuda is indeed a fourth possibility and I think we might consider sending a ship there for supplies at some future time. But for now, I consider it too far away to be practical. Master Rolfe, please record that the possibility of returning to Bermuda was considered and concluded to be infeasible at this time."

"The immediate problem," he continued, "is whether we can stay here at Jamestown. To do so requires that we feed ourselves and defend ourselves against the Indians."

The Governor paused. He turned to Captain Percy. "Could you tell us how Powhatan managed to have large supplies of corn, despite the famine, when Ratcliffe had his disastrous encounter at his village."

"Powhatan has an empire with thousands of subjects. He taxes them heavily and one of the principal objects to tax is corn because it can be transported and stored. He uses this food for his own use, for trade, and for rewarding his favorites. The men and women around him will not go hungry."

"And there is nothing we have that he wants?"

"Copper is useful to him but he is a shrewd trader and has accumulated much of it in the past three years. And of course, he covets weapons of any sort."

"Well, obviously we will never provide him weapons. For now we must plan on producing food for ourselves. In that regard, you heard Rolfe and Horton tell us yesterday that food would require a full growing season. Am I correct, Master Rolfe?"

"Yes, sir. Even then, we do not have enough seed to plant food for two hundred people."

"And then our capability does not extend to growing food for the entire colony, about two hundred persons?"

"No, sir. Because we have so little seed."

"What about hunting, Captain Percy?"

"Deer are not as plentiful as I had hoped. The Indian people depend on them for clothing as well as food. They are skilled hunters and have driven away or killed the deer that otherwise might easily be hunted by us. They have even killed the hogs we loosed on a nearby island. No, I would not recommend hunting unless you have a large group of men who can defend themselves. We have lost too many of our hunters."

"Well then," continued the Governor, "what about foraging?"

"Indeed, we would not be alive today without that," said Percy. "There are trees in the woods which have provided nuts and some wild vines producing grapes. But last fall the trees hardly produced and unless there is rain we cannot expect them this year."

"Could you instruct us about fishing? That should be productive."

"The further one proceeds downstream, the better the fishing becomes. The fish retreat downstream during the cold of winter, probably to move to warmer waters. Oysters inhabit the lower reaches of the rivers because they only exist in salt water. At present, I believe our best possible source of food is from the water and the best place for that is at Point Comfort, near Fort Algernon."

"It appears to me," said the Governor "that Point Comfort affords some advantage over Jamestown because of better fishing as well as the generally healthier conditions there. Do all agree?"

"But, to remove to Point Comfort would make us vulnerable to the Spanish, would it not?" He paused to give an opportunity to anyone who wished to comment.

"Master Rolfe, please make note that despite the advantages of a move to Point Comfort, they are not sufficient to overcome the exposure to attack."

"Now, since our food supply is inadequate here at Jamestown, we must consider departing by ship. I would like to hear your comment on that alternative, Captain Newport."

I sensed a relief in the spirits of the men in that room. Somers and Newport were sailors. For them the sea was a natural means of escape from our dismal situation. Captain Percy likewise seemed relieved. Perhaps he had thought Governor Gates to be an inflexible general, too concerned with his own reputation to consider retreat. Percy obviously favored a departure, and as soon as possible. But he knew he did not stand high in the Governor's estimation because he had presided over such calamities as had occurred during the past year. Let the grisly facts speak for themselves; he would not press for withdrawal. Only Yeardley seemed disappointed with the way the deliberations were going. But I had long realized that he was a very ambitious man; not inclined to give up, nor would he shrink from a clash with the Indians or any other attacker. Captain Newport said, "We will have to use the two small pinnaces from Jamestown to carry the additional sixty settlers. I assume the pinnaces are seaworthy, or can be made so. Then," he continued, "there is the matter of food. We don't have sufficient stores to last the voyage to England."

His remarks were greeted with silence. I looked at Sir George Somers. The Governor had rejected a return to Bermuda but Sir George was not going to reopen that subject. He had another proposal. "We might consider sailing up the coast to Newfoundland. There will be English ships there for the abundant fishing. At the least, we can feed the starving and arrange for passage to England."

"There is a prevailing current which would help us," said Captain Newport.

"Is there any other comment on Sir George's proposal?" asked the Governor.

Captain Percy was quiet. He was not going to jeopardize the proposal, which might seem a retreat to the Governor, by his endorsement. In this respect I believe he was wise because the Governor was not in a good mood. It was galling to have to return to England after the almost miraculous journey to Virginia.

"Gentlemen, it appears that there is only one way in which we might sustain ourselves here. That is by fishing, provided the fish are plentiful enough. If not, the best course open to us is to sail up the coast to Newfoundland and eventually to England as suggested by Sir George."

"Because of the weakened condition of the survivors we found here we cannot delay preparations to leave while we seek the outcome of fishing. Therefore I intend to follow both courses simultaneously. Captain Newport, I want you to put all the longboats at your disposal, along with men necessary to man them, to fishing the river from here to Point Comfort, and beyond if need be."

"In the meantime, Sir George, please see to the repair and outfitting of the four pinnaces. We are confident of the *Deliverance* and *Patience* which brought us here from Bermuda but the *Virginia* and *Discovery* will require more attention."

"We will devote a week to these two activities. If fishing has not proved sufficient in that time we shall proceed with loading. Do you have any comments?"

"Just one, Governor," said Captain Newport. "We cannot possibly transport all the cannon at the fort in these small vessels."

"Leave that to me, Captain Newport. I will decide about the cannon."

~11~

Toward the end of my second week as a member of the guard my attention was distracted by a disturbance within the walls of the fort. There was loud shouting and a small group had gathered near the front of the church. I moved quickly off the bulwark and toward the commotion. Men were moving, as I was, to the group that was gathering about a tall but lean man who was doing the shouting while others had stopped whatever they were doing and simply stared at the scene.

"I tell you there is no God! There is no God! How could there be a God who would first make us and then set us here to starve? Answer me that."

He stared about the circle at men who I presumed to be his friends for they were trying to reason with him. "Calm yourself, Hugh. I merely said that God would save us."

"Save us! If there were a God, he has certainly decided to damn us. To which I say, damn him!"

"All right, that's enough." It was the captain of the guard. "Take him to the guard room," he said to two soldiers who had run up and seized the man.

"You needn't force me. I am not mad," said the man. He shook his arms free and walked, not without dignity, I thought, considering his situation.

"Who is he?" I asked of one of the friends who had tried to restrain him.

"Hugh Price. And a good man he is too. But a bit hotheaded sometimes."

"Indeed, I can see. I also see that he is a non-believer."

"True enough. But until today he has kept that to himself."

I thought that perhaps Price would be punished publicly for

his blasphemy. But the Governor must have felt lenient when told of the man's previous conduct. In fact, after a few hours in the guardroom, where he no doubt assured the captain of his intention to keep the peace, he was released and later that afternoon I saw him leave the fort with a man I recognized as a butcher who had been with us on the *Seaventure*. The butcher was armed with a weapon so I presumed that he was intent on proving to himself that game could be found.

On the next day, I was told that neither Price nor the butcher had returned to the fort according to men who lived nearby. A brief search was made of all the houses to be certain they had not returned to some other building and spent the night. When the search was completed with no sight of the two men, I was instructed to go with three soldiers of the guard to see if they might be found.

I followed the path leading in the direction that I saw Price following the previous afternoon leading the butcher who followed with his gun. They were an incongruous pair, Price being so lean and the butcher a corpulent man, one who was quite conspicuous in Jamestown. But the woods had swallowed them up so I instructed the men to form a line abreast. Presently, we came to a tidal marsh that we crossed, as it was low water, and moved slowly up into slightly higher ground. Now the underbrush became thicker and our movements slower.

"Master Rolfe," called the soldier who was on our extreme left. "Over here!"

I moved quickly toward the sound of his voice.

"Over here, sir. Behind these trees."

Lying on the ground at the foot of two large cedar trees was the unmistakable corpse of the butcher. He lay on his back with three arrows sunk deep into his considerable bulk and a fourth protruding from his neck. There was no sign of a struggle indicating that Indians had killed him from ambush. His weapon was missing.

On the other side of the trees, just a few yards away, lay the mutilated corpse of Price. His body had been ripped open and his insides strewn nearby, covered with dried blood. There was but one arrow in him that must have pierced his heart. It was difficult to believe that this was the same man I had seen the day before, lean but very much alive. From the marks on his body, I judged that he had been ravaged by wolves. I had seen sheep gutted in much the same fashion back in England.

We made a sorry sight going back to the fort. The largest of the soldiers managed to carry the body of Price while two moved along slowly with the corpse of the butcher. I followed closely carrying our weapons while thinking we were ourselves quite vulnerable if there were enemies concealed in the underbrush. After what seemed an interminable time we reached the clearing outside the fort. A cry went up from the bulwark; and, by the time we reached the gate, Captain Yeardley and a small group of men were waiting.

Yeardley instructed that the bodies be left outside the walls and soon men with shovels were busy preparing for their burial. It was only natural that afterwards there was talk about Price having brought God's wrath upon himself by his blasphemous talk only a day before his death. Why else, they said, would his body be ripped apart while the animals spared his companion, the butcher. I could not speculate on these things. What I was certain of was the truth of the statement that it was not safe for settlers to be beyond the walls of our fort.

I did not tell Sarah about the death of the two men. I was growing more concerned for Sarah's health and did not want to upset her. I had hoped that when we finally reached Virginia she would begin to recover. Instead, she tired easily and spent most of the day lying on her bed in the tiny sleeping area of the house. I was thankful for the friendship of Mistress Horton and her maid Elizabeth who showed her every kindness.

It was like Sarah to think of someone other than herself. She had never truly wanted to come. She would have been content to spend her life at Heatcham, the home of my family. Instead of coming to the flourishing place I had expected, we had found quite the opposite. The efforts of my countrymen, though costly in lives and treasure, had not succeeded in gaining a toehold in what should have been a perfect place for Englishmen to establish a new dominion. Was this poor stewardship on our part, as I suspected, or was it the will of God that we would not succeed here? Could we not tend a part of this country and spread the word of God to the natives? Surely it was not meant to be the domain of Spanish conquerors that cared only for riches.

I spent the remainder of the day doing what I could to make Sarah comfortable. I made sure that there was plenty of wood for the fire as it was very cool in the evenings. I made some small repairs to the walls of the house so she would not feel a draft if a wind arose. Then I made her some tea and she asked if I would read to her from the Bible and the prayer book as she did not feel strong enough to attend services at the church.

On the following morning the bell summoned us to morning prayers. The Governor addressed us afterwards to say that unfortunately the trial at fishing had been a failure, that not a single sturgeon had been caught, and that the few fish caught had not been sufficient to feed the fishermen much less the entire settlement. The Governor informed the assembly that his goal was to depart after three more days. There was still much to be done. Besides doing our best to make the ships seaworthy and loading them, it was necessary to dispose of the cannon.

Only the smallest of the cannon could be carried on our pinnaces and used to any effect. The largest guns, and there were fifteen of them, could not be left to fall into the hands of the natives or any Spanish who might arrive before we could return to Jamestown. I was told the Governor scorned any proposals to destroy the guns. Nor would he approve of their being dropped into the nearby James River. This left only one alternative, that we bury the cannon. There was a large ditch between the fort and the river intended to make access to the fort difficult for an attacking enemy. Many days of work had been done in the excavation of this ditch and it was logical to take advantage of it to temporarily dispose of the guns. In some places it was necessary to widen the ditch but that was still easier than starting a fresh pit elsewhere.

For a day every shovel available to us was in constant use. Even the Governor and Sir George Somers took their turn in the digging just as they had at the pumps on the *Seaventure* during the great storm. The effect on all of us was immediate; if the commanders would bend to the task with a will, so could we. Even as the ditch was widened, we were about the task of removing cannon from the bulwarks and moving them to the gate. The ground was hard from the dry weather and easily supported the carriage wheels of the guns as we dragged them across the interior of the fort to the river gate. Outside the gate the going was more difficult as the ground sloped toward the river and we had to be careful that the guns did not roll over into the ditch before we had them in the proper location. We well knew that a man's foot could easily be crushed if caught beneath a gun carriage. But we were blessed to have sailors and carpenters, who were familiar with block and tackle, could steady a load against the nearby palisade, and gently lower the heavy loads into place without damage to the gun or to any of us. Then, of course there was the back breaking effort to fill in the ditch. By taking turns, so that no one was asked to do more than he could bear, the job was done.

We could load all four of the pinnaces simultaneously because the water was deep enough close to the shore to bring the boats within reach of a short gangplank. The single pier that we had was quite small and only served to make loading a little more efficient.

Sawn planks, shingles, resin, and ash for making soap were about all that we had to take by way of cargo but Captain Percy insisted that we have something to show the Virginia Company in London. We worked until dark the evening of the June 6, 1610, and then went to our rest knowing that we would sail in the morning.

"Do you think we will return, John?" Sarah asked me.

"I feel sure of it. We will, if we are fortunate. But surely other Englishmen if not us."

It was a clear night. The moon was new and shone above us in the west over the river. Nearby pine trees and the great forest beyond acted like a sounding board for the west wind.

"Perhaps we will have a favorable breeze tomorrow," I said. "I hope so, John." She was soon asleep.

Morning light crept slowly through the trees, preceded by

the call of birds. It was a cheerful sound for what I expected would be a cheerless day. All about us was a bustle as men moved more swiftly than usual; no one wanted to be the last to be ready. We had been ordered to strip the houses of all our possessions. I was excused from guard duty because I needed to attend to my wife. I noticed that the soldiers were busy going through the houses, checking to see there were no fires left burning nor anything of value left for the Indians. After a brief assembly and prayers we began our movement to the ships. Two drummers stood at the gates and their drum rolls accompanied the procession. First came the sick, followed by the able bodied, and then the soldiers. The Governor was the very last, walking with his usual dignity. If there were natives watching from the woods they did not see a defeated man in Sir Thomas Gates, rather a man who ceded nothing and intended to return.

The *Deliverance* was the last to cast off. As she moved slowly into the river channel, a volley of muskets was fired from the stern. Once again, we were underway.

~12~

There is always a sense of excitement at the beginning of a journey. When we left England almost exactly a year ago spirits soared. We all shared a feeling of elation. But as we began our descent down the James River, on our way to the great Chesapeake Bay and then to the ocean, the feeling was more of relief, relief that Jamestown was being left behind. Even those who had been there only a few days realized that it was a place of sorrow and death. I could not help but notice some of the looks that were exchanged by some of the earliest settlers. For the first time I saw faint smiles where before there had only been long faces. They did not tempt fate by exulting, lest our ship go aground or some other event cause the Governor to rescind the order to depart.

The seamen worked with a will to maneuver our ship into the most favorable breeze and current. They worked as men do who have been away from their calling for some days and also shared the general desire to put this place behind them. They could not work up a wind, however, and we were dependent upon the tidal current to carry us downriver. After a few hours even the tide ceased to help us and they had to drop anchor before the water would carry us back upstream. "Not to worry, John," said James Swift, the sailing master. "Two days is the most we should be in the river. Then we will be on our way to Newfoundland to make a fisherman out of you."

"Why should I be in a hurry," I replied. "What could be more pleasant than a journey on the *Deliverance.*"

Although I did not speak the whole truth, there were worst situations one could imagine than being in the channel of that broad river. It was the clearest of days with no haze at all. The shorelines enclosing the sparkling water were like bright green ribbons stretching to the next bend. Where creeks entered the river there was marsh grass reaching to a man's height. At other places the shallow, tan colored bluffs were etched into the green where the river had eroded the banks. I wished that Sarah were on the deck to enjoy the sunshine but she was not strong enough to stay away for long from her berth below. I had been with her until she fell asleep.

Late in the day we passed the Isle of Hogs where the colony had kept some of its livestock in better days. When it became warmer those of us on deck sought what shade we could. There was no point in becoming overheated when the water we had to drink was so bitter. Our plan was to take on more water near Point Comfort where there were some nearby springs. The sailors had rigged canvas by the hatches in hopes of deflecting some air into the spaces below. I obtained a bucket and carried some water from the river below to bathe Sarah's face and hands. She was made uncomfortable by a fever that never left her.

We passed the entire day and the following night making our slow progress, stopping for the flood tide, and then proceeding. I did not sleep well for Sarah seemed more feverish than before. She called out in her sleep, asking for Bermuda, our child who had died. When I drew her close she would wake and take some comfort that I was there.

One thing was constant, the creaking of the timbers of our ship. They were comforting, in a way, because they reminded us where we were, on a journey and doing something to improve our chances of survival.

About an hour after the morning light had filtered down from the deck above I heard a commotion on deck. The barefoot sailors were running about and there were shouts. Knowing I had slept all that I was going to, I slipped out of our bed and found my way in the half light to the ladder than led to the deck.

"It's a canoe," said one of the soldiers.

"No. Damn your eyes. It's a boat."

We had made slow progress downstream because there was

no breeze during the night. But as predicted we were about halfway down the river to a place called Mulberry Island. As with Jamestown it did not appear to be an island but more like a small peninsula pointing downriver.

I moved to the rail where I could see what the sailors were watching. It was indeed a boat, not a canoe, coming out of the sunrise on the horizon. Because of the light behind it, details were not clear except that it was being rowed and therefore was not Indian.

"Send for the captain. It may be Spanish."

But before the captain reached the deck someone had seen the flag of St. George flying from the helm of the longboat. It was English but not a boat recognized by any of the crew.

When it drew alongside the man who climbed quickly up the ladder identified himself as Captain Edward Brewster.

"I have a message for Governor Gates."

"I am Governor Gates."

"Lord De La Warr sent me from Point Comfort when he heard that you were preparing to depart. His instructions, which you will find in this message, are for you to return to Jamestown and await his arrival there."

"Indeed. Let me have the message."

The message must have been brief because it took Governor Gates but a moment to read its contents. He turned to Captain Newport.

"Signal the other ships to send a boat to us for instructions. We are returning to Jamestown."

"Tell me, Captain Brewster, where is Lord De La Warr now?"

"Probably en route already. When we arrived at Point Comfort we learned that the pinnace there was being prepared for departure with you for Newfoundland. I was sent immediately to intercept you, hoping that I might arrive before you left Jamestown."

"If I may say so, we were all relieved to hear of your recent safe arrival from Bermuda. Everyone believed that you had been lost at sea."

"Thank you. But where is Lord De La Warr now?"

"I left Point Comfort yesterday morning and I expect that he too is now underway for Jamestown." We were soon to come about and begin our trip back up the river. There were groans from below deck when the passengers heard the news.

"What is it John?" Sarah asked.

"Lord De La Warr has come to rescue us. We are going back to Jamestown."

"I don't understand."

"It is a resupply. He has brought stores, I am sure. And with more men we will be able to defend ourselves from the Indians."

"I truly did not look forward to another ocean crossing, John."

"Neither did I. But very few feel that way now. Perhaps some food will raise their spirits."

Knowing that relief was on hand, the Governor gave orders to double the rations for the day. It was still meager but nonetheless appreciated. After a day and a night with no wind a fresh breeze rose from the east, favoring us on our return up the river. People began to take more interest in what was happening. So we were returning; and what could we expect to find? Jamestown as we had left it or would the Indians have burned it already? What kind of man was Lord De La Warr? Would we stay at Jamestown or move to some other place?

I was warned by my brother before leaving England that it was not wise to put much stock in rumors, particularly when people are tired or sick. So I resolved to await developments rather than waste time in idle speculation. I had the choice of seeing our return to Jamestown as a disaster, which many others did, or I could view it as a fresh chance. The situation had obviously changed, and changed dramatically. We were again being offered an opportunity to achieve our purpose of establishing a new dominion in a country that offered great possibilities.

Because our breeze did not fail us we easily reached Jamestown by evening. It appeared untouched so we could begin the process of unloading. The first to go ashore was Captain Yeardley with a group of soldiers. They would reconnoiter to be sure we were not walking into an ambush. Apparently there was none and in a few minutes we saw him appear at one of the bulwarks motioning for us to come to the fort. The Governor walked quickly up the bank and stood at the gate.

"Come along then," he said as we reached the gate. "Go to the same quarters you previously occupied. Good evening, Mistress Rolfe, I hope you are feeling better."

"Thank you, Sir Thomas. I shall manage."

"Good evening, Mistress Horton. I hope you are well."

"I am well, Sir Thomas, but distressed with our situation. I thought we were gone from this wretched place."

"We have been delivered from our previous situation, ma'am, and I trust this will become a less wretched place for you."

Robert Horton tipped his hat to the Governor and took his wife's arm to move her past the Governor who was obviously intent on raising the spirits of the people. Mistress Horton was wise enough to say no more within earshot of the Governor.

"I don't see why you are upset with me, Robert," she said later that evening as we sat by the fire.

"I am not upset. But surely you see that the Governor was acting under orders. He had no choice but to bring us back here."

"Who is this Lord De La Warr?"

"Someone who has been given authority over the colony. Don't forget, for all they knew in England, Sir Thomas was lost at sea."

"Do you suppose Lord De La Warr is displeased with the Governor?"

"We will no doubt find out when Lord De La Warr arrives," Robert said. "At least he should be pleased that the fort was not burned."

"We should all be pleased for that," I said.

~13~

A whole day passed before the arrival of Lord De La Warr. We spent the time in preparation. Unoccupied houses were made ready for the new arrivals. Captain Brewster had said there were three ships: *De La Warr*, *Blessing*, and *Hercules*. Their names meant nothing to me but James Swift reminded me that *Blessing* had been one of the ships in our fleet that sailed from Plymouth in 1609. With their arrival the number of settlers would be increased to over four hundred.

When Lord De La Warr arrived he proceeded directly to the quarters of our Governor where they met in private. In the meanwhile, the passengers and crew from the three ships came ashore and assembled in the church. It was difficult for all of us to find a place inside and a few had to stand by the door and windows where they could hear the services. Lord De La Warr, a ruddy faced man with a dignified, even haughty carriage entered with Governor Gates. By his appearance I estimated De La Warr to be much the younger of the two men, perhaps by as much as fifteen years. I thought Lord De La Warr also had the appearance of a military man as he walked slowly to the seat reserved for him. He sat near the rude pulpit occupied by Reverend Bucke and watched the preacher appraisingly as he delivered his sermon.

The Reverend delivered what I considered an appropriate message on the care of a merciful God for his people. He admonished us to be thankful for our deliverance from the perils of the ocean and that Lord De La Warr and his followers had made a safe ocean crossing in time to succor us before we had to withdraw from Virginia. There were prayers of thanksgiving and I believe that a feeling of calm descended on the people when we reflected that we could indeed be thankful for being reinforced from England. The hearts of our countrymen had been moved to send us aid and we could thank Providence for that.

We then heard an officer read the commission of Lord De La Warr by which he was designated as governor. Afterwards, Sir Thomas Gates rose and read a brief statement relinquishing the post of governor and presented Lord De La Warr with the seal. All this took but a few minutes but left us with no doubt where the power now lay in our colony. There was utter silence when Lord De La Warr rose to speak.

"I greet you in the name of your fellow countrymen who have made this resupply by three ships and three hundred settlers possible through the investment of their treasure. We have heard in England of your suffering and privation and are saddened by the deaths of so many of our countrymen."

"Some of the losses suffered here are due to sickness and mere misfortune. But certainly not all can be so excused. Much of the blame can be attributed to unwillingness to work for your own support, to your unwillingness to pull together in a mutual venture that requires cooperation for success, to your unwillingness to give up idle pastimes or unprofitable activities."

"I tell you this. Today, the 10th of June 1610, marks a new day in this colony. The law now is to be both moral and martial. I shall have it published shortly in written form and it will also be read to you. It shall govern conduct and set forth the strictest punishments that I warn you will be enforced for acts of disobedience. Now, I do not desire to raise my sword against any of you. I should much prefer to do so in defending you from your enemies so look to your actions that you not be cut off for being delinquent in any way."

"Because we have ample stores with us now to sustain the deserving, as well as ample punishments to deter the undeserving, you should be of good cheer. With God's help we shall succeed. I look to every person to do his or her part."

As he concluded he looked slowly about the church as if to fix every one of us in his memory. We all realized that Lord De La Warr had spoken in earnest. He then left the church to make an inspection of the fort. We were instructed to stand by our houses where we might greet him as he progressed. He moved with the same vigor with which he spoke, passing through the camp with barely concealed contempt for what he considered to be of shoddy construction or unkempt appearance. I heard him giving Sir Thomas orders for early restoration of cannon to the bulwarks. In the meanwhile, we would have to depend on the ships' guns for defense.

True to his word, Lord De La Warr had a written copy of the laws posted where it could be easily read. Among the many provisions of the moral law: Religious services were to be conducted daily and persons were to be appointed to report those who were negligent in their duties and service to God. Fines would be imposed for not attending services.

Punishments, including death, were listed for sodomy, adultery, rape, or fornication. Whipping was prescribed for those guilty of slander against the Virginia Company. Sanitation regulations were listed so that the fort not be poisoned with ill airs.

Punishments were listed for failing to repair for work or failing to remain at work during the required times. We were required to be on guard against any treachery by the Indians and to report such treachery to Jamestown immediately. The death penalty could be imposed for a variety of offenses including heresy, murder, thievery, unauthorized trade with the Indians, robbing Indians, and sedition.

To this were added martial laws which applied mainly to military offenses such as misbehavior before the enemy. Also prohibited were the wasting of powder and shot or personal feuding.

It was plain that Lord De La Warr was not only a determined man but one who had taken care to have legal authority for imposing his will upon the settlers. With his authority established he next set about organizing his subordinates to carry out his mission. Because he was now Governor it was necessary to assign some other position to Sir Thomas Gates whom he designated as Lieutenant General. He designated Sir George Somers and Christopher Newport as Admiral and Vice-Admiral respectively. Captains over fifty men were appointed including George Percy, Edward Brewster, George Yeardley and several others whom I had never met. Various other appointments were made for special positions including John Martin to be master of the iron works. It was said that that this last appointment was a humiliating demotion for Captain Martin. Indeed, Captain Percy treated Captain Martin with barely concealed contempt because of his lack of courage in dealing with the Nansemond Indians prior to our arrival. The resulting fiasco caused the slaughter of Lieutenant Sicklemore and his men.

There was much commotion about the fort as the military companies were organized and drilled by their captains and sergeants. I expect that any Indians who may have been watching us were impressed by the number of soldiers and their weapons. At this time I was not assigned a military duty because there were so many military men that arrived with Lord De La Warr. Instead I was assigned to a work party charged with constructing more houses for the new arrivals. Newcomers had filled all the unoccupied quarters but there was need for more so that some of the new arrivals continued to sleep on the ships that brought them. Among these was Lord De La Warr, who sometimes came ashore to see that his orders were carried out but at other times called his subordinates to meet with him aboard the *De La Warr.*

The most senior of these subordinates were appointed to Lord De La Warr's council. They met soon after his arrival to determine how to meet the settlement's future need for food because we could not depend indefinitely on the stores brought on the ships. I suspect it was at one of these meetings that Sir George Somers again brought up his proposal to return to Bermuda. Thomas Powell had told us that the Sir George would be sailing soon.

"The Admiral asked me if I wanted to go back to Bermuda with him," said Thomas.

"And what did you say to that?" asked his wife.

"I said I had a wife to think of now and asked if he would let me stay here."

"What did he say?"

"Well, he stood there twisting his mustache while he knows that I'm stewing. Finally, he smiles and looks at me and says it's all right for me to stay. Even though he plans to be gone and come back quickly he says he doesn't want you to be fretting, my dear."

"Well, bless me. I am surprised. As much as he likes his food I did not think that the admiral would go without you."

"Say a little prayer that he does not change his mind."

"Do you suppose you could make a little broth for Sarah?"

"How is she?"

Elizabeth looked at me before answering. "No better. The fever does not leave and she has chills." Thomas made a broth and we tried to get her to drink. But it was no use.

"Did you know, John that Lord De La Warr brought a physician with him?"

"I did not, Thomas. But I will seek him out. Where can I find him?"

"He is probably back on Lord De La Warr's ship tonight. But I expect he can be found in the fort tomorrow. His name is Dr. Bohun."

Thomas pointed out Dr. Bohun the next day at morning prayer. As a member of the Governor's personal staff, he departed the service with Lord De La Warr and I lost sight of him among the crowd in the church. But I looked for the group whom the Governor had gathered around him outside and waited while he instructed them in a loud voice on improvements he wanted to have made in the fort.

"This church must be enlarged. I want Reverend Bucke to discuss this with the builders and show me his plans when he has made a proper sketch. I want the work to begin as soon as the additional houses for the people have been completed." He then strode off with Sir Thomas Gates in the direction of the south bulwark where the first of the previously buried cannons was being restored to its position.

"Dr. Bohun."

The physician turned and looked up at me. He was rather short but of sturdy physique. He had a pleasant expression and courteous manner.

"What may I do for you, sir? I am afraid you have the advantage over me."

"I beg your pardon. My name is John Rolfe. I came from Bermuda with Sir Thomas Gates on the *Deliverance.*"

"I see. If it were not for that detour you might be called an ancient settler."

"Hardly, although I do feel that it has been an age since I left England. I pray, Dr. Bohun, that you might find time to visit my wife. She gave birth to a child in Bermuda who died before we left that place. She is now troubled by a fever, has grown very weak, and is barely conscious."

"There are so many sick here that I scarcely know where to begin. If you will wait here I will get my medicines and you can take me to her."

As we walked to our house, Dr. Bohun questioned me about Sarah. When we entered the house, Mistress Horton was at her bedside; I never left her alone now. When he had asked more questions and examined her, he handed some herbs to Mistress Horton and asked her to make some tea, using one of the herbs.

"She needs liquids because of the fever. Because her throat pains her, this tea will make it easier for her to swallow and perhaps to eat something more substantial." He then pointed at a powder that he said should be taken for the fever.

Two days passed and Sarah seemed to be doing better.

"How do you find the new governor, John."

"A very able man, no doubt. He is pushing the men to improve our situation."

There was the sound of a volley being fired.

"What was that, John?"

"That must be a salute for Sir George Somers. He is sailing on the *Patience* to Bermuda. And Captain Argall is to accompany him with the *Discovery.*"

"Sir George is a kind man."

"Yes, he was very kind to us."

"He brought us safely to Virginia."

"But for him we might still be in Bermuda."

We went on talking about Bermuda. Now that it was June

87

we were beginning to have very warm days in Virginia. In Bermuda there always seemed to be a breeze off the ocean. Not so at Jamestown; it seemed especially warm this afternoon. Sarah asked if we could leave the tiny house. Mistress Horton and I made a comfortable place for her to sit outside where she soon drifted off to sleep.

That evening the fever mounted higher than ever. Sarah became delirious and there was little that Mistress Horton or I could do to comfort her. We bathed her face and fanned her and then she began to suffer chills.

"Oh we are lost. We are lost," she muttered.

"What is she saying, John?"

"I think she is back in the shipwreck."

"Mistress Horton, I can hardly feel her pulse. Would you ask your husband to go fetch Reverend Bucke?"

"Yes, of course."

"Bermuda," said my wife. "I want to see Bermuda."

I felt sure she was speaking of our baby. Those were her last words. By the time Reverend Bucke arrived she was gone.

~14~

We buried Sarah outside the fort near a small grove of cedar trees where so many other settlers had been buried and where the funeral rites were still performed frequently. It was a sunny day and the woods were bursting with the richer, darker green colors of late spring. The sunlight areas where the trees had been cleared contrasted vividly with the shade in the woods. But it was a melancholy scene despite the bright sunshine.

I was pleased that both Sir Thomas Gates, our prior Governor, and Lord De La Warr, the new Governor, attended out of respect for Sarah even though Lord De La Warr and Sarah had never met. Most of the funerals had been held surreptitiously in order that Indians who might be watching should not be aware of the death toll. We had two enemies, the hostile Indians and sickness, and it must have been the strategy of Chief Powhatan that he had only to wait until sickness overcame us and he would be rid of the English intruders on his territory. So it was natural that we had tried to conceal our losses.

Lord De La Warr, however, was not a man given to any action that could be called timorous or even stealthy. His reinforcements were sufficient to overcome fear of the hostile chief, in his own mind at least, and he did not intend to show any sign of weakness to his enemy. Granted he had soldiers in the woods to prevent a surprise attack but that was a normal military precaution. So Sarah's funeral was well attended by many of the recent arrivals as well as those who knew Sarah from the days on the *Seaventure* that now seemed so long ago.

The Reverend Bucke read the familiar words from the

burial service in a measured cadence. I had asked that there be no eulogies but he read comforting words from the book of Revelations. With a heavy heart I sprinkled a handful of dust on the crude coffin that had been fashioned by the carpenters of the *Seaventure* the day before. Most settlers, I realized later were buried in a simple shroud, often from an old sail. The prayers ended and I accepted the condolences, first from our leaders, including even gruff Christopher Newport, and then others who had known Sarah. As we walked slowly back to the fort I could hear the men shoveling earth into Sarah's grave.

Our shared adventures had brought me close friends. The Hortons, William Strachey, and Richard Bucke were especially kind to me in my bereavement. I blamed myself for bringing Sarah to Virginia, thinking that her death could only be attributed to the rigors to which she had been exposed.

"Certainly, we should grieve for her, John," said Bucke. "But to blame yourself is to assume that you caused the shipwreck, or the conditions of Bermuda's birth, or the sickness that is so prevalent around us. These things are the forces of nature and there is little we can do but endure them."

"As a minister I think you are saying these things for my comfort, Richard. And what you say is true: that I am not responsible for nature. But I should have had greater foresight. It has been so different from what I expected."

"Of course it is different, John. We have been deceived; but more than anything we are the victims of self-deception. We should have realized that we traveled on oceans that are almost uncharted. We do not even know if we are on an isthmus near another great sea or if we are on a huge continent? We should have known that it was no easy matter to provide food for ourselves. Instead we expected natives to give us anything we needed for sustenance in exchange for miscellaneous trinkets."

"To me," I said, "our relations with the natives have been particularly disappointing. I had hoped we were coming to teach them and help them. Instead, except for a few in the distance near Point Comfort, I have not even seen them here. Machumps disappeared shortly after our arrival in Virginia and I do not know what tales about us he may have carried back to his people."

"The story of Machumps and Namontack is not unlike the story of Cain and Abel.

Machumps was envious of Namontack who was blessed with a gentle spirit. So Machumps killed him, I believe, out of jealousy."

"It's entirely possible."

"Don't we see the same pattern in our own society?" continued Bucke. "Envy and jealousy drives us to hate one another. No, I do not think those two young men to be that different from Englishmen I have known."

"If they are so like us, how can they be so treacherous, at one moment our friends and the next our enemies. Such actions must spring from their heathen spirits."

"I am surprised to hear you say that, John. Isn't our English history full of treacheries?"

"Spoken like an Oxford don. But let us not argue the point. A more important question is how are we to survive here if the Indians are hostile."

"Are you sure that all the Indians are hostile? It has not always been this way. The first settlers were welcomed by the Indians."

"True. But the underlying treachery was there. I understand the theft of tools and weapons has gone on for a long time."

"I can understand how a heathen might be moved to steal an iron tool if all that he had were made of wood or stone."

"Ha! Now it is my time to be surprised at you, Richard. There is a commandment against thievery. How can you justify it?"

"I did not justify it. I simply said that I could understand it."

"Even if they take weapons for the purpose of attacking us?"

"These men have to hunt, John. They see great advantage in having a gun."

"More likely Powhatan wanted the weapons to use against us. His word was spread and our weapons began to disappear."

"If Powhatan's rule is so absolute, how can we influence him to change? Captain Percy tells me that the sailors have given away so much copper in exchange for little that the

Indians have all they can use."

"It is difficult to say. I think that perhaps our leaders may attempt to use force."

"It is a difficult problem. But come. I want your opinion on quite another matter. I have been asked by Lord De La Warr to submit a proposal for improving our church. Tell me what you think of this?"

He showed me sketches of an enlarged building. The floor plan showed a rectangular structure twenty-four feet wide and sixty feet long. This allowed for more pews and a choir. There was a chair designated for the Governor in the choir. There would also be more windows.

"It appears you have increased the size without elevating the roof."

"True. We can thereby use what already exists and simply increase the length. Notice the furniture."

"I see that it calls for pews of cedar and a communion table of black walnut."

"For our carpenters who built the *Deliverance* and the *Patience* they should pose no great problems."

"Particularly if Lord Delaware's men brought nails with them."

"I have already learned that they did. But Frubbisher and his men will have little use for them in the finer furniture. Do you approve of my sketch."

"I do indeed."

"I would like to have you help me in supervising the work. Would this interest you?"

"Certainly. We have almost finished the building of additional houses. I will ask permission to work on the church."

And so it was arranged. Lord De La Warr approved Reverend Bucke's design with an added requirement for fresh wildflowers to be placed in the church each day. For my part, I appreciated Bucke's request for my assistance. I think he believed I needed the activity and we had the opportunity for talk about the work. I was glad to have more to do. It took my mind off my loneliness.

"How much longer before the roof is finished, Rolfe?"

I turned quickly to see who addressed me. It was the Governor who had taken me by surprise. Ordinarily his movements were accompanied by the sounds of his escort.

"I had them remove part of the thatch this morning, sir. It had not been prepared properly. Still, it should be finished by Sunday."

"Good. We can accommodate more people even if the pews are not finished. Perhaps you would care to have dinner aboard the *De La Warr* this Sunday?"

"I would be honored."

"Good. I am pleased with the progress here."

He walked off toward the storehouse before I could tell him that the progress was due to the carpenters who had worked together so much over the past year. I would not have mentioned the diligence imparted by the new Governor's strict demands for a day's work by all of the settlers.

Sunday morning gave Lord De La Warr another opportunity to impress every soul in Jamestown with his position and authority. A quarter hour before ten o'clock we had been called by the bells to the center of the fort where we awaited the arrival of the Governor. By then he had departed his ship in a longboat and was being rowed the short distance to shore. Members of his guard of honor, which I estimated to be at least fifty men, were forming along his line of march, first to the gate of the fort and thence across the marketplace to the entrance to the church. The guard wore resplendent red uniforms.

I could not help wondering what the cost of all those uniforms must have been. It was a display of wealth as well as power.

The assembly of the guard was accompanied by the loud commands of their officer and sergeants as the men were aligned in two perfect rows. The sun caused a bright reflection on the helmet and polished breastplate of the commander as well as the on the ornate halberds carried by the men. At the order of the commander, the drummers stationed at the gate began to play while Lord De La Warr and Sir Thomas Gates walked solemnly to the church. At the door they were met by the captains of the several companies of soldiers and then processed into the church. When I entered the church was already half full of worshippers. The Governor sat in the choir on a chair draped with rich green cloth and his senior officials sat nearby. It may have been a church of simple construction but the congregation seemed quite splendid to me.

I suppose it was natural for the Reverend Bucke to refer in his sermon to the twelve tribes of Israel reaching the promised land. He recounted how Jehovah had given Moses the Commandments to be the law for the people and then went on to suggest how we should regard the divine and martial laws that had been set forth by the Governor. Without suggesting that they were of divine origin, he nevertheless argued that experience had shown that settlers in a new land needed strict rules. I felt sure that these words were pleasing to Lord De La Warr. Bucke then went on to describe how Joshua had to deal with the Canaanites, causing the Governor to pay even closer attention. How often, I thought, do we heed those things that most closely conform with our own notions. Gentle treatment of the natives had not produced good results; we would now treat them differently.

After the service, the congregation watched Lord De La Warr and his leaders proceed ceremonially, with beating of drums, through the lines of soldiers back to the boats. William Strachey beckoned me to join him in one of the boats that carried us to the *De La Warr.*

"I am pleased you could join us today, Master Rolfe," said Lord De La Warr as were seated at his table. "You know all the gentlemen present, I believe."

"I do, my lord."

"Sir Thomas tells me that you have previously served on occasion as secretary to my council. I would like to have you or Ralph Hamor continue to do so when Master Strachey is not available."

"I would be most pleased."

Lord De La Warr then proposed a toast to the King. After we had reseated ourselves he asked to be excused from further toasts because he was affected with the gout and Dr. Bohun had limited his wine. This was said good-humoredly enough and the conversation turned to events of the past week. At this point, the first course, consisting of fish, was served. Lord De La Warr's cook had contrived to prepare an excellent sauce for the fish. The cook was further challenged by a sauce for the beef that was decidedly not fresh.

After we had finished the pudding, Lord De La Warr questioned Captain Newport about conditions upriver. He wanted to know about the location of Indian settlements. "It is already late in the planting season. We need land for farming that is away from the unhealthy conditions at Jamestown."

"There are several places I can think of between Jamestown and the falls that are about fifty miles upriver."

"I have another suggestion," said Sir Thomas Gates.

"Let us hear it, Sir Thomas."

"We might consider occupying land downriver. There are fewer Indians downstream who might oppose us."

"You have in mind to occupy Kecoughtan?"

"It is worth considering. There are large cleared areas there."

"It was once the site of a much larger Indian village," said Captain Newport.

"Recently?"

"Before the English arrival. It is believed that Powhatan attacked it and drove the people away. At any rate his son, Pochin, now occupies it with a small force."

"We will consider taking it if Powhatan's hostility continues," said Lord De La Warr.

~15~

Lord De La Warr was a man accustomed to being obeyed. And, within the confines of Jamestown, he could see evidence that his will was done. Hours of work and worship were strictly enforced, work was purposeful and was achieving desired results. Beyond the palisades, however, lay the woods where De La Warr's men did not venture without concern for their safety. It was plain that even a short distance from Jamestown, the will of Lord De La Warr meant nothing. In that region the will of Powhatan made itself felt in direct opposition to our desire to prosper or even to survive.

The situation must have seemed puzzling to the Governor. Had not Powhatan given his allegiance to King James and received a crown of copper from him? By temperament I believe Lord De La Warr was prepared to send troops to compel cooperation but felt obliged at least to try to reestablish a working relation with Powhatan. He decided to do this with a letter. William Strachey assisted with its preparation and described its contents to me.

The letter to Powhatan listed the various outrages committed against the settlers. Thefts and killings were enumerated and while direct involvement was not blamed on Powhatan, it was clear that he had a responsibility to control the actions of his people.

"Our Governor is no diplomat, John," said Strachey.

"I can understand that. Our people are being killed."

"Well, the Governor said that if it continues there will be reprisals.

He also demanded the return of weapons that the Indians have stolen."

"Do you think that will happen?"

"Who knows? At least the threat is plain enough. If the weapons are not returned, Lord De La Warr will send men to recover them."

Two of the ancient settlers were chosen to deliver the letter. These brave souls had previous experience in trading with the Indians and had some knowledge of their language. They went without a guard since a confrontation would have defeated the purpose of the message. They were gone for three days and, although I was beginning to wonder if they would return, the palisade guard hailed them in the late afternoon of the third day and escorted them to the presence of the Governor.

"Was there a reply?" I asked William Strachey.

"Of sorts. I suppose there is no reason to be discreet. It will be known soon enough."

"Tell me,"

"Well, perhaps our Governor seemed disagreeable in his letter but Powhatan is downright insulting. He said our men could either remain in Jamestown or should return to England. Those who venture outside the settlement can expect to be shot."

"My God! That sounds like war."

"Then he added the ridiculous demand that if there were further messengers they were to bring him a horse drawn coach."

"What?"

"A horse drawn coach like those used in England."

"It doesn't sound as if Powhatan cares much for the good opinion of our Governor."

"If his intent was to annoy, he was eminently successful. Our Governor, whose disposition is choleric to begin with, is positively raging. I left his presence as soon I could."

To me, the exchanges of messages had seemed pointless. It had the effect, however, of marking a change in the relations between the natives and us. It formalized the enmity that existed and would no doubt continue as long as the leaders did not feel that there was sufficient gain from making peace.

Both Lord De La Warr and Sir Thomas Gates were military

men. Both of them felt the need for action, particularly in the face of Powhatan's provocation, although I think Lord De La Warr was more given to precipitous action. They both felt a need to retaliate and both probably felt that, given the unhealthy conditions at Jamestown, establishing settlements at other locations was desirable. There were many examples from the English experience in Ireland of seizing land for a settlement that could be defended by fortifications. Conditions in Virginia were similar- a landing could be made, land taken, and defensive works constructed. There was no explanation given in early July when Sir Thomas Gates with two companies of soldiers loaded aboard ship but I expected action. I asked William Strachey who was accompanying the expedition where it was bound.

"I could not say for certain but you recall Sir Thomas Gates' proposal to seize Kecoughtan?"

"Yes."

"I believe that is where we are bound. If not to take the village then perhaps some land nearby."

So it was no surprise to me to see Sir Thomas sail downstream with his men. Later I learned that their passage had been without unusual incident. When they reached our fort at Point Comfort that had been named Fort Algernon they were beset with strong winds from the north. At the fort they learned that a longboat had been blown loose from its mooring and lost. Knowing the value of the longboat, Sir Thomas gave orders to sail along the south shore in search of it. They felt themselves fortunate to sight the longboat on the morning of the 6th of July and sent Humphrey Blunt in a canoe to retrieve it. To their surprise Indians seized Blunt when he reached the longboat and dragged him into the woods.

Captain Yeardley then went ashore with a group of soldiers where they discovered the body of Blunt who had been slain by the Indians. To the minds of many this recalled the slaughter of Lieutenant Sicklemore and his men by the Nasemond Indians earlier that year.

The senseless killing of Humphrey Blunt caused Sir Thomas Gates to seek revenge less the Indians interpret his forbearance as weakness. Although Blunt had been killed south of the James River, Sir Thomas moved to act on the north side where the village of Kecoughtan was an attractive target. The troops were landed at Fort Algernon where they were unopposed and marched the few miles to the vicinity of Kecoughtan on the 8th of July. Then, on the early morning of July 9th, they prepared to take the village. As a ruse, a drummer was sent ahead of the troops in an attempt to draw the Indians out of the village. The drummer was a clever fellow who could dance while he played and gave the impression that the English came in friendship. When the Indians came out to where the drummer was playing they were rudely surprised by a fusillade from the soldiers. Five of the Indian men were killed while the remainder in panic ran for the nearby woods. It was all over in a matter of minutes according to William Strachey.

I was saddened when I heard the details of the seizing of Kecoughtan. The Indian village had been one of the few places where we truly had been greeted in friendship by the Indians under the control of Powhatan. Their warm welcoming of the original settlers in 1607 was already part of the lore of the colony. But our leaders were thinking ahead about what we needed for survival. In their minds the cleared fields around Kecoughtan were of extreme value. They wasted no time in making the village a part of the colony. Ten men, including the Reverend William Mays, were left to establish an English settlement. I believe including a rector indicated the desire to make this settlement permanent.

Back at Jamestown, in the days that followed we saw more of the Indians than we had previously. Almost daily there were visits of small groups who would come as close to us as possible without any warning. If we saw them and responded by picking up our weapons, one of them would cry, "all friends," and attempt to show us some offering such as bread or a small fowl. We were then expected to offer them something in return. In the meantime, they gazed about at the activities of the settlement with great curiosity, probably in order to report when they returned to their villages.

It was under these conditions that I had my first opportunity to observe the Indians closely. I was involved in the construction of one of the several new houses outside the walls of the fort. Hearing a clicking sound, I turned to face an Indian whom I suspect was at least six feet tall since he was several inches taller than I. The first thing I noticed was the color of his face that had been painted or stained with bright red dye that extended to his shoulders. The right side of his head had been shaved while the hair on the left side hung almost to his waist. The hair was glossy, probably from grease that had been applied to it, and there were two strings of gleaming white shells suspended from his hair by copper rings. The clicking sound I had heard must have come from the movement of these shells. In his hand were more of the shells that he extended to me. I was so taken aback by his appearance that I ungraciously declined his offer by shaking my head. He then offered them to one of my fellow workers who took them and smiled admiringly before handing them back.

While this exchange was going on I noticed that we had another visitor. The second was shorter and was probably a boy in his teens. While our attention had gravitated toward his more striking companion, the boy had found his way to a carpenter's box that contained some of our tools. He was idly picking his way through them as if they were his own. He disdained a saw and a plane before his attention settled on a hatchet. Even as I shouted at him to stop he slipped the hatchet under his waistcloth, turned, and began to walk away.

"Not so fast," said John Laydon, grasping the boy by the arm.

The boy shook himself but it was no use. John was too strong for him and reached quickly to retrieve the hatchet. Now the boy was furious. His older companion then extended the shells to John Laydon, evidently offering them in trade. John's response was to make a sweeping motion with his hands, indicating he wanted the Indians to leave.

At that moment two members of the guard who evidently had heard my shout rounded the corner of the palisade. They escorted the pair away from the fort and stood watching while they disappeared into the woods. The Indians would not be hurried. They went at their own pace, leaving no doubt that they were angry.

"Those are Paspaheghs," said Laydon, "one of the two tribes we see most. The others are Chickahominys. Of the two, I would say the Paspaheghs are the worse. They were the ones who attacked us in force soon after we first landed at Jamestown."

These bothersome visits continued. What seemed most strange to me was that on the same day when several visitors might approach our camp, Englishmen would be ambushed if we ventured too far in the woods around Jamestown.

"They do it because they think they can get away with it," said John Laydon. "In the starving time when so many people were sick there was hardly anyone to stop them from coming into the settlement. Also, we did not have the strict Governor we have now."

The continual thievery fueled the anger of Lord De La Warr. Not only had Powhatan refused to return stolen weapons, he tried to get more from us. He knew that he was being harassed and he knew the source was Powhatan. His patience was exhausted by the thefts so that when a particularly notorious Paspahegh thief was caught near the palisade gate in the act of stealing a weapon he determined to have a trial.

He convened the council to hear the case in the center of the marketplace at four o'clock in the afternoon. This allowed for as many of the settlers as possible to observe the administration of justice. Like the Indian I had seen earlier, the thief was tall and strongly built. He wore his hair in the usual fashion but instead of shells he wore several bones and a feather for decoration.

Witnesses to the several offenses of the culprit reported to the Governor and the council. They testified to the theft of two pistols, an axe, and a bag of coins, all on separate occasions. The Indian had also injured a guard while he was being subdued. The words of the witnesses were translated by an interpreter to the Indian who merely shook his head, regardless of what was said to him. When offered a chance to explain his actions through the interpreter he said that he had taken nothing; everything he carried away had been given to him.

The Governor and council retired into the guardroom to deliberate. When they returned the Governor announced that the offender had been found guilty and that in punishment his right hand was to be struck off. I do not believe that any of us felt the sentence to be excessive considering that thefts of weapons were involved. There was no delay in carrying out the sentence. A chopping block was produced and a soldier called from the guardroom carrying a broad axe. The Indian was told to lay his forearm on the block which he did with great dignity. At a nod from Captain Yeardley, the axeman lifted his axe and brought it down on the man's wrist with a loud whack as the iron drove into the wood.

There was an involuntary gasp from the crowd as we saw the hand fall off the block. The Indian calmly reached out with his remaining hand to pick up his severed hand. Then he rose to his feet and surveyed the onlookers with a sneer. Doctor Bohun moved toward him to minister salve to his wrist but he shook his head and pulled his injured forearm close to his chest. Not a syllable had escaped his lips.

The Paspahegh faced the Governor while waiting to be dismissed. "Go back to your chief," said Lord De La Warr. "Tell him a similar punishment awaits every thief at Jamestown." The interpreter translated the Governor's words. The Indian stood motionless until a guard at either shoulder escorted him to the gate. No translation was required for the look of contempt on his face.

I expect that what we had witnessed that day was the subject of conversation around every fireplace in Jamestown that evening. I know it was at ours. Both the Hortons and the Powells had attended the trial but Mistress Horton had managed to slip away before the punishment.

"Got what he deserved," was Robert Horton's only comment.

"How can you say that, Robert? The poor man will probably die," said his wife.

"But, Mistress Horton, that Indian probably used one of those pistols he stole to ambush our men."

"Hush, Thomas," said Elizabeth. "Can't you see Mistress Horton is upset?"

Although I had offered to move from the house after my wife died, my friends refused to hear of it. I was grateful to them. The concerns expressed by these women were a softening influence in a life lived in an untamed place. We were daily affected by violence and privation. These conversations seemed my closest real link to the gentle life I had lived at Heacham Hall.

The conversation changed to the weather. It was becoming very warm. We only needed the fire now for cooking. Thomas offered to share some pipe tobacco with me. He had traded for some with one of the recently arrived soldiers.

The visits by the Indians stopped.

~16~

Our daily routine was to rise, consume a breakfast of cornmeal mush and tea, to which might be added some cheese since the most recent arrivals had brought goats with them. We would gather for morning prayers at the church after which we would repair to our various work details. Some of the men were involved with the loading of material of commercial value aboard the *Blessing* which was to return soon to London. I could see the value of straight timbers that could be used for ships' spars but wondered how much iron ore would be found in the large quantity of earth that was loaded aboard ship.

In the afternoon, after a meal of bread and some kind of stew of meat or fish, those of us who had been assigned land worked on the planting of seed brought by Lord De La Warr. Compared with cutting and shaping logs I found this work to be pleasurable. John Laydon shared this feeling.

"What do you think of these garden sites, John?"

"They will do fine if we get rain. And now that we have some goats and chickens we can do some manuring."

"I hope some of those chickens are good laying hens. I haven't had an egg since we robbed bird nests in Bermuda. Speaking of things I would like, John, I would enjoy some tobacco again. The little bit I bought is almost gone."

"I don't think you would like the Indian tobacco much. But it is better than nothing."

I liked John Laydon and respected him for his common sense.

"I understand Sir Thomas Gates will be going back to England with the *Blessing*. Do you wish you were going with him?"

"There is nothing for me there. Or for Anne either."

"So you have no regrets about coming to Virginia?"

"No, except that so many of the people I came with have died. And the ones Anne came with have not done much better."

"How have you managed to avoid being sick?"

"We have not avoided it altogether. I had the flu several times and Anne did too but it was never the bloody flu. But we have not gotten the fever, either one of us. You watch, now that it is getting warm people will start to get the fever."

On the 20th of July, 1610, the *Blessing* left with Sir Thomas Gates aboard. It was explained to us that he would be seeking more settlers and supplies for us back in London. I did not doubt his ability to do so. Sir Thomas was a man who inspired belief. For my part, I regretted his departure. I had not forgotten the leadership that he and Sir George Somers had provided in the shipwreck and then on Bermuda.

I had another reason for not wanting Sir Thomas to leave: he had gotten to know me and seemed to respect my ability. If I were to make my way in the colony and eventually become a leader myself it would be because I had gained the favor of those in command. Lord De La Warr knew who I was but not much more.

We were seeing less of Lord De La Warr. His health had caused Dr. Bohun to recommend that the Governor continue living aboard ship rather than on the island. It seemed that he suffered from the flu as well as gout. William Strachey told me the Governor seemed to tire easily and made fewer trips to Jamestown island from his ship. Strachey saw him frequently, however, because of his position as secretary of the colony. To be truthful, I was a little bit jealous of Strachey. When he had gone with Sir Thomas Gates on the expedition to seize Kecoughtan I thought that I might be called by Lord De La Warr in the interim to perform secretarial duties. But it had not happened.

Because our leaders were military men, they were seeking a military solution to our problems with Powhatan. The easy success in taking the village of Kecoughtan added to their enthusiasm. I could not say we were intoxicated by success but there was an atmosphere of confidence in Jamestown after Sir

Thomas Gates' victory. The morale of the soldiers at Jamestown was high and they spent at least part of every day in military drills and training. Some of this training was in marksmanship with the objective of making every soldier an expert with the musket. Targets were set up so that every man fired his weapon at the beginning of his guard shift as well as at the end. Scores were kept so that the men who did best were recognized for their shooting skills.

Near the western bulwark there was a cleared area that was used for drills. The companies of fifty soldiers were deployed over the ground in various formations such as those they would use while on the march or when closing with an enemy. During the most complex maneuvers, the captains would personally take charge of the drills as they would no doubt command these formations in battle. Mixed with the commands were the leaders critiques of their men. Some led by encouraging, others led by scolding. I noted that the sergeants were quick to provide the scolding if the hapless soldiers were slow or clumsy in their movements.

In early August there was a rumor that another military operation was about to be undertaken. During the day there were frequent visits by the officers to Lord De La Warr's ship where they conferred. Also several barges were made ready to transport men, a sure portent of troop movement. We knew something was eminent but where would the soldiers be sent? On the night of August 9, sensing that something was about to happen, I walked around the palisade to the waterside and seated myself on the bank. The mosquitoes were thick in the heavy evening air. Knowing that I could not sit there long, I walked along the bank toward the gate as a column of soldiers emerged and began to load in one of the barges. It was a large group, perhaps as many as seventy in all. The first men took their places at the oars while those who followed them filled in the center of the wide barge. When it was full, a second barge was loaded in the same way after which they pushed off from shore and began to move slowly upstream. They had no lights on the boats which could serve to warn watchers from the shore and in a very short time they were lost to view.

We still were told nothing of what might be the objective of the troop movement. The only acknowledgement of their departure was Reverend Bucke's prayer the next morning for "the safe return of our comrades." I tried to catch the eye of William Strachey as he left the service the next morning but, because he was with the Governor's entourage, he was gone from the church and out of sight before I came outside.

It was in fact two days before I was able to talk to Strachey. By then the soldiers had returned. The soldiers were in high spirits and the sounds of their ribald laughter could be heard throughout the settlement. Finally, the news of their operation was revealed to us following church service. There had been another victory over the Indians. This time, our men had attacked the village of the Paspaheghs and driven them out without any losses to our troops. A quantity of corn had been seized and brought back in the barges to Jamestown.

Later that day, William Strachey sought me out in the field where I was tending to plants that needed weeding. We had received some rain that was encouraging but it, of course, nourished the weeds as well as the crops. "Somehow I think you enjoy tilling the soil, John Rolfe, more than any of the other pleasures Jamestown has to offer."

"Is that an honest appraisal or do I detect a bit of sarcasm?"

"Some of both, John."

"Regardless, this is my assigned occupation. But what keeps you from yours? Doesn't Lord De La Warr require your services?"

"The Governor is not well today. The good doctor Bohun has bled him and prescribed rest because he did not sleep well last night. To tell you the truth, I spent part of the night in the company of the Governor and I did not rest well myself."

"You were upset?"

"It was not a comfortable time; hard to describe really. You see, I was present when Captain Percy came to deliver his report on board Lord De La Warr's ship."

"About the fight at the Paspahegh village?"

"Yes, Percy came aboard and reported to the Governor in his cabin. He had taken time to change his clothes so that he looked more the part of a courtier than a soldier. Then he managed to flatter the Governor in that ingratiating manner he has where he indicates that he and his listener are above the common sort of people."

"Well, they are, aren't they?"

"Yes, but he is so damned smug about it. Eventually he was satisfied that he had accomplished that and was ready to report. He started with their departure from Jamestown by barge and described how they moved upstream to the mouth of the Chickahominy River. They disembarked there and he allowed the men to rest so they were fresh when they attacked at first light in the morning."

"Did he have a guide to take them to the Paspahegh village?"

"Yes, but not a very reliable one. In fact, he was an Indian prisoner who was manacled and guarded closely lest he led our column astray. Percy's description included the type of formations they used. He and the Governor digressed into a short discussion on the merits of a close versus an open formation. But finally he had his troops arrayed before the village and himself located with the colors. "

"It sounds like a parade."

"True; how he managed not to alert the village is beyond me. He then had Captain West fire a single pistol shot which was the signal for the fusillade to be fired into the village. The Indians ran out from their lodges and the men fired their arrows while the women and the children ran. But, as you can imagine, it must have been a lopsided affair. Sixteen Indians were killed in the melee."

"And we lost no one?"

"No. In a few minutes the Indian men were killed or fled and the soldiers began to search the village for food. Then they fired the lodges and destroyed as much of the standing crops as they could."

"This may sound strange, William, but it does not seem to be a fair fight."

"It isn't. But it is the only way we can win. The Indians will not stand up to us. Their tactic is to retreat into the woods and ambush us from behind cover. Our only way to damage them is to attack their villages."

"Was that the extent of the fighting?"

"No. There was more. On the return to Jamestown, Percy had some of his troops put ashore under Captain Davies who marched inland and destroyed more lodges. A lot of damage was done. The fight was carried to Powhatan for a change."

"I suppose the operation was a great success?"

"Yes, but you have not heard the worst part." Strachey paused as if he did not wish to continue.

"What else happened."

"Somehow, the soldiers captured the queen of Paspaheghs who was trying to escape from the village with her small children. They brought the queen and the children to the barges and actually loaded them aboard. With all the corn that had been seized, there was very little room."

"I can understand that. I saw the loaded barges when they departed Jamestown."

"So the soldiers set up a clamor to kill the queen and the children. Percy was evidently in a quandary; although, of course, he did not say so to Lord De La Warr. He just said that he called a council of his officers to discuss the matter."

"Good Lord, why did he have to do that?"

"Because, my dear Rolfe, the man is a weakling. The council concluded the children should be killed. They were thrown overboard and shot in the water."

"My God, how horrible. Is there more?"

"Yes. Lord De La Warr asked why the queen had been spared."

"What did Percy answer?"

"That he thought she had value as a hostage. Which was reasonable enough; but the Governor told him that a blow had been struck at the Paspaheghs and that the queen should be killed."

"Did Percy oppose that?"

"Yes, but the Governor was adamant. He insisted that she be killed immediately and even specified that she should be burnt. That, to my surprise, caused Percy to take a stand. He insisted there had been enough cruelty and she should die by shot or sword. Thereupon Captain Davies was ordered to take the queen to shore and kill her."

"So the queen was on the Governor's ship?"

"Yes, but he never even saw her."

~17~

To me, Lord De La Warr's killing the queen of the Paspaheghs was more than mere cruelty. It was reckless and foolish in that it raised the hostilities to a higher level of violence. I was depressed by this thought and scarcely noted the arrival later in August of a pinnace commanded by Captain Samuel Argall. He had departed earlier in the summer with the mission of finding food off the fishing banks farther north along the coast. He had succeeded in bringing back a cargo of fish and was, of course, welcome for making this addition to our stores.

I would probably make little note of Samuel Argall if were not for an important part he played later in my life. In truth I was not drawn to the man. He always seemed to be acting in his own interest rather than for the common good. Nevertheless, I had to credit him with talent. He was only a few years older than I but had already become a successful sea captain. He was credited with finding a better route from England to Virginia, a route that avoided waters frequented by Spanish ships. Perhaps I was jealous of the respect he received from the leaders of the Virginia colony.

It was now late summer and we continued to work hard on the improvement of Jamestown that had been directed by Lord De La Warr. The palisade walls had been completely repaired and the bulwarks reinforced. We continued to work on new buildings within and without the palisade. The blockhouse, a strongpoint near the narrow entrance to the Jamestown peninsula, was reinforced. Because we had received some rain our crops were continuing to do well. It was a busy time and I was glad for the activity which made the time pass quickly.

Jamestown continued, however, to be an unhealthy place. Scarcely a week passed that we did not lose settlers to sickness. I was distressed that Mistress Horton became ill with the fever. We thought that she would not survive the alternating fever and chills that racked her in early September. Thanks to the ministrations of Elizabeth Powell she survived but in a weakened condition.

I was still called upon occasionally to take the place of William Strachey as secretary to Lord De La Warr's council. Sometimes I would be early and find the Governor alone.

"Come in, Rolfe. I trust that you are well."

"Yes, thank you, my lord. And yourself?"

"Well enough, except for this wretched cough and the gout. But they never seem to leave me. Tell me, have you heard the news of the men who were sent to search for minerals?"

"No, my lord."

"Well, you might as well hear it from me. They were wiped out except for one man."

"How could that happen?"

"From the best I can glean from the only survivor, they had made their way upriver as far as the Appomatocs. There they saw a party of Indian women on the shore. The women were naked and beckoned the barge to pull into shore. With very little deliberation our men decided to stop to disport with these sirens. They were then lured into the lodges and attacked."

"And then?"

"There is little to say. The one survivor is a man named Thomas Dowse who evidently is quick on his feet and managed to dodge a shower of arrows on his way back to the boat. "

"What will we do now, my lord?"

"I will discuss that with the council this evening. I want to continue our search for minerals. We must make this colony profitable. But it will not be easy. The men who were most knowledgeable about minerals were on that miserable barge."

At that point the members of the council arrived and they began their deliberations. Some were for an attack on the Appomatocs. To my surprise, the Governor opposed an attack. It was certainly not that he feared the Indians. I think he just wanted to proceed with the business of establishing another settlement. Others thought it was a risk to spread our manpower too thin by sending out another expedition. All agreed that the death rate proved how unhealthy a place Jamestown was. It was decided to send more men upriver to the falls.

Captain Brewster, an officer in whom Lord De La Warr had great confidence, was put in charge of the party that was to move upriver to the vicinity of the falls. He did this with great care to avoid the Appomatocs. He began the construction of a fort there as a safeguard against Indian attacks and within a few weeks he was joined by Lord De La Warr for whom the fort was named.

I was not surprised that the Governor removed himself from Jamestown. He was not a well man. In his absence, Captain Percy was named commander at Jamestown. I felt sure that Lord De La Warr must have felt uneasy in giving over the command to Percy, the man who had been in charge during so many of the earlier misadventures of the colony. But with Gates and Somers both gone he had little choice.

Perhaps it was my imagination but I felt that a subtle change came over the colonists who remained at Jamestown. They sensed that the firm hand of De La Warr was removed from them and that Percy was a pale copy of the unwell but nonetheless demanding Governor. Percy was more concerned with which gentlemen he would invite to dinner at his quarters than with repairs and improvements at Jamestown. He felt obliged to form an advisory council who were mostly men like himself, concerned above all with their own comfort and privilege. I feel somewhat guilty in voicing such a criticism of Captain Percy because, being a gentleman myself, I was on several occasions invited to his table. When I enquired later how we came to enjoy such delicacies and fine drink I was informed that each supply that arrived from England included a special shipment to Percy provided by his wealthy brother.

In the absence of William Strachey, who had accompanied the Governor to the falls, I was asked to be secretary. Because I was not drawn to Percy, I was not eager to accept the position but felt it unwise to decline.

At the meetings of the council we read messages concerning the settlement at the falls. They had succeeded in establishing their fort, although it was much less substantial than ours at Jamestown. Explorations were proceeding in search of precious metals, commodities that would have put the Virginia colony on a sound financial basis. All of us had learned, however, to be less optimistic about the chances of finding gold or silver.

The men upriver had not managed to escape from want since game continued to be scarce and neither had they escaped from the continual oppression of the natives. In one of their clashes Captain William West, the cousin of Lord De La Warr, was killed. We heard no reports, either good or bad, on the health of our Governor so we did not know what effect, if any, had resulted from his removal from Jamestown.

Those were the conditions that existed as we passed the fall of 1610 and prepared for another winter. We had the same leader in Captain Percy who had been in charge during the preceding disastrous winter but there were sufficient stores on hand to get us through the cold weather ahead. We did not have cheerful prospects but conditions were improved.

The hostile Paspaheghs had probably delayed seeking revenge for the killing of their queen until after their fall hunting season. We were told that they were accustomed to gathering large groups of hunters who would drive the deer before them until they became the targets of waiting bowmen. Success brought them hides for warmth and meat for the winter. With the hunt finished, we became their quarry.

They chose to attack our blockhouse, the most isolated part of our fortifications. To his credit, Captain Percy became aware of the Paspahegh activity and increased the guard. He directed Captain Powell, whom he put in charge, to take prisoners if possible. For once, it was our men who lay in ambush rather than the Indians.

The chief of the Paspaheghs, who had the imposing name Wowinchopunck, led the attack himself. His appearance, according to Powell, was no less imposing than his name and was intended to strike fear in the heart of his enemies. He had painted his skin black and attached horns to his head, causing him to look like the Devil himself. Our men were so well concealed that John Waller, an especially brave individual, was able to spring from cover and seize Wowinchopunck. Waller called on his comrades for help in subduing the chief which caused other Indians to emerge from the underbrush. In the struggle, Captain Powell saw that the chief could not be held and so he pierced him with his sword, not once but twice. Although the Indians managed to carry him away from the scene of the fight, we did not see how Wowinchopunck could survive his severe wounds.

The loss of their leader must have been a severe setback to the Paspaheghs. Indeed we were scarcely bothered by them for the remainder of the winter. In that season, the lack of foliage made it more difficult for the Indians to attack us by surprise. But we maintained our vigilance, knowing that there had been no change in their animosity towards us. The drilling of the soldiers and the practice of marksmanship continued even as the season grew colder.

January and February were bitter cold. On many days it was too cold to work and, in the absence of Lord De La Warr little was accomplished. We struggled just to keep a supply of wood for the fires that burned both day and night. Although our people did not become sick with as great a frequency as they did in the summer, there were always some who were seriously ill and our numbers steadily continued to be reduced by deaths. I estimated that over one hundred had died at Jamestown since I had arrived the previous May.

Sickness was not confined to the common sort. Workmen, soldiers, and gentlemen were afflicted without consideration of their station. The most outstanding example of this was our Governor, whose sickness has been previously mentioned. In late March he returned to Jamestown from Fort De La Warr.

"I doubt he shall be here long," said William Strachey.

"Is he close to death?" I asked.

"Not that close. But Doctor Bohun is counseling him that he must leave for a better climate or he will die soon. I must say he looks wretched. But then he never has been well since he arrived."

"Do you think he will leave?"

"Absolutely. There is a place in the West Indies called Nevis where there are healing baths. His hope is to go there to recover and then return. Moreover, he plans to take his guard with him."

"All of them?"

"All fifty. After all, he equipped them in those brilliant uniforms and has paid them so he feels they are his."

"That is true but it hardly seems likely that they will be needed on the short journey to the Indies."

Lord De La Warr was not the sort of man who excited admiration. He was too much the martinet and lacked the common touch. But he was a strong leader and, I thought, greatly to be desired compared with George Percy. It must have chagrined him to have to withdraw from Virginia. He turned over the leadership of the colony to Percy and left without ceremony.

Although the Indians were no longer sending men to Jamestown attempting to trade and spy on us, I believe that they observed us from a distance. Surely they noted the arrival and departure of ships and no doubt saw that Lord De La Warr and his men had departed downriver. They probably regarded this as an opportunity to do us harm. But this is speculation on my part. It is a fact, however, that shortly after this departure they chose to attack us. Once again, it was the Paspaheghs, the tribe that was still smarting from the loss of its king and his entire family.

The entire event had a bizarre, nightmarish quality about it. On the evening of the attack it had scarcely grown dark when I heard cries coming from the direction of our outlying blockhouse. These were unintelligible to me and therefore had to be Indians. Occasionally, I could hear one of our men shout to them in reply saying "begone" or words to that effect. The noise was intermittent but as it continued I could detect a taunting tone in the Indians shouts.

After what seemed to be at least an hour I heard the sound of a group of soldiers being assembled near the gate closest to the blockhouse. I walked out of our house toward the gate in

115

time to see this group, about a half dozen men, march off into the darkness. Obviously, it had been decided to reinforce the blockhouse. I thought that was a sensible precaution, given that no one knew how many Indians were in the woods, well concealed in the night.

The taunting cries continued throughout the night, disturbing the rest of many of our settlers. No doubt they also disturbed the guard at the blockhouse who unwisely decided that at daybreak they would respond to the Indians when the soldiers could at least see their adversaries. So they ventured forth, only to find the Indians receding into the woods. The decision to pursue the Indians was fatal because our soldiers were lured into a ambush in which they were cut down by the arrows of perhaps a hundred bowmen.

The fighting must have been as short as it was deadly judging from the chorus of shouting from the site of the ambush. An entire company of soldiers who had been mustered specifically to go to the relief of the blockhouse was soon marching in the direction of the Indian shouts. They cried "Paspahegh" repeatedly as they withdrew, evidently savoring their revenge upon us.

The company that went to reinforce the guard arrived only in time to recover the bodies of the ambushed men. The burial outside the walls of the fort was the largest that I had attended since coming to Virginia. It was a gloomy affair. It brought home the fact that our Indian adversary was a skilled fighter and tactician. He had convinced the blockhouse guard that only a few of the enemy were without, so few that they had to retreat when pursued. Then they massed so many bowmen that they overwhelmed our men even though armed with muskets.

After this victory who could say how much pressure the Indians would exert against us. Would they be satisfied with their revenge? I did not see how we could establish the Virginia colony successfully without peace. But how would we achieve peace?

~18~

On May 19, 1611, Sir Thomas Dale arrived at Jamestown with three ships laden with settlers and supplies. Of all the men I met in Virginia, this man was to make the greatest impression on me. He was perhaps fifteen years older than I and had spent all of those years as a soldier. He had a martial bearing and what I have heard soldiers refer to as the habit of command. He was tall and lean, with dark hair and a short beard. The settlers quickly learned that he meant what he said and learned to fear him because he would impose the most dreadful punishments for offenses against the martial law.

All of Sir Thomas Dale's adult life had been spent as a soldier. He served with the Dutch, and with English forces in Scotland and the Netherlands. His excellence as a soldier had resulted in a captain's commission and later a knighthood. We soon realized that he was as devoted to his God as much as to his king. His devotion was apparent through the support he gave the church. He insisted that both The Reverend Bucke and The Reverend Whitaker, who had come to Virginia with Sir Thomas Dale, were accorded the highest respect. Any sort of blasphemy was not tolerated.

On the day following his arrival, which was a Sunday, a special service of thanksgiving was held in the church. After the service a formal ceremony was held at which Percy surrendered his commission and Dale caused his to be read. Following the ceremony, Sir Thomas directed that the officers and gentlemen were to remain in the church as he wished to address them. He stood in the middle of the nave where we could all see and hear him well. He spoke without any notes, looking at each of us in turn as if to burn his words into our consciousness.

"Gentlemen, I think it well that I should address you so that you learn my assessment of the conditions we face together. As a soldier I have always found it profitable to share knowledge with my subordinates in order to work better together."

"Our three ships made the crossing from England in eight weeks, thanks to the blessings of Almighty God and the skill of Captain Newport. This voyage included a brief pause in the West Indies where we were refreshed by wholesome food and water. As a result, we arrived with three hundred men in good physical condition ready to work and to carry out any military operations required of them. The favorable journey also resulted in the healthful passage of our horses, cattle, and other livestock."

"There are many things which need to be done here at Jamestown in order to make this a more self sufficient place. I refer to the repair of buildings and the construction of new ones. Many of you will be involved in this effort, about which you will hear more details later."

"We will carry out attacks against Indian villages where they are a threat to our safety and well-being. In this regard, I hardly need to point out that offensive operations by us are more likely to promote our security than allowing the natives to attack us at will. We will be successful in this, not only because we have well-trained men but also because we will make our men less vulnerable to Indian arrows. I intend to use armor that I was able to obtain from the Tower of London before leaving England. Our enemies will find that men who previously were pierced and halted by their arrows can now withstand them without injury."

"Finally, since this is a communal enterprise and we depend so much upon one another, you must prepare to embrace the moral and martial laws to a higher degree than you previously thought possible. These laws were propagated by Lord De La Warr and I shall have them read again periodically to all of our people."

"A thief can expect the direst punishment, to be broken on the rack before being hung. I will not distinguish amongst degrees of thievery because I believe a thief is a thief whether he steals a farthing, a pound, or a neighbor's horse. A man who steals food from our common stores can expect to be starved to death. A religious blasphemer can expect to be burned at the stake."

These last remarks were indeed a warning. That evening I cautioned both the Hortons and the Powells to be extremely careful; that our new leader was a man who believed in severe punishment. We had come too far and been through too much to sacrifice our lives or our health for some offense.

On the day after his arrival, Sir Thomas Dale summoned the council to meet with him. I was included because I sometimes substituted for William Strachey as secretary. We were a somber group, not downcast but careful not say anything which might draw the ire of our commander.

"Captain Percy, it is my understanding that no corn has been planted at Jamestown. How is that so?"

"It is our intention to plant corn but we had first planted vegetables, Sir Thomas."

"I want the planting of corn to begin immediately. Whom do we have here who is a farmer?"

"Master Rolfe," said Captain Percy, looking toward me.

"Well, Master Rolfe, I shall look to you to oversee the planting of corn."

"I am not at all pleased with the condition of our buildings. I can tell that you have able carpenters here but more care is needed for buildings that are falling into disrepair. I refer specifically to the church and storehouse, two buildings that are very important to our welfare. I also want a house built for the purpose of dressing sturgeon. I understand they were rare last year but this year we are blessed with their return. I also find that the pier that you use for the unloading of ships is undersized and should be improved. Captain Newport, can you see to that?"

"Yes sir."

We went to work with a will, first because we wanted to please Sir Thomas Dale and also because we were motivated to get a good crop. I estimate there were about eight acres that we set out as the first area of corn planting. Sir Thomas came to inspect the work as he said he would. He was not pleased that we had been unable to use the plow he had brought but understood that more effort was needed first to remove stumps. We were to see more of him than we had Lord De La Warr whose health was a constant problem.

After the planting of corn I proceeded to plant a vegetable garden. I gave some seeds to John Laydon who had been helpful to me. He was interested in anything that might produce some food.

"Would you like some tobacco seed, Master Rolfe?" he asked me one day.

"What did you say?"

"Tobacco seed."

"Where will you get the seed?"

"From a friend. He is too sick to work. It is for Indian tobacco."

I had heard that Indian tobacco was very strong and bitter. But as I was anxious to have some tobacco again, no matter how strong, I accepted Laydon's offer and set out some of the tiny seeds to germinate. First I made a hole in the ground with my finger in which I placed several seeds. Later I would remove the sprouts from the ground, separate them and replant the individual sprouts.

I resolved to learn more about the cultivation of tobacco.

~19~

Our days after the arrival of Sir Thomas Dale were filled with labor. He made the strictest demands on us; and, while we knew that what he drove us to accomplish was for the benefit of the colony, what he asked seemed to strain the limits of human abilities. His attitude was naturally transmitted to his subordinates which resulted in an oppressive atmosphere. For my part, although I was often in charge of work details I tried always to remember that I was working with free Englishmen.

The labor was intense but we began to see results: living conditions were somewhat improved and we were beginning to have more food. The first yield of our gardens brought us vegetables and we had fresh fish to supplement our rations of meat. There were now thirty cattle at Jamestown that were making their contribution in the form of cheese and butter.

Two men were singled out for punishment for relatively minor offenses. One had shirked a work detail while the other had been apprehended by the guard while relieving himself within the confines of the palisades. Both received twenty-five lashes for punishment that was administered after morning prayer on the day after their apprehension. We were all required to witness the whippings although I noticed that Mistress Horton and several of the women hid their faces. The man accused of leaving his work party had a sickly look about him. In his condition I wondered if he was strong enough to survive such punishment. One could not help feeling compassion for the poor creature as he was helped back to his quarters by his friends.

About a month after his arrival, Sir Thomas Dale must have felt that enough progress was being made at the settlement to warrant the beginning of military operations against the Indians. It was his opinion that the Nansemond tribe, who lived south of the river , should be attacked to avenge the massacre of settlers in the previous year. It was recalled that Lieutenant Sicklemore and his men had been found murdered with their mouths stopped up with bread. In every encounter, the Indians south of the James River had proved to be fierce combatants. With characteristic zeal Sir Thomas decided they would be the objective of his first offensive.

Two companies of fifty men each were to attack the village of the Nansemonds. One company was chosen from the troops who had crossed the Atlantic with Sir Thomas. The other company was chosen from those that had come to Virginia earlier to make use of their experience. I was not surprised that Captain George Yeardley's company was the one selected. He had returned with the troops from the fort established by Lord De La Warr at the falls and I sensed was eager for a new mission. Perhaps he volunteered or perhaps Sir Thomas, being a veteran soldier, observed the high quality of discipline that Yeardley had instilled in his men. Whatever the reason, they were chosen and prepared by fitting themselves in the armor that had been brought from England.

Observing them load into barges, I had to admit the soldiers were a formidable sight. Their gleaming helmets added to the height of each man while their body armor made them broader and stronger looking. I knew that they must have been sweating profusely beneath the armor but each of them knew its value in defending against the arrows they were likely to meet. Across their chests were bandoliers of powder and shot that would enable them to fire successive volleys. A few men were also equipped with round targets, or shields, with which they were to ward off enemy arrows while the other soldiers reloaded.

When the men were all loaded into barges, Sir Thomas Dale, who had been observing the preparations, signaled for a longboat to be drawn up to the pier. He and his captains were splendidly attired in bright uniforms and armor. Sir Thomas even had a plume in his helmet that I thought would make him an especially attractive target. They did not bear muskets but had swords and pistols. After they entered the longboat it quickly pulled out into the river and moved downstream, followed by the barges. They had timed their departure for a favorable tide and within a few minutes were receding from our sight.

The operation against the Nansemonds was over quickly and within three days our men had returned in their barges with a quantity of corn. The news of a decisive victory was published and no doubt greatly embellished upon by our returning soldiers who were in good humor despite going through a dangerous and fatiguing experience. I made a point of seeking out George Yeardley to hear first hand what had happened.

"They are brave fighters, probably the most warlike Indians we have encountered. They saw us coming long before we landed and had a large number of bowmen on the shore ready to receive us."

"Didn't that make them an attractive target?"

"Yes, perhaps it did. But our troops are not accustomed to shooting from barges so our firing was a little ragged. And the range of our muskets is not much greater than the range of their bows so we thought it best to get ashore as quickly as possible. But they managed to bring down arrows on the barges as they landed and a few men were wounded."

"Did the armor help?"

"God, yes! Not only for the protection it afforded us but also for the effect it had on the Indians."

"What do you mean?"

"They were dismayed to see the arrows bouncing off the breastplates and the helmets. So they fell back and we pursued. But we were careful not to be led into an ambush. We knew how to reach their village without being caught in a killing ground so we slowly made our way toward the village."

"But they continued to fight?"

"Oh, I give them credit. They kept on fighting. Besides their leaders who were encouraging them they had their shamans who were doing their best to use witchcraft against us."

"How?"

"They were trying to conjure up rain. They knew we were dependent on burning fuses to ignite the powder of our muskets. You could identify the shamans from their extreme use of paint and decoration. They looked like so many devils, running about with rattles and making all the noises they could to attract the devil. One was throwing burning torches in the air."

"But I suppose it did not rain?"

"Not a drop. They had to fall back but all the time they were losing men. We had some wounded, including Francis West, but not seriously. Sir Thomas Dale had a close call, however. Being at the head of our formation, he was the target of many arrows. They bounced harmlessly off his armor. One arrow, however, struck on the helmet just above his eye. We came that close to losing our leader. An inch lower and he would have been a dead man."

"How many did they lose?"

"I estimate fifty Indians were killed out of possibly two hundred bowmen. They will be a long time recovering. We took what corn they had and burned the village."

"How will we ever live with these people in peace?"

George Yeardley looked at me for a moment before answering. "Don't you realize, John Rolfe, that this is a military campaign? We are here to take land because the Indians, realizing that we have come to stay, will make no compromise."

"When will it end?"

"When they realize we can take what we need by force and defend it."

There was no doubt that the operation had been a success.

Shortly after his return from the attack on the Nansemonds, Sir Thomas Dale proved that his promise of strict punishments against offenders was no idle threat. One of the soldiers who had not participated in the operation had been apprehended in the quarters of the absent soldiers where he was rifling their possessions. For this grievous offense, and to Sir Thomas there was no baser crime than barracks thievery, the offender would be broken on the rack.

I had heard of this device and had it described to me but had never witnessed its application. It consisted simply of a wooden frame at either end of which were mounted axles about which ropes were coiled. Nooses on these ropes could be fixed to the wrists and ankles of the offender lying between the axles. Turning the axles placed an unbearable strain on the joints of the poor wretch subjected to punishment.

I was thankful that the women had been excused from witnessing the punishment and only wished that the rest of us had not been required to attend. Although the women were excused they could not have helped hearing the screams from the victim as his arms were pulled from their sockets. Fortunately, the poor man was no longer conscious when his body was removed from the rack and he was hanged. His body was left hanging for the remainder of that day.

As if we needed a reminder that we were under martial law, we were required to hear a reading of the articles the following morning. Besides thievery, desertion, and work offenses one had to be careful to avoid any sort of blasphemy. Sir Thomas Dale was as scrupulous in defending God as he was our King.

"I am only thankful that I have very little to do with the man," said Mistress Horton.

"Hush, my dear," cautioned her husband. "You must be careful not to say anything that might be considered treasonable."

We were seated in our house and I believed we were safe enough from eavesdroppers. Still, Robert Horton was right in cautioning his wife. There was no point in challenging the martial law that was being enforced by Sir Thomas Dale.

The only concession to her husband's caution was to lower her voice somewhat.

"I don't care what you say, he is a cruel man. The way he looks through you with those pale eyes is hardly human. Of course, he has had no more traffic with me than to wish me good morning. To be sure, I want to keep it that way."

"That is enough on that subject," said Robert. "Let's see if John can tell us anything about the black magic being practiced by the Indians."

He was referring to stories going about Jamestown that described a strange incident following the recent foray against the Nansemonds. A group of soldiers, including Sir Thomas Dale himself, had happened upon an isolated Indian lodge in the woods. They went inside to rest briefly and find respite from the sun. Within a few minutes strange feelings came over all of the men. They thought they were in combat and that their comrades around them were the enemy. With that, they set about to pummel one another as if their lives depended on it. Fortunately the hallucination did not continue and their wits were restored. They recognized one another and were thankful that no one had been seriously injured by his fellows.

"It is true evidently," I said. "I have it directly from two of the officers who were present."

"Humph," said Robert. "There has to be a rational explanation."

But there was no explanation. Weeks went by and a similar incident occurred during an expedition when soldiers were preparing fortifications around their camp site. Sounds came from the woods around them caused them to believe that Indians had surrounded them. Then they began to hallucinate and, in their confusion, once again mistook one another for enemies. After pummeling one another for a short time, the illusion faded and they returned to normal.

Afterwards, some believed that they had indeed been surrounded while others thought that the Indian sounds were part of the illusion. There was no explanation; and, while the soldiers laughed about it, there was unease that the Indians were using some form of black magic.

~20~

I must admit that in the year that I had been in Virginia I had given little thought to the threat that the Spanish made to our settlement. It was known to all of us that our site at Jamestown had been chosen for its location upriver from the coast where we could easily be attacked. In our day-to-day life, however, we were more concerned with the more immediate threat of attack by Indians and in obtaining enough food to stay alive. We were told that the Indians at Kecoughtan spoke of attacks by the Spanish in the past, but that had been many years ago.

And so it was a great surprise to have a longboat arrive at James town carrying three Spaniards. They were under guard, of course, and caused quite a stir when the longboat pulled up to the wharf. I had gone to the wharf when I heard the shouts of the guard calling for the officer of the day who was Captain Yeardley.

"Sir, I have three Spanish prisoners aboard by order of Captain Davies." Davies was the commander at Fort Algernon.

"Where did they come from?' asked Yeardley.

"They came ashore from their ship and were taken in an ambush by Captain Davies. We think they had not seen our fort."

"Leave them in the boat and take it to Sir Thomas Dale's ship. That is where he is and he will give you orders."

"Yes, sir."

The longboat pulled away from the wharf. I had a chance to see two of the Spaniard's faces. One of them wore beard and mustache. From his clothing and bearing I took him to be senior to the other two. Neither of the men I could see looked very happy to be at Jamestown, which was natural, I suppose. I wondered what quirk of fate had brought them here. The third man was facing away from me so I could scarcely see him.

The ships that had brought Sir Thomas Dale and his supply to Jamestown were still here. Men were loading them with lumber, shingles, and pitch for the journey back to England. I could understand why the London Company did not want the ships to return empty. And so Captain Christopher Newport waited, rather impatiently I expect, before making another of his many Atlantic crossings.

It was natural to interrogate the Spanish and Captain Newport was a logical choice to be one of the interrogators. Besides him, Captain Percy and William Strachey were assigned to the task. Strachey told me later of the confrontation with Molina who was the senior of the three Spaniards. Molina did not seem overwhelmed by being questioned by the three men and the English lieutenant who had escorted him to Jamestown.

"He told us he was stationed in the Indies and had been sent to search for a lost Spanish ship."

"What did Captain Newport say to that?"

"He asked how any Spanish captain could sail as far north as the 37th parallel without knowing that he was lost."

"Did he get a satisfactory answer?"

"Molina said that the ship's rudder could have been damaged or he could have been aground on a shoal. Captain Newport laughed and asked how any ship could survive being caught on a shoal offshore. To this Molina replied that he agreed with Newport but that the guns of the ship could be salvaged. Captain Newport did not call Molina a liar but it was clear he did not believe a word. At that point, Captain Percy accused Molina of being a spy."

"Which I presume he denied."

"Emphatically."

"How did he allow himself to be captured?"

"The lieutenant from Fort Algernon repeated that they were captured by Captain Davies in an ambush. But that was just the beginning of the story. Molina asked for a pilot from the fort to guide his ship to a safe anchorage. He offered to remain with Davies, along with his two companions, until the anchorage was accomplished."

"That sounds reasonable."

"So it must have seemed to Captain Davies. However, no sooner had our pilot boarded the Spanish ship than they hoisted sails and left."

"That must have been a great upset for Molina. Come to think of it, it must have been almost as great a shock to Captain Davies."

"True, because the Spanish have one of our men who know everything about us. As for Molina, he now acts as if a simple mistake were made, that there must be a logical reason for it, and that he wants to be returned to Spain as soon as possible."

"I don't like the thought that they have one of our pilots."

"It is not a good situation. We continued with our accusations which he continued to deny. To hear him speak, he is a man of peace who wants to see peace between our two countries. Although we spoke to him rather harshly at times he always gave a soft answer. I would guess that he is highly placed except for his countrymen sailing off without him."

"And he gave no clues to what his shipmates were about?"

"Only that they were searching for a lost ship."

"Well, his shipmates could be meeting now with other ships to plan our destruction, could they not?"

"Indeed they could. But he maintains that he is a man of peace and there is ample land for our two countries to share in the Americas. For my part, I take him for a highly born Spaniard. He wears fine clothes and understands our language. Despite his education and position I believe he is naïve, that he came to learn about our colony and carelessly allowed himself to be captured. We had a little better luck questioning his companions."

"Did you get a confession?"

"Not really. But the second Spaniard, whose name is Perez, said that we were not in danger of attack this year. We took that as an admission that the Spanish have plans of some sort and he knows about them. We got very little from the third man, whose name is Lembri. There was something strange about him. I am not even sure that he is Spanish."

"What does Sir Thomas think about these men?"

"He is concerned that there is more than one Spanish ship lying offshore. He thinks that Molina definitely came to learn about us and that there is a possibility of attack."

"So what is to be done with our Spanish guests?"

"Sir Thomas gave orders that they be confined on separate ships. Perhaps we will get more out of them later."

The talk in Jamestown for the next few days was about nothing but these spies. I call them spies because I believe that was what they were. Despite their claim to be searching for a ship, they had come ashore at Point Comfort and they had departed suddenly when they had secured a pilot who could be used to their advantage. I thought of the many problems facing Sir Thomas Dale and was glad I did not bear his responsibilities.

Mistress Horton and Elizabeth Powell were upset by the thought of an attack by the Spanish. They considered them to be especially cruel and that they would treat English women very badly.

"That's foolish," said Robert Horton. "You are in daily danger of an attack by Indians who treat prisoners much worse. Besides, it is an attack that will probably never come. We waited for the Spanish to invade England in '88 and it never happened."

"You were protected by Queen Elizabeth's navy then," said his wife.

"The Spanish need protecting from themselves. They did not know how to handle their ships in either a fight or a storm."

I had been a small child at the time of the Spanish Armada and could speak with no direct knowledge. But Robert Horton had been a young man who remembered it well.

A week after Horton expressed his opinion, events apparently proved him wrong. We were awakened by trumpets and the rolling of drums. The tolling of the church bell summoned us to assemble. This was unusual because of the early hour.

I was still groggy from sleep and had splashed cold water

on my face to clear my head. There was a bustle of activity not heard on other mornings as people dressed hurriedly and ran toward the church. Some carried their weapons thinking we were under attack by the Indians. The soldiers were already in formation by companies. By contrast with the silent soldiers the rest of us milled about behind the formations asking one another what was happening. Women and children were in the mass of people with the occasional infant voicing its unhappiness at being suddenly awakened.

We were obviously not assembled to fight a fire or we would have been given instructions immediately. Nor did it appear that we were under attack. I saw Captain Yeardley step up on a platform where the entire assembly could see him. "Give me your attention," he said. "At just after daybreak a boat arrived from Fort Algernon. It reported that yesterday, in the afternoon, a fleet of nine Spanish ships entered Chesapeake Bay. A force that large could only have one purpose: to attack us. An emergency session of the council has been called and is now meeting."

"You are to return to your quarters at this time and make your breakfast. You should prepare enough food for the entire day because you may not have another opportunity. When plans for our defense have been prepared you will be reassembled for instructions. Are there any questions?"

"Will we be issued firearms?"

"Yes, but our supply is limited. When we next assemble you should bring any weapons with you that you own. If you do not bring them you may find yourself issued a pike or sword to which you are not accustomed. Now, if there are no further questions, commanders take charge of your companies."

The rest of us stood and watched as the soldiers marched off to their separate areas. There was a certain comfort, I supposed, in being a soldier. You had your orders and you carried them out. We walked back to our houses. I was not surprised to see Mistress Horton in tears.

"I knew it," she sobbed. "The Spanish are coming. Nine shiploads of them are enough to overrun us."

"You must not worry, ma'am," said Elizabeth Powell,

trying to comfort her.

"Isn't it enough to try to stay alive here? What have we done to deserve this?"

"I'm sure it's nothing that you have done. Please sit yourself down."

Sitting down seemed to quiet the poor woman. Elizabeth brought her something to eat but I noticed that Robert Horton kept his distance. He probably did not wish to be reminded that only a few days earlier he had scoffed at the idea of Spanish attack.

Elizabeth said there was little we could take with us to eat except for some bread. She did not have time to make more. I was not thinking about food; my mind was more on what we had been told about weapons. I had my sword and a pistol that I checked to see was in firing order. We were all rather quiet. Concerns that I had about work and my feeling of loneliness disappeared in the uncertainty of the moment. We had no idea what this day held for us. In about an hour we were called back to receive our instructions. Once again Captain Yeardley addressed us.

"It is the decision of the council that we will make our defense aboard ship. Each of our three ships will have at least two companies of soldiers aboard in addition to the crew. Women and children will remain here within the fort with a guard to see to their safety."

A loud murmur arose from the settlers who were not soldiers. It was caused more by surprise than consternation. Probably the soldiers shared our surprise but did not voice it.

"Silence. You must realize this is necessary for the defense of our ships. It also permits us to carry the fight to our enemy rather than allowing ourselves to besieged." We were rather quickly assigned to ships and began the slower task of loading. Powder and shot were issued from the storehouse to sustain us if it were a prolonged fight. Only one ship could come to our small wharf at a time so smaller boats were used to transport men and supplies. By noontime it was mostly done and I once again found myself aboard the *Deliverance*. I thought of the many hours we had spent working to build this ship in

Bermuda, using some of the timbers from the *Seaventure*. Being aboard raised my spirits; I recalled how God had delivered us through many calamities and I trusted that we would not now be brought to ruin by the Spanish. Although I had never been in a naval battle, nor a battle of any other sort for that matter, I felt that we had a better chance aboard ship.

Immediately upon hearing of the impending attack, Sir Thomas Dale had sent Captain Brewster and Lieutenant Abbott with a force of forty men in boats to obtain information about our enemy. They were already on their way downriver before the meeting of the council. I think this act demonstrated the forceful nature of our leader; he was not going to be without information. In the early afternoon we were able to see the small boats working their way back to Jamestown. All we could do was wait, wondering what news they would bring.

The leading boat finally drew up alongside the *Prosperous* which was our ship farthest downstream. Shortly we heard a cheer go up. What had happened? Had the Spanish failed to come upriver? We could only wait until Captain Brewster's boat approached us. We could see him clearly, standing in the bow, as he came alongside the *Deliverance*.

"The ships are not Spanish. Governor Gates has returned."

A roar of approval greeted these words. We had been spared a bloody fight, a fight with a very doubtful outcome for us. There were more cheers resounding from all the boats. We now had to face the tedium of returning to shore and unloading but no one minded. By five o'clock were ashore once more, greeted by more smiling faces than I recalled ever seeing at Jamestown.

We had scarcely returned our equipment to our houses when we heard shouts from the waterfront indicating the arrival of the first vessels. All of us immediately returned to see the ships except Mistress Horton. She announced that she was worn out by the events of the day and was taking to her bed. Her husband said he would remain with her but she urged him to go, allowing that the day had ended much better than she had thought it would.

We seated ourselves along the river's edge and watched the

arrival of the ships. The sun was slipping lower in the sky and the wind was dying with the day, making for a slow approach to the anchorages. The first and largest of the ships was evidently the flagship carrying Governor Gates. When it anchored a boat was quickly lowered over the side to carry him to shore. Sir Thomas Dale awaited him there with a military escort. The two men moved into the fort where I presume they exchanged the news they each had for the other.

I was content to watch the arrival of the other ships. There were only six instead of the nine that had been reported earlier. The captains knew they were being watched from shore and moved their ships as smartly as they could to their anchorages.

All this was accompanied by an incredibly beautiful sunset whose crimson glow diffused over the water. It was a captivating scene, combining the grandeur of nature with the beauty of the sailing vessels. Soon the small boats were at work, delivering passengers to shore where they would make their new home. I prayed that they would have an easier time than so many who had preceded them.

Jamestown was lit that night with bonfires and torches. People taking their first steps in their new land exchanged greetings with seasoned settlers. By orders of Sir Thomas Dale, wine was dispensed from the storehouse in honor of the arrival of Governor Gates and this great supply. For the first time I had the sense that we would not fail, that the seeds planted at Jamestown by England would take root in American soil and prosper.

I had hoped to greet Governor Gates that evening when his fleet arrived at Jamestown. I continued to admire him for his leadership and wished to remain in his good graces. Because of his height and commanding presence he should have been easy to find. I was standing on the edge of a crowd of gentlemen, obviously looking for someone, when William Strachey saw me.

"Hello, John Rolfe, for whom are you searching?"

"I had hoped to catch a glimpse of the Governor, perhaps to give him my regards."

"I'm afraid that you won't see him tonight."

"Is he ill?"

"He has returned to his ship. Have you heard the news? His wife died on the passage from England."

"Lord have mercy."

"It's true. He brought his wife and children with him from England. But his wife died and was buried at sea."

"Poor man."

"The children are to return to England I understand."

Sir Thomas Gates and I had shared the hardship of shipwreck at Bermuda. Now we had something else in common, both of us had lost our wives as a result of coming to America. I knew something of the desolation that he must have felt. There was also the temptation to become mired in feelings of guilt. For me, the only way to overcome these feelings had been to lose myself in work, but even though the pain was lessened by activity, the thought remained that my ambitions had brought us to the far country where she died. William must have guessed where my thoughts were taking me. "Come along, John, and have a cup of wine with me."

~21~

The new arrivals slept aboard ship on their first night at Jamestown. There had not been time for them to unload on the evening of their arrival, and in truth, there was not sufficient room for all six hundred of them at Jamestown. Our settlement would have burst at the seams to find a place for that large an increase in population. So they had made their way back to the ships that night with many shouts echoing over the water following their celebration of a safe passage over the Atlantic.

The colony's leaders had assembled the next morning for a church service after which there was a meeting to discuss plans. I was invited to attend because I was considered to be knowledgeable in the planting activity at Jamestown. At the church service I found a seat on the aisle where I hoped that Governor Gates would see me when he exited the church. At first I thought he would pass me by as he was in conversation but he paused momentarily, and as he did so, I caught his eye. He reached out to shake my hand.

"There's John Rolfe, one of my Bermuda stalwarts. I trust you have been well?"

"I have, Sir Thomas. May I say how glad I am to see you again."

He moved on as others greeted him. I thought how characteristic it was of him to refer to Bermuda. He was one of those leaders who bound others to him. By contrast, Captain Percy who followed in his wake had passed me by without the slightest acknowledgement of my presence. Although I was a gentleman I was not sufficiently important to merit his attention. I told myself that someday I would rank high enough to claim the attention of the Percys of this world.

Governor Gates opened the meeting by having the order read that designated him as Governor. This was followed by an order that bestowed the title of Marshal upon Sir Thomas Dale. There had been speculation about the relationship that was to exist between the two leaders. Gates was clearly the superior but there was ample authority for Dale to operate in any sphere that the Governor designated for him.

"Gentlemen," said the Governor, "you must be aware from the size of this supply, six ships and six hundred people, that there is solid support for our enterprise in England. But, in all modesty, I have to say that I labored hard to gain that support in the absence of material returns to the investors. Such support cannot go on indefinitely, and therefore, it behooves us to do all we can to make our activity financially successful."

"To that end, I see that we must continue our efforts in three areas: security from Indian attack, obtaining sufficient food, and producing goods that have value in England. Marshal Dale, could you advise me on your activity during my absence?"

The newly appointed Marshal of the Virginia colony was quick to respond to this invitation. He enumerated the many repairs and improvements that had been made at Jamestown, improvements that strengthened us militarily such as a new blockhouse and a munitions building and ones that helped with the production of food such as the sturgeon curing house. I saw nothing in his statements that could be considered boasting, even though the work accomplished and continuing had been considerable. Rather he was a man of great sincerity and singleness of purpose. He spoke of the executions of thieves and the punishment of malingerers in a matter of fact way. To him it was nothing unusual but for the settlers at Jamestown it had been a great spur to activity.

"Then there have been expeditions against the Indians that I trust will meet with your approval. Foremost among them was an attack on the village of the Nansemonds. In this foray we avenged ourselves upon them for their previous slaughters of colonists. While the number of their warriors killed numbered about fifty we lost none of our own but had only several wounded."

"I congratulate you on your success."

"Much of that success, your excellency, was due to armor which protected our vital parts from their arrows. There was, however, an unusual event on that expedition that I wish to make you aware of."

"And what was that?"

"We have long suspected that the witch doctors of the Indians had the power to perform unusual acts. On this occasion it was demonstrated on our expedition against the Nansemonds when a group of us entered an Indian longhouse where we were put under a spell. Thank God it was short lived because our men fell to fighting one another and would have done serious damage had not the spell ended as quickly as it began."

"Do you believe this was witchcraft?" asked the Governor.

"Without doubt. But perhaps you should hear the opinion of the Reverend Whitaker."

All eyes fastened on the priest, a very learned churchman who had accompanied Sir Thomas Dale from England.

"That this sort of spell was cast is an undeniable fact, Governor Gates. And it occurred on more than one occasion. More recently, Marshal Dale and a group of soldiers had a nearly identical experience while on an expedition farther up the river. The fact is that the Indian priests do practice witchcraft. They are well acquainted with Satan himself. They are a great cause of our difficulties with the Indians because they urge them to do us grievous harm. It is at their command that the Indians make war or peace."

"We would do well to learn more about these men," said the Governor.

"They recognize two gods, a god of good and a god that governs the evil of this world. They reason that the god of good requires little from them because, being good, he will bless them regardless. Their god of evil, or Okee as they call him, is greatly to be feared and they chose to devote their worship almost exclusively to him, taking great care not to offend him, and calling on him for help in their various schemes."

"So it was the power of Okee that was present in these strange events?"

"I prefer to think that it was Satan, though perhaps by a different name. God willing, I shall find out their secrets. When I have done so, I shall publish them for all to know."

The Governor said nothing. Perhaps like me, he thought the Reverend Whitaker sounded overconfident.

I was called upon to describe the progress in planting. We were already gaining beans, peas, and cabbage from our gardens and the corn appeared to be growing successfully although we had not received as much rain as desired. I did not mention my small planting of tobacco.

There were other brief reports on the livestock and on the supplies that had been brought on the ships. I had learned to regard quantities of ship's stores with suspicion. There was often depletion due to rot or infestation of rats and other vermin. Even so, the colony appeared to have sufficient to feed our increased population for several months.

When the reports were finished, Governor Gates informed us of his plan for the future.

"Gentlemen, are now able to make a significant advance in the development of the colony. It has been recognized both here and in London that Jamestown is not the most advantageous location for our principal settlement. By establishing another settlement further upstream we will decease our vulnerability to the Spanish as well as finding a more healthful location for our settlers. I propose to give the name Henrico to this new settlement in honor of Prince Henry and that a force of at least three hundred men be dispatched for its foundation. Marshal Dale shall command this expedition and supervise the work there. I leave it to him to select the companies of troops he desires for his command. The expedition should depart in early September."

A loud murmuring spread throughout the room. Most of us had suspected there would be a new settlement. Indeed, there had been several previous attempts. I suspect many of the captains of companies were wondering whether Sir Thomas Dale would select them to go with him.

"Marshal Dale, do you have any comments at this time?" asked the Governor.

"I thank you, Governor, for the honor of commanding the force to establish Henrico. With your permission I would like to have the troops march upstream rather than go by ship. For the men who have been on ship it will toughen them as well as acquainting them with the country. It will also furnish the opportunity to encounter and defeat some of the hostile Indians in the vicinity."

Sir Thomas Dale never forgot that he was first of all a soldier. I would hope that he welcomed the new settlement as an opportunity to seek peace with the Indians. I knew, however, that I had to keep such thoughts to myself. We were still at war with the natives.

Thus began a period of preparations. There were many rumors of who was to be among the troops commanded by Marshal Dale. I knew that Captain Yeardley would be vying for such a position even though he had come to Virginia as commander of troops for Sir Thomas Gates who would be remaining at Jamestown.

Neither the Powells, the Hortons, nor I were selected to go to Henrico. At least initially, it was a military operation to be followed by a time of construction. I believe that Thomas and Elizabeth Powell would have liked to leave Jamestown but when Mistress Horton developed a fever, Elizabeth Powell would have refused any opportunity to leave the bedside of her former employer. I could only admire her devotion, particularly as I did not think Mistress Horton to be seriously ill. But as the days passed I saw that I was wrong; the fever did not leave her and she had little appetite for food.

On the third day I asked Elizabeth, "How is your patient faring?"

"She was extremely hot last night but the fever did not break."

"It's a shame that Dr. Bohun is no longer with us." The good doctor had left with Lord De la Warr who was seeking a cure in the islands.

"I don't miss him at all," was her tart reply.

"Come now, Elizabeth, he is a skilled physician."

"If he was so skilled why was Lord De la Warr always so sick?"

I had no answer for that.

"All he would have done," continued Elizabeth, "was bleed my poor mistress. What she really needs is being made comfortable so her body can throw off this fever."

A week passed with Mistress Horton growing feebler. During most of this time she recognized no one and was often delirious. I despaired for her life because the fever had killed so many of our settlers. But, under the patient care of her husband and Elizabeth Powell she gradually improved as if called back to life from the brink. We regarded her recovery as a miracle and I asked Reverend Bucke to offer a special prayer of thanksgiving that she had been spared.

In early September, the main body of troops, that numbered about three hundred, left to march to the site of the new settlement of Henrico. They carried little more than what they would need in combat since their baggage was to be transported by ship. Marshal Dale and a few members of his personal staff traveled on the ships. Dale had chosen Ralph Hamor to accompany him as his secretary. Hamor had been one of the original passengers on the *Seaventure*. He was a few years younger than I but well-educated. His father had a large investment in the colony, I was told; but, I do not think he received preferment for that reason. I was disappointed not to be appointed secretary but was told that my efforts were needed at the plantings of Jamestown. I consoled myself that there would be other opportunities to gain preferment in the colony and that I was respected as a man who understood planting, an essential activity for our eventual success.

The troops were a brave sight as they marched out of Jamestown that day. I was among the spectators at the gate watching them depart. There was a drummer with each company and a pair of men with fifes at the head of the procession. I noticed that Captain George Yeardley had succeeded in being selected for the expedition. The men had a fine military appearance, particularly as they wore armor. None of them, however, looked more the part of a soldier than Yeardley. From his appearance and manner you marked him as a man who would someday achieve high position. Not only was

Yeardley participating in the expedition, he had been chosen to command the force, probably because he had been in Virginia longer than most of the other captains. As commander, he was entitled to have the flag bearer marching near him, along with aides who could carry his commands to other officers.

Not the least in importance to the small group around Captain Yeardley was an Indian who would act as interpreter. This man, who had been captured on the campaign against the Nansemonds was named Copotone. From the time of his capture he had taken pains to cooperate with us and, for reasons of his own, indicated that he did not want to return to his tribe. He had proven useful and as time went on gained the trust of our leaders. I regarded him and men like Machumps who had made a few visits to Jamestown as useful connections to the Indians whose friendship we needed for the ultimate success of our settlement.

One week after the departure of the ships and soldiers, a boat returned with a message from Marshal Dale specifically ordering certain individuals to proceed immediately to Henrico. We were needed for various reasons, mine being advice on the land to be used for planting. I said a hurried goodbye to Robert Horton telling him that I expected to be gone for only a few days and that I had to depart without delay on the boat that was waiting to take us.

The trip upriver caused me to again marvel at the magnificent waterways of Virginia. I felt sure that they exceeded those of England in breadth and size of tributaries. The rivers of the Chickahominys and the Appomattocs alone were broad avenues of water and there were many other streams that contributed to the flow of the James River. A skilled sailor commanded our boat and used sail, oars, and tidal currents to speed us on our way, occasionally resorting to oaths and blasphemies. If reported to Marshal Dale he would have suffered much for his tongue but the man was so obviously good natured that I had to believe he meant no offense.

At Henrico I was escorted to the tent of Sir Thomas Dale who welcomed me and turned me over to Captain George Yeardley.

"Yeardley has command of the troops engaged in construction of the palisade around the settlement. Others are building the blockhouses and the living quarters. I want you, Rolfe, to accompany Captain Yeardley and select the ground near the palisade to be cleared for planting. His men will do the work as soon as they finish their present project."

I left with Captain Yeardley after congratulating Marshal Dale on the site he had selected for Henrico. It was high ground, well drained, and easily defensible on three sides because of the river that curved about it. The river limited the amount of palisading required although it was still considerable. I could not help being impressed with the amount of work already done by George Yeardley's men.

"At this rate you will be done with your palisade in a few days," I said.

"The Marshal expects results. Work hours are from daylight until dark and that makes sense because we are most vulnerable until our defenses are in place. I have explained that to the men but I am sure some of them do not appreciate it, particularly the new ones. Some are already wishing they had never come to Virginia."

"Was your march from Jamestown eventful?"

"There were a number of villages along the route and our orders were to destroy them, which we did. One skirmish remains vivid in my memory. I have always admired bold leaders who dressed to impress the enemy as well as their own men. In this fight the Indian leader was adorned in a most unusual way. He had feathers stuck on his skin over almost his entire body and on his shoulders he had fixed the wings of a swan."

"On his shoulders?"

"Yes. The Indians had already loosed a volley of arrows at us and we were deploying to take them under fire. Then our feathered enemy appears in front of his men, exhorting them to fight. Because of his wings you could almost imagine him trying to fly. His men were not as brave as he, however, and they retreated after a few exchanges with our troops. Our interpreter, Cocopone, says that this man is named Munetute and that he has the reputation of being immune to any danger from our bullets."

"And is he?"

"So far. I would say at least twenty-five shots were fired at him since he makes such a noticeable target but he was never hit. I can attest to that."

"Could this be more witchcraft?"

"I don't think so. I would say he has been lucky but his luck may change."

~22~

Upon my return to Jamestown, after informing the Hortons and Powells of my return, I went to inspect the plantings, including my Indian tobacco. I was intrigued by the sturdy plant. The leaves were so broad and firm that I told myself this soil must be especially suitable for its growth. My enthusiasm had grown during the season of planting.

Knowing that the Indian tobacco, even if successfully grown, would be inferior, I determined to see if I could buy some seed for the species of plant grown in the Indies. Accordingly, I had taken advantage of Governor Gates convoy being at Jamestown and approached every captain to see if any of them might have some seed he would sell to me. It was common practice to bring plants and seeds to England, especially from exotic foreign places like the Indies. I talked to all but two of the six captains before finding one who had a small quantity of tobacco seed.

"Did I understand you have seed from the tobacco grown in the Indies, sir?" I asked Captain Bagnal, who, like myself hailed from Norfolk in England.

"Yes, it came originally from Trinidad. Unfortunately, I have only a small quantity of it."

"The seed is so fine, captain, that only a small quantity is required. May I ask if you would be willing to sell me some?"

"You may ask all you want but I am loath to part with it. I understand it is being grown in England, though not as successfully as in the Indies."

Captain Bagnal could tell that I was determined to have some seed and he charged me dearly for it. I think the fact that he had known my father who had been prominent in commerce influenced him to sell me what was little more than half a cup. I thanked him profusely and offered to send him some of my crop as a gift if I succeeded.

"If this adapts to Virginia, and I see no reason why it should not, I look forward to sharing a pipe with you someday in the future. It will not be this year because there is not enough time but, God willing, these seeds shall sprout in my garden in 1612."

"I wish you well, John Rolfe," said Bagnal as he put my two gold sovereigns in his purse. "I had no idea that seed would end up in Virginia. I know you will tend it carefully."

I was sure that he was pleased with the tidy profit he had made on his miniscule cargo.

Even if I never made a profit myself, I thought that I would be able to enjoy smoking the tobacco that I could grow next year.

In the meantime, I continued to work on my small crop of Indian tobacco. I began the process of cutting and curing the leaves. Even with the strong Indian tobacco there was a variable result, depending on the curing. Some of the leaves even rotted and were worthless. I tried to recall what amount of curing seemed to work best but with little success. I determined that when I planted my crop next year I would keep records in order to be able to analyze the results.

What can I say about the Indian tobacco? I knew it would be strong, which it was. But it was better than no tobacco at all even though a single pipeful was sufficient to satisfy my appetite for smoking. Some of my friends could not stand the taste and amused us with their reactions as they made wry grimaces and quickly passed their pipes to someone else.

William Strachey came to speak to me one evening in September.

"I plan to return to England, John."

"Why now? The prospects of our venture are much better now than when we came. And you have become a seasoned settler." A "seasoned" settler was one who had survived the first year in Virginia and therefore chances were that he would remain healthy.

"I go for the convenience of the company. I am to carry back the laws that have been established here and explain their operation to the investors in London." On the night before his departure, William ate with us at our house. Thomas Powell prepared a delicious meal of roasted duck, corn, and steamed vegetables.

"I must compliment you, Thomas, on the duck. It is as good as any to be had in London," said William.

"And I'm sure you will be having some soon in that very place."

"That assumes that the trip home will not be as long as the trip we had on the *Seaventure*."

"Pray, don't even think such thoughts," said Mistress Horton.

"Thank you for your consideration, ma'am. I would not want to live through another shipwreck. But, in retrospect, I must say that it was almost a magical experience. Perhaps miraculous is a better word. It all seems like a dream now."

"If a dream, it was a nightmare," said Mistress Horton.

"When I have written my history I must show it to some of my friends who write for the stage. I have a modest holding in Blackfriars Theater. Perhaps it would help to stir up interest in Virginia."

"It has done so in the past," said Robert Horton.

"But so much of our story has yet to be written, William," I said. "We have yet to make peace with the Indians and we are yet to return the investment in the company."

"True. But who knows when these things shall come to pass. In the meantime I must seize my best opportunity."

William Strachey was a man in a hurry to make his name and fortune. Perhaps I was sensitive to his feelings because I too was eager to be known and to acquire wealth. Despite his skill as a writer that I hoped would bring him success, I thought the best chances of advancement were in Virginia where a man did not need to be an aristocrat to distinguish himself. Captain John Smith had proven that and I thought that George Yeardley would likewise prove it. When the present obstacles to our success were overcome, who could foresee the limits of Virginia's greatness?

We toasted William Strachey that night and cheered his ship

when it lifted sail the following morning to set off downstream with the tide toward Fort Algernon and the Atlantic. Although he repeated that he thought he would be back in Virginia I wondered to myself if we would see him here again.

As we had seen the previous year, it was possible to have hot weather in Virginia as late as September. With the heat came another outbreak of sickness at Jamestown. We had more sickness since the arrival of new settlers with Governor Gates. It was not unusual to see the outbreak of sickness among the unseasoned but I was surprised when Thomas Powell became ill.

I became alarmed when his sickness progressed quickly to the bloody flu. He had no appetite, although he was a man fond of his food, and his sickness soon weakened him severely. At the suggestion of Mistress Horton, her husband Robert and I obtained permission to sleep in one of the houses occupied by soldiers while the two women nursed Thomas. He and I would come by the house at some time during the day when Thomas was less likely to be asleep.

He did not live five days after he took to his bed. Elizabeth had borne up well until he died and then she broke down. I think if it had not been for Mistress Horton, Elizabeth might have died too. She had scarcely slept during his illness and probably had taken little food. She was so distraught and feeble that she could not attend her husband's burial. It was just as well. Despite the comforting words read by Reverend Bucke there was a depressing sameness about the funeral service that we had heard so many times.

We were not reduced to the numbed state that we had found the settlers in at Jamestown in 1610 but we were always reminded of our mortality. The steady occurrence of burial services, particularly in the hot weather would not allow us to forget the fragility of our lives. I thank God for the Reverends Bucke and Whitaker who ministered to us through these difficult times.

Whitaker had accompanied Marshal Dale to Henrico. I wondered how he felt about the severity of the punishments that were a staple of life at Henrico. We had heard reports of two men who, for the theft of food, were sentenced to be chained to trees until they died for lack of food or drink. It was an unmerciful punishment, to say the least, since their death agony would be stretched out for days.

Just before Christmas I had the opportunity to visit Henrico a second time. I had been sent by Governor Gates to deliver dispatches to Marshal Dale. Upon arriving at the new settlement I was amazed at the difference since my previous visit. In addition to the lengthy palisades there were quarters for all of the three hundred men and women who now lived there. There were also large blockhouses that helped to defend the town from Indian attack.

"How would you like to move to Henrico, John Rolfe?" asked Marshal Dale.

The question took me by surprise. I thought it wise not to appear unwilling to move if Sir Thomas Dale wished. "Why, I would like it very much. I believe that more of the colony's activities will shift to this area."

"Good man. I could not agree more. My main reason for suggesting it is to have your services before planting time in the spring. I will speak to Governor Gates about it, unless you wish to speak to him yourself."

"I shall ask the Governor when I return, sir. When would you like for me to be here?"

"As I said, I value your suggestions with regard to planting. I would say February at the latest."

"I greatly appreciate your asking me, sir. I feel honored."

"I think I will have you quartered with Ralph Hamor. He has a rather small house all to himself. I believe he would be glad for your company."

"An excellent suggestion, sir."

Hamor was bright and well thought of in the colony, as he now held the position of secretary. I hoped he would not feel that I was competing with him for preferment.

During the return journey downstream to Jamestown I considered the relocation ahead. In truth, I would be pleased to move. I had come to America to find adventure and fortune and removal to Henrico seemed a step in the right direction. I considered that the land that should be available for my forthcoming experiment with Trinidad tobacco should be at least as good as that at Jamestown. More and more of my thought was given to tobacco. Having learned the process of planting, I considered how to vary the process in order to produce the best crop. Curing appeared to offer the most potential for experimentation while cross-pollination with the Indian tobacco might result in the product best suited for production in Virginia. Beyond my thoughts of producing a superior product was the realization that tobacco would be an incomparable cash crop with potential markets in England as well as Virginia.

I had another reason for thinking it good to move from Jamestown. In the months since Thomas Powell had died, Elizabeth had recovered from her grief. I was finding myself increasingly attracted to her. She was indeed a pretty woman with a lively spirit that would make a suitable wife for someone in our settlement. I could not help being aware of her presence since we lived in the same house. She had grieved for her husband but with her naturally buoyant spirit was aware of the increasing attention being paid to her by the unattached men of the settlement. It was only natural that she should take another husband.

I did not want to admit it to myself, because of my belief in social advancement, but Elizabeth was not a suitable person for me to marry. Although intelligent, she was an uneducated person whose station in life had been that of a lady's maid before her marriage to Thomas Powell. Moving from Jamestown would spare me the potential of becoming more interested in Elizabeth Powell than I should.

Governor Gates was receptive to Marshal Dale's proposal that I should go to Henrico. I waited until an evening in late January when we had finished supper to tell my friends.

"I cannot believe that you would go off and leave us, John," said Mistress Horton. "It's been two and a half years since we sailed together on the *Seaventure*," added her husband.

"I feel that I have no choice. Marshal Dale has asked for me expressly."

"We will miss you, John," said Elizabeth Powell.

I wondered if I detected a reproachful note in her tone. Had I given her any reason to mistake my feelings for her that were only the feelings of a friend? I thought not but we had been together so much that there were bonds that grew out of simple familiarity. I knew that I would always hold both Elizabeth and Mistress Horton in the highest regard and would do nothing to hurt them. I regretted that I had to tell them but if I waited until just before my departure I thought that they would be offended.

Having told them, I was amazed how quickly the time passed before it was time to leave Jamestown. On a bright winter morning in late February I found myself prepared to go on board the pinnace *Discovery* that was bound for the settlement upstream. At the pier to say farewell were the Hortons, Elizabeth Powell, and Reverend Burke.

"Goodbye, John Rolfe," sniffed Mistress Horton.

"Goodbye, John, And God bless you," added Elizabeth dabbing at her eye with her handkerchief.

"Dear friends," I said. "It is not as if I were bound for England."

"Nor on your way to Heaven either," added Richard Bucke.

"Indeed not," I said. "I will only be a few miles up the James River. I will be sure to visit you in Jamestown and I hope you will come to Henrico."

I kissed the two women who seemed to brighten and shook hands with Robert and Richard.

"Good luck with your tobacco, John," said Robert Horton. He had watched me tending my small crop of Indian tobacco and knew how much store I set by the crop I intended to plant with my seed from Trinidad.

With much waving they bid me farewell as the captain ordered the sails of the small ship to be raised. We slowly gathered speed and headed up the river. I watched my friends head back toward the fort. In the days to come I would never think about Jamestown without emotion. It was a place of sorrow, the place where I lost my wife Sarah and friends who had sailed with us from England. It was a place of danger where mistakes in judgment had cost men's lives. And it was a place of want although conditions were slowly easing. By contrast with these turbulent emotions. I could not help being aware of just how small Jamestown was. It was a tiny place in the great expanse of forest and water as we moved slowly up the river toward Henrico.

~23~

From Jamestown to the Chickahominy the James River maintains its breadth of several miles. From the Chickahominy upstream it narrows considerably to perhaps half its former width until reaching the mouth of the Appomatox, about twenty-five miles distant. Through these reaches it has gentle curves that break up what might otherwise be a monotonous journey. But after the mouth of the Appomatox the River again narrows, this time to a width of a few hundred feet. Whereas changes in course have been gentle they now become much more convoluted as the James sweeps in great looping curves.

There is much more relief in the terrain and Henrico was sited by a soldier's eye to gain the advantage of both elevation and the protection of the river that flows around it. It was only natural for our soldier leaders to name the town for Prince Henry on whom England was placing its hopes for the future. This outpost of our civilization appeared to me as a resolute statement of our intention to persevere in Virginia. It was the English reply to Powhatan who had said he would only allow our presence in Jamestown.

My impression as we arrived that day at Henrico was one of activity. Although it was still winter men could be seen everywhere busily constructing new buildings and preparing construction materials. Smoke rose from kilns where brick makers were at work. I imagined that there were plenty of volunteers to stoke the kilns in the coldest weather. Rather than using a saw pit, logs were being sawn into boards on scaffolds. I suspect that was easier to erect a scaffold than dig a pit in the rockier soil of Henrico. Other men were making clapboard and shingles. There were several clapboard buildings but I noted that most of the living quarters were of wattle and daub as at Jamestown.

I went directly to the guardhouse where Ralph Hamor greeted me. "Welcome, John, I trust you had an uneventful journey."

"Thank you, it was pleasant enough."

"Marshal Dale is not available to see you this morning. He has gone out with a patrol to check our defenses. We continue to be harassed by Indians. Almost daily there is some sort of attack. We cannot even send out hunting parties unless they are guarded.

"There is not that much resistance near Jamestown."

"True. Perhaps it is because we are closer here to Powhatan's village or perhaps he recalls his demand that we not venture from Jamestown. But, we are on our guard and we will prevail I am certain. Now, allow me to show you our quarters. I believe Marshal Dale told you we would be quartered together."

We walked past several houses on the same street to a small timber and daub house measuring perhaps eight feet by ten feet. At one end was a fireplace and there were crude beds on either sidewall. It had a thatched roof that appeared to be in excellent condition and enough room under the eaves to store any belongings from the damp.

"It's quite comfortable, really," said Hamor. "Six soldiers normally are housed in a space this size. I shared it earlier with Michael Sizemore who died of an infected wound."

"I feel most fortunate to be here."

"You will find Marshal Dale to be a demanding taskmaster. But he has a gift for choosing able people for his staff and you should feel complimented that he has asked for you here."

"I am indeed."

"His power at Henrico is so absolute that he is unquestioned in anything that he chooses to do. Much of his power is exercised through punishment of malefactors. It is through the power to punish that he has been able to accomplish so much here in a few short months. He is also quite religious. I would say the Reverend Whitaker is his closest confidant. We attend church not once but twice daily and three times on Sunday. There is no time for bowling in the streets at Henrico."

"What are his plans for the future?"

"I will leave it for him to tell you. He is not guarded in that respect."

Sir Thomas Dale, the Marshal of Virginia, did not return from his exertions in the field until late afternoon. I was at the guardhouse to greet him when he dismissed the officer and men who had accompanied him. Although they had been gone the entire day he showed no evidence of fatigue. The same was not true for his men who looked as if they had been led on a merry chase. Dale's forcefulness and energy were apparent in his bearing and in every movement he made. I had heard that he began his career as a common soldier and earned his commission the hard way, in service overseas.

"Welcome, Rolfe. I trust your journey from Jamestown was uneventful."

"Thank you, Sir Thomas. It was."

"We have some sort of action here each day; but it serves to keep us alert. We have much to talk about but it can wait until supper."

Ralph Hamor told me that an invitation had been extended to me to join the Marshal's mess. Other members who gathered around Sir Thomas' table that evening included Captain George Yeardley, Captain Edward Brewster, the Reverend Alexander Whitaker, and Ralph Hamor. I was particularly pleased that Whitaker was in the group because he was my age; and, although I had not known him in England, some of my friends had attended Cambridge University with him. He was a man of great learning, as was his father.

Yeardley was, of course, an old friend. I did not know Edward Brewster well, he having arrived with Lord De La Warr and having spent much time away from Jamestown in explorations upriver. He was an energetic and ambitious soldier, much like George Yeardley but without Yeardley's social graces. He seemed devoted to Dale and was most attentive whenever the Marshal spoke.

"You saw me return from the field today, John Rolfe, which was unusual. I rarely lead the patrols myself but it is a rare day that we do not have some sort of patrol leaving Henrico. We have found it necessary lest we have a daily shower of arrows somewhere in the fort. We still receive a few arrows but do not allow the Indians to gather in mass so they can do us some real harm."

"Were you successful today?"

"Only in the sense that we kept them from attacking the fort or ambushing our men outside the palisades. We saw a few and we pursued them but I am convinced that no Englishman will ever catch an Indian once he has begun to run."

"Why is that?"

"For one thing, we wear armor. For another, the Indian is a hunter who has to be able to run down a wounded deer that may require miles of pursuit through the woods. No, our most effective tactic is to attack their villages. If they stand and fight, we will win. If they depart, we destroy the village."

"Do you have it in mind to campaign against a village?"

"Yes. But, baring unforeseen circumstances, my intent is to wait until we can not only attack and destroy but also settle the lands of that village."

"Would you attack Powhatan himself?"

"No, unless he forced my hand. My intent is to attack the Appomattocs. We will defeat them and settle an old score."

"Will you do that this spring?"

"Not very likely. We have much to do in our settlement here. Now let us discuss another matter," continued Dale. "As you all know, Governor Gates and I have employed Draconian measures in order to maintain discipline and carry out the simple tasks we must do in order to survive such as building palisades and houses. I have observed, however, that in the production of food by communal means, we have not been so successful. There are too many ways to shirk. You can drive a hundred men to attack a village but you cannot drive them to plant a field nearly so successfully. Somehow, successful agriculture requires devotion, devotion that is not forthcoming from the men we have here."

"Do you mean to say," interrupted Alexander Whitaker, "that these men cannot farm? There are farmers scratching out a living in England that are mere brutes compared to these men."

"I believe the key word in my remarks was devotion. How do we obtain devotion that is required to get a truly worthwhile return from the land?"

No one spoke. I believed that the answer was an obvious one but I preferred that someone else should provide it.

"Why not give the men who farm a share of the produce?" offered Ralph Hamor.

"Lord De La Warr favored such a plan but was not here long enough to implement it."

"But how do we meet the needs of the settlement?" said Marshal Dale. "Not everyone can be a farmer."

Hamor hesitated. "The man who farms returns a fixed portion to the settlement. All that he makes in excess is his to do with as he pleases."

"Congratulations, Secretary Hamor, you and I are in agreement," said Dale. He looked around the table. "Does everyone agree?"

The Reverend Whitaker and Captain Yeardley nodded, as did I.

"How about you, Captain Brewster?"

"Sir, I know nothing of such things."

"So, you abstain. Well, there's an honest man. Now I would like to hear from Master Rolfe."

"Sir Thomas, I believe providing ownership of land to these men would be the wisest step you could take in turning these forests into productive farms."

"But I did not say ownership."

"But why not? Consider the stakes. We are not in a position where we can afford to fail. In England these men could not aspire to land ownership except through inheritance or many years of toil. Here is the opportunity to obtain land simply through producing crops and paying a fixed remittance to the settlement. Any man who has the slightest interest in farming will jump at the chance."

"I believe you are right. But how much land to the man?"

"I would say three acres. Enough to produce a worthwhile crop but not so much as to overwhelm him with the initial labor required."

"And what would he pay to the settlement yearly?"

"Two barrels of corn."

Marshal Dale stroked his chin with his right hand. "Make it two and a half barrels."

Everyone laughed. While no one said it we could not help thinking that a plan like this was less onerous than the communal labor to which everyone was now subjected.

"Very well, Rolfe. We shall give the land to successful farmers. I want you to chose the land that will be distributed. We will need timber to impale it lest the Indians or our own livestock make free to plunder it. But do not concern yourself with timber that is in such plentiful supply. Choose the best land for our farmers to work."

"Yes, Sir Thomas."

"Our talk tonight, for the most part, has dwelt on two topics, security from the Indians and food," said Marshall Dale.

"These are necessary for our survival," said George Yeardley. "We have no choice."

"I for one would prefer peace," said Alexander Whitaker. It was some time since I had heard such a thought expressed by an Englishman. It was my preference also but I had learned to be silent in the company of soldiers.

"You might have peace, Reverend, if you could somehow influence the thoughts of Powhatan," said Yeardley.

"And his brother Oprechancanough," added Edward Brewster.

"That may be a difficult task but we must accomplish it someday. And when it is," said Whitaker, "what do we then do?"

"We might save the souls of these heathen," continued Whitaker. "It will not be an easy task, Sir Thomas. I was with you when your men were surrounded and the heathen priests worked their magic on you. There were evil spirits abroad that night. There is no doubt these men are acquainted with Satan. Not only do they know him but these priests consult Satan on

157

any matter of importance. Nevertheless, they have reasonable souls and intellectual faculties."

"Reverend Whitaker," I asked, "do not the actions of these priests make these people barbarous, an accursed generation?"

"In their present state, yes. But it need not continue. Consider the condition of our ancestors in Britain before Christianity was brought to our island. I say that bringing these Indians to God is the great task remaining before us after we have achieved peace and have solved our problems of producing food."

"I think you are overlooking one thing," said Marshal Dale.

"What is that?"

"That the settlement of Virginia has come about as the result of investments of private adventurers. Thus far, there has been scant return on those investments. If there are not products of value, be it minerals, furs, or bounteous crops that can be sent to England, then the colony will fail from lack of support. We simply cannot split enough clapboard to pay for the settlement of Virginia."

We were silenced by the logic of the Marshal's remarks.

"Our great need, the economic justification of Virginia, is also our great opportunity. Those who solve this problem will be richly rewarded."

~24~

I became accustomed rather quickly to my new life at Henrico. This was an easy thing to do because we were so caught up in the work of building a new city. There were three entire streets within the palisades and work was continually underway to build new houses or improve the earlier ones. Some were of two stories, having a first story of brick and second story of timber. It was not hard to encourage men to work on these houses; they were our main source of comfort and protection from the elements.

My own time was mainly spent in the clearing of fields and apportioning them for assignment to individual farmers. By now we had suitable pens for much of our livestock. These were important not only for protecting the creatures but also for retaining the manure that was needed to make planting a success. Because Marshal Dale directed most of his questions about farming to me I found myself more and more directly involved in all phases of the work.

By becoming the overseer of much of the planting, I had the latitude to tend to my special interest. That interest was my experiment with tobacco. I had retained some of the seed from Indian tobacco as well as the seed from Trinidad. In order to compare them, I planted both types. This involved the entire process that I had undertaken the previous summer. First tiny holes were made in the ground in which I placed a few seed. Then I had to wait for the seed to germinate so that the tiny sprouts could be separated and transplanted.

In the spring, wildfowl returned from the south in great abundance. No advice was needed from me on the harvesting of this bounty. Hunting parties brought back great quantities of geese and duck that were shot from hunting stands along the river. There was sufficient for every man to feast on wildfowl.

Marshal Dale took advantage of these fresh provisions from the sky to entertain Captain George Percy who was soon to return to England. Percy was known for the table he kept at Jamestown. In an effort to repay his hospitality Marshal Dale invited Percy to visit Henrico before his departure.

"I trust that all is well at Jamestown," said Marshal Dale at dinner.

"There is definite progress. Governor Gates has directed more attention to fishing with the return of warm weather."

"Do you have any thoughts on Virginia that you would share with us before departing?" asked the Marshal.

Percy reflected. "If we had it to do over, we should never have chosen Jamestown for a site. It's a damned unhealthy place. I'll never forget the way those poor devils sickened and died." He paused while we all were silent. "Then too," he continued, "we never should have been governed by a council. Our present arrangement, where a governor is in command, works better. You and I, as military men, understand that."

The talk shifted to memories of the Netherlands where both Dale and Percy had served before coming to Virginia. Percy allowed that he might return there if his services were required. I was thankful that Marshal Dale did not ask him if he intended to return to Virginia.

The next morning we said farewell to Captain George Percy as he prepared to board the shallop that would return him to Jamestown. I was surprised and pleased when he addressed me by name as he shook hands. I later remarked on this to Ralph Hamor.

"That is the first time he has ever called me by name."

"It is a sign you are coming up in the world."

"What do you mean?"

"George Percy wants to stay on the good side of everyone who amounts to anything. His recognition means that you have made a place here."

"What nonsense," I said. I pretended to be oblivious to such considerations but secretly I was pleased.

160

By late spring all of our crops were doing well. We had received sufficient rain. Fear of drought had been my main concern after the dry summers experienced previously. I encouraged our farmers to make successive plantings so there would be extended harvest periods and was gratified that most took my advice.

My experiment with tobacco appeared to be proceeding well. By summer both the Indian and Trinidad tobacco plants were several feet in height but the Trinidad was taller by almost a foot. The Trinidad also had a fuller leaf and the leaves had a greater network of supporting veins. I was pleased that Ralph Hamor took an interest in what I considered a luxurious growth.

"By heavens, John Rolfe. You will have enough tobacco for an army. I hope you will remember your friends at harvest time."

"You would be surprised how quickly an army could puff away these plants. As for my friends, I will remember them most who help me with the crop."

"What would you have me do? I am no farmer and I would not wish to damage any of your plants."

"What needs to be done is simple enough but it requires much bending over. First, there are what we call suckers that have to be snapped off. They are these small offshoots at the base of the plant. If allowed to remain they will sap the energy of the plant. Second, we have these infernal worms that will ruin the leaves given the chance."

Hamor was as good as his word. With his gangly frame it was no easy task for him to bend over but I became accustomed to the sight over the next few months. He enjoyed smoking tobacco as much as I did and worked for many hours without complaint.

I had kept good records on the farm in England. In Virginia, I became even more meticulous. I assigned letters to the rows of tobacco plants and numbers within the rows to individual plants. When the tobacco had blossomed early in its growth I had cross-pollinated between some of the Indian and the Trinidad tobacco. I had in mind to identify the healthiest plants and to use their seed for future plantings.

More land was selected on both sides of the river for impaling and future settlement. Once impaled, the land would be used first to enclose livestock that required greater pasturage. One could not help wondering what the Indians thought of our claims upon what had been land over which they had roamed freely in their hunts. They might use impaling on a limited scale around their villages but never to the scale that we did to enclose vast tracts.

Marshal Dale would have liked to employ two thousand Englishmen in the work and indeed wrote to England asking for more men. Lacking them, however, it fell to the three hundred men that were under his command to expand the English presence in Virginia. On the south side of the James it was his plan to have five centers, or forts. One of these was to be a hospital and another the manse for The Reverend Whitaker. Work began on the manse which was named Rocke Hall.

Although we had moderate rainfall that cooled us from time to time, there were months in the summer of 1612 when we endured oppressive heat. We thanked God for good water at Henrico because we depended on it to slake our thirst. Despite my primary interest in the work in the fields I found myself seeking shade when the opportunity presented itself. We were all conscious of the heat, especially George Yeardley whose men were becoming ill from the long hours under the unrelenting sun. Finally, he prevailed upon Marshal Dale to allow work earlier in the morning in order to escape the heat of the afternoon. Yeardley was a patient man and I will never forget his perseverance in persuading Dale to change the hours of work.

"Yeardley," said the Marshal, "your men are all seasoned. They are accustomed to Virginia. Why should they be getting sick at this time?"

"They cannot drink enough water to keep their bodies cool. They are struck down by the sun."

"So you would have them stumbling about in the dark instead."

"Only until the weather moderates. Perhaps for a month. Then we can go back to normal hours."

"How will the work get done?"

"The work will get done, sir. Pray remember these are Englishmen who are not bred to work in this heat."

"All right, Yeardley. I've heard enough. Reverend Whitaker, I desire that weekday services be conducted only in the afternoon since we will reserve the morning hours for labor. Will you see to it?"

"Yes, Sir Thomas."

"Very well. I need not tell you, Captain Yeardley, that although I have approved your suggestion, I will be watching closely."

And watch he did. Dale also burned under the Virginia sun; but he burned from an inner fire. When I consider how much was done at and around Henrico in that first year I am amazed that a single man could drive his fellow men to do so much. It is true that in Yeardley and Brewster he had disciplined and loyal subordinates who did what was asked of them. It was also true that we were motivated to produce our food and make ourselves safe from the Indians. But the building of a city that was ever expanding was accomplished because it was demanded by one man, Marshal Dale.

Not all could stand the pace. Our men were aware that beyond us, in the woods, the Indians lived in their villages where no one was subject to the punishing and unceasing labor of the English settlers. Three of our men decided to slip away to join one of these villages where the Indians were known to be friendly. They left on a Sunday when they probably thought they would not be detected as soon or pursued as vigorously as on a workday. Nevertheless, immediately following the Sunday morning service, patrols were dispatched on both sides of the river to find the deserters.

By the end of the day they were back in Henrico, not having even reached an Indian village. For their punishment they were sentenced to be burned alive on the following morning as decreed by Marshal Dale. Theirs was the most grievous offense and they were to receive the most severe punishment.

The Reverend Whitaker was willing to intervene on behalf of one of the prisoners. He visited the men on the eve of their

163

execution and found that one of them was only seventeen years old. He pleaded with Marshal Dale that the young man had been influenced by the older pair and because of his previous record was deserving of mercy. I was surprised when Marshal Dale granted the appeal and I believe it was due as much to the eloquence of Alexander Whitaker as it was the facts in the case. Dale was a hard man but he would listen to reason, particularly from persons whom he trusted.

So the young deserter received a severe flogging and was required, along with the rest of us, to witness the burning of his companions. It was a gruesome event from beginning to end. The two men had to be carried to the stakes, all the time resisting by twisting and kicking. They must have known there would be no further mercy and vented their anger on their fellow men who were participating in their execution. When they were finally tied and blindfolded, Whitaker approached them to hear if they would make peace with God. They were unrepentant, however, and mouthed vile curses on all, particularly Marshal Dale. We then had to listen to their screams of agony as they died in the flames.

In the early days of the Virginia colony men had the choice of working or consuming their time in idleness. Under Gates and Dale, however, the choices were harder: unremitting labor or severe punishment. I lamented the fact that the choices were so stark and longed for the day when men would be freed from them. But I kept my feelings to myself.

At the beginning of fall I was ready to harvest my tobacco. No children ever looked forward to a feast or holiday more than Ralph Hamor and I anticipated the first pipe full of tobacco from my planting of Trinidad. Our anticipation was increased by the sight of the leaves that had changed in color to a rich gold.

On a cool evening in fall after supper Ralph and I stood on the bluff overlooking the James River. There was a bite of autumn chill in the air.

"Ralph, I believe we might try a pipe of tobacco this evening."

"You cannot mean it. I had thought your curing process would never end."

"It may not have. But we will try it and see."

We sat before the fire in our house where I took a small board on my lap and proceeded to shred a leaf of Trinidad. I shredded what amounted to about a cup of tobacco and passed the board to my friend. "Help yourself."

"No, after you. I know how long you have awaited this moment."

"Very well. But let us not stand on ceremony. After all, you have put up with my fretting over this patch of tobacco all these months."

We soon had filled our pipes and lit them with tapers from the fire. I drew on the pipe until it was glowing and I could draw my first breath of the smoke. I cannot tell you the pleasure of that moment. There was no bite, no bitterness, only a mild and pleasant taste accompanied by an aroma I would call delicious for want of a better word. I could see that Ralph Hamor, like I, was transported by the experience.

"Marvelous, John Rolfe. I congratulate you."

~25~

I could hardly believe my good fortune. It had been a gamble to plant Trinidad tobacco in Virginia soil hoping for good results. Fortunately, the soil had the suitable combination of elements and nutrients, and the climate had the moisture and temperature needed by the plant to produce bright leaves of tobacco. From my farming experience I knew that many relocated plants did not do as well.

The idea of establishing plants in new locations was not new to me. My countrymen had brought many herbs and even trees to England; some made the transition successfully, others had not. Tobacco could be grown in England but the results were inferior. On the other hand, it appeared that tobacco seed from the Indies could successfully make the transition to Virginia. The implications of this fact were enormous. At the personal level, it meant that I could meet my own needs. For the settlement, it meant that we could establish a market in Virginia. On a larger scale, if our product was of high enough quality, it was possible to assume that Virginia tobacco could be sold in the English market. That market now depended on imports controlled by Spain. It was enough to make my head swim as I pondered how to proceed.

I asked Ralph Hamor to speak to no one about the tobacco. At first he protested, saying such a secret was impossible to keep. But he assented when I said I only wanted to wait until the following evening when we might share it with Marshal Dale at his table. Without conceit I believed this was a major development and I did not want Dale to learn of it second hand.

As expected, sharing the tobacco with Dale, Yeardley, and Brewster was a great success. Actually, Brewster declined my offer, saying tobacco did not agree with him. He did remain at table, however, as the others puffed away and I received a second confirmation of the success of Trinidad tobacco in Virginia. Dale himself seemed especially pleased.

"Splendid, John. Your labors in the field have rewarded you handsomely. We must send some to Governor Gates."

"Of course, Sir Thomas. I know he enjoys a pipe."

"And complains as much as any man when he cannot get tobacco."

I could tell that Marshal Dale's mind had already moved beyond thoughts of sharing tobacco with friends. As he sat in a small room in Virginia that was filled with a pleasant aroma he doubtless thought of the thousands of pipe smokers in England whose demands for tobacco could be met by a product we were capable of producing.

"How should we proceed, John? Can we send some of this to England now?"

"I would not recommend it. I am not satisfied with the curing process and really need to experiment further to get the best results. Also, I wish to determine which of my plants provided the best tobacco."

"Well, when would a shipment be made to England?"

"I expect next year, in 1613. I can plant enough to get a good shipment from the best plants, cured in the most favorable way."

That was the beginning of an intense period of experimenting with my plants. I selected seed from the healthiest plants for my next year's planting. It appeared that cross-pollination had produced good results but I was not satisfied.

While I was generous with my gifts of tobacco to Governor Gates and my friends at both Jamestown and Henrico, I sold some of the remainder. I have always thought that people value an object more if they have paid for it. As long as people paid for my tobacco I knew that they appreciated it; whereas if I gave it away it might have been accepted just to keep from offending me. Besides, I surely could not sustain everyone's tobacco needs out of my own pocket.

It was a good harvest at Henrico that year in all respects. Marshal Dale's experiment with individual cultivation of land had been an unqualified success. All the men undertaking to plant three acres had been successful in producing their two and a half barrels of corn for the settlement except the men who got sick and died. Those who recovered did not lose their land because temporary arrangements were made to tend the crops. All told, it was a season of relative plenty with cabbages, beans, and cauliflowers from the gardens and as many walnuts as we wished to gather in the woods. We were especially glad for the wildfowl that gave us plenty of flesh to eat without having to kill any of our livestock. These were needed for breeding purposes.

When the crops were in and the cold weather had begun, Marshal Dale made his plans for his attack on the Appomatocs. None of us had forgotten the treacherous murder of Lord De La Warr's men who had been lured by the Indians on shore as they passed their village. The sight of the naked Indian women, waving for the Englishmen to join them, was too much for the foolish settlers. Only one had escaped the trap to return safely to Jamestown.

I was glad not to be included in the expedition against the Appomatocs. Their village would be burned and their crops would be seized. Those who did not flee would be slain. I did not feel real sympathy for the Appomatocs. Besides killing Lord De La Warr's men, they had been responsible for numerous attacks on Henrico. It was all part of a war that began with Powhatan's slaughter of Ratcliffe and his men. It had begun during the starving time and continued without ceasing. It was especially ugly, not only for the terrible losses that had been afflicted upon both sides but also for the tension which lay over the land. In truth, we could go nowhere without being anxious for our safety.

Our men went to the village of the Appomatocs in December as planned. They were successful in their attack and captured large quantities of corn that were later brought to Henrico by boat. By this expedition Sir Thomas Dale not only obtained revenge and gained security for our settlement but also extended the acreage for our settlement during the following year. It was land only a few miles distant from Henrico and had great potential for agriculture.

In February of 1613, I was able to visit my friends at Jamestown. I had seen them but very sparingly during the past year. The Hortons greeted me warmly when I went to the familiar house within the fort.

"It is only a year that you have been away, but it seems much longer," said Robert Horton.

He looked pale and less robust. I was glad he was not living at Henrico where the demands on the settlers were more severe. Only the young men were able to endure the labor at Henrico.

By contrast, Mistress Horton was looking healthier. She had also lost weight but it became her to do so. I hoped that by surviving the fevers she had gained some resistance.

"Elizabeth will be glad to see you," she said. She regarded me steadily. "She has married again, you know."

I suspected that she was aware of my attraction to Elizabeth. I felt a pang of regret that I hoped I did not betray with my expression. Perhaps I had been foolish to let my head rule my heart. After all, this was Virginia where class and position made little difference. If I had not held myself back I might today have had a wife, a spirited young woman with whom I would have been happy despite my own foolish ambitions.

"No, I did not know she had married."

"Yes, to George Grave, the carpenter."

I remembered Grave well. He had done much of the work on the church at Jamestown.

"For months we had men around here pestering the poor girl night and day. Particularly those soldiers. There was one sergeant that I thought was going to fight George over Elizabeth."

"I hope that did not happen."

"No. Someone told one of the officers about his threats and the sergeant was warned off. So nothing happened." She paused as she saw Elizabeth and her husband approaching. "Look, here they come now. Aren't they a handsome couple?"

Once again Mistress Horton's eyes scanned my face. This time I permitted myself a smile as I prepared to greet Elizabeth. She handed a basket to her husband and ran toward me with her arms outstretched.

"John Rolfe, how good to see you." She hugged me tightly and kissed me on the cheek. I was aware of the fullness of her strong young body against me.

"Elizabeth, how dare you marry without me here to bless it?"

"This is Virginia, John. A person has to seize the moment before it passes."

"I only jest, Elizabeth. I have truly never disapproved of anything you ever did."

Turning to her husband, I said, "Nor could I ever disapprove of you. Congratulations!"

"Thank you, John." said Grave.

He was an affable man, always good tempered and usually smiling as if to offset his sober surname. His good nature had served him well, through the shipwreck and days on Bermuda to the hardships of life in Virginia. He was of medium stature but possessed unusual strength that enabled him to handle the heavy timbers of the pinnaces we built in Bermuda and the buildings in Jamestown. Like many skilled carpenters, he made tools seem to be extensions of himself. Although Grave was physically different from Thomas Powell, Elizabeth's first husband who had been slight of build, the two men were similar in their easygoing personalities. Had this similarity been important in the attraction of Elizabeth to George Grave? I suspected it had.

It was good to be with my friends again. I could relax with them more easily than in the company of Sir Thomas Dale at whose table I ate most of my meals. We talked far into the night. They told me that the Spaniard Molina was still a captive at Jamestown. Although he was normally confined aboard a pinnace, he was often given his parole to walk freely about within the walls of the fort. George Grave had seen him several times at the church where he would watch Grave at his work.

"I think he is fearfully lonesome," said Grave. "He really

has nothing to do and they keep him separate from the other prisoner. The third one died last summer."

"I think Governor Gates has come to believe Molina is not a spy," said Robert Horton.

"Then why has he not sent him back to England?" I asked.

"Why take a chance? If he is returned to England he will probably be returned to Spain and then be free to report all that he knows about us."

"That sounds reasonable," I agreed.

"The Governor is wise," said Robert. "Why leave such a decision to the men at court?"

"While you are here at Jamestown, John," said Mistress Horton, "you will no doubt see Captain Argall. He is here again. What a dashing man."

"I remember Captain Argall," I said. I recalled that he had found a safer Atlantic crossing. More recently, I learned that he was related to Lady De La Warr as well as a high officer in the Virginia Company. These connections had no doubt helped him gain the position of pilot of the Virginia Company, He was successor to Captain Newport. I fought my desire to belittle his position as being due to his family connections.

"For all that he is a dashing man," said Robert Horton, "he has proven his worth to us."

"In what way?" I asked.

"Governor Gates sent him north, up Chesapeake Bay, to trade with the Indians for food. He has just returned with a pinnace full of corn. Over a thousand bushels they say."

"He went clear out of Powhatan's kingdom," said George Grave. "To a tribe called Potomacs. They must have had a good harvest last year."

"And they gave it all for a few pieces of copper," added Horton.

"Captain Argall must be a good businessman as well as a sailor," I said.

"I dare say he would have seized the corn if they did not trade," said Horton.

"I think he has given us cause to celebrate," I said. "Will you share my tobacco?"

171

While the women cleared the table we filled our pipes and began smoking. In a short time we had so filled the little house with smoke that Mistress Horton opened the door.

"I declare, John Rolfe," she said. "Now that you have your own crop of tobacco you can literally smoke us out of house and home."

"Please say no more, my dear," said her husband. "He has brought us real tobacco, a rare gift."

"I must say it smells better than that awful weed you grew when you were here," said Elizabeth. "No wonder everyone is talking about it."

On the following day I attended the Governor's meeting with his council. The recently returned Captain Argall was present since he was a member of the council even though frequently absent on missions assigned by the Governor. Sir Thomas Gates was his usual dignified self.

"Welcome, John Rolfe, and thank you for the report which you have carried from Marshal Dale. I am pleased with his success against the Appomatocs. Also with the success of his farming program which you have no doubt aided considerably."

"Thank you, Sir Thomas."

"I understand that much of the land taken that is south of Henrico will be good farmland."

"Unquestionably, Sir Thomas. The river has enriched it by flooding for generations."

"And you are proceeding with your plans to plant more Trinidad tobacco next year?"

"Yes. And I have asked sea captains to bring me seed of other West Indian strains of tobacco as well."

"Good. We have been blessed not only with success at Henrico but also by the trading expedition of Captain Argall in the northern region of Chesapeake Bay."

"Perhaps you can tell us," said the Governor turning to Captain Argall, "how you came to be so successful."

"Through no great merit on my part I assure you, Governor Gates. In the first place, I traded with people who had not been subject to the drought conditions endured in recent years by Powhatan's people. So their chief had a great plenty of corn to trade. The second way in which I was unusually fortunate was that these people have not been trading with other Englishmen whom, I regret to say, will give away their treasure for a song. And so, by selecting copper that the king came to covet as soon as he saw it, I was able to extract a great price."

"Did the king regret his trade?" asked the Governor.

"Apparently not. I remained for several days of feasting. Moreover, I left a young officer as hostage, one Ensign Swift, as a token of good will. In addition to learning the language which will make him more useful to us, he will learn much about what is happening in the tribe."

"That is not James Swift?" I asked.

"No, James Swift is still sailing with Captain Newport. For all I know, they are in the East Indies now." I heard that Newport had left the Company after a dispute over supplies.

"Do you not fear for the life of such a hostage?" I asked.

"There is some risk, I suppose," said Argall fixing me with his eye. I had not intended to ask what might be considered an unfriendly question. "And so, if the Governor sees fit to send me to the Potomacs again in the spring, I expect to find Ensign Swift ready to aid materially in any endeavors. Who knows what we might find at that time."

I left the meeting greatly impressed by Captain Samuel Argall. I could see why he had found favor with the leaders of the Virginia colony.

~26~

"Shallop on the river," cried a voice from the watchtower.

I was outside the Henrico palisade but near the bluff so it was easy for me to take a few steps and view the visitor. Although it was almost a certainty to be from Jamestown it was still a source of interest until we could discover who might be aboard. The boat was several hundred yards distant but I could see that most of the men aboard were soldiers. That was a sign that someone of importance was likely to be aboard. But he was probably not Governor Gates. The Governor usually sent a messenger to prepare us for a visit.

As the shallop pulled into shore, I recognized Captain Argall whom I had last seen in February. He was the first passenger to debark, stepping confidently to shore to be saluted by members of our guard. He must have returned from his visit to the Potomacs that he had told us he would make in April. I wondered what news he might bring us. Had he achieved another coup by trading for a shipload of corn? Was the chief of the Potomacs preparing to wage war on Powhatan? Had a supply fleet arrived from England? There was no point in my standing there on the bluff gawking like a schoolboy. I would go to Marshal Dale's quarters and find out.

When I knocked on the door and was bidden to enter Sir Thomas looked up at me with a quick glance. "Have a seat Master Rolfe. I have sent Ralph Hamor to summon Captain Yeardley and Captain Brewster. Do you have any idea what news Captain Argall may be bringing us?"

"Not in the least, sir, except that it probably has to do with his latest expedition to visit the Potomacs."

"That is as good a guess as any," said the Marshal. With

that young man, however, it could be anything."

Captain Argall reached the Marshal's quarters at the same time Ralph Hamor arrived with Yeardley and Brewster. We could hear their good natured exchange of greetings outside along with some banter from Yeardley about bringing back more corn. I could not hear Argall's response but it occasioned laughter from the others. They then trooped into the Marshal's house where the greetings continued and Marshal Dale extended a warm welcome to Captain Argall.

"Well, Captain, what news do you bring? I presume it is good."

"It is so good that Governor Gates wanted me to bring it to you personally. He thought you might have questions about what has happened."

"I am ready to hear whatever good news you bring."

"I have returned from the Potomacs with a most important captive."

I could see that Argall was enjoying the telling of this tale. He had our complete attention.

"And who might that be?"

"Pocahontas, the daughter of Powhatan."

"I have heard of her, of course, from the reports of John Smith. And the ancient planters speak very highly of her. They say the first settlers would have perished but for her."

"She is now at Jamestown, Marshal Dale, aboard the *Treasurer*. Although we strive to make her comfortable, I can tell you she is not a happy passenger."

"I should think not."

"Governor Gates has sent me to advise you of this and to request that you return with me to Jamestown where we can decide how best to proceed in our dealings with Powhatan."

"Of course. But first tell us how this came to be."

"You were aware that I was to return to visit the Potomacs for continued trading. Well, as it happened, I set out on my journey on the 19th of March instead of April because I wanted to explore the northern portion of the bay above the river of the Potomacs. For the sake of brevity I will say that I found the entire reach of the bay to be navigable by my ship *Treasurer*.

175

Many of the creeks on the eastern shore are shallow for a ship such as mine but they can be navigated easily with shallops."

"When I returned to the Potomacs I found Ensign Swift to be in good health and full of news about the tribe. The most important news he had to share with me was that an Indian princess named Matoaka was the guest of Jopassus, chief of the Potomacs. My interpreter, being present at my conversation with Swift, immediately said that Matoaka was another name for Pocahontas whom he remembered as the favorite daughter of Powhatan. I wanted to know the nature of Pocahontas' visit."

"Swift assured us that Pocahontas was in the good graces of Powhatan and that she was visiting the Potomacs for the purpose of trade, It seems that Powhatan is as aware as we that the Potomacs had several good harvests and large supplies of corn. Powhatan, on the other hand, needed corn for his people but had many pieces of copper he had obtained from the English at Jamestown."

"I had scarcely heard about the presence of Pocahontas nearby when I resolved to capture her by whatever means necessary."

"If I were going to be successful, it was necessary to secure the cooperation of Jopassus. I decided not to delay but to approach him forthwith and say I must have Pocahontas as a captive. I explained that her father Powhatan held at least six English captives and by holding her we could bargain for a safe exchange."

"What was Jopassus' reaction?" asked Marshal Dale.

"Negative, as I expected. He said it would mean war with Powhatan. They have been enemies for years but an uneasy truce exists now that Jopassus wishes to maintain. I asked him if he did not value our friendship and said we could no longer be friends if he did not help in the capture of Pocahontas. He professed to desire our friendship but was afraid there might be war. So I told him that we would defend him if Powhatan should make war on the Potomacs. I told him of the defeats that we had inflicted on Powhatan because of our muskets and the protection provided to us by armor. I left him to think about our offer because I could see that he was not convinced."

"The next day Jopassus said he was reassured by our offer of an alliance. Still, it would not risk allowing Pocahontas to be captured unless it could be made to appear that it was not his doing. Knowing that if I could just get Pocahontas aboard the *Treasurer* she would be my captive, I asked Jopassus how that could be arranged. After much talk he proposed a scheme that I think shows what a cunning rascal he really is."

Captain Argall held the rapt attention of all of us. I could not help but have a feeling of distaste, however, for what I was hearing. One of our captains and an Indian chief were plotting the betrayal of an innocent young woman who by all accounts had befriended the English. How did Jopassus differ from Judas who had plotted to betray our Saviour? I wondered if Argall had any doubts about the morality of what he was doing. Then I rationalized that English lives might be saved from what Argall was trying to accomplish.

"It seems," continued Argall, "that Pocahontas was a friend of the wife of Jopassus. Although Pocahontas had been aboard English ships, her friend had not and it was decided that she would beg her husband Jopassus to allow her to go aboard. Jopassus was to argue against going aboard, finally relenting, but only on the condition that Pocahontas accompany them. I thought the plan quite devious."

"So it was agreed to perform this little play?" asked Marshal Dale.

"There was still some hesitation but it was overcome by the offer of gifts. They were nothing more than a small copper kettle for Jopassus and some beads for his wife. The following day Jopassus appeared with the two Indian women. I found Pocahontas to be most comely and possessing a lively spirit. The two women seemed very impressed with the appearance of the *Treasurer*. I of course invited them aboard and Jopassus declined. His wife immediately protested and a fierce argument began, followed by tears. You could not have seen better theater in London or Paris. I thought Jopassus was going to beat her as he threatened to do more than once if she did not desist. I finally interjected myself into the family argument by saying how much it would please me to entertain them aboard.

Jopassus capitulated but only on the condition that Pocahontas would accompany them. To this she readily agreed."

"When my visitors were aboard, I could scarcely conceal my elation. I had previously instructed several of my most trustworthy men that, once aboard, Pocahontas was not to be allowed to go ashore. So we proceeded about the ship with me showing them the various spaces aboard. They were particularly delighted by the navigation instruments which they regarded as having magical properties. The tour was followed by as sumptuous a meal as was in my power to provide. I might add that throughout the meal, Jopassus was so pleased with the success of his clever plan that he kicked me repeatedly under the table."

"Because the visit aboard ship had proved to be so enjoyable, I invited my guests to spend the night. I could tell that Pocahontas was somewhat apprehensive but she reluctantly agreed because Jopassus and his wife seemed eager to stay. Several of my officers gave up their berths so the Indian guests could be accommodated. In the morning Pocahontas seemed anxious to go ashore and it was then that I had to tell her she was to continue as my guest. Jopassus and his wife each made token protests that may have fooled Pocahontas but I am not sure. With great dignity Pocahontas reminded me that she was the daughter of Powhatan, the greatest of all chiefs. Furthermore that he would not only be outraged by her capture but also by the means by which it was achieved.

"Put you down, did she?" said the Marshal.

"Indeed. She allowed that the other Englishmen she had met had been men of their word. She must have been referring to Captain John Smith. Whoever they were, it was clear that I was not one of the honorable Englishmen. I have to admit I was impressed with her demeanor. She never became excited or showed any fear."

"At that point, Jopassus swore mightily that he would never have come aboard had he known it would end with Pocahontas being carried away against her will. He asked that his wife and he be put ashore which I was glad to do."

"I accompanied Jopassus to his village, having issued

instructions for securing Pocahontas in one of the cabins of the *Treasurer*. At the village I spoke with one of the Indians who had accompanied Pocahontas to visit the Potomacs. He agreed to carry a message to Powhatan. By the message I informed the chief that his daughter was captive but would be returned unharmed to him when all Englishmen whom he held captive were returned with their weapons to Jamestown along with a large quantity of corn."

"Well done, Captain Argall," said Marshal Dale. "You proceeded directly with the business."

"In a few days I had an answer. We would be provided all we asked for if we came to Powhatan's village."

"But I take it that you did not comply since you say that Pocahontas is presently at Jamestown."

"Yes, sir. I reasoned that Powhatan's invitation might be a trap. No one has forgotten the experience of Captain Ratcliffe who went to trade with Powhatan. Did you know that my interpreter, Henry Spelman, was actually present and witnessed that massacre? But I do not wish to digress. If I were to avoid compromising the ransoming of Pocahontas, I could not risk going to Powhatan's village. Besides, Governor Gates might have other conditions that he wished to impose."

"And is she in good health?" asked Captain Yeardley. "Sometimes these savages do not bear captivity well."

"She is well. A bit pensive, I should say, but well."

"I congratulate you, Captain Argall," said the Marshal. "I think I speak for all of us when I say that you have accomplished a remarkable action that will be of great importance to the Virginia Company."

There was a chorus of approval. I did not join in because of the lingering distaste I felt for the treatment of an Indian woman who without question had been our friend. I now regretted my reticence because Argall noticed it. Men like him feed on approval and flattery. I am sure that his dislike for me began at this moment.

"How say you, Master Rolfe? Do you approve of the way I have brought a precious captive to Jamestown?"

"I am sure I could not have done half so well," I replied.

Argall stared at me coldly. He knew I had not meant him a compliment. But why would he take offense unless his own conscience disturbed him?

"Come, come, Argall. Everyone means you well," said the Marshal. "What does Governor Gates desire to do next."

"He wishes to consult with you before taking any action. I believe that he feels that we are in an extremely strong position because we have the young woman. For that reason alone Powhatan is not likely to take any violent action against us. Besides, he has indicated a willingness to trade for her."

"Is seven the number of prisoners and runaways that Powhatan holds?"

"Yes , sir."

"You can make that eight. We had another runaway day before yesterday," Marshal Dale added. "In my opinion a runaway is not worth trading for, except to give him the punishment he deserves. Be that as it may, our position versus Powhatan has improved greatly. I look forward to discussing it with Governor Gates."

~27~

Marshal Dale left Henrico the following morning to go with Captain Argall to Jamestown. There was no effort to keep secret the news of the capture of Pocahontas. On the contrary, word was published throughout the settlement because it was an undeniable success for the Virginia colony. A few years earlier, such an event would have been unthinkable. Even in the spring of 1613 it seemed unreal.

"What a stroke," mused George Yeardley.

I knew without asking that he was speaking of Samuel Argall's achievement.

"The man was born lucky," said Edward Brewster. "She fell into his hands."

"Not quite. He learned she was visiting the Potomacs and took the initiative to get her aboard his ship. Then he managed to get her away without a struggle in which she could have been injured."

"Wasn't it luck that Jopassus would betray her?" Brewster insisted.

"Maybe, but what if the man is lucky? You can't hold that against him."

As I listened to the two officers arguing I thought of the difference between Argall and Brewster. Brewster was ambitious and brave, qualities that he shared with Argall. But Argall had something more, perhaps one could call it imagination or the ability to see the potential gain of seizing an opportunity.

"I still don't think he did anything anyone of us could not have done."

Brewster sat gazing steadily at Yeardley. He was a short,

compact man who possessed great physical courage. I could tell that he had voiced the final thought of his argument, that he could have done as well as Argall. Personally, I had my doubts.

I did think, however, that George Yeardley could have achieved this coup as easily as Argall. He had the imagination and the presence to beguile an unsuspecting person.

He also had the grace to placate his friend, Edward Brewster.

"I have no doubt you would have snapped her up, Edward. But don't be anxious about it; there will be other opportunities to deal with Powhatan and that brother of his."

On his return from Jamestown we learned just how the Governor and Marshal Dale were dealing with Powhatan.

"We thought Captain Argall had expressed our demands well. He asked for all English captives held by Powhatan, the weapons and tools taken from us, and a large quantity of corn. We simply repeated these demands so Powhatan would be sure that they came from the Governor himself."

"He must be concerned if Pocahontas is indeed his favorite," said Yeardley.

"I think he is concerned. He sent Machumps to Jamestown to see if she was being treated well. I don't like that fellow. He is sullen and disrespectful."

"Then he has not changed much since I first met him on the *Seaventure*," I said.

I repeated to Marshal Dale the story of how the two Indian boys had been aboard that ship. Before we left Bermuda, where we were shipwrecked, Namontack disappeared and we suspected Machumps had killed him, but we had no proof.

The Marshal nodded his head slowly as if those events were no surprise to him.

"Well, he had plenty of opportunity to see and talk to Pocahontas. I must say she now appears to be in good humor. Acted as if she had no concern about the people who are holding her. There really is a good feeling toward her at Jamestown. Part of it from her reputation as a friend to the English and part to her natural good nature."

"And Machumps has returned to Powhatan saying all is well with his daughter?" asked Ralph Hamor.

"Unless he chooses to lie to Powhatan and I expect that would be a dangerous thing. As a matter of fact, after Machumps departed, Governor Gates told me that he planned to give Pocahontas the freedom of the fort, provided she promised not to escape."

I was sitting opposite Edward Brewster, who greeted this remark with a slight widening of his eyes. I was sure that he would not have taken such a chance.

There was little to be done except wait. We would not expect Powhatan to launch an attack on us while we held his daughter. But we couldn't be sure and could not relax our security. We would continue our work: building, planting and performing the tasks necessary to stay alive.

We were going to do more than the minimum to survive; Marshall Dale would see to that. He had plans for five forts to be built around the land impaled on the other side of the river. There was also to be a hospital for the care of settlers who became sick, particularly new arrivals. He told us of these plans with his customary directness.

"With the coming of warm weather and longer days we should make good progress."

His remark was greeted with silence. I wondered how many men would die from exhaustion and disease in the warm weather he mentioned. I estimated we had already had eighty who died at Henrico.

"Rolfe, I want you to go to Jamestown and find some more carpenters who would like to join us here."

"I would be happy to do so, sir."

"Most of the men here are soldiers and work quite willingly but they need carpenters to teach them the skills they lack."

"John," asked Alexander Whitaker, "I wonder if you might inquire there for a woman to be my housekeeper at Rocke Hall? I have a cook, Mistress Grimes, who is quite satisfactory but the only others available for household duties here are mere children. I would like to employ an older woman."

So I found myself going to Jamestown on what was really a recruiting mission. I had not told anyone at Henrico but I knew exactly who I had in mind to persuade to make the move.

George Grave was the ablest carpenter that I knew at Jamestown and John Laydon was also a carpenter. Their wives, of course, would be welcome too. And I hoped also that Mistress Horton could be persuaded to come to become housekeeper for the Reverend Whitaker. To my great regret, Robert Horton had not survived the previous winter. A position with Alexander Whitaker might please her, particularly if the Graves came to Henrico.

Jamestown in the springtime was always a pleasing sight. The green leaves provided a backdrop to the fort that appeared to be so tiny as we approached it from upriver. Why should such a soft landscape be so perilous for any Englishman who left the protection of the fort and meager street of houses that stretched eastward from its wall? Sooner or later we had to make peace with Powhatan but I could not see in the spring of 1613 what would bring peace.

Leaving the shallop at the dock I walked quickly to the gate of the fort and to the familiar space in front of the church that was called the marketplace. Governor Gates did permit a market on Saturday afternoon but there was none today. Probably there was little to sell this early in the season. How familiar it all looked. A few children were playing in the afternoon sun. Two small boys were imitating soldiers at drill.

I turned toward the eastern bulwark in the direction of the house Mistress Horton now shared with George and Elizabeth Grave. On my left, in front of one of the tiny houses that I now considered to be quite comfortable homes after almost three years in Virginia, was a group of four women talking in a lively fashion as women will. The contrast with Henrico where no one was idle during hours of daylight made me pause. I looked at them and recognized Anne Laydon. I must have stopped abruptly and caught their attention because Anne turned and called to me.

"John Rolfe, what brings you to Jamestown?"

"To see your good husband, among other things. How are you both?"

"We have survived another winter for which we thank God. As you probably know, Robert Horton was not so fortunate.

Come here, I have someone I want you to meet."

As I walked the few steps to where Anne was standing I noticed that one of the women was dressed in Indian fashion. I knew immediately that it must be Pocahontas Who else could it be? She had every quality you could expect in a princess: dignity, confidence, and an expression that conveyed good will.

"Pocahontas," said Anne, "this is John Rolfe."

I was at a loss for words. I could do nothing but incline my head in a short bow.

"John Rolfe," she said, smiling.

I recovered somewhat and mumbled something, "At your service."

She laughed. The other women laughed. Then we were all laughing. I tried to think of something else to say without success. Anne Laydon came to my rescue.

"Pocahontas is showing us the beadwork on her robe. It is exquisite."

Her robe was a light brown deerskin with a fringe of tassels about two inches long. Around the fringe was sewed what appeared to be tiny shells of purest white. The shoulders and front of the robe were decorated with even smaller blue beads that formed swirling patterns. I thought I recognized the form of birds in the beadwork and made some remarks of admiration. She also wore a simple necklace of copper and white shells. I could not help noticing that her dark hair was worn in a single long braid.

"Perhaps she will show you how to do such beadwork," I said.

"I hope so," said Anne. "She has also shown interest in our clothing. Elizabeth Grave is making her a dress."

"I can see she has won new friends already."

"I consider myself an old friend. Pocahontas sent us food during the winter of 1607. And she warned us when we were about to be attacked."

"Without question," I said, "old friends are best. Thank you, Anne, for introducing me. I must go now to call on Mistress Horton and others."

I bowed to the women. "Goodbye, Pocahontas."

"Goodbye, John Rolfe." Then she laughed. She covered her mouth to hide her smile. The other women were smiling too. I felt like a schoolboy. Did she have this effect on everyone? I had paid her too much attention but I could not help but admire her.

These thoughts were still in my mind as I called on Mistress Horton. That good woman greeted me warmly and invited me to come to supper that evening. George and Elizabeth would be there, of course, and I asked her if she would have the Laydons join us afterwards. She thought they would but we could not keep them late as the Laydon's daughter was very young.

I spent the remainder of the afternoon visiting the ship that was anchored at Jamestown. I was delighted to find that it was Captain Bagnal's ship. It was he who had sold me Trinidad tobacco seed. He welcomed me aboard and after hearing that my crop had been successful asked if I had some that he might sample. We were soon sharing the fragrance of my Virginia grown crop of which I was rightly proud.

"Well, I congratulate you, Master Rolfe. This is almost as good as the Spanish grown tobacco you find in England. I have some more seed but I don't suppose you would be interested since you are now producing your own."

I am sure that he knew full well that I was interested, as any planter worth his salt would be. "This is a different variety, I suppose?"

"Yes. It is called Varina. But I only have a small amount. The Spanish farmers are very jealous I understand. It's the field workers that manage to send it out now and then."

After more discussion Captain Bagnal managed to relieve me once again of two gold sovereigns for a small amount of seed. I knew what might be accomplished with it, however, and did not begrudge his bargain. It was possible this strain could prove even better than the first he had sold me.

"By the way, do you have much of this tobacco on hand?" asked Bagnal.

"Some, but I can sell it easily here in Virginia."

"Why not let me carry it back to England? I dare say it will bring you a better price."

"I had thought to experiment more with growing and curing."

"You can work on improving as you like, but why not see what this will bring?"

"Very well. But it will only be a few barrels. When do you depart?"

"I expect to be here another ten days."

"I estimate I could send five or six hundred pounds."

"I will have room for it; and if I don't, I will make room."

I was pleased with Captain Bagnal's eagerness to ship part of my tobacco crop. He was one of a breed of men who had enriched many merchants, including my own father, by their willingness to take a risk on importing goods from overseas.

As I gathered at table that evening with my friends I felt relaxed and comfortable. There was not the need to be on guard as one always did in the presence of Marshal Dale. The Graves and Mistress Horton were my shipmates from the *Seaventure* who had worked so hard together to reach Virginia. I had known the Laydons ever since arriving in Jamestown three years earlier. Their four year old daughter, Virginia, was sleeping soundly on a bed nearby.

"She has grown in the past year, Anne."

"She has begun to help me with chores and that gives her a good appetite."

"Not that anyone in Jamestown needs an appetite," said John Laydon.

"True enough, John," I said, "and that brings me to what I want to talk to you about."

I paused. How would I introduce the idea of leaving Jamestown?

"I would like for all of you," I said looking around at the group I knew so well, "to consider coming to Henrico."

"For a visit?" asked Elizabeth. "I would like to. George has been there but not I."

"Not for a visit but to live and work there. There is better land and it is healthier."

"We hear awful things about Marshal Dale," said Mistress Horton.

"It's true he is a strict disciplinarian but I think he is more concerned about the soldiers than ordinary folk. He has already provided land ownership to those who work it."

I could see that the opportunity to own land was important to my friends. In England, they could work an entire lifetime without hope of gaining ownership.

"There is plenty of good land. And there will be more available from what was taken last December from the Appomatocs."

"But we have duties here in Jamestown, John," said George Grave. "How can we just pick up and move to Henrico?"

"That is a good question, George. The fact is I have been sent to find two good carpenters and also a housekeeper for The Reverend Whitaker. George and John are the carpenters, and you, Mistress Horton, I hope might consider being the housekeeper."

"But I was thinking of returning to England," said the good woman. "In fact, it might be best for me to go on the ship that is here now."

"Oh, Mistress Horton," said Elizabeth, "you must reconsider. Reverend Whitaker is the most learned man. I have heard him talking with Mr. Bucke and it made my head spin. They can speak on any subject. Mr. Whitaker could convert Powhatan himself if given the chance."

"Please stay," said Anne Laydon. "We can all live nearby at Henrico."

"I will have to think about it."

Anne's remark about living nearby indicated interest in moving. No doubt she had unpleasant memories of Jamestown.

"George, you and John are needed as carpenters. We have many workers at Henrico but need skilled carpenters to supervise the building. You will have time though to plant your own land. Marshal Dale wants the land to be farmed by as many as possible."

George looked dubious. John Laydon was evidently more adventurous.

"Is it good fast land, John? Not just tidewater marsh?"

"There is plenty of fast land. I am planting it now and can

attest to the amount of corn in has produced for any man who would till it."

"Then I am willing to go," said Laydon, looking at his wife who nodded agreement with a smile.

"Let's do it, George," said Elizabeth. "It's time to move on."

"All right, Elizabeth, if John Rolfe thinks it best for us, I agree."

"Mistress Horton" said Elizabeth, "won't you come too?"

"I'll have to think about it."

~28~

"When will the carpenters from Jamestown join us?" asked Marshal Dale.

"I expect them here within a week."

"A week! I expected them to come back with you or require only a few days at most."

"It was the best I could arrange with Governor Gates, sir. He has these men supervising workers now and wants to be sure that the work they are doing will be properly continued." I did not mention that both men had families to consider. Marshal Dale would expect that wives would facilitate rather that encumber their husbands' departures.

Perhaps my expression betrayed my thoughts. I was about to bring up the subject of my tobacco shipment when the Marshal said. "Both these men have wives don't they?"

"Yes, sir."

"Humph! Do we have a house available, Hamor?"

"Yes, sir. We have a vacant house because of deaths during the past month, Unfortunately, it is very small."

"Well, see if you can move men to get a second house. John Rolfe has spoken highly of these men that he has recruited, Grave and Laydon. They will be important to us and I want to encourage more to come from Jamestown. We need more people on our land."

Marshal Dale never ceased to surprise me. He seemed to alternate between actions that were harsh and those that were enlightened. I was pleased that he was taking these pains on behalf of my friends who, of course, would need a place to live. On the other hand, Mistress Horton had seemed hesitant about Marshal Dale, as would anyone who had heard of his severity. I believe that he was convinced that the men under his command were motivated by fear of punishment. There was no doubt that they were motivated because they labored or marched at his command, until overtaken by exhaustion. By their labor they were carving a settlement out of the wilderness. But now that the settlement was showing signs of success, who would want to live there if it entailed such sacrifice? The Marshal would have to soften his manner. Perhaps he was beginning to.

While I was glad that my friends were coming and that they would be appreciated for what they could bring to Henrico, I had little time to speculate on what occupied the mind of Marshal Dale. I had only a few days to prepare my tobacco to send to Jamestown. Captain Bagnal had given me four barrels from his ship, *Blessing,* that I would use for shipment. Having these barrels was important because it saved me much labor in making my own. We had only one cooper at Henrico and his labor was in great demand to create barrels for the storage of corn.

My method of packing the tobacco in barrels was to roll the leaves into strings that were then coiled like a rope directly into the containers. It was time consuming but it permitted me to make good use of the available space. The lids of the barrels were pressed down firmly to pack as much in as possible. I thought myself successful when I tried to lift a packed barrel that must have weighed over one hundred fifty pounds. My four barrels would then exceed six hundred pounds. I left the exact determination of the weight to Captain Bagnal who would act as my agent in selling the tobacco.

Although we had saved sufficient tobacco for our own use, Ralph Hamor seemed disconcerted that I was rushing to take advantage of Captain Bagnal's imminent sailing for England.

"I thought you were going to wait until you were more satisfied with the curing process."

"I was, Ralph, but Robert Bagnal appears to be an honest man as well as a shrewd one. In his judgment, this tobacco will sell in London. Why not find out?"

"What do you think it will bring?"

"Good tobacco is so much in demand that the best has sold

for as much as a pound sterling for a pound of the best leaf. Now, suppose we only get a quarter of that, say five schillings. My six hundred pounds of leaf would bring one hundred fifty pounds sterling."

Hamor was stunned. "What did you say?"

I repeated my calculation.

"I had no idea there was so much in those barrels."

"There are a lot of risks. The market could change, the tobacco could be spoiled, the ship could be lost. You know the danger of storms as well as I."

"I know that you could make a tidy profit if all goes well."

"Let's not count on that eventuality. Let's just see what happens."

My tobacco was sent to Jamestown on one of two shallops. Marshal Dale himself was in the other. He was going to meet with Governor Gates and was escorted by a squad of soldiers. Before departing he congratulated me and wished me success. It was his vision that, in the future, cargoes from Henrico would be loaded here on ships bound for England rather than on small shallops.

A farmer enjoys what is probably the most satisfying occupation on earth. From a handful of seed and properly prepared soil he undertakes to begin a process that, carefully tended and blessed with God's sunshine and rain, will bring forth fruits and grain in abundance. Seeing the ripe crop before harvest is a moment of great satisfaction. When the crop is harvested and is on its way to market is another moment of satisfaction. I had enjoyed those moments on our farms at Heacham Hall and now had the same feeling even though my crop was not en route to one of the market towns in Norfolk. It would be months before I knew the outcome of the shipment.

In the meantime I had plenty of work to occupy my mind. New fields on the north side of the river were being cultivated and I wanted to get my new tobacco seed in the ground as well as tend to my already planted tobacco. There was much record keeping related to those activities.

Marshal Dale's return coincided with the arrival of my friends from Jamestown. I was particularly pleased to see that

Mistress Horton had come with them to be housekeeper for the Reverend Whitaker. Ralph Hamor had managed to arrange for houses for both George Grave and John Laydon. Mistress Horton would stay with the Graves until a place was ready for her at Rocke Hall. Ralph Hamor and I hurriedly arranged for fires to be laid in their new homes.

Marshal Dale invited Mistress Horton to join us for supper that night so that she might be welcomed to Henrico by the Reverend Whitaker. Once again the Marshal was showing consideration that one might not have expected.

I had grown to admire Alexander Whitaker who came to Virginia with Marshal Dale and accompanied him when he began the Henrico settlement. He had vigor that animated his slight frame and lighted his eyes, but what distinguished him primarily was his intellect. I did not see how he could be excelled in either oratory or written discourse. His father was likewise a minister and well known for his learning, having been a teacher at Cambridge University for many years. I suppose it was natural for Alexander to follow in his father's footsteps, just as I had followed those of my father. He was at home in the pulpit as I in the open fields.

"What shall I do for the natives, Mistress Horton? That is the question of my ministry."

"Well, Master Whitaker, I know that you may pray for them, as I have heard Reverend Bucke do on many occasions."

"I might have done that in the comfort of my parsonage in England. And. I have prayed for them here but I fear I have not brought the word of God to them."

"If you were to do so, could they understand?"

"Are you questioning my ability to communicate, Mistress Horton, or their ability to comprehend?"

"If your communication were perfect, sir; indeed, if you spoke the very same language, could they comprehend?"

"Oh, I truly believe that they could. How do they differ from you and me? They have all the requisite senses to live in God's creation. They see, smell, and hear as well as you or I. They certainly communicate with one another as well as you or I. Why would God, after granting them these faculties, deny them the ability to comprehend the good news of the Gospel?"

"What you say may well be true, Alexander," said Marshal Dale, "but I believe the problem of communication is not yet solved."

"That is undeniable."

"And so, how can it best be solved?"

"On my part, I have been studying their speech. I have, of course, the lexicon of Indian words prepared by Thomas Harriot of the Roanoke colony. And I have endeavored to learn from conversation with Cocopone who interprets for Governor Gates, as well as from a few words with Machumps during his infrequent visits."

"You might get help from Henry Spelman, Captain Argall's interpreter," suggested George Yeardley.

"I have tried, George," said Whitaker with a smile, "but I find that young man is uncomfortable speaking with a priest."

"If you will forgive this suggestion, Alexander," said Marshal Dale, "we could arrange with Powhatan to exchange you for one of his priests. That would facilitate your learning process."

We all laughed. I wondered if some such thought had ever occurred to Whitaker.

"I have considered suggesting this but feared that, if it came to pass, the experiment might result in converting you to worship of their God Okee."

More laughter filled the room. The Reverend Whitaker could give as well as he got.

"I tremble to think of such an outcome, "said the Marshal, "and will take a different tack. You know that we have tried to induce Indians to let us have their children in order to instruct them and send them back to their parents as Christians. But no Indians have been willing to do so. I must say that I can understand that because we are so different."

"But consider out present position. We have at Jamestown, Pocahontas, the daughter of Powhatan. She seems well disposed towards us. Further, she seems to be a person of exceptional spirit and intelligence. What if she were to learn our language, our customs, and, above all, our religion?"

194

"Why, sir," said Mistress Horton, "she could do all these things."

"I agree, ma'am. I believe that having done those things, she could be a most persuasive friend for us. She is said by Governor Gates to show interest in all our customs. When she eventually returns to her father she could perhaps even persuade him to let us have children to educate. I have discussed the proposition with Governor Gates. As you all know, conditions of her ransom have been sent to Powhatan. Although he has agreed to the conditions, he has not complied. We do not know when he will comply but, if he has not done so within another fortnight, we want to bring her here to Henrico. Once here, we would like to put her under your tutelage, Alexander, with the objective to be her education and her conversion."

"I would consider that a privilege, Marshal Dale. It could be a lengthy process, however, since it would involve teaching her our written language if she is to be truly grounded in our religion and have the ability to teach it to her own people."

"She could do it," said Mistress Horton. "I have seen enough of her at Jamestown to know that she has the mind for it. Indeed, I would say she thirsts for it."

"If she came to Henrico and lived at Rocke Hall, Mistress Horton, much of the responsibility to teach her our ways would be yours," said the Marshal.

"That responsibility would be a pleasure."

"As for you, Alexander, you would be teaching her the English alphabet so that she may read. Are you willing to undertake such a fundamental task?"

"Sir, I came to Virginia prepared. I brought hornbooks and slates thinking that I might teach Indian children. Why should I be shy of teaching an intelligent adult? To me this opportunity seems but another manifestation of God's Grace. Who can say what doors it will open for us?"

"Think of the dangers this colony has undergone, sir. The Virginia settlement was dying when Sir Thomas Gates arrived from Bermuda. God saved him and the passengers of the *Seaventure* from the terrible storm and guided them safely to

Jamestown. Then Lord De La Warr arrived with men and supplies when return to England seemed the only possible course. And then you came, Marshal Dale, to save the colony when Lord De La Warr's health forced his return to England."

"We have not spent forty years in the wilderness, as did Moses, but surely the hand of God has been upon us as it was upon Israel. And now we are asked if we can teach the way of God to the daughter of the most powerful chief of the native tribes. For me, the answer to this question can only be yes. Yes, with a thankful heart I would undertake to instruct her so that she may become our sister in Christ."

If Marshal Dale had called upon us then to stand, lift our glasses, and toast Pocahontas I would have sprung to my feet. Why should I have been so enlivened by the proposed coming of Powhatan's daughter to Henrico? I had only seen her once, and that briefly. Was it the stirring words just said by Alexander Whitaker? Probably not. I believe that I was moved by the thought that Pocahontas was indeed our friend, that she had proved it by deeds, not just words, and that she was genuinely drawn to us. In the darkness that seemed to exist between us and her people she was a light that offered hope of approval, understanding, and peace. I knew I was not alone in my desire to see that light.

~29~

I was greatly encouraged by the success I had so far with the planting of Trinidad tobacco. Not only had members of the Virginia colony praised it but also Captain Bagnal had been certain of a market for it in England. For my part, I was determined to make it better through whatever means were within my control.

First I wanted to get the newest seed that Bagnal had brought me under cultivation. I had already made plantings in March and April with Trinidad seed. Now I would plant the Varina type along with a third planting of Trinidad. My object in having several plantings was to find which planting time was the optimum. I also wanted to determine the best distance between plants. I had already learned that the Trinidad plants, because of their greater size, benefited from more generous spacing.

I had carefully measured the size of plants the first year and left space in my planting journal to compare plants grown on the same ground in successive years. How long could the ground support strong plants without having to lie fallow? I also was careful to record the drainage conditions on each part of the land I used. If this tobacco was to compete with Spanish tobacco it was important to learn as soon as possible what conditions resulted in the best leaf.

Ralph Hamor willingly joined me in my labor. He was more of a scholarly man than a farmer but he was adapting to spending part of each day in the fields. He understood the potential this plant had for being a valuable commodity and took a keen interest in the entire process from planting to curing.

"I don't see what the phases of the moon have to do with planting, John Rolfe. I can understand the effect of cold, and sunshine, and rain. But you leave me behind when you speak of the moon having an effect on plants."

"I don't suppose you have trouble understanding tides do you?"

"Well, yes, if you must know, I do have a little difficulty understanding tides."

"I don't mean completely understanding them because they are truly complex. But whether in Virginia or Bermuda, haven't you noticed that the highest tides occur at the time of the full moon?"

"Yes, of course."

"Well, if the moon can have such an effect on the seas, why can't it have an effect on the water in and around plants?" He shook his head. "I'll have to leave that to you planters. Just keep telling me what to do."

Marshal Dale had assigned two other men to help me with the tobacco crop. There was so much labor involved that Hamor and I could scarcely keep up with it. I had selected the men myself knowing there would be some who preferred farming to cutting wood day after day. The settlement had impaled large tracts of land by setting timbers in the ground to form a large fence, similar to the palisades at Jamestown. Several miles of palisade now existed on the other side of the river where Alexander Whitaker had his parsonage.

The use of timbers there to create forts and a hospital now required the efforts of men like George Grave and other carpenters. With the pressures of planting and recording I found that the days passed quickly. The spring weather was ideal for outdoor work and much was done to enlarge and improve the Henrico settlement. Marshall Dale, although never satisfied, at least seemed pleased with the progress. Following our morning church service he rose to address the congregation.

"All of you are aware that Pocahontas, the daughter of Powhatan, is now at Jamestown. She is our hostage and certain conditions have been communicated to Powhatan as the terms of her release. I have learned from Governor Gates that some of these conditions have been met. Eight prisoners held by Powhatan have been released to us along with a few stolen tools. Of the large number of our weapons known to have captured or stolen, only a few have been returned, and those returned are in pitiable condition, not fit for use.

Because neither the other weapons nor the quantity of corn we demanded have been provided, the Governor has rejected Powhatan's partial compliance with the conditions."

"Governor Gates has decided, in response to my request, to send Pocahontas to Henrico where she will be instructed by the Reverend Whitaker, and other members of this congregation, in the teachings of the Christian Church. She has indicated a willingness to receive this instruction and an interest in learning more about our way of life. All of you can assist in making her feel welcome. I want to caution you, however, against making her the object of unwarranted curiosity or any sort of disrespect. Those who have met her know that, on the contrary, she deserves the respect of all of us. I expect her arrival tomorrow and I expect you assist her in any way that you can as she joins our community. Our success in winning her to our way of life can bring many benefits both to us and to her people."

Direct speeches by Marshal Dale to the people of Henrico were not common. He was used to having his wishes transmitted through his captains or by written proclamations.

It was as if the conversion of Pocahontas to Christianity were a battle and we were all his troops in the coming campaign. No matter what we thought of the "battle," there was no doubt of its importance to Marshal Dale.

Despite his warnings about curiosity there were a small crowd who somehow managed to find their way to the landing on some pretense of business when the shallop bearing Pocahontas arrived at Henrico. The Reverend Whitaker was there, of course, along with Mistress Horton and Elizabeth Grave. Captain Yeardley detailed two squads of soldiers to form a guard of honor. That drew a few small children and provided a sufficient excuse for their mothers who pretended to be looking for their offspring who had somehow escaped from their chores. I had no real excuse for being there so I observed the scene from

199

across the river where I was tending tobacco plants.

Although I understood that Elizabeth had made a dress for Pocahontas, she must have chosen not to wear it on this occasion, being instead in the deerskin skirt and robe that I had seen at Jamestown. As soon as she stepped from the shallop, George Yeardley, resplendent in his plumed helmet and cape, greeted her He did not move with more grace than she, however, and she regarded the waiting soldiers of the guard while all other eyes were fixed on her. Once past the guard, she ran to greet Mistress Horton and Elizabeth. Then they all moved up the hill to the home of Marshal Dale.

I must confess that I thought all this bother for the sake of a single young woman excessive, even though she was the daughter of a king. I had come from England to America for many reasons; but not the least of these was to escape the burden of the aristocracy which I found stifling. But I did not dwell on this. After all, the presence of Pocahontas gave us something else to think about in our rather bleak existence. And from all reports she was friendly and unassuming.

At first I did not see her frequently. During the first summer she spent at Henrico she occasionally attended church services with Mistress Horton. It was reported to Marshal Dale that she was progressing well in learning our language and he told us that he had been pleased to communicate with her. He and Alexander Whitaker had in fact been learning as much about the Indian religion from her as the reverse. She told them that the Indian priests who dressed most hideously to imitate their devil, or Okee, might aspire to have an afterlife with him. Ordinary people, however, were thought to have no afterlife and perished in their graves. There were three great temples near the village of Powhatan where only the greatest chiefs and priests were entombed. Ordinary folk were not admitted and made sacrifices of appeasement when they even came near the temples.

The Marshal was generous in his praise for both the Reverend Whitaker and Mistress Horton. He thought them able tutors for he said it required as much or more skill to teach a bright pupil as to teach a laggard.

"The Marshal praises your efforts most highly, Mistress Horton. He says your pupil is progressing even better than he had expected."

"It is no trouble to teach this lass. She can sound every letter as clearly as a bell and has learned to recognize each one."

"So you are enjoying your new occupation?"

"I only wish I could learn her language. It is like music, John."

"Music?"

"Oh, you know what I mean. Some foreign tongues are harsh and forbidding. Not hers. I was teaching her to recognize the letter "c" and to sound it out. So I used the word copper as an example of the sound and pointed to a copper ornament she wears on a necklace. She repeated "copper" and then said their word for copper, "mattassin.""

"But you don't think you will learn her language?"

"I doubt it. That is not what the Reverend Whitaker and I are supposed to be doing. Besides Pocahontas has her mind set on learning ours. She uses her new words at every opportunity. It is only occasionally that she will say something in her native tongue and then usually to herself."

"Do you believe, Mistress Horton, that she is truly set on learning our ways?"

"I do. She has told me several times that she wants to be baptized. I think she is sincere."

"Could she not be simply learning our language to use against us when she is released?"

"It is possible, I suppose. But it does not fit with what people like Anne Laydon know about her from the early days in Jamestown. I do not suspect her of guile. Speaking of guile, that Captain Argall who tricked her will never be her friend. She may treat him politely but I sense her resentment of him."

"I think that is understandable, don't you?"

"Of course. I don't like the man; but that is between you and me, John ."

"Why do you think we have gone several months now and not heard any further response from Powhatan to Governor Gates' demands?"

"How would you expect me to answer that question? I have no idea what he may be planning. You should know more about that than I do."

"Has she spoken of him?"

"No, but because I spend so much time with her I wonder what is going through her mind."

"Surely you do not spend all day doing lessons."

"No. She is an active creature and needs to move about. She likes to help in the garden and has taught us some things about planting. And she even helps with the cooking."

"Quite a change for a princess."

"I don't think so. She says she is used to work."

"What does the Reverend Whitaker have planned for her."

"He says that when she has learned the Lord's Prayer she may attend the Sunday catechism."

I suspected that would take some time. I was invited each Sunday afternoon to Rocke Hall where we were rehearsed in the articles of faith. I began to have more sympathy for the Indian woman. Many English people found the catechism quite daunting. To a person accustomed to neither the English language nor the Church of England a session might seem overpowering.

My mind was filled with other things. The tobacco plants required almost continual care. One of the two additional men assigned to help me had become ill and, although I had requested and received a replacement, the new man was not as diligent as his predecessor. I hoped an early recovery would enable me to return the replacement to Captain Yeardley.

When my sick worker, whose name was John Dixon, had been absent for nine days I went to the hospital that had been built at Mount Malado because I understood he had been sent there. The hospital building, that was even larger than the church at Henrico, was built primarily with the intent of enabling new settlers to recover from the sea voyage from England and sicknesses they might undergo before they were seasoned to Virginia. But, even though our location was healthier than Jamestown, many of the settlers at Henrico became ill, particularly in the summer months.

As I entered the door of the clapboard building that resembled a large barn, I encountered a solitary clerk seated at a desk. He lifted his gloomy face and peered at me.

"What can I do for you?" he asked.

"I have come to enquire of John Dixon. I have brought him some sassafras for tea."

"I am afraid John Dixon can drink no tea. He died last night."

"He's dead? I was here only the day before yesterday and saw him appearing better."

"Perhaps he appeared so to you. The surgeon bled him that same evening when the fever grew worse. He then fainted and never recovered."

"Lord help us, he was a strong lad but two weeks ago."

The clerk eyed me as if I were holding him responsible for Dixon's death. "The surgeon pronounced him dead himself."

I turned and walked slowly toward the door. I looked down at the small package I had brought. "Here is the tea I brought. And some cakes. Would you give them to some other patient?"

"Certainly, sir."

~30~

It was the beginning of the weekly catechism, conducted by Alexander Whitaker in Rocke Hall, his house across the river from Henrico. It was Sunday afternoon and the group gathered in the main room of the house. In addition to the marshal, Captain Yeardley, Captain Brewster, Ralph Hamor, and myself, our circle had been widened to include Pocahontas, who had learned the Lord's Prayer to the satisfaction of Alexander Whitaker. Mistress Horton who accompanied the young Indian woman in public also attended. Whitaker had begun the catechism by saying that Pocahontas' progress in bettering her understanding of our language had been remarkable. He believed that attending the catechism would benefit her both in understanding our language and Christianity and that we might gain insights into the beliefs of the Indian people whom we hoped to convert to the Kingdom of God.

"What do we learn about God as creator from the revelation to Israel?" asked Whitaker.

"We learn that there is one God, the Father Almighty, creator of heaven and earth, of all that is, seen and unseen," responded George Yeardley.

Addressing himself to Pocahontas, the Reverend Whitaker said, "We believe that there is but one God, Pocahontas, and we ask you to leave behind the Indian belief in other Gods."

"That I do gladly. Your God must be greater than Okee or any of our other Gods."

"We agree, but tell us why you believe our God is greater."

"He gives you so much help. Your boats are greater than our canoes and your guns greater than our arrows. Even your houses are better than ours."

"He does help us, it is true. But things such as the building of ships and houses can be learned. These things can also be forgotten but God remains the loving God who creates us."

"Why do you say, Master Whitaker, that there is only one God and then you also speak of Satan?"

"Satan is not a God although he is a very powerful force. He is a fallen angel who rebelled against God just as we sometimes rebel against God."

"But you do not worship him because he is not a God?"

"We do not worship him for the reason that he separates us from God. But I believe that your people worship Okee whom they believe has the power to do much evil."

"That is not so, Master Whitaker. They believe that Okee has the power to do much evil, and so they give him gifts."

"Why do we not hear more of your good god Ahone?" asked Marshal Dale.

"Because he is good and our people do not need to be afraid of him. Do I need to be afraid of one who is truly good?"

"Yes, if you offend him."

"But we see that bad things can happen to you even if you mean no harm to the gods. So we ask the priests to help protect us against gods who may do us evil."

"How do the priests do that?"

"They have been taught secret words to speak to Okee or other gods. We cannot understand them and dare not try."

"Have you been in the great Pamunkey temple, Pocahontas?"

"No. I have been with my father when he went but I could not go in. He told me there were many fearsome carvings there and that it had seven priests."

"Do the Indian people have a word for sin?" asked Whitaker.

"What is sin?"

"I will direct your question, 'What is sin?' to another person, Pocahontas," replied Whitaker. "Would you answer the question, Captain Brewster?"

"Gladly. Sin is the seeking of our own will instead of the will of God, thus distorting our relationship with God, with other people, and with all creation."

205

"How does sin have power over us?"

"Sin has power over us because we lose our liberty when our relationship with God is distorted."

Seeing that Pocahontas wore a puzzled expression, the Reverend Whitaker asked, "What is it, Pocahontas?"

"I do not know 'relationship'. Tell me what this means."

"A relationship is a bond that ties you to another being. You, for example, have a relationship with your father Powhatan. This is such a strong relationship that we say you and he are relatives. You and Mistress Horton also have a relationship: you are friends which means that you care about each other and want good things for each other."

"We say that friends are the same spirit in two bodies," said Pocahontas.

"I do not know a better way to define friendship," said the minister.

"Why do you call God, 'father'?"

"He told Israel that there is one God, the Father Almighty."

"Israel? What is Israel?"

"A group of tribes, of which there were twelve, lived many years ago, and still live far across the ocean in the direction of the sun."

"Did the tribes fight?"

"Oh yes. Yes and God gave them great victories so long as they obeyed him and kept his commandments."

"Commandments?"

"When your father told you 'do this', what did you do?"

"When I was a little girl I would do as he said. But not always; sometimes I would run in the woods and hide."

We all laughed, except for the marshal. Eventually even he managed a smile.

"Well, what he told you to do was a commandment. And when you did not do as he said we say that you broke his commandment. But then what happened after you broke his commandment?"

"Sometimes I would come back and say I was sorry and perhaps cry or make him laugh. If I thought he was really angered I would sometimes sleep in the woods."

"But you always returned?"

"Yes. I knew he would not always be angry forever."

"We must learn more about commandments, Pocahontas. Mistress Horton will talk to you about them before next Sunday. These are commandments from God, our Father in heaven."

So saying, the Reverend Whitaker closed the catechism with a prayer. It had been a briefer period of questions and answers than we were accustomed to but he did not wish to overwhelm his new pupil. Instead of further questions he continued with a discourse on our obligations to our fellow man.

I found the Sunday catechisms at Rocke Hall to be a refreshing change from our daily labors, particularly in the hot summer of 1613 when the days were so long and we worked so hard to comply with the demands of Marshal Dale. I had always attended catechism with some small anxiety, similar to that of a schoolboy, concern that I might be unable to respond correctly to the questions. Gradually, this discomfort disappeared and I asked myself why it was that I felt more at ease. Partly it was due to the liberality of Alexander Whitaker who was less interested in the rote response than to impart understanding in the minds of all of us. But the principal reason, I believe, that all of us came to look forward to these sessions was the presence of Pocahontas.

I wondered how it was that Pocahontas was able to enter into not only our presence but also our culture as unreservedly as she did. Did she suspect that Powhatan was going to let her remain unransomed, month after month, even after he had returned English captives to us? As she adopted more of our ways was she thinking she might serve him in the future as an ambassador to the Englishmen? Was it simply an interesting game to her or was she sincerely drawn to us? These kinds of thoughts were only speculation on my part. More obvious was the power of her personality. She had a largeness of spirit that enabled her to accept instruction in language and religion from Alexander Whitaker without surrendering her opinions or view of the world. She would even tease him on occasion if he began to pontificate by interrupting the discussion with remarks that were at once abrupt but not unkind.

We had reached the autumn equinox and the heat of the Virginia summer had begun to abate when Captain Bagnal arrived by ship from England in Jamestown. He sent a message advising me that my tobacco had been well received, bringing a price of eight shillings per pound. Although less than the price of the finest Spanish tobacco, this exceeded what either he or I had expected for Virginia tobacco in the London market. He congratulated me on my success and hoped that I would soon have additional crops for export.

I could hardly contain the news. I turned to Ralph Hamor who was busy reading dispatches he had received from Jamestown. "You will not believe this, Ralph."

"I would believe anything you told me, John Rolfe."

"My shipment of tobacco fetched eight shillings per pound on the London market for a total of two hundred forty pounds before paying the transport and factor's charges."

Hamor put down his papers and stared at me. "That is hardly to be believed. I congratulate you on your success."

"I think we can do better, Ralph. Captain Bagnal's letter says that the finest Spanish tobacco is selling at eighteen shillings per pound."

"At that price tobacco is almost worth its weight in silver." He slowly shook his head from side to side as he pondered that thought. "Unbelievable."

"I truly mean it when I say that we can do better. The tobacco I shipped was coarser than what we are producing this year. We are getting rounder and finer leaves. What we did last year is not an accident. We have done it again and done it better."

"Please stop saying, 'what we have done'. It is you who have done it."

"It was my idea, I admit, to use seed from the Indies. But you helped, as did John Laydon. And Marshal Dale has encouraged me here at Henrico."

"Have you told him the news?"

"No, I have not. Is he at his house?"

"No. He may have gone to Rocke Hall. He is taking much interest in the schooling of Pocahontas. I will let you know when he returns."

Marshal Dale, accompanied by Alexander Whitaker returned just before the evening church service. I had no opportunity to speak with him beforehand but approached him as he left the church.

"May I have a word with you, sir?"

"Can it wait until supper?"

"Of course. But I think it will interest you greatly."

"Very well, come along with me. We can talk as we walk. I have asked Captain Yeardley to meet with me at the house."

"Perhaps I should wait."

"No. What he and I have to discuss is nothing new. I continue to be disturbed by Powhatan's unwillingness to ransom Pocahontas."

"Very well, sir. I will try to be brief. I wish to report that my shipment of tobacco to London brought a price of eight shillings per pound of tobacco."

Marshal Dale stopped in his tracks and stared at me. "Good Lord have mercy. That is the best news I have heard in months. That puny shipment was only four barrels, I believe you told me."

"Yes, sir. But all of it was sold."

"I believe you may have found an answer to one of our most pressing questions, Rolfe: how is Virginia going to support itself? How much was gained from this transaction?"

"There is a balance with the London factor in excess of two hundred pounds."

"How much tobacco did you ship?"

"Six hundred pounds."

"How much can you ship from this year's crop?"

"I would estimate over a thousand pounds. And I expect it to be a higher quality."

Dale resumed walking. "How many men do you need to help you with the crop?"

"There are four of us now, including Ralph Hamor and myself."

"Do you need more?"

"One more because I am taking more care with curing than I did before and Ralph cannot spare much time from his other duties."

"You shall have another man, of course. This is astounding news. The value of a man's labor in tobacco is many times what he can bring in other crops. And therefore we shall plan on even more plantings next year. Congratulations, Rolfe, you have done us a great service."

When we met for supper that evening I received more congratulations from my friends. Yeardley and Brewster, being military men like Marshal Dale, treated the whole matter as a miracle of some sort. Hamor and I, knowing the labor involved, were no less gratified but recognized what had been required to make develop a marketable crop. The truth was probably somewhere in between these views: that a tiny seed so small as hardly to be seen could, with care produce a plant of great value.

~31~

News of the success of Virginia tobacco spread rapidly throughout the Henrico settlement. I was accorded status in the eyes of my countrymen, if not that of a hero, at least that of a person of special interest. Before and after church services, men and women questioned me about the crop: Where had I bought the seed? Did I expect to do as well this year? Could they plant tobacco too?

In the evening, if I walked out to look on the acres planted in tobacco, I would see people standing at the edge of the fields looking at the plants. Some were possibly doing mental calculations on the value of what they saw on the London market. Others were looking closely at the plants to note the difference in size, number of leaves, or structure of the leaf.

Another worker was provided to help me with my crop. I had plenty for the men to do. The plants still contended with weeds for nourishment. There were also grubs and caterpillars that attacked the leaves. These had to be removed by hand and destroyed or they would return. It was a loathsome task, that I found particularly tiring, and I was glad to have help.

I began the harvesting of leaves before the first frost. Our practice had been to leave them in piles for curing. I was not satisfied with the process and experimented with hanging leaves on pieces of string. Some of the women at Henrico provided me with string made from flax they had planted in their gardens.

I was pleased, as a man who had spent his life on a farm when not attending school, to have stirred the interest of other persons interested in agriculture. These men were the salt of the earth, in my opinion, and I valued the opportunity to converse with them about farming. But they were not the only ones interested in my crop. Marshal Dale, who had immediately seen its importance to Virginia, was full of questions on how to insure the toehold that Spanish tobacco strains had managed to gain on Virginia soil. He took me to Jamestown to confer with Governor Gates.

"Congratulations, Rolfe, your tobacco will be a boon to the Virginia Company."

"I am pleased to be of service, Sir Thomas."

"I enjoy the pipe myself although not as much as some men. When I was last in London, it was even more the rage that when we left in 1609. That being the situation, how can we best profit from it? Send them more tobacco, of course. Have you given that much thought?"

"Marshal Dale has asked me the same question."

"Rolfe has not had the opportunity to think about anything else," said the marshal.

"At Henrico he is besieged by people who want to share his prosperity. I have asked him how we might proceed in future years."

"I would be pleased to hear it," said the Governor. "I thought John Rolfe would make his mark in Virginia when I first saw him on the *Seaventure*."

I was flustered by the kind remarks of Governor Gates.

"Thank you, Sir Thomas. I will have more seed at my disposal than I will be able to plant next year. I would suggest that what I have to spare may put in the Company storehouses at Henrico and Jamestown to be shared by qualified farmers at either site."

"I can instruct the farmers at both Henrico and Jamestown on its proper planting and care."

"Excellent. Do you foresee any difficulties?"

"The seed must be protected to prevent damage or theft. We must be alert for vermin that can reduce the crop's value."

"Anything else?"

"We want to enhance the name of Virginia tobacco by improving our strains and our quality. Someday you may wish to establish inspectors to ensure that only quality leaf is exported."

"In good time, Rolfe, in good time," said the Governor. "For the time being we will concentrate on enlarging the crop."

Turning to Marshal Dale, the Governor asked, "Do you agree with Rolfe's proposal to expand growth by providing seed to qualified farmers at Henrico and Jamestown?"

"I do indeed."

"Then let us proceed. But first let us join in a toast." He filled three glasses from a decanter on a table.

"To John Rolfe and Virginia tobacco."

This was very heady praise to me. But I felt secure in the knowledge that last year's success was not an accident. Indications were that this year's plants were even better, at least from the small quantities that Ralph Hamor and I had been able to test. My helpers worked with a will to harvest the leaves and complete the curing process. When I was not in the fields I was making records in my journals on the results at various locations.

I probably could have been excused from attending catechism but I continued to look forward to it. By late November Pocahontas had recited the Ten Commandments to the satisfaction of both Alexander Whitaker and Marshal Dale. As her sponsor, Dale took a strong interest in her education. He was attentive to her responses to questions after our minister had explained the meaning of each commandment in detail.

She was quick to grasp a concept even if it was incompatible with her native culture. Idols and images, for example, which were forbidden to us were plentiful in every Powhatan village. Most were grotesque, however, and I think she had no difficulty rejecting them. On the other hand, she might have found a beautiful idol representing our God to be acceptable. She even advanced this idea on one occasion but was quickly admonished by Alexander Whitaker.

On the last Sunday in November I arrived at Rocke Hall early for the catechism. Mistress Horton and Pocahontas greeted me and bade me to be comfortable by the fire. When Mistress Horton excused herself I was alone with Pocahontas for the first time since she came to Henrico.

"Many good things are said of you, John Rolfe."

213

"We are not supposed to judge one another.'

"How can we not judge? We see a man do a good thing. Are we not to honor him?"

"The Bible says the Lord shall be our judge."

"You do not like it when people say good things about you?"

"Of course I do," I replied with a smile.

"If you do not, I will speak no more."

I laughed. I had been teasing her and now she was teasing me. "Please speak if it makes you happy."

Now she was smiling. I could not help noticing the merriment in her dark eyes and the way she tilted her head when she smiled. "Well, they say you are a very good farmer. The best farmer at Henrico."

"I would like to be a good farmer but I would never say I was the best."

"Why not? Then all the people look up to you."

"People think you are good for what you do, not for what you say."

"You can do both when you are here at Henrico. But if you come to my village you should not say too much."

"Why not?"

"Because in my village only the women are farmers."

"Why is that?"

"The men must hunt or fish. The hunting makes them walk and run much, sometimes for many miles, sometimes for many days. So the women farm the fields at the villages because they must care for the children."

"So the men never farm?"

"Sometimes they grow the tobacco."

"But the women's farming is important, isn't it, Pocahontas?"

"Yes, it is. The corn we plant can be dried and we eat it in the winter. If a man is a good hunter and has a wife who can grow corn and peas and squash, he can live well and be happy."

"So the women always stay at the village?"

"Not always. At this time of year..." she paused to search for a word. "How do you call it when the summer is gone but it is not cold?"

"We say autumn."

"We say *taquitock*, the time of year for the big hunting. Then the whole village goes with the men to hunt deer because they are gone for many days, up near the mountains. When many join together they can kill many deer."

She made a circle with her arms. "The men go around the deer. Then the men come closer and closer until the deer are easy to kill."

"We do the same thing in England."

"Then why are you not a hunter like the men in my tribe?"

"I am able to hunt, as are most Englishmen, but we have too many people and not enough deer. So we raise cattle, and pigs for our meat."

"I do not mind eating cattle or pigs, John Rolfe, but they have no fur. When our men kill a deer or beaver they have the fur. Do your people not want fur?"

"Indeed they do. They would pay for the fur of beavers. I believe that your people could trade furs with the English."

"Would you send our furs to England?"

"Yes, just as I intend to send the tobacco that I grow to England."

"Will you go back to England?"

Before I could answer I was interrupted by the arrival of Alexander Whitaker.

"Good afternoon, John. I trust that Pocahontas and Mistress Horton have been entertaining you?"

"I could not have had better company."

I told Whitaker about Pocahontas' remarks on the large scale hunting by her village. He expressed interest in their skill with the bow and arrow, commenting to us that it was not that long ago that it was the primary weapon in our own country. Pocahontas told how young boys made small bows when very young and were then taught their use by the older boys. They also became expert stalkers at an early age because they were expected to bring home small game they could kill for the family cooking pot.

At the catechism that evening, Whitaker questioned us on the Kingdom of God.

"Who are members of the Kingdom of God," asked Whitaker.

"All who believe that Jesus Christ is the Son of God and

215

keep his commandments," answered Marshal Dale.

"But you already have a king. I have heard you speak of King James in England," interjected Pocahontas.

"True, he is our earthly king and even though we are not in England we are members of his kingdom. We obey him in earthly matters. But God is our heavenly king and no matter where we are, we are members of his kingdom."

"Do you want my people to worship your God?"

"That is why I have come to Virginia, Pocahontas. To spread the good news of his kingdom and our salvation through Jesus Christ."

"And my people can still have Powhatan as their king?"

"Yes, of course."

"You are a very good teacher, Master Whitaker, and when my father Powhatan sends for me I will ask him to invite you to his village. He will give you a very great feast and you can talk to him about God."

"Thank you, Pocahontas."

Alexander Whitaker and Marshal Dale had every right to be proud of their pupil. Pocahontas not only seemed desirous of accepting our religion and entering into our culture, she also appeared to understand the implications of her assimilation. She would, in effect become an emissary from the English to her native people. She would be bringing a religion based on love rather than fear and an opportunity for them to benefit from the advances of our civilization.

I had known from the first time I saw Pocahontas that she was someone to be admired. Now I understood why English settlers had feelings of affection for her. Like them, I enjoyed being in her company. I was flattered that she had shown interest in me by commenting on my success with tobacco. When I felt my first stirrings of interest in her as a young woman I told myself she was too young; she was at least ten years younger than I. She had only the rudimentary education acquired over the months spent at Rocke Hall. She was the product of another race, religion, and culture. I could only envision her as a friend.

Besides, I had much work to do.

~32~

We harvested and cured enough tobacco so that our second year's shipment to England was double that of the first year. It amounted to just over 1,200 pounds. Besides what was exported, I retained two hundred pounds for our use in Virginia. Although that amount would have allowed almost a half pound for every man in the colony, I was confident it would be consumed. On average, I found the quality of the leaf to be much improved and noted that the brighter the leaf, the better the tobacco.

Thanks to the policy of Marshal Dale to allow individuals to manage their own plots of land in return for an annual contribution of corn to the storehouse, we were faring better in our harvests. Men and women worked with a will, both to produce and to preserve food. Hunters returned from the river with their hunting bags filled with ducks and geese. The geese were particularly appreciated at our Christmas feasts, having savory flesh when roasted and served with oysters that were brought upriver from Point Comfort.

Pocahontas continued to enter into our way of life with enthusiasm. Having recited the Lord's Prayer and the Ten Commandments, she now labored to memorize the Apostle's Creed so that she might become a member of the Church. Not surprisingly, Marshal Dale was as strict as any parent would be in insisting that her recitation be perfect. The Reverend Whitaker would perform the laying on of hands although he was not a bishop; indeed we did not even have a prospect of having a bishop in Virginia. Nevertheless, I say without undue prejudice that we could not have had bishops from England of better education, understanding, and devotion than the

Reverend Whitaker at Henrico and the Reverend Bucke at Jamestown. Nor could Pocahontas have had a relative or friend more concerned for her education than these ministers.

If Marshal Dale and Pocahontas, who spent many hours together during which he tutored her in spoken and written English, ever discussed her father's seeming indifference to her captivity, they gave no sign of it. The marshal seemed in control of his impatience, either because Governor Gates restrained him or because he sensed a continuing advantage in holding Pocahontas prisoner. Did Powhatan dare to launch a major attack on us while we held the daughter who was said to be his favorite? It appeared he did not; or was it because Marshal's Dale's troops, with their armor and muskets, had proven superior to his bowmen in combat? For whichever reason, there had been a slackening of attacks on us.

As usual, Marshal Dale found an outlet for his enormous energy. He had been reconnoitering the terrain downstream from Henrico at the confluence of the James and the River of the Appomatocs where we had defeated that tribe a year earlier. I had confirmed for him that the land was more favorable for farming than any near either Jamestown or Henrico. The land he favored possessed the further advantage of being bounded almost entirely by an oxbow of water so that a palisade across the neck with a length of merely two miles protected land with about a ten mile perimeter. He gave this place the name Bermuda Hundred; and, with the harvest done, decided to begin work for a new community in December of 1613. You can imagine the long faces of the men at Henrico who, believing they might have a respite from their labors in the winter of that year, learned that they would begin the two mile impalement and cutting of timbers for houses. It required an effort, I am sure, for most of them to hide their sour looks from persons like me who spent much time in the company of the senior officers. One gets accustomed, however, to detecting the murmurs of discontent even though they are muted.

There was an advantage in doing that type of work in late autumn. With most of the leaves gone, the felling of logs and trimming them for posts was easier. But it was a hardship to leave what had become relatively comfortable houses in Henrico for the temporary huts that would be used by the work parties. There was some outright grumbling but it did not last long. No one dared to give any sign of what might be considered as mutinous conduct.

Leadership of the work parties was given to Captain Yeardley. He began the work with his usual energy. In December the ground was not yet frozen and he wanted to begin the impalement lest freezing weather make it impossible to get the stakes into the ground. A good beginning was made and by the middle of January the long, snakelike palisade was well begun over the low lying land that was to be our next area of settlement. Within Bermuda Hundred we laid out several large acreages that would be farmed by groups of men and families.

I helped to lay out the farmland that would be tilled in the spring of 1614. In addition to allocating three acres of land for each man to farm, we planned to distribute the livestock so that it would be carefully tended and be a source of manure for the various holdings. Although he was a harsh man, Marshal Dale prided himself on his fairness, striving to give each man an opportunity to succeed without giving undue advantage to anyone.

During my visits to Bermuda Hundred I stayed with Captain Yeardley in one of the temporary houses that had been erected for the work parties. As usual, I found that conversation with him came easily. He was interested in more than making war on the Indians and always seemed pleased to learn more about planting.

"Will you be here much longer, George," I asked.

"I doubt it. The ground is so frozen now that we cannot dig postholes. That stops building construction. We have laid up a good supply of timbers though and should be able to make good progress when it grows warm enough. By the way, how much tobacco were you able to barrel for shipment?"

"We shipped 1,200 pounds. It should bring an even better price than last year."

"Are you capable of expanding the crop?"

"Yes. Why do you ask?"

"Just curious. It seems the way to make this colony profitable."

"I agree, and I believe that everyone, including Marshal Dale feels the same way. He has cautioned me, however, not to become overly enthusiastic about planting very large acreages."

"Why, may I ask?"

"He believes we must first assure our ability to produce our own food."

"I cannot fault that policy. No one has forgotten the starving time and we are still not at the place where we can say that we have plenty."

"He intends to have plantations in this region on both sides of the river. Spread out so that sickness or calamity in a single spot would not wipe us out. All these plantations are to have their established herds, of course. We would not be dependent on Jamestown."

"And do you think this is feasible?"

I hesitated before answering George. We had shared too many dangers for me not to trust him. Nevertheless, I was reluctant to say anything that might sound like a criticism of Marshal Dale.

"I think it entirely feasible. The land is good, the climate temperate with enough sunny days to permit several crops a year. So far, we are expanding our holdings despite the opposition of the natives. Perhaps that can continue. To continue indefinitely, however, we need to conclude peace."

Yeardley was silent. He reached for his tobacco pouch, turned his gaze from me as he filled his pipe, and regarded me again after it was lit. "I believe that is true. If Powhatan so desired he could muster hundreds of bowmen and do us great mischief."

This admission from Yeardley encouraged me to think that our leaders would welcome peace.

As the winter deepened, I found that more and more I was drawn to Rocke Hall. At first I told myself that it was because I enjoyed the company of Alexander Whitaker. It was true that I found him interested in my planting and indeed in all the

220

activities of the colony whether military or civil, spiritual or temporal. He was my age and had attended Cambridge. Although I had not, but instead owed my education to the tutelage of churchmen nearer my home in Norfolk, I was familiar with that university and had visited several of its colleges. With the passage of time, however, I had to confess to myself that I was drawn to Rocke Hall more by Pocahontas than by any other attraction.

I anticipated her cheerfulness and her welcoming smile each time I saw her and delighted in her adaptation to our speech and customs just as everyone who saw her at Henrico. She had a way of looking at me that made me think she understood me and approved of me.

I asked myself why it should be important to me to have the approval of a young Indian woman ten years younger than I. Her people were uneducated and capable of inflicting unspeakable cruelties on their enemies. They worshipped false gods and devils and had not even the rudiments of a written language.

Perhaps Alexander Whitaker first challenged my prejudices. He saw in the Indians all the good qualities they possessed as children of God. In his eyes they had minds, bodies, and spirits just as capable of serving God as did the English. He and Marshal Dale had instructed Pocahontas and I had witnessed their pleasure when she was baptized. Whitaker influenced me, as he did all the members of our company. It was Pocahontas herself, however, who did the most to dispel any doubts we might have had about her right to be an equal in our eyes. She did this with her intelligence, her largeness of spirit, and her happiness to be in our midst.

There was more. I was fully aware that she was a woman and that she seemed attracted to me. It could hardly have been an accident that I found myself alone with her, even if only for a few minutes, on my visits to Rocke Hall. And, although she never visited me at the house I shared with Ralph Hamor, she did come to my fields on several occasions while I was there working. At these times she would ask me what I was doing and make some small comment if the Indians had another way.

She did not tarry long but I found myself soon in the habit of looking to the edge of the field where it was her practice to come sometimes and stand patiently regarding me until I noticed her presence.

I began to realize that I was in love with Pocahontas and was greatly disturbed. What could possibly be an honorable outcome of such emotion? I had already glimpsed what I thought was the reaction I would receive from others. It was on an evening that I went to Rocke Hall to return a book belonging to Alexander Whitaker. Or at least that was the pretext of my visit. When I knocked Elizabeth Grave opened the door,

"John Rolfe," she said. "Please come in."

"Thank you Elizabeth. How good to see you."

I had not seen her in several weeks. She now worked at the hospital regularly. "I trust you and George are well."

"We are."

"And at the hospital?"

"We have only a few patients at this time of year. But one of them is Jane, Mistress Horton's helper. She and Reverend Whitaker and Pocahontas have gone to see her. They should be back soon."

"I have only come to return a book. I need not stay."

"Mistress Horton tells you are here several times a week," she said without smiling.

I could not help noticing her coolness.

"That is true. They always make me welcome."

"It is a pity Pocahontas is not here to entertain you."

There was no mistaking the hint of sarcasm in her manner. I chose to ignore it as best I could. Elizabeth and Mistress Horton were among my oldest friends in Virginia.

"Please extend my thanks to Reverend Whitaker for the loan of the book."

"I will tell him."

It was a brief exchange and I hoped Elizabeth's attitude was not shared by Mistress Horton. Perhaps Elizabeth harbored thoughts that, although I had not courted her after the death of her husband, I was paying considerable attention to the young Indian woman. I could not guess if her resentment might have that origin or if Elizabeth simply did not approve of any English male being attracted to an Indian woman.

What was I to do? I found little encouragement if I looked to the Bible. The wives of Esau were from the Philistine tribes and led to his estrangement from Israel. Likewise the downfall of Solomon could be attributed to his marriage with strange women. But how could anyone who met Pocahontas think of her as strange? They could not. Not only for her open and generous character but also for the fact that she had renounced her native religion to become one of us. What value was our friendship if we did not completely accept her?

These doubts distressed me but did not deter me from either thinking of Pocahontas or from seeing her. She had become the main attraction in my life. More than the rich landscape, the golden harvests, the spirit of adventure, the high opinion of my fellow man, or even the times of worship, I valued the opportunities to be in her presence.

~33~

"Have you never married, Pocahontas?"

"Yes, I was married to Kocuom."

I was not surprised that she had been married. She, being young and attractive, would surely have suitors, particularly since she was the daughter of a chief.

"Was married? Did he die?"

"I know not. Maybe. But, because I am a captive of the English, I have no husband."

"I see." I supposed that Pocahontas was referring to the customs of her people. Who was I to question them? I was at a loss for words. But she was not. "Mistress Horton says that you had a wife who died."

"Yes. She died soon after we came to Virginia."

"I am sorry."

"I should never have brought her to Virginia. I could have left her in England until I knew that it was safe for her to live here. However, she wanted to come and we came to stay."

"You mean for always?"

"Yes."

"Do you think you will marry again?"

"When my heart tells me," I replied.

She tried to change my mood which had become somber. "I think if you were an Indian man you would have several wives."

"Why do you say that?"

"Oh, you would be a great hunter and a warrior. You would marry a first wife and then, after you had many great hunts and all the people knew you were a great warrior, you might have some other wives. You might even become a chief."

"Thank you Pocahontas, but you flatter me."

224

"What does 'flatter' mean?"

"To flatter is to speak words to please another but words that may not be true."

"I will tell you it is true that my father has many wives."

"How many, Pocahontas?"

She hesitated before answering. "Oh, sometimes six. And sometimes maybe even ten. He has many wives."

"Really?" I knew Powhatan had several wives but I had no idea he had that many.

"Yes. But they are not his wives forever. He will marry the daughter of village chief and then when she has a child he will send her back to her people. That way he has many children and many people who love him as a father."

"How does he feed such a big family?"

"He has more than enough to feed them. Every village must send him corn. Every village has a field that is planted with food to be sent to him. And every hunter must send him furs."

"In England we call these taxes."

"Taxes?"

"They are what you have to give the king."

"Tell me more about your English king."

Pocahontas had a seemingly inexhaustible curiosity about things English. Alexander Whitaker had some books with illustrations of buildings in England. Drawings of large buildings and city streets fascinated her. She expressed wonder at buildings of brick or stone and especially of churches with tall steeples. A ballroom with chandeliers and ornate furniture seemed unbelievable to her.

"It is so large. How can this be?"

"It is just a room in a large building."

"My father has a large bed."

"I expect he does."

"Do you not believe me?" There must have been doubt in my voice.

"It came from England and was given to him by Captain Newport."

I had forgotten the four poster bed that had been a gift to Powhatan from the Virginia Company before I came to Virginia.

"And does he sleep in it?"

"No, he keeps it in a temple along with his other trophies."

"Then it must be a large temple."

"Yes, but not so large as your buildings in England."

The Reverend Whitaker was very interested in the Indian temples and asked Pocahontas questions about them. Unfortunately, she had not been allowed to enter them and could not answer from direct knowledge. She knew that the bodies of dead chiefs and priests were taken to the temples and that there were many images of Akee in them along with lesser gods. The priests spent much time in the temples where they offered prayers and interceded for their people.

Whitaker was also conscious, I am sure, of my growing affection for Pocahontas. Indeed, we all liked her. Unlike Elizabeth Grave, however, he did not appear to view my feelings in an unfavorable light. I believe this was because he considered Pocahontas to be our equal in every respect. He delighted in her response to education and ability to adapt to our customs of dress, speech, and manners. But even more, he valued her largeness of spirit, her generosity, and her kindness. It was in Alexander Whitaker's presence, in fact, that I first seriously entertained the possibility of marriage to her.

"Don't you think, John, that Pocahontas provides a powerful example of the Indian's ability to adapt our ways?"

"I do not see how any person could do better."

"With her ability to live in both cultures I see no reason why she could not have an English husband."

I stared at Alexander Whitaker. I said nothing and neither did he but I believe that he smiled slightly before turning away.

I should have taken courage from the tacit encouragement of such a good man as Whitaker but instead I began a time of great anxiety. I knew that while there were good people like him who would approve and support such a marriage there were others who would view it as the reaching of a lonely man for carnal pleasure. Others would say I was seeking the advantage that might come from marriage to the daughter of a powerful chief.

I reproached myself for such cowardly thoughts but they would not leave me. My primary concern as a Christian was that I might be taking a wife from a people who worshipped strange gods. None of these concerns, however, were great enough to dissuade me from my desire to be with Pocahontas, to marry her if possible.

How was I to go about it? After a week of stewing in my thoughts until I thought I would go mad if I could determine no logical course of action, I unburdened myself to Ralph Hamor. I will not recite my long explanation to him of how I came to be so confused and unhappy except to say that he listened patiently to my explanation and then slowly filled his pipe as he regarded me.

"First of all, John, why not stop your pacing and enjoy some of this excellent tobacco produced by your own hands?"

"Of course, Ralph. You have listened well and I believe appreciate the agony that I feel."

"Yes, and I believe that we can cut to the chase, if you will forgive the expression. In my view, it is totally understandable how a man could fall in love with Pocahontas. She is an endearing person and will have other suitors if she remains with us although perhaps none as worthy as you. Do you believe that she shares your feelings?"

"Yes."

"But you are reluctant to pursue your suit without a clearer understanding of how to proceed?"

"Ralph, I don't know what to do. We are, after all, holding her hostage. We don't know how her father would react. I don't know how Marshal Dale would regard it. And of course, I regard her so highly that I would not upset her."

"Of course not. Well, you cannot go dashing off into the forest to seek her father's approval. And you risk upsetting her by proposing at this time. These suppositions lead me to the conclusion that you must proceed first to gain the approval of Marshal Dale. She is, after all, his captive and, perhaps more important, he regards himself now as her protector."

"I believe that you are right. But how should I proceed? I can't just walk up to him and say, 'I want to marry Pocahontas.'"

"That would be too abrupt and I would not suggest it. You need to seek his approval in a most deliberate, reasoned way."

Try as I would, I could think of no comfortable way of

approaching Marshal Dale. After several days, I gave up and decided that I would just wait for an opportunity. I hoped to find a moment when the subject could be introduced that would offer a chance for success without prejudice to my cause. It was late March and Governor Gates had sailed from Jamestown earlier in the month to return to England. I had not attended his departure but, of course, Marshal Dale had. Dale was now the highest authority in the Virginia Colony. He was obviously pleased with the freedom of action that he had, even though I knew of no obstacle that Governor Gates had ever put in his way. Under these conditions I thought there might be a favorable moment for me to present my request. That moment occured sooner than I anticipated. It followed an evening meal when the officers had excused themselves and Hamor, knowing my desire to be alone with the Marshal, made some excuse to leave the table.

"I believe that we are making real progress, John."

"There certainly is progress, sir."

"I wish we had five hundred more settlers, people to put out on the land."

"Do you mean more families?"

"Of course." He seemed to reflect for a long moment. "How I miss my wife. I was married to Elizabeth less than a year when I came to Virginia. But, that is a soldier's life."

This was the first time he had mentioned his wife in my presence. I could not imagine a better time to introduce the subject foremost in my mind.

I was about to speak when he said, "I have decided that Powhatan has kept us waiting long enough."

"It has been a long time, sir."

"I believe that he is trifling with us. It is time for us to force an answer from him. What does he want, peace or war?"

My heart sank. When Marshal Dale spoke in this fashion he followed it soon with action. I felt it best not to mention my desire to marry Pocahontas. He went on to discuss his plan to transport troops by water to Powhatan's village and said he had already told Captain Argall to prepare his ship.

"But you will learn about this soon enough, Rolfe. You shall certainly be a member of the expedition."

~34~

"So, you didn't have the nerve," said Ralph Hamor.

"No, I didn't."

"Well, if you wanted to talk to him, you would never have had a better chance than tonight."

"Probably not. On the other hand, since he is busy planning an expedition he probably could find any number of reasons to deny my request."

"Maybe." Hamor seemed let down.

"I believe I should write him a letter."

"A letter?"

"Yes, a letter. You see, what I fear is I may say something he disapproves of if I approach him in person. By writing out my thoughts I can choose my words most carefully, marshal all the arguments I can, and, unless I am greatly mistaken, present my entire case."

"I understand what you are saying, John, and while I believe you speak well enough to present your case, you must be the judge of what is best for you."

And so, I decided to write to Marshal Dale. The letter was successful in that it ultimately won the approval for me to seek the hand of Pocahontas. Nevertheless, I regret writing it. I regret writing it because Ralph Hamor himself later published the letter. It became a part of the records of the colony, a letter that makes me out as an obsequious ninny whose utmost concern seemed to be his own piety rather than the happiness of the woman he loved. It was a letter that, in the eyes of a later reader, could hardly be exceeded in wordiness and fawning appeal for the favor of the recipient. I shall always regret it; but it had one saving grace: it worked.

Because our days were spent in preparation for the expedition, I spent three evenings in composing the letter. I was like a man with a fever until I finished. When I offered it to Hamor to read and to make suggestions, he refused saying he could not do justice to a missive on which I had spent such labor. But he was willing to carry it to the Marshal when the time came.

Marshal Dale's plan was a simple one. He would employ the *Treasurer*, captained by Samuel Argall, to carry his troops to Jamestown where soldiers aboard two shallops would swell the force to one hundred fifty men. Then we would sail down the James, and around Point Comfort, up Chesapeake Bay to the Pamunkey River and then upstream to Powhatan's village that was on the west fork of the Pamunkey. Pocahontas would accompany us. Her ransom was still the main bargaining element in dealing with Powhatan. Even if Powhatan's affection for her had diminished, a factor we had no way to evaluate, the safety of his daughter had to be important to his prestige.

"When they come to meet us, as I am sure they will, we will put it to them simply: they can have peace or war, it's their choice," said the marshal, looking around the small group he had gathered in his quarters. Captains Yeardley and Brewster were there, along with Captain Argall, Ralph Hamor, and I. We were fortunate that Yeardley and his company had not returned to England with Governor Gates; they were seasoned men with a dependable leader. I had never been comfortable in the presence of Argall, and was now even less comfortable because of Pocahontas' disdain for him, but did my best to conceal my feelings.

"May I ask, Marshal Dale," asked Argall, "what the roles of Masters Hamor and Rolfe are in this command?"

"They are my staff, Captain Argall. Any instructions you receive from them shall have the effect of being my orders."

"Aye, sir," responded Argall without emotion. He would have been wiser not to ask.

We departed Henrico on the last day in March. Spring had arrived and some glimpses were to be had of white-blossomed dogwood trees along the shore but it was a dismal day with rain and mist obscuring most of the view. Despite my feelings toward Captin Argall, it was comforting to know that he was an experienced navigator. He stood on the deck throughout our passage to Jamestown where he could hear the men sounding the river depth from the bow before passing his commands to the helmsman. I also admired the way his crew managed the sails to bring the *Treasurer* smartly to the pier at Jamestown. The captains of the two shallops at the pier came aboard to receive sailing instructions from Captain Argall. The Reverend Bucke had come to the pier to wish us Godspeed.

"Hello, John Rolfe," he said as he saw me on the quarterdeck.

"Richard Bucke, I pray that all is well with you."

"And with you. How is Pocahontas?"

"Well, I believe. She is below with Elizabeth Grave." The Marshal had thought the expedition might be a strain on Mistress Horton and brought Elizabeth instead as her companion.

"Good. How is Alexander Whitaker?"

"Well, but he complains of not getting enough exercise to be in the best physical condition. Look, there is Pocahontas now."

She and Elizabeth Grave had emerged from the cabin. The rain had stopped and there were patches of blue sky above us. Both women were dressed in gray and wore gray and white caps. Elizabeth had a shawl to protect her from the breeze but Pocahontas seemed not to need one. They both waved and called out to Reverend Bucke as our ship pulled away from the pier. The rector seemed a little flustered by such attention from two attractive young women. This did not go unnoticed by the soldiers gathered on the deck, several of whom mimicked the women good naturedly.

We had been at Jamestown less than an hour. Marshall Dale and Captain Argall were desirous of at least reaching Point Comfort, at the mouth of the James River, by nightfall.

Morale of the men was high. All of them had met Powhatan's warriors in combat before and, although they respected the skill of the native bowmen, they felt confident unless they were greatly outnumbered. The expedition was a change from the heavy labor and the routine life in our small settlements. As the sun emerged from behind the clouds that slowly drifted eastward, they crowded on the decks. Some of the men nearest the rails pointed out places where they had been or the occasional natives whom they saw near the shore. As for me, I recalled vividly Mulberry Island where we met members of Lord De La Warr's relief expedition as we were abandoning Jamestown to return to England. Sarah had still been alive then but her strength was ebbing fast. I put those thoughts behind me. It did no good to brood on the past.

As we moved downstream I marveled again at the width of the waterways in Virginia. Before we reached Point Comfort the James had become several miles wide. John Smith's explorations had shown that there were other rivers of comparable size, all of which flowed into the huge Chesapeake Bay. I recalled Captain Christopher Newport saying that near the mouth of the James it widened into a natural roadway and that someday entire fleets of English vessels might anchor there. Now that Samuel Argall was our mariner I appreciated the gruff Newport even more than I had before.

I descended to the main deck to speak to Pocahontas and Elizabeth.

"Do you like being on shipboard, John?" asked Elizabeth.

"Yes, I like to feel the roll of the ship."

"Didn't you have enough of rolling in the great storm?"

"Yes, enough for a lifetime. There was never a greater storm than that."

"Oh, you two frighten me very much," said Pocahontas in mock fright. "I wanted to go someday across the wide water."

Elizabeth and I laughed. We doubted that Pocahontas had any fear.

On the second day of our journey we began the trip up the Pamunkey. We had anchored inside the mouth well after dark believing it better to navigate the less familiar waters during daylight. The land appeared similar to that along the James except there were bluffs nearer the mouth of the river. Once again our captain steered close to the channel in order to avoid shoals. Along the shore we glimpsed Indians. Here they were more likely to be in the open and few made an effort to conceal themselves. I wondered if they had seen our little fleet last night at anchor; and if so, was word being passed up to Chief Powhatan about our movements.

By the afternoon we had reached a fork in the river. We sailed into the southern fork near which Powhatan's village, Matchcot, was located. Many Indian men were beginning to gather along the shore. We were near enough to the riverbanks to hear their shouts. Our interpreter Cocopone advised us that their remarks were insulting, a fact that we might have deduced without the need for translation. When asked for their meaning he simply said the Indians asked why we had come. Marshal Dale had him reply that we had come to deliver Pocahontas to her father in return for weapons and corn that had not been delivered to us as agreed upon; and, if we did not obtain satisfaction, we were there to fight. This was followed by more derisive shouts that Cocopone said taunted us about the slaughter of Captain Ratcliff and his men that had occurred nearby, and predicted a similar fate for us. By then a large group of Indians with bows had assembled, with one of them launching an arrow that nearly reached the *Treasurer.*

The first missile was followed by several volleys of arrows, some of which fell on the deck. An arrow struck one of our soldiers in the forehead causing him to fall to the deck with much bleeding. I looked down from the quarterdeck and was relieved to see that Pocahontas and Elizabeth had gone to their cabin. Marshal Dale's reaction to the attack was immediate; he ordered two of the ship's cannon to open fire and directed Captain Yeardley to bring musket fire to bear on the closest enemy. The cannon fire tore through the crowd of Indians, felling five or six, and causing the rest to run for the cover of nearby woods. Meanwhile Captain Argall ordered crewmen to lower the ship's boats and Captain Brewster assembled his men to go ashore.

I did not accompany the shore party, although Ralph Hamor did. He later reported that the soldiers burned about forty of the

Indian houses, but only after removing whatever food and booty they could find. Personally, I regretted the bloodshed I had witnessed but at least Marshall Dale had made known his serious intentions: he had come to make peace or to make war.

We had no more contact with the natives that day but found the next day they had dramatically changed their approach to us. Whereas they had been insulting and were daring us to fight, they now acted aggrieved and asked what cause they had given us for offense. They invited us to come ashore and talk, asking again what was the purpose of our visit. To this Marshal Dale agreed but he put nearly a hundred of his men on shore so that there would be no chance they would be overrun. I was in the longboat with him and Captain Yeardley and stood near the Marshal as he conversed with the Indian leaders, using Cocopone for his interpreter. Pocahontas accompanied us ashore and was recognized by all the Indians.

In the group of Indians, who approached us quite boldly, were two men whom, I was told later, were brothers of Pocahontas. They conversed with her excitedly and were obviously interested in her appearance. For her part, Pocahontas acted with great dignity. She later said that she had chided her brothers that her father had not paid her ransom that should have been insignificant to him.

Although these were sons of Powhatan, they could not speak for him. Because he was not present it was agreed that messengers from Marshal Dale should go to Powhatan, men who were familiar with Dale's demands and could return with Powhatan's answer. I was surprised when Marshal Dale chose me, rather than one of his military officers, to be his emissary.

"You are thoroughly familiar with our proposal for the return of Pocahontas, John Rolfe. We want the return of any Englishmen and any English weapons along with five hundred bushels of corn. I suppose you can attest as well as anyone to the good health of his daughter and assure him of her speedy return to his village. If he refuses our requests we will march on his village. You may take any man you choose with you and Cocopone for your interpreter."

In the few minutes that I had to prepare myself I chose

William Sparkes, a soldier who had been assigned to work with me on my tobacco crop, to accompany me on my mission to Powhatan. I had found Sparkes to be very dependable; and, above all, he was discreet. He was not likely to blurt out a foolish remark that might be regretted. I also took time to speak quietly to Ralph Hamor.

"Listen carefully, Ralph. I have something to ask of you."

"What is it?"

"You recall the letter that I showed you that asks Marshal Dale's permission to marry Pocahontas?"

"Of course."

"When you return to the ship I want you to give him the letter. You will find it in a packet on my berth."

"Are you sure this is the time?"

"I am not sure of anything at this time. But I believe it's possible that Pocahontas may be returned to Powhatan and I want to prevent it. Will you give Marshal Dale the letter?"

"You may depend on it, John."

It was agreed that one of Pocahontas's brothers and a companion would remain with Marshal Dale as hostages toward the safe return of Sparkes and me. Personally, I felt no anxiety about myself and, to all appearances William Sparkes was unperturbed by the thought of being in the hands of Powhatan's men. I was more concerned about the possibility that Pocahontas could be returned to her father since the Indians appeared to be in a conciliatory spirit.

This was my foremost thought as I walked with our Indian guides along the river. Actually we walked only a short distance along the Pamunkey before we moved inland to higher ground. We were soon on a well-worn path that followed a gentle ridge leading to an Indian village. I estimate we had walked about three miles. I presumed this to be the village of Powhatan but I was wrong. This was the village of Opechancanough, the brother of Powhatan. There were very few men visible in the village. I presume they were among the large group of warriors that had encountered us at the River. We saw women, children, and a few old men. We were brought to the door of an Indian lodge and instructed to enter.

"What are they asking us to do, Cocopone?"

"They want us to go in and rest. Messengers are being sent to the village of Powhatan to find out where we are to meet with him."

"How long must we wait?"

"I do not know. With such an important chief we have to wait upon him."

I did not mind waiting. It gave time for Ralph Hamor to deliver my letter to Marshal Dale.

~35~

We waited throughout a long afternoon, resting ourselves in the Indian house. When Sparkes and I grew tired of waiting we decided to leave the confinement of the dark and smoky space that was lit by only the flame of a small fire at its center and the small opening that was so low we had to bend double to make our exit. We were the immediate focus of attention for two warriors who were standing nearby, obviously with the intent to guard us. Cocopone had been conversing with them and asked if we wanted something to eat or drink. We declined but indicated that we were rested and wanted fresh air.

Cocopone had learned that this was the principal village of Opechancanough, second only to Powhatan in prestige and importance in the Powhatan empire. He pointed out a nearby house that he said belonged to the chief and where he would no doubt meet with us when he was ready. It stood at the head of a row of houses and was not only larger but sturdier in appearance. Opposite the row of houses was a large cleared area with a circle of poles imbedded in the ground that I supposed were used for ceremonies or dancing. Probably most of the men of the village were in the group that confronted our force at the river; only women and children were visible and they all seemed occupied with their chores.

We strolled slowly along the wide clearing in front of the houses. I suggested to Sparkes that we should not be too inquisitive about the village lest our interest be misinterpreted. We engaged one another in conversation, commenting on the gardens where we could see Indian women tending their crops. I reckoned that the nearby gardens had been cleared several years earlier because the trees had not only been felled but also burned, leaving more room for planting.

In the evening, shortly before dark, we were summoned to the house of Opechancanough. It was decorated with carvings and colorful images, some of which were quite fearsome. We were offered comfortable seats, covered with furs, where we sat opposite men whom I presumed to be minor chiefs of the Pamunkeys. We were not kept waiting long for Opechancanough for whom we all rose to make our greeting.

At one glance I could see why he had made such a strong impression upon every Englishman who had seen him.

He was quite tall, well over six feet, and carried himself erectly so that he seemed even taller, even though we had risen at his entrance and I found myself looking up at him. Although I had seen many tall Indians, his height was a surprise to me. I could not estimate his age but to say that he was in his middle years or beyond although he was obviously still strong. His expression was haughty, if not arrogant, and seemed especially calculating because he regarded you from beneath eyelids that drooped. This was a chief who did not derive his power just from having a powerful brother. He was a force in his own right. By his appearance and his manner he commanded our attention so that no one moved until he signaled for us to be seated.

A conversation began between him and Cocopone that went on for several minutes. At length there was a pause and Cocopone looked to me and began to explain.

"The chief asked who you were and I told him about you. Then he asked why we were here and I tell him again about Pocahontas and how the English have come to bring her back to Chief Powhatan and that you have come to speak to him."

"What does he say?"

"He asks what we want from Powhatan. I tell him the prisoners, the guns, and the corn. Then we can have peace between our people."

"Does he not already know this?"

"Maybe. Anyway, I tell him again."

"Ask him when I can go to speak with Powhatan."

To this question I would have expected a short answer but I

was wrong. The conversation went on for several minutes. Both men raised their voices so that I became concerned for Cocopone. There was no point in antagonizing our host. He looked unpleasant enough to begin with.

Their conversation stopped. Cocopone turned to me while Opechancanough regarded me with his baleful eyes.

"The chief says that Powhatan will not see you."

"But it was agreed that I was to go to meet with him."

"I know that and have said so."

"Why can I not see Powhatan?"

"Our host, his brother, has already spoken with him. He says that Powhatan agrees to have peace; that he has returned the prisoners with their weapons. But he has no corn now and it is best now for everybody to go home and plant corn."

"So there will be no exchange for Pocahontas?"

"Chief Opechancanough says he will talk to Powhatan again and maybe that will happen."

"I think I understand what you are telling me, Cocopone. He says that Chief Powhatan will not meet with us. That he knows our demands but has no corn. That Powhatan wants peace but we must wait to see if an exchange can be arranged for Pocahontas."

Cocopone nodded.

"Then I ask you to repeat what I have just said to him. I must return to Marshal Dale without seeing Powhatan and we must be sure there is no misunderstanding."

I watched Chief Opechancanough as Cocopone repeated my remarks. This time there was but a brief assent by the chief. He then clapped his hands and food was brought for us to eat.

It would have been useless for me to protest that I had not been able to see Powhatan and that the response to Marshal Dale's demands was unsatisfactory. Opechancanouggh left no doubt in my mind that the matter had been discussed sufficiently and was considered closed for the present time. Besides, I personally would not have liked to have Pocahontas returned to her father and any delay was welcome to me. I believed that I should not give my host the impression that I was disappointed with the response received and endeavored to display the utmost of equanimity in my manner. On his part, he displayed no emotion whatsoever; and, while we were fed well and treated courteously, it was without any show of warmth from the chief.

We spent the night in Opechancanough's village and returned to the river the next day. I was soon aboard the *Treasurer*, making my report to Marshal Dale. It was a brief report, even though I tried to give him my impressions of Opechancanough and the way in which we were treated.

"Oh, he is a devious character, no doubt about it. Every man since Captain John Smith who has met him says the same. But we must give the devil his due: he is very capable and he is a survivor. Do you think he is reporting Powhatan's views accurately?"

"I have no reason to doubt it. There was enough time for him to see Powhatan while we were kept waiting in his village."

"But there is a factor in these proceedings that is not known either by Powhatan or by Oprechancanough."

"What is that, sir?"

"The fact that you wish to marry Pocahontas."

"That is true."

"And you have made this fact known to me in your letter that was delivered yesterday by Ralph Hamor. I must say that you have stated your reasons for proposing this union in great detail. But as you say in the letter it is a holy matter and there are many considerations. I commend you for your zeal and your willingness to proceed without fear of opinion. I only hope you have not been made uncomfortable by the anxiety that you have felt."

"I count it a small price for my affection for Pocahontas."

"If you have no objections, I would ask Pocahontas to join us."

I nodded agreement. I was too overcome to speak. Although he had not said so specifically, I assumed he approved of my request to marry.

He walked to the door of the cabin and told the sentry standing there to request the presence of Pocahontas.

"We must discuss this with her before we can plan how to proceed."

"I understand, sir."

The door to the cabin was opened for Pocahontas who swept into the room with her characteristic energy and expectation. She curtseyed prettily to the Marshal and smiled at me. I wondered how anyone could resist her.

"Thank you for joining us, Pocahontas. I have some important questions to ask you."

She stood very still. The smile had left her face as she regarded us gravely. "I am ready for your questions."

"Please do not be upset. This is a pleasant matter to discuss. It regards a request that I have received from Master John Rolfe that he be allowed to seek your hand in marriage."

"My hand?"

"That is a way of saying that he wants to marry you."

"Then he must ask me."

"I am sure that he will. But before I give him permission to do so, I must tell you that I must ask your father, Chief Powhatan, for his approval."

"Why? You have taken me away from my father."

"True; and I hope you believe we have tried to treat you well. And if Powhatan agrees to your marriage it may help to bring us peace. If he does not agree, it could bring trouble. Do you see why we should ask?"

"Yes. We can send my brothers. I will speak to them and tell them what they must say."

And so the brothers of Pocahontas were chosen for this important mission. It was obvious that they had the greatest solicitude for her well being and I have no doubt that she instructed them carefully about how they were to approach their father.

I had some misgivings about placing the matter in Powhatan's hands. He had, after all, obstructed us by not complying with the demands for the ransom of Pocahontas. Then he had refused to see me when I was sent as emissary from Marshal Dale. Why should he now prove cooperative? What if he said no? What would we do then?

Pocahontas did not seem to share my concern. Obviously she knew her father better than I and could anticipate his actions better. The matter was out of her hands from the time her brothers waved goodbye on the shore and began their journey to Powhatan's village. There was nothing she could do about it and she refused to be anxious.

Marshal Dale seemed to share the confidence of Pocahontas in a happy outcome. Did he believe that there were especially good reasons for Powhatan to agree to our marriage? Whatever doubts he might have had were concealed as he entertained us with his officers at dinner in his cabin that night.

In the morning the envoys to Powhatan returned. He approved of the marriage, saying he gave her as a sign of his good will and his desire for peace. The brothers would attend the wedding.

~36~

"Will you marry me, Pocahontas?"

"Yes, I will be your wife and you will be my husband."

We were both silent. I had finally asked the question I had not dared to ask before, not without her father's approval, even though I believed that Pocahontas loved me and would consent to be married. Since the messengers had arrived with Powhatan's consent to the wedding of his favorite daughter to an Englishman, I had felt a deep sense of relief. All my anxiety was gone with the fears of imagined difficulties. Now we were embarked on the return to Jamestown. Pocahontas and I stood at the rail of the *Treasurer* which was sailing down the Pamunkey River. Although a small guard was posted on the ship, there was a general air of relaxation from the tension of the previous days. Word had passed quickly of the cessation of hostilities.

Pocahontas was the first to speak. "John, what would you do if my father had said no, that you could not marry his daughter?"

"I believe that God has cleared a path for you and me. I believe it is his will that we should be man and wife. So I will neither question how this came to be nor fret over what might have happened."

"Fret?"

"Oh, that is to be afraid of little things."

"Let us say that we will never be afraid of little things."

"We have too much to do for that. Pocahontas, let us suppose I were an Indian man and that I fell in love with you and wanted to marry you. Would I go to your father for permission?"

"First you would have to prove that you had enough goods to have a wife and that you could provide food for me. You would give me presents and be willing to pay my father and mother for me."

"I would pay for you?"

"Yes, because you would be taking me away from my father and mother. How much you would pay is something you would talk about with my father."

"I suppose your father would demand much for you."

"My father is already a rich man. He would not ask much for me but he would want to know that you are a great hunter and a brave warrior. After you had given him presents that you had agreed upon, he and my mother would bring me to the house that you made for us. Then he would join our hands together and give me to be your wife."

"And that is all?"

"He would ask your promise to take care of me. Then your father would ask me to promise to be good to you. After that your father would break a string of beads over our heads and we would be married."

"Do you think your father will come to our wedding?"

She hesitated, tilted her head as if she were in deep thought, and then said slowly, "I do not think that he will come."

"Why not?" I asked.

"I know that my father cares about me. Since I was a child, my people have said that I was his favorite. But he did not pay the English what they asked for me and that made me sad. I thought that he was angry with me but now I think that he wanted to see what would happen."

She looked up at me. "And something good has happened. You and I are to marry and maybe this will help bring peace."

"Powhatan must be very wise."

"Yes, he is wise. He believes that it is wise not to go anyplace where he can be tricked or surprised."

"What do you mean?"

"He has never gone to the village of the English. Even when Captain John Smith was here, he would not go to Jamestown. Captain Newport asked Powhatan to come to

244

Jamestown because your king had sent him a crown and many gifts. He would not go and so the English had to come to Werowocomoco. He did not want an English crown anyway."

"The English came to Werowocomoco?"

"Yes, they thought it was important to give Powhatan a crown, even though Powhatan said he did not need one. He was already king of his people. Then they also brought the big bed. It was very big but I do not think Powhatan ever liked it. There was one present that he did like."

"What was that?"

"A red coat. He wore it many times." She smiled, as if remembering, "The other chiefs would also like red coats."

"So, you do not expect him to come to our wedding."

"No, because he is very careful. He will not say he does not trust you and he may give some other reason but I think the real reason is that he is very careful."

"What about Opechancanough?"

"I cannot say. I do not feel that I know what he is thinking. He is a man of surprises."

"I daresay we gave him a surprise when we sent the message that we wanted to marry."

"Nothing would surprise Opechancanough."

"I think your brothers were surprised when they saw you the other day."

"They had not seen me in a long, long time. They thought I would be unhappy because I was a captive. But I was not unhappy. Mistress Horton, Elizabeth, and Master Whitaker have been very kind to me, making me one of their people. Marshal Dale has been like a father and has taught me so I could be baptized. But you have been the best because you have loved me. And because I love you too, I am happy.

"My brothers were surprised to see me wear the clothes of the English. Why should I not want to wear English clothes? The English things are better. You have books that people can read and understand. Your boats can cross the widest waters. Already your farmers can grow more corn and peas and even better tobacco than we can."

"I thought you did not seem happy to see your brothers."

"Oh, I was glad they are well but I was displeased that my father had not paid my ransom. I wanted them to know I would be pleased to stay with the English."

Pocahontas' manner had changed when her brothers returned yesterday with the news of Powhatan's approval of our marriage. Whereas she had been almost haughty, now she was conciliatory and well-disposed toward the two men. Both appeared to be slightly older than she and it was easy to imagine they had once been her protectors when she was a little girl. She made a point of introducing them to all of us and of making flattering remarks about their skill as tireless hunters. When Marshal Dale invited them to eat with us and remain aboard the *Treasurer* overnight they seemed pleased to accept.

The main topic of conversation last night had been the place and date of the marriage. Marshal Dale, who no doubt had already planned these details, made a skillful pretense of allowing us to participate in the planning.

"The wedding must take place in church," said the Marshal. "Where would you rather be married, Pocahontas, Jamestown or Henrico?"

She hesitated and looked at me. I was no help, and gave the slightest of shrugs to indicate that it did not matter. She in turn, smiled at Marshal Dale and replied, "You must choose, Sir Thomas."

"Either place would be quite fitting I believe. We have been at Jamestown longer and I believe the church there is better appointed. Moreover, it is the church of Master Bucke, our senior clergyman."

A look of concern crossed Pocahontas' features.

"What is it, my dear?" asked the Marshal.

"Master Whitaker has been my teacher."

"True, and he will help to marry you. You need not worry. Both the Reverends Bucke and Whitaker will marry you to John Rolfe."

This pleased her. It pleased me too to have both men participate. Although I liked Whitaker, and admired him for his scholarship, Bucke had been my friend in time of great hardship.

"Then we must decide the date," continued the Marshal. "I

would propose in a week's time."

I knew that must seem a short time for the preparations, even though I would have married Pocahontas that very day, given the opportunity.

"Could I suggest two weeks?" offered Elizabeth Grave. "There will be feasting to prepare for as well as accommodations and the clothing of the bride."

"I am sure you know more about the latter than I. Very well, I suggest a compromise: the wedding should be in ten days. Is it agreed?" He looked about, and seeing no dissent, declared, "The wedding shall take place in ten days at Jamestown."

We had bid farewell to the brothers of Pocahontas that morning, hoping that we would see them again in Jamestown in just a few days. She told them they could bring as many of her family to the wedding as desired to come. Afterwards she told me that she has said this to show no feelings of bitterness or rancor. She also said that Powhatan would send whom he pleased, even though not likely to attend himself.

Ten days proved to be sufficient for our preparations, although there was no time to spare. We had to travel down the Pamunkey River, into Chesapeake Bay, and then up the James River with consideration of course of the tides that were ever present to help us or to hinder. Marshal Dale decided that we should be in Jamestown three days prior to the wedding. Pocahontas and I made a brief visit to Bermuda Hundred to view the home that Marshal Dale had designated for us. I was familiar with the site but wanted her to see it. She was enthusiastic and happy even though the building fell far short of the home I hoped to provide for us one day. There was ample well-drained land between the James and Appomatox Rivers. Most of it had been cleared except for chestnut and mulberry trees that soon would be bearing fruit.

After the visit to Bermuda Hundred I saw little of Pocahontas. Mistress Horton and Elizabeth Grave needed her for fitting the dresses that were being prepared for her, particularly her wedding dress. She submitted to this with her usual good nature I was told when I enquired about her. Word having passed throughout the area that we were at peace, Pocahontas began to have Indian visitors. They were awed by her English dresses and would sit on the floor at Rocke Hall watching her as long as Mistress Horton would permit them.

The day of our wedding dawned clear and bright at Jamestown. The fresh green of the trees and grass made me feel that nature had adorned herself for the great occasion. It had rained heavily the previous day but now the air was washed clear of any moisture and was cooled by fresh breezes that swept across the James River from the southwest. A scattering of dogwood trees peeped from the edge of the woods showing their white blossoms that were shaped like crosses. On the grassy areas of the riverbanks that had not been grazed by our cattle there were golden wildflowers in profusion with occasional patches of pink or blue.

Marshal Dale had declared the day to be a holiday. Relief from work and the expectation of a celebration contributed to the sense of well-being that prevailed in Jamestown. Captain Yeardley had brought his company to be a guard of honor for the occasion and other settlers had come from Henrico for the diversion of the wedding that was to be at three o'clock in the afternoon. Adding to the dreamlike quality of the day was the sight of brightly dressed Indian men and women who walked freely about the settlement, both outside and within the palisades. The brothers of Pocahontas had come and brought with them Opachisco who was to represent Powhatan at the wedding. Opachisco was another brother of Powhatan but not as tall as Opechancanough whom I had met two weeks earlier. Pocahontas said that he was her favorite uncle and they spent an hour together during which he brought her news and greetings from her friends. She also explained to him his role in the ceremony where he would give her in marriage.

At three o'clock most of the population were assembled at the new church that stood outside the palisades of the fort. The church could not accommodate everyone so the spaces near the doors and windows were occupied by onlookers who hoped to see or hear some portion of the ceremony. The guard of honor lined the walk from the governor's house to the church along which Pocahontas and her uncle would pass on their way to the ceremony.

Ralph Hamor had agreed to attend me and bore the ring I was to give to Pocahontas. When all the guests, including Marshal Dale who was resplendent in his uniform, had taken their seats, Hamor and I took our places before the altar. The Reverends Bucke and Whitaker were robed in white while all about the church I saw the faces of my friends who had become Virginians with me in the four years since we arrived from Bermuda.

The brothers of Pocahontas were there, dressed in buckskin with their faces painted brilliant red. The elder, Naukaquawis, was especially resplendent. Surely, the church had never been so brightly decorated with flowers found around Jamestown than it was that day. But then, I asked myself, when had there been such a joyous occasion?

Only the arrival of Sir Thomas Gates with reinforcements and supplies, had been so momentous.

From outside the church we heard the command of the honor guard that meant that Pocahontas was on her way to the church. I glanced toward Richard Bucke who smiled at me in reassurance. All eyes had now turned to the door as we waited for her entrance. I cannot describe the emotion that filled that building. Remember, this was the woman who when hardly more than a child had saved the colonists at Jamestown in its earliest days. She befriended us at a time when we had no friends. And now she appeared at the door to our church. She was dressed in a tunic of muslin, a flowing veil and a robe of rich material from England. Around her neck she wore a beautiful necklace of freshwater pearls sent to her by her father. To every man his bride is radiant but I believe none could surpass the brilliance of Pocahontas as she entered the church on the arm of Opachisco. They moved as one down the aisle with her smiling graciously while he carried himself gravely with downcast eyes. She paused and made the briefest of bows to her brothers who now stood beside Marshall Dale.

I recall clearly the exchange of vows, placing the ring on the hand of Pocahontas, and kissing her at the conclusion of the ceremony but no part of the wedding remains clearer in my mind than the sight of her as she walked down the aisle to join me at the altar. Those were a few moments of distilled clarity magnified by a sense that God was granting us a union that was our destiny. Our lives would be forever linked no matter what the future. That this wedding was occurring almost defied belief and yet it was happening.

Perhaps those in Jamestown that day had some sense of reprieve that added to the joyousness of the occasion. If this wedding could occur, why could we not have peace?

As the church bells pealed and the festivities began we sensed that anything was possible.

~37~

Now that there was peace between the Indians and us, Marshal Dale's plan to expand from the Henrico area to Bermuda Hundred went forward rapidly. Henrico had been chosen as a site that could be easily defended; but, defense was no longer our first consideration. Bermuda Hundred was about ten miles downstream from Henrico along the winding river but only ten miles overland. This was land near the confluence of the James and Appomatox Rivers that was better suited for farming. Moreover, we were able to farm land that already had been cleared by the Indians over hundreds of years.

Our house was close to the bay formed by the two rivers. William Sparkes and three other men lived in a nearby house. I had contracted with the Virginia Company for the services of these men. Although they worked for me they were expected to produce an annual contribution of two barrels of corn for the company. I assigned them land for the production of their quota. As before, Sparkes showed himself to be a willing worker and we worked well together to make our land productive. We also built the small pier on the creek where we kept a boat.

I set about the planting of corn and tobacco with enthusiasm while Pocahontas created a garden near our house for herbs and vegetables. She had the confidence that came from a childhood when she had been expected to help with planting. She delighted in showing me an herb that was unfamiliar to me; I was expected to learn the Indian name because I had no other name for it. But otherwise Pocahontas avoided the use of her native language when speaking with me. She was still more interested in unraveling the mysteries of English.

Mistress Horton was still our neighbor because Alexander Whitaker had moved his household to Bermuda Hundred, having left the Henrico Church in the care of William Wickham. Likewise George and Elizabeth Grave lived nearby where George was engaged in the construction of the Bermuda Hundred Church. I greatly regretted that the Laydon family had remained at Henrico but at least Pocahontas still had as neighbors the two women who had befriended her most at Henrico.

It was, as usual in early Virginia days, a time of hard work. But it was rewarding because we could see the results of our labor. In early summer our crops were responding to the sun, rain, and fertile soil with which Providence blessed us. We had made a pen for our two cows and five goats and there was ample grazing land within the impalement of the Bermuda Hundred settlement. On some days one or more of my men were called upon to help harvest the large quantities of fish that appeared in the rivers. The company provided salt for preserving fish but our main enjoyment was to have fresh fish for roasting. Occasionally a sturgeon would be among the catch, an occasion for a feast. Our days were long but as summer drew nearer we were accustomed to finding shelter from the Virginia sun at midday. After a few hours rest we resumed working until sundown.

I felt sure that Marshal Dale must have been congratulating himself on the events that were coming about largely due to his initiative. Every fortnight since the agreement of Powhatan to his daughter's wedding Marshal Dale had been receiving gifts from Powhatan or Opechancanough. They were accompanied by expressions of friendship for Marshal Dale whom the chiefs now considered to be their brother.

Perhaps his successes in opening new lands to settlement and in dealing with the Indians led Marshal Dale to overreach himself. His boldness and self-confidence were attributes that were essential to establishing a new settlement. Lord De la Warr had exhibited the same qualities that would not permit us to surrender to hardship and danger.

Marshall Dale was harsh but he would use all the resources

at his disposal to achieve success. As he attributed at least some of his success to my marriage to Pocahontas he may have reasoned that another marriage would bring further benefits.

It was a great surprise to me to learn that Marshall Dale asked Powhatan to permit him to marry another of his daughters. He already had a wife in England and, even though he might desire to achieve a more lasting peace with Powhatan or the happiness now enjoyed by Pocahontas and me, a union with one of Pocahontas' sisters could only be considered bigamous. How would such a marriage be accomplished? Certainly not through the offices of Alexander Whitaker, a man of great piety, or Richard Bucke who would never consent to officiating at an illegal wedding. It was a matter, of course, in which my opinion had never been sought and which Marshal Dale never chose to discuss with me. Indeed, I would not even discuss the bizarre business in these pages were it not for the insight it gives us to the character of Powhatan himself.

I learned of the matter from Ralph Hamor who was sent by Marshal Dale to be his envoy to Powhatan and kept an account of his mission. In his journey he was to be accompanied by Thomas Savage, a young man who had been given to Powhatan by Captain Christopher Newport and who lived with the Indians for three years. Savage spoke the Algonquian language fluently, given the time spent with the Indians, and had been well-liked by Powhatan himself. Hamor also had two Indian guides who could take them to Matchcot, Powhatan's village on the Pamunkey River.

Hamor told me they made the journey on foot. After they crossed the James River they did not need a boat until they arrived at the Pamunkey which they had to cross to reach Matchcot. When at the Pamunkey, one of the guides gave a great shout and a dugout canoe was sent for them.

As they reached the opposite shore, Thomas Savage whispered to Hamor that they were being greeted by Powhatan himself. The chief had impressive stature, about six feet in height, with the massive chest and arms of a strong warrior. He addressed himself first to Thomas Savage whom he seemed happy to greet. He called him his child and chided him for not visiting him in the four years since Savage had returned to Jamestown. Then he paused and said that in all that time he had not seen Namontack either who had gone to live with the English and never returned from England.

Turning to Hamor, Powhatan reached for his neck, causing him some alarm as he wondered if Powhatan meant to cut his throat. As it happened, he was seeking to identify Hamor by a necklace that he had sent to Marshal Dale as a gift. The marshal had replied that any envoy from Dale who did not wear this necklace for identification was an imposter and should be made a prisoner. Hamor had never heard of such an arrangement and hastily fabricated an excuse, saying that Marshal Dale did not believe the necklace necessary when he was accompanied by Indian guides who could identify him. Powhatan accepted this excuse graciously and then bade them accompany him to his house. Around them in every direction were Indian men, each with his bow and a quiver filled with arrows. No Oriental potentate has a more impressive bodyguard.

In his house, Powhatan seated himself on a mat that served as his bed while two young women sat at his right and left hand. He offered Hamor a filled pipe who, after he had taken several draughts of the strong Indian tobacco, passed the pipe back to Powhatan. Then he began a pleasant conversation, asking about his brother, Marshal Dale. He also inquired about Pocahontas and John Rolfe, how we liked, lived, and loved together. Hamor replied that his brother was well and that Pocahontas and John Rolfe were very well. Then he was bold enough to repeat what he had heard Pocahontas say on several occasions: that she was so content that she would never change her life to return and live with Powhatan. At this remark, Powhatan laughed heartily and said that he was glad of it.

Powhatan then asked Hamor to reveal the purpose of his unexpected visit. He responded that he could only discuss his mission in private, since it was a matter of great importance. Powhatan ordered all his attendants to leave except the two young women who were forbidden to leave his house.

Hamor then proceeded to present Powhatan with a succession of gifts from Sir Thomas including pieces of copper, strings of blue and white beads, combs, fishhooks and a pair of knives. He did this slowly enough so that Powhatan could examine the gifts individually and be satisfied of their high quality. When he saw Powhatan was pleased with what he had brought, Hamor told him that the fame of his youngest daughter's beauty had reached the ears of his brother who had no greater desire than that she be permitted to return with Hamor to Bermuda Hundred. His object was that she would become his companion, wife, and bedfellow. This would also greatly please Pocahontas who would dearly love to see and be near her sister. Hamor could tell that this message was agitating Powhatan greatly and that he barely permitted him to complete his request.

With the greatest of dignity Powhatan expressed his thanks for the gifts although he allowed that they were not as ample as those previously given to him by Captain Newport. He said it was quite impossible to give his daughter to Marshal Dale because he had already sold her to a great chief who has taken her away three days' journey from him. He had sold her for two bushels of beads made of oyster shells. When Hamor countered with the suggestion that Powhatan recall the daughter and we would pay treble the price in more precious objects, he firmly declined.

He said his youngest daughter was now his greatest delight and he could not live without seeing her. If she went to live with the English he would never see her again because he had made a firm resolve never to visit the English. Moreover, he could give no greater assurances of peace than he had already given. Too many of Dale's men and too many of Powhatan's men had already been killed. No, even if he should have justification for war he was now old and would gladly end his days in peace. So, if the English should offer him injury, his country is large enough that he would remove himself farther from us. Thus, he said, I hope my brother will be satisfied.

When I heard these words from Ralph Hamor I was stunned. I could not believe that Marshal Dale, already married, could propose marriage to a young girl hardly more than a child. To this day I have not understood it. How could a man whose whole being was based on the concept of authority propose an action in direct conflict with our legal and religious principles? It was a matter, however, that he never spoke of and no one spoke of it in his presence. I doubt that anyone was ever able to take full measure of this man.

Another event occurred during Hamor's mission to Powhatan that was unusual. On the second day a man approached him whom he took to be an Indian by his appearance and his dress. But, to Hamor's surprise, the man was one William Parker who had been captured by Powhatan's men three years earlier in the vicinity of Kecoughtan. He pleaded for help and Hamor promised to secure his freedom. When confronted with evidence that he had not returned all the English prisoners, Powhatan became indignant and threatened not to provide guides for Hamor's return to Bermuda Hundred. To this Hamor replied that his failure to return safely would result in reprisal against Powhatan by Marshal Dale.

I could not help but admire Ralph Hamor for his skill as an ambassador. He had taken on a difficult mission and, while he had not won a bride for Sir Thomas Dale, he had won the release of a captive whose very existence had been denied by Powhatan The most lasting benefit, however, of Ralph Hamor's embassy to Powhatan was the declaration of the chief that he would not make war. He had already retreated from Werowocomoco to Matchcot on the Pamunkey. There was more land still available if he desired to withdraw further from the tidewater area of Virginia. The prospects of peace looked good as long as Powhatan lived. At this point, his leadership appeared to me to be a blessing and I could only wish him a long life.

~38~

Ralph Hamor had scarcely returned from his mission to Powhatan when he informed me that he intended to return to England.

"I trust that you have not felt the displeasure of Sir Thomas Dale?" I asked.

"Definitely not. In fact, I am beginning to believe that he now realizes how Powhatan has saved him from what would have been a very unwise marriage."

I could only shake my head. The matter still seemed incomprehensible to me.

"So what is your reason for returning to England at this time?"

"My father is not well. For some time he has been a director of the East India Company. I believe the responsibility has weighed heavily upon him. It has been five years now since I last saw him."

"And do you plan to return to Virginia?"

"Absolutely, John. I believe that my future is here. I believe that yours is also; but you already know that."

"It is indeed. England has a foothold now. I would not be anywhere else."

I did not look forward to Ralph Hamor's departure. He was possessed of a good mind and a courageous nature. He had been a great help to me in my tobacco planting, giving freely of both physical assistance and honest criticism.

Pocahontas was greatly interested in the thought of Hamor's return to England although she was not pleased that he would be sailing with Captain Argall on the *Treasurer*.

"How long is the journey?" she asked Ralph Hamor.

"About six weeks. On a June crossing we are likely to have favorable winds."

"You will sail all the way to London?"

"Yes, when we reach England we will probably sail up the River Thames. It depends upon the winds."

"Tell me about London." She was fascinated by the thought of that city.

"We have told you about Whitehall Palace and St. Paul's Cathedral. But you need to know there are also small streets, crowded with shops, having upper stories hanging over the shops so that one can scarcely see the sky. In some parts of London there are so many people on the streets you can scarcely walk."

"I think I would like the palaces better."

"I think you would too," said Hamor. He looked at me and smiled. "I think you had better make your fortune before taking Pocahontas to London, John."

"Your father lives in a big house," Pocahontas said to Hamor. "You told me that yourself."

"It is true," he replied.

"How did he make his fortune?" continued the inquisitive young woman.

"Now, Pocahontas," I interjected, "as a courteous lady you should not ask someone the source of their family's money.

"Then how will I find out?"

"You may ask someone else," I replied.

"I do not like this custom. I think the Indian way of talking is better. You are my friend, Ralph Hamor. You are not hurt, are you, if I ask you this question?"

"Not in the least. My father has made and sold clothing for many years. He began as a tailor, as his father had before him. But he found that he was good at selling the clothes. So, he paid others to be the tailors while he sold the clothes and made a lot of money."

"That sounds easy," said Pocahontas. "If it is really easy then anyone could become rich. So, maybe it is not really easy."

"Many people in England become rich," said Hamor. "They often do it by buying and selling as members of a group or corporation. If a group are the only ones who have the right to sell furs, for example, they are said to have a monopoly. They may become very rich."

"Monopoly," said Pocahontas. "That sounds like an Indian word."

"It is a word that I believe your father would understand well," I said.

I could not help noticing Pocahontas' questions about England. While before our marriage I had thought it interesting for a young Indian woman to wish to visit my country, I now, as her husband, began to think of how I could make such a journey possible. Ralph Hamor's joking remark about first making my fortune was a chance remark that hit quite close to home. I wanted to be more firmly established in the new world before a return visit, however desirable, to the old.

Ralph Hamor departed for England as he said he would. Although I did not believe that my friend William Strachey would ever return to Virginia, I fully expected Hamor would.

Both men were enthusiastic about Virginia but three years had passed already since Strachey's departure.

Two men who had befriended me had been secretaries of the colony and I was pleased when Marshal Dale made me acting secretary.

"I expect my action will be ratified by the Virginia Company," said the marshal.

"Indeed, you have on many occasions acted as the secretary in the absence of either Master Strachey or Master Hamor. But more importantly, they will want to recognize you for the services that you have performed for the colony."

"If you are referring to my marriage to Pocahontas, sir, I must say that I do not consider that to be a service."

"Of course you do not," said the marshal, with more than his usual sensitivity. "It would have been more appropriate to say that the Virginia Company recognizes your status in the colony. As well they may, for I have written reports that reflect upon you quite favorably. And the fact that Ralph Hamor, who shares my high opinion of you, is now returning to England will be to your advantage."

259

"Ralph Hamor will report on the great potential here for producing crops of all sorts, in huge quantities, provided we get the people. We need more settlers. It is my belief that a commercially viable tobacco industry can be developed. In this regard, I am reminded that our sovereign, King James, has strongly criticized tobacco."

"I have read his tract on the subject. Do you think it has made an impression on his subjects?"

"It is a strong condemnation without doubt. Despite the arguments against tobacco, smoking has grown in popularity. The King noted that the power of imitation draws people to tobacco. I agree with him and cannot but notice how many persons, once initiated, are unable to discard the habit. Since so many are drawn to it, it makes little difference that the King wrote a tract years ago condemning it."

I was continuing to use my opportunities to experiment in the cultivation of tobacco. There was so much land available at Bermuda Hundred that I was able to pick and choose my location for tobacco plots. I looked for meadows that did not show signs of recent cultivation. I made a point of avoiding planting where woods blocked the exposure to the sun. A gentle southern slope seemed ideal because there was sunlight and drainage without much danger of erosion.

Pocahontas showed interest in my tobacco. As I expected, she favored the Indian technique of making small hills around plants. She also suggested cutting the tops off the plants so that the growth would be concentrated in the leaves.

"Your plants are so tall," she commented in the late summer. "They are two times as big as the Indian tobacco. You are a very good farmer."

"Thank you very much, Mistress Rolfe, but given the seed and hard work, any farmer could produce the same."

"I do not think so. You think of all the ways to make it better. Look how beautiful these leaves are." She reached out to touch a large leaf. As she did so it became apparent there was a large worm on the leaf.

"That worm admires the tobacco just as much as you do," I said as I took the worm from the leaf and killed it. "I do not know what they call this in London but I call this Virginia brightleaf."

"You must go to London to hear with your own ears," said Pocahontas.

"In good time," I replied. "There is much work to do."

I was glad to have William Sparkes and the others working for me. Now that their quota of corn was assured, I could use their labor to assure the success of the tobacco crop. As much as men could do, of course. The rest was up to God. We could not control storms that swept over the land in the late summer. But we had been spared hail when the tobacco plants were small and there was no drought in the growing season. We had much to be thankful for.

Our harvest was good that year in every respect. Corn, squash, and beans were available in abundance. We had fish that we ate fresh or preserved using the salt produced from drying ponds. With the cold weather came ducks and geese in great flocks. The wisdom of Marshal Dale's policy to allow individuals to grow their own crops was apparent. He was determined not to repeat the starving time and even restricted the growing of tobacco to smaller plats for concern that planters would neglect food crops. I was treated as an exception to this policy because of the work I continued to do in improving the tobacco. Even so, between the settlers' crops and mine, we managed to produce 2,500 pounds of brightleaf for export to England.

In the winter of 1615 it became apparent that Pocahontas was with child. This was a cause of great happiness and thanksgiving for us. As she was a very active person, I expected Pocahontas to slow down in her activity but she did not. This was a matter of concern for me as well as Mistress Horton who counseled her to take more rest. Elizabeth Grave had altered dresses for her that she wore to church but much of the time she dressed in the deerskin tunics of her tribe that were quite warm as well as comfortable.

"Pocahontas," I asked, "should we not send word to your father that you will soon give birth to our child?"

"I have already done so. I should have told you so. Soon he

will send women to be with me."

She was right. In early March, two women appeared at our house accompanied by Machumps. One was her sister Mattachanna who was about her age and one was an older woman, an aunt whose name I have forgotten. At the meal we shared that evening the conversation was mostly in Algonquian. Neither of the women guests spoke English and Machumps rarely spoke. I wondered how he had ever found sufficient favor with Powhatan to be sent to England. He would only speak when I spoke to him and then only to make the barest reply. After learning that Powhatan was well and that there was much snow at Marchcot, I gave up conversation and listened to the pleasant voices of the women. They were obviously happy to be with Pocahontas and that she would soon become a mother.

"I am glad they are here, Pocahontas. We can make them comfortable here in our house."

"They will not stay in the house. They will stay in the barn and will be warm with the animals." In the autumn I had built a small barn that sheltered our livestock.

"But that is not necessary. They will be more comfortable here."

"They wish to be with me. I will be in the barn too. Machumps can stay here with you."

It had not occurred to me that Pocahontas would follow the Indian custom of withdrawing to some secluded place to have her child. I fully expected her to call on Mistress Horton and Elizabeth Grave to assist her. But I was wrong and I made only a faint attempt to dissuade her. They spent the first night in the barn and were there when Mistress Horton came to see Pocahontas the next day.

"Can't you do anything, John?" she said. "There are even places where the wind has driven the snow through the walls of the barn."

"She told me it was too warm in the house so I don't think it bothers her. I have learned that when Pocahontas makes up her mind she is determined. I went to build a fire for them but her aunt drove me out. She said they would build a fire when they needed it."

262

"I suppose that awful Machumps is staying with you."

"He is, but he is really no bother. I have already passed the limits of conversation with him."

I had not seen Machumps for several hours. I busied myself chopping wood. At least I could take the women some firewood. The skies had clouded over so that there was no sun and it began to feel colder. They would need a fire soon. I was startled to have someone at my side whom I had not seen approaching. It was Machumps, who was holding two recently killed rabbits in his right hand. When I looked at the rabbits he held them up to my view. Then, still holding the rabbits in his right hand, he pointed to the barn where Pocahontas and the women were. Bending over the woodpile, he skinned the rabbits quickly on a log before taking them to the barn. I followed with the wood I had chopped. Machumps did not attempt to enter the barn but dropped the rabbits in the snow by the door. He called our something to the women that I suppose informed them of the fresh meat. Following his example I laid the wood by the rabbits.

After eating a silent supper with Machumps in the house, I spent the evening reading the Prayer Book and the Bible. I was sure that Mistress Horton had spread the word through the community of our Indian guests and the withdrawal of the women from the house. In my heart I felt Pocahontas was right in looking to her Indian family for help at this time. I hoped that no one with the best of intentions would attempt to interfere. Who, after all, could be of more help to Pocahontas than her kinspeople?

In the early morning I was awakened by Machumps. He beckoned for me to come quickly. I hurriedly put on my shoes and cloak, clamped a hat on my head, and followed him from the house. It was the time of twilight before dawn and the snow had a blue tint to it as we walked to the dark shape that was the barn. I prayed that all was well, not having been told anything by my silent companion.

In the barn we paused to accustom our eyes to the darkness. I could hear the cattle stirring. There was a fire that illuminated the three women kneeling on the furs they had brought with

263

them from the house. Pocahontas was between her aunt and her sister, holding our son on the morning of his birth. Looking up at me and holding him so that I could just see his face, she said, "Here is your son, John Rolfe."

I dropped to my knees and reached out my hand to touch a tiny hand that was protruding from the fur wrapped around him. I could not see his eyes that appeared to be shut but stroked his thick dark hair. This brought a cry from the infant that caused the three women to laugh.

"Go now," said Pocahontas. "I will bring him to the house."

Outside it was already brighter. It was going to be a beautiful day. Our world was going to be filled with beautiful days. I thought of that other child born among the animals in a stable long ago. I hurried to the house to prepare my son a welcome.

~39~

Pocahontas had definitely followed the Indian custom when she withdrew from the house to give birth. This caused me to wonder how Pocahontas would raise our son, by following the Indian or the English customs. I thought it best not to inquire but simply to observe. At first, I believe that she was drawn to the Indian ways, if only by the presence of her sister and aunt.

Shortly after returning to the house, Pocahontas's aunt produced a cradle board, to which the baby was bound after first placing a fur pelt on his backside to give him some comfort. It was the practice of the Indian women to treat their infants thus so they could be easily transported on the back of the mother or placed upright against a tree or pole.

I noticed, several days later, after the other women had left to return to Matchcot, that Pocahontas removed our son from the cradleboard. She placed him in the cradle that Mistress Eason had sent from Jamestown in anticipation of his birth. To me, this was a sign that Pocahontas intended to raise him in the English ways. And why not? She had chosen the English way of life and her son was an Englishman. Please do not interpret my statement as an assertion of superiority. I firmly agreed with the Reverend Whitaker that God created the Indian with all the same human attributes as we possess. And I greatly admire many of the attributes that are valued in the Indian culture such as courage, self-reliance, and an appreciation of nature.

"Are you pleased with your son, John?" Pocahontas would ask. She smiled as she said it because she was never in doubt about the answer to the question. I was enchanted by both my wife and my son. From his earliest days he bore a great resemblance to her and as the months passed our neighbors commented on how much they looked alike.

"You know I am pleased with my son."

The songs that Pocahontas sang to Thomas as she held him in her arms were Indian songs. He was a healthy baby and I thought that he grew at an astonishing rate. Those were happy days. For the first time in the six years that I had been in Virginia I was at home, as a man should be, with his wife and family.

"How would our child be raised, Pocahontas, if he were brought up in Matchcot?"

"In the village of Powhatan, or any other Powhatan village, he would learn to be a hunter. His father would make him a little bow and little arrows."

"Not with arrowheads, I hope?"

"Not at first. But when he could hit a leaf or something very small with an arrow, then he would have sharp arrows. His father would take him hunting to teach him. He would teach him where the animals came, how to wait very still for the squirrels, and how to call to turkeys."

"And the mother would no longer teach him?"

"She would make him practice. She would want him to learn soon so he could bring food for the family. She would tell him stories of mighty hunters to make him brave."

"I fear that Thomas will not receive this training."

"It would be good for him to learn the Indian way of hunting. It would help to make him strong and not to be afraid. I would like for him to do this and it makes me sad that he will not. But he will grow to be a good farmer like you."

"I have heard that there were secret ceremonies and trials that young boys must endure before they become men."

"Yes, but I am not sorrowful that he will not do them."

"Do you know about these secret ceremonies?"

"Only a little. They are called "huskanow," and at the beginning the entire village will attend so I have seen the beginning. First there is a feast. Then all the people are in two large circles around men who are painted different colors and wear horns on their heads. The people dance and then the men with the horns shout and do strange things to make the people watch them. After this they bring the young boys, whose faces and bodies have been painted white, into the circle. The men with the horns surround the boys and beat them with rushes."

"What a strange ceremony."

"It is only the beginning. The people return to the village but the boys are kept in the woods for many months. They are made to eat things that make them do strange things. Some of them become wild and they are put in cages. A few of them die."

"Why is this done?"

"They learn not to be afraid. They become men and are treated like men when they come back to the village to live. They are now ready to fight for the tribe when there is war."

"I see what you mean about not wanting this for Thomas."

"Do you do something like this in England?"

"Not really. A young man who is lucky may go off to a university. Or a young man may become an apprentice for seven years in order to learn a trade such as being a tailor or a silversmith."

"That is not the same."

She was curious about our society and wondered how much our society in Virginia reflected that in England.

"I have heard you speak of Lord De la Warr. He must be a very great man to call him Lord."

"He is a member of the nobility. Our king has the power to make someone a noble. In England there are many nobles and rich persons who own most of the land. In order to farm the land a farmer must pay money to the noble who then becomes richer and more powerful. Here we are all being given the right to farm land that we will own."

"Someday will you have noblemen here?"

"Perhaps, but I hope not. There is more opportunity for men like me if we do not have a great many noblemen."

"But, won't they come here?"

"Some, like Lord De la Warr. But most will stay in England where their money is."

Pocahontas seemed to accept that. In her mind, I believe, England was beginning to take shape as a place like no other, filled with exotic people, buildings, and incomparable wealth. Though I tried to explain that there were many people who struggled to earn their daily bread I am sure it did nothing to dampen her imagination.

Sir Thomas Dale, who was a man given to enthusiasm, had done a great deal to stimulate the imagination of Pocahontas toward English life. I judged the two greatest passions in his life to be patriotism and religion. If would be difficult to say which passion was the greater, particularly as they seemed to become intertwined in some respects. Part of his enmity toward the Spanish came from his dislike of Catholicism. Thus his desire and drive to make Virginia a successful colony grew in part from his desire to deny this territory to the Spanish.

Marshal Dale had as great a part in bringing Pocahontas to Christianity as did Alexander Whitaker. He took considerable pride in her conversion and even boasted of his effort on her behalf. Pocahontas had strong feelings of gratitude for this. Personally, I feel that Pocahontas was not given sufficient credit for her own actions. She was not a child, after all, but a mature individual, accustomed to making decisions for herself. Who knows who was the strongest influence; perhaps it would be more appropriate to say it was God who had brought her to be a Christian.

As you would expect, both Marshal Dale and the Reverend Whitaker were pleased by the baptism of our son. We thought it was fitting that he should be named Thomas and were gratified when Marshal Dale agreed to be his godfather. We asked Mistress Horton to be his godmother, a request that gave the greatest joy to that good woman. The ceremony took place in the church at Bermuda Hundred.

The largest number of settlers in the colony now lived in the vicinity of Bermuda Hundred and for this reason, Marshal Dale made it his one of his two residences. There was also the Governor's house at Jamestown. Sir Thomas Gates had built it using brick made locally. The marshal used the residence when he was in Jamestown and it was also occupied by Captain Argall who stayed there when he was not on away on his ship.

As we moved into summer, I made a practice of visiting our

other settlements where some of the settlers' land was planted in tobacco. This enabled me to watch over the newest plantings and make sure that the tobacco was properly tended. In early July I accompanied Marshal Dale on his shallop on a trip to Jamestown with the intent of surveying the tobacco plats. Pocahontas accompanied me since Mistress Horton offered to watch over Thomas.

"Marshal Dale has only three soldiers with him, John," said Pocahontas as we took our seats in the shallop.

"There has not been an attack on us for over a year, since before we were married."

"I would be more careful."

"Would Powhatan also be more careful?" I asked.

"Of course he would. He would have twenty men at least."

She was right. It was the prudent thing for a chief, whether Indian or English, to avoid capture. Powhatan's policy of cautiousness had enabled him to rule for many years. I prayed that nothing untoward would happen to Marshal Dale. We needed his strong leadership.

"Who would want to fight on such a beautiful day as this?" I said. "We have a good wind at our backs to take us to Jamestown."

"You must not think I am afraid. I just want Marshal Dale to be protected."

She said no more about it. Soon she was engaged in conversation with the marshal who was the last to come aboard the shallop.

As we passed the mouth of the Chickahominy River we saw Indians close to the shore who were working on fish traps. These ingenious devices were constructed of stakes driven in the river bottom that supported nets arranged so that fish could easily proceed into the trap but found it difficult to get out. Now that there was peace, the Chickahominys were extending their traps further into the river.

Captain Yeardley, who had come earlier to Jamestown was waiting to greet us as we docked at Jamestown. As usual, George Yeardley was especially courteous to Pocahontas. Like the marshal, he always addressed her as Lady Rebecca, her Christian name.

"You must bring Thomas with you when you travel, Lady Rebecca."

"He is too young to be a soldier, Captain Yeardley. He does not walk yet."

"That should not deter you. Captain Yeardley was soldier when he was barely old enough to walk," said Marshal Dale.

We all laughed. A lighthearted remark was rare from the marshal. There was some justification for his statement because Yeardley was a seventeen year old recruit when he served with Marshal Dale in Holland.

Turning to me he said, "I have some matters to attend to now, but could you and Lady Rebecca meet me at the Governor's house in an hour? I have something to discuss with you both."

"Of course, Sir Thomas. We will be there."

Although I devoted the next hour to inspecting the tobacco crop, my mind was on the meeting with the marshal. Did he have some new agricultural scheme to propose? I kept him well-informed of the condition of the tobacco so I hardly imagined he wished to discuss that. Perhaps he wished to discuss the idea of having a school for the Indian children. I knew that was a goal he would like to achieve. Several leaders in the colony had long thought that the way to win over the Indians was through education of their children. The difficulty was in getting the Indian parents to submit their children to our schooling.

As we entered the Governor's house, Pocahontas asked me if I had any idea what the marshal wished to discuss with us. She was as curious as I was but I had no new ideas. Instead of answering her question I commented on the new floor that had been laid in the great room of the Governor's house.

"You must make a floor like this for us," was her reaction.

"I will someday. I promise."

"How do they make the wood so beautiful?"

"It has been rubbed with oil."

"I think we should sit on the floor."

"We will sit as the marshal sits," I said, knowing that the marshal would sit on a chair.

The question was quickly resolved when the marshal entered and we sat on the chairs he indicated for us. Pocahontas complimented him on the new floor.

"Thank you, Lady Rebecca. But I did not ask you here to see the new floor. I could have conferred with you at Bermuda Hundred but, because I knew you were coming to Jamestown today, I thought we could talk while away from the distractions of Bermuda Hundred."

"As you are aware, I have been here in Virginia for four years. The work I have undertaken here has been the most difficult work of my life, but I thank God that he has blessed my efforts. What I am proposing to do is to return next year to England. I will leave the colony much better established than it."

"Marshal Dale," said Pocahontas. "You cannot leave us."

"Do not forget, my dear Rebecca, that I am married, just as you are. You would not keep me longer from my wife, would you?"

Pocahontas shook her head slowly.

"Do not be sad, either of you. What I want to ask you is this: would you like to accompany me when I return to England next year?"

We were both taken completely by surprise. While I knew Pocahontas would like to visit England, and I wanted to take her there, I thought such a trip was far in the future.

Pocahontas looked to me to make a response.

"What would be the reason for Pocahontas and me to go?"

"You are living proof that Englishmen have nothing to fear by coming to Virginia. For years there was real danger. Much has been written about it. Too much, and much of it is lies. Can you imagine the effect on the London populace to see you, a prosperous settler, along with your Indian bride, the daughter of a great chief."

"I had never thought of such an idea," I said.

"Well, I have," replied the marshal. "To make it all the more convincing we must take some other Indians, perhaps some of Lady Rebecca's kinspeople."

"I want to go," said Pocahontas. "I want to take my sister and her husband too."

"What about my tobacco," I asked. "I cannot leave it now."

"There will be any number of volunteers to take your place in the fields. Besides, have you considered the opportunities that you will have to visit the London market? There, after all, is where Virginia tobacco is sold. You will profit from such a trip."

"You are right, of course, Sir Thomas," I said. "It is a brilliant idea."

"There is another good reason in justification for a visit to England by the Rolfes," continued the marshal. "We have talked many times about a school for Indian children. There is sympathy for such an institution in England. But a school, with schoolmaster and books, requires a patron, someone to pay the bills. It is difficult to find such a patron while here in Virginia but I feel sure that you can find willing patrons in England."

"I would like for Indian children to become Christian like me," said Pocahontas.

"It is a worthwhile dream and, with God's help, we can make it a reality. Don't you agree, John?" said the marshal. "I have had it in mind for some time but now we can make it come to pass," he exclaimed, bringing his fist down on the arm of his chair. "I am delighted that you are agreeable. I will write today to the London Company to seek their approval. In the meantime, we have plenty of time to plan and to prepare ourselves."

~40~

As we approached harvest time in the autumn of 1615, I regarded the tobacco crop with the knowledge that it would accompany me to England. I would have to devote special care and attention to it because there would not be time to produce another crop if we sailed before harvest in 1616. I thought we were fortunate in the growing season of 1615, having neither too little nor too much rainfall. I exhorted William Sparkes and the men to be especially careful to protect the mature plants and to treat the leaves carefully during the curing process. I was pleased with the size and quality of the leaves that had been produced from plants grown from specially selected seed.

In our conversations, Marshal Dale had impressed upon me that I had several responsibilities to consider while in England. To begin with, I was the consort to the Indian princess of Virginia. Then too, I was to be a man of business engaged in the selling of tobacco. As if these were not enough, I was also the Secretary of the Virginia Colony. In that regard, he expected me to prepare a report to go to King James himself. The report should describe the various settlements that comprised Virginia as well as our activities and prospects. There was plenty of time to prepare the report since we would deliver it ourselves in England.

"You know how I have strongly recommended that more settlers be sent here," the marshal reminded me. "I believe that you should make our situation known in detail. Report the exact number of persons living at each settlement. I want the King to realize how few persons are holding so much land for England."

I was familiar with the six main settlements except for

273

Dale's Gift which was on the eastern shore of the Chesapeake Bay. It was engaged primarily in fishing and making salt, activities that were important to our maintaining a stable supply of food. I made it a point to visit there. Also, when at the other settlements I grew more familiar with activities other than the production of tobacco which had been my first interest.

At the beginning of my report I called attention to the fact that the Virginia colony whose prosperity I was now describing was the same that had floundered badly for several years. A curious reader might question how this was so. I had the temerity to explain that at the outset we had an aristocratic government whose leaders were filled with envy and dissensions, that their actions choked the seeds and blasted the fruits of all men's labors. I stated that it was in this government that happened all the misery. If I seemed swift to condemn it was because I had witnessed first hand the fruits of this government. I reported that under the absolute government of our military leaders we had progressed, particularly in the construction of towns and palisades for the protection thereof.

I labored long on the wording of this portion of the report. I realized that what I was presenting to the king was opinion, even though Marshal Dale and I were convinced that they were correct opinions. I obviously did not wish to antagonize the monarch who was the chief of the aristocracy in England. Would he be offended by the reference to "aristocratic government" whose leaders seemed unable to cooperate and to avoid dissension? It was well known that King James not only believed in the divine right of kings but also used the aristocracy to bolster his rule. He was well known for his anger when antagonized. Would he not be antagonized by our production of tobacco, a plant that he considered loathsome?

It seemed the better part of valor not to dwell too long on the failures of the early colonial government but simply to convey to the reader that having moved to a more effective administration, the settlers in Virginia were able to benefit from the fertile land, waters, and climate. Fortunately, the disasters of the early years were not repeated. I then devoted myself to the facts of our situation that could be laid out in an objective description.

I listed the crops that presently engaged our efforts and described how two men by their labor produced a harvest exceeding fifty English pounds in value. This was no exaggeration and I hoped would suggest to his majesty the benefits that would result if he filled our landscape with industrious settlers. At present there were but 351 men, women, and children in all Virginia. Our six settlements except the aforesaid Dale's Gift were located along the James River. I listed each of these settlements, beginning with Henrico that is ninety odd miles above the mouth of the river. We at Bermuda Hundred, the largest settlement, are only ten miles downriver from Henrico, and Shirley Hundred is but three or four miles downriver from us on the opposite shore. It is then thirty-seven miles downriver to Jamestown and another thirty-seven to Kecoughtan that is located at the mouth of the river. There is an officer in command at each of these settlements and all but Shirley Hundred are served by a minister.

I spent many hours laboring on this report to make it informative without taxing the patience of King James whom I knew to be a man of scholarship and intellect. I thought it best to conclude with an appeal to bring Christianity to the natives. It would be another and perhaps the most significant of the opportunities open to the English people as we proceeded with the work ahead of us.

Pocahontas looked forward to the opportunity to go to England from the very day Sir Thomas Dale had brought up the subject. She had no doubt that the proposal from the marshal would be agreed to by the company in London, whereas I wondered if the expense of bringing us, along with a retinue of Indians, would be approved. I knew that having a group of ten or more Indians was considered important by Marshal Dale in order to make the favorable impression he desired. He believed that the presence of a single Indian might indicate coercion whereas a larger group of visitors indicated peaceful relations. The presence of Pocahontas alone, no matter how impressive an individual she might be, was simply not enough. Though I agreed with the logic of his thought the provisions necessary for the accommodation of a retinue would be considerable. I had not even begun to think of the difficulties that might be involved with controlling such a group.

Pocahontas was more involved with preparing herself for the interesting events she foresaw in her future. Surely she would meet people of high rank and responsibility. She was aware that she would be, for most English people that she met, the foremost representative of her race and therefore the object of great interest on their part. To some degree, the Indians of Virginia would be judged by the impression that she made. She turned to Alexander Whitaker, who had provided much of her religious education, also to be her mentor on society. I could not disapprove of this because his educational attainments exceeded mine. She also called upon Mistress Horton to increase her knowledge of what she might expect to encounter. She showed not the slightest anxiety for what lay ahead but only what I considered an intelligent interest. She had not been awed by any Englishman she had ever met and I did not expect that even a meeting with King James himself would ruffle her composure.

She agreed with Marshal Dale that a retinue of Indians from her tribe would be desirable and naturally gave some thought to whom they might be. Her favorite sister, Matachanna, who had attended her at the birth of Thomas, was a logical choice and apparently a suitable one to everyone concerned. This was a matter in which Powhatan had a voice because the Indians were his subjects and no doubt he had ideas of whom he would prefer to send. As expected, Powhatan decreed that Tomocomo, the husband of Mattachanna, would also go to England. Although a stranger to me, Tomocomo was well known to Pocahontas.

"He is a good man," she said, "but he thinks Tomocomo is very important. If we do not pay him much attention, he is very unhappy."

"That sounds like a lot of Englishmen I know," I replied.

"You know he is a priest, don't you?"

"Pocahontas, I know nothing about the man."

"Well, he has been able to heal sick people. Also he speaks to the god Okee and many people are afraid of him. But I do not believe in Okee anymore. Tomocomo speaks much to Powhatan and Powhatan tells him what to do."

"I suppose he will be the leader of the Indians that go with us."

"Yes, but he does not command me."

Pocahontas did not seem concerned about taking our infant son on the long ocean voyage. He would only be a year old at the time of the journey. I could understand this because Pocahontas had never made an ocean voyage. She had never been beyond Chesapeake Bay. And so we lived the remaining months before the trip with her not knowing what lay ahead and me praying silently that the ocean would prove kinder than on my last voyage.

Marshal Dale had long ago sent word to England of his intended return. He expected that someone would come to replace him as the acting governor. Perhaps even Lord De la Warr himself would come. But, come what may from England, Sir Thomas Dale was going home. If a replacement were not on hand by the time of departure, he would name Captain George Yeardley to succeed him. I thought this was a logical choice and personally agreed even though Marshal Dale did not seek the opinion of anyone in his selection.

Another decision made by Marshal Dale was that the Spaniard Diego Molina would return with us to England. Molina had been our prisoner since soon after Marshal Dale's arrival in Virginia. Besides Molina, only one other survived the detention in Virginia. That was Lembri who was suspected of being a spy. This suspicion had existed from the date of his capture at Point Comfort when one of our men accused him. He had not been executed, however, in hopes that he might reveal his identity and information about the Spanish.

Molina was confined at Jamestown. He was not heavily guarded because there was little likelihood that he would run off to the Indians. Hope was continually in his breast that he would be returned to England and then to Spain. Lembri, on the other hand was heavily guarded and was kept separate from Molina. His situation was more desperate and he was more likely to attempt to escape.

During the first week in May we assembled the group of Indians at Jamestown that would constitute the retinue of Pocahontas in England. Tomocomo was second only to Pocahontas in rank among the group. Besides his wife Mattachanna there were three other Indian women and four Indian men. All of them, including the women were tall, well-proportioned people. The men all had partially shaved heads and long hair in a single braid. Tomocomo was distinguished by the skin of a snake he wore coiled about his head and the bones that were intertwined in his braid. I could not help remarking on the appearance and the vitality of the group. It was as if Powhatan had chosen them for their appearance. Two houses were assigned to the Indians as a temporary residence while awaiting departure. At any hour of the day, English settlers, particularly the children, could be seen at these two houses where they stared openly at the Indian men and women. It was hard to say who had the greater curiosity, us about them or they about us. Curiosity led to closer inspection and soon our people were intermingled with them, examining each other's clothing and making comments that were mutually unintelligible.

Marshal Dale had chosen his departure season well. There was a series of sparkling spring days at Jamestown during which the *Treasurer* was laden and made ready for the journey. The barrels containing my shipment of tobacco were securely stored in the hold but far enough above the bilge so that there was little chance of damage from water accumulating in the ship. After all the care lavished on this tobacco, I could not afford to have it damaged during shipment.

Ship arrivals and departures from Jamestown were always an event for the settlers. Arrivals meant the possibility of new settlers, and at the least, the advent of news from England for all and the possibility of letters for a few. Departures were less exciting but even so were enough to bring spectators to the waterfront. Our departure aboard the *Treasurer* differed from the usual because of Pocahontas and the Indians. They dressed themselves in their finest clothing for the occasion. As they moved out of the gate of the fort and walked onto the pier they were applauded by the watching colonists. They were a memorable sight, Pocahontas, the living legend, leading her tribespeople on their journey to London.

It was also a memorable occasion for another reason: Marshal Dale was leaving the colony. While there was some enthusiasm shown, and even a feeble attempt at a cheer, this was not a crowd saying farewell to a favorite. Too many had suffered punishments or indignities for minor offenses during his years of administration. The presence of Acting Governor Yeardley and a company of troops prevented any overt rudeness or misbehavior. In a way it was unfair because whatever prosperity Virginia enjoyed at his departure was very largely due to the leadership of Sir Thomas Dale. Still, autocrats are rarely appreciated.

When all his passengers were aboard, Captain Argall gave the commands that freed us from the pier and headed the *Treasurer* into the channel to begin its trip downriver to the Chesapeake Bay and then to the ocean. How familiar the river seemed. Five years earlier we had made our way upstream to find Jamestown in a shambles. Since then the river had been our main highway – to connect our settlements, transport our crops, and mount expeditions against the Indians.

Pocahontas and I stood on the quarterdeck that evening as we watched the river widen into a broad reach above Point Comfort. She had decided to revert to the use of a cradleboard for little Thomas during the voyage. He had learned to walk but was not ready for the challenge of a rolling deck. From her back he had watched a spectacular sunset behind us with the red of the sky reflected in the water of the James River.

"We should see a light at Kecoughtan," I said, as I looked to the north.

"I see no light there," said Pocahontas "but there is one ahead of us," she said as she pointed toward the bow of our ship.

"That is Point Comfort."

"Will we stop there?" she asked.

"Not unless there is a signal to Captain Argall."

There was only a single gun salute fired from Point Comfort for the *Treasurer*. We returned the salute as the ship glided into Chesapeake Bay under full sail. I heard Pocahontas speaking in Algonquian to Tomocomo who had approached her. After a brief exchange he disappeared in the darkness.

"He wanted to know if Captain Argall will stop sailing now that it is dark."

"What did you tell him?"

"That he will sail all night. I remember."

She was referring to the voyage she made with Argall when he had kidnapped her. I knew that Pocahontas still resented Argall but I had made up my mind to get along with him. I think both Argall and I realized that we had important positions in the colony and it was to our advantage to cooperate. There had been too many examples of foolish conflicts among the English.

The following morning we passed the capes and were in the ocean. Until then, neither Pocahontas nor any of the other Indians had been on the ocean and it quickly earned their respect. What had seemed a rather large ship no longer seemed so large as they felt the thrust of the huge waves that carried us up and then hurled us forward into a mass of swirling water. All of them, whether men or women, had been taught not to show fear but it was plain that they were awed by the power of the sea.

It was our custom to have morning prayer on deck. Each day Marshall Dale would conduct this service from the prayer book. All of the Indians attended except Tomocomo. Pocahontas told me the Indians did not resist or resent attending because they had come to acknowledge that our god was very powerful. They did not go so far as to think he was the only god but thought it prudent not to offend him. As for Tomocomo, I thought it understandable that he not attend since he was a priest and was loyal to his own gods. At different times he could be seen on the deck, chanting and tossing tobacco in the sea. His sacrifices of tobacco were usually at times of rough weather. When it was especially rough, he was more likely to be joined by some of the other Indians who, like him, would try to propitiate Okee.

By the time our voyage was nearing its end, it was apparent to me that a contest of sorts was being played out between

Pocahontas and Tomocomo. It was a contest for the leadership of the Indians. Tomocomo was exerting himself to keep them loyal to the old ways while she was eager to explore the ways of the English. She was willing to adopt the English ways as she demonstrated by her dress and language. There was no lack of respect between the two. Neither would say anything negative about the other but each was promoting their view, subtly for the most part, to influence the others. In this I think Pocahontas had the advantage because all of them were going to a new and strange place where her influence might be very useful in making one's way among the English people.

The Indians had a reminder how strange and sometimes terrible the English could be. On the very morning that land was sighted, all were gathered on deck to view the dark sliver of England that projected ever so small above the horizon. The buoyant spirits of the seamen were beginning to be shared with the Indians who at first viewed England with some trepidation. Suddenly the voice of Captain Argall boomed from the quarterdeck saying that all the ships passengers would gather on the main deck to witness an execution. This came as a complete surprise to me as I had heard no mention of any trial or even of any crime that might merit so drastic a punishment. When it was reported to the captain by his deck officer that all the passengers were present, the doors to the main cabin were opened and Lembri, the pilot who had been captured with the Spaniard Molina, was escorted to a rude platform of trestles set below the yardarm of the main mast. Two seamen hoisted Lembri onto the platform where a third fastened a noose about his neck.

"Lembri," said Captain Argall, "it is my duty to execute you by hanging for the crime of treason. Do you have anything you wish to say?"

Lembri was unagitated. If he had held hopes of being returned to Spain, the dashing of those hopes had not drained his spirit. I heard later that during the voyage his captors had plied him with strong drink under the influence of which he had confessed his Irish origin and that he had been a pilot for the Spanish in the armada that attempted to invade England.

Eying the captain who stood only a short distance from him, Lembri said in a ringing voice, "The only thing I wish to say is: damn you, Captain Argall; damn Marshal Dale; and damn King James of England."

These words produced as great a shock in the audience gathered about him as the swift move of the executioner to blindfold Lembri and then jerk the rude trestle out from under him. Within a minute his body was swinging like a pendulum in time to the rolling of the ship.

~41~

We arrived at Plymouth on June 3, 1616, almost seven years after the departure of the *Seaventure* from that port in 1609. When we had set sail in our brave fleet to meet the challenges of the new world beyond the ocean I could never have imagined the scope of the events that lay before us. There had been harrowing adventures such as the great storm and shipwreck as well as the war with Powhatan. We had lost loved ones and companions to sickness, hunger, drowning or enemy arrows. There had been bitter privation and severe military discipline. But there had been successes: the discovery of land of great fertility with wide flowing waterways and the carving of a foothold for England on what must be a great continent. For me personally, there was the solid satisfaction of adapting tobacco plants to Virginia that were proving to be of high quality and might prove even better. The thought that filled me with the greatest emotion, however, was that I had married the incomparable Pocahontas. I still found it hard to realize that I was her husband and that we were the parents of Thomas, now a healthy one year old boy.

We exchanged salutes with the fort and took aboard a pilot who would guide the *Treasurer* to an open pier. All of us lined the rails, naturally, to obtain a better look at Plymouth and to observe the docking. I felt a lift of my heart, that I am sure I shared with my countrymen, as I saw our nation's flag flying from so many ships and buildings. What our Indian passengers felt I cannot imagine.

Seeing Tomocomo near me, I turned to him and asked, "What are you doing with that stick, Tomocomo?' He was holding a rather large staff in one hand and a knife in the other and was busily engaged making notches in the staff with his knife.

"I see Englishmen for chief Powhatan."

"What do you mean?"

"He tell me to tell him how many men and women are in England. I make a cut in stick every time I see English man or woman. Then when I go back he will know how many people are here."

He was very serious. I did not have the heart to tell him he would require several sticks a day when he reached London and perhaps a whole boatload of sticks before we returned to Virginia. He had devised what seemed a logical system and, in some parts of the world, what would be a practical system. I would leave him to discover for himself how practical it would be in England.

When we were finally made fast to the pier, a gangplank was thrust out and we made ready to disembark. By protocol, Sir Thomas Dale, should have been the first to leave the ship. He declined, however, saying that Pocahontas should precede him. He even indicated that I should accompany her but I insisted that he debark before me which he did. On hand to greet us was the Admiral of the port, Sir Lewis Stukely, a dignitary of impressive girth and military appearance.

"Sir Lewis, may I present Lady Rebecca, daughter of King Powhatan of Virginia?"

"Welcome to Plymouth, Lady Rebecca. I am at your service."

"Thank you, Sir Lewis," replied Pocahontas, smiling at the admiral who was no doubt astonished to see a copper skinned woman in conventional English dress.

"Sir Thomas," remarked Admiral Stukely, "you will forgive me if I ask for your instructions before we withdraw for refreshments at my headquarters."

"Certainly, sir. In what way can I be of assistance?"

"It would be most convenient if you could tell me how you wish to proceed to London. You may go overland, a distance of over 170 miles, or you may sail aboard the *Treasurer,* a longer journey but a much more comfortable one. I might add, that by sailing, you will be able to disembark on the Thames below London and then proceed by barge."

Sir Thomas Dale, who had first conceived the plan for Pocahontas to visit England, was not blind to the greater opportunities for impressing the public by arriving in London on a barge, possibly even a royal barge. It would be easier to warn friends of our exact arrival time and, as the admiral said, the prospect of a more comfortable trip on the *Treasurer*.

"We would be most grateful, Sir Lewis, if you would send a courier to advise the Virginia Company hat we will depart Plymouth on the *Treasurer* and would be pleased to be accommodated on the barge."

"It will be done," he said, extending his arm to Pocahontas. "And now, allow me to welcome you to England properly."

To Sir Lewis Stukely went the privilege of being the first person after our arrival to be captivated by Pocahontas. She sat in the seat of honor next to him at table where he found conversation easy with an attractive, vivacious woman whose command of English far exceeded what he might have expected. Despite her youthfulness, she was accustomed to being in the company of men of high position. She treated the admiral with respect but was not awed by him. For his part, I believe he was disappointed that we were to spend so short a time at Plymouth. Even as we ate the luncheon provided by Sir Lewis, men were working at the dock to replenish the stores of the *Treasurer* so that we could sail the next day.

It required two full weeks for us to round the southern coast of England and make our way into the River Thames. Apparently someone highly placed in the Virginia Company had interceded for us because a royal barge was provided for our use on the Thames.

"I expect Lord De La Warr had something to do with this," said said Marshal Dale as he viewed the brightly painted barge.

"Not to mention your own position as governor of Virginia," I added.

"It's true I was governor, but only acting governor. Lord De La Warr is governor for life. He is held in high regard at court. Always remember, Rolfe, the importance of having friends in high position."

"I will, sir," I said, agreeing to a principle that I had long recognized as being important to a person's advancement.

What a colorful sight we must have been in the barge. The crew were in their livery of crimson and gold. Sir Thomas Dale wore his uniform with a plumed hat and Pocahontas her dress with full skirt and high-ruffed neck. The Indian contingent was resplendent in white buckskin and bright paint. Tomocomo wore both a snake and the head of a hawk in his hair. He was bound to create a stir in London.

Now that we were between the banks of a river where people were clearly visible, Tomocomo had resumed his census, making notches quickly in his stick. By the time we reached the palaces at Greenwich, however, he had no further room for cutting on the stick and, with a disgusted expression, consigned it to the river. I sympathized with the poor fellow. What might have been a practical technique when numbering a tribe in coastal Virginia had been sadly deficient in England.

I was sufficiently familiar with the sights of London to point out important landmarks to Pocahontas.

"What is that big house?" she asked, pointing to the Tower of London. "Is that a castle?"

"It has been a castle for several kings," I replied. "But now it is used as an armory and a prison for enemies of the king. It is called the Tower of London."

"I would not want to be a prisoner there."

"You are in no danger of ever going there, I assure you."

"And what is that, over the river?" she said pointing to the structure looming before us.

"That, my dear, is London bridge. It is probably the most famous bridge in the world."

"It looks like it is made of stone."

"It is."

"And there are houses on it, many houses."

"Many people live on the bridge and work in the shops there. Captain Yeardley told me that his father's shop is on the bridge."

Tomocomo approached us and touched Pocahontas on the arm. He pointed to the south tower gate of the bridge where the heads of executed felons were displayed on staffs rising high in the air.

"Those men were criminals, Tomocomo. Their heads are to warn thieves who come into the city."

Tomocomo nodded. He understood perfectly.

The barge now turned and proceeded toward the wharf of the Tower of London. My first inkling that Lord De La Warr might be there to greet us was sight of his company of soldiers in their red uniforms. This was the same company that he had brought to Virginia; it had paraded numerous times at ceremonies in Jamestown. The sight of the soldiers had drawn a crowd of onlookers. Even more people crowded the banks after the Tower Artillery fired a welcoming salute. The firing of the salute startled some of our Indians who were still not accustomed to the idea of salutes. The great puffs of smoke and the noise emanating from the Tower made them uncomfortable. Little Thomas, who was being cared for by Pocahontas' sister Mattachanna began to cry. But he was soon placated and caught up in what was going on around him.

Lord De La Warr was not the only one on hand to greet us. Lady Dale, who had hardly seen her husband during their entire marriage, was on the wharf. Beside her was Sir Thomas Smythe, the Treasurer of the Virginia Company, along with several government officials.

"John, is that not Ralph Hamor?"

"I believe you are right, Pocahontas."

"I will be glad to talk to him again."

I gazed at the faces of the crowd of welcomers but was unable to find my brother Henry.

"You see, Pocahontas, you already have friends here in England."

She looked at me and smiled. "Sometimes you treat me like a child, John Rolfe."

Approaching the wharf and debarking was done much more quickly from a barge than from the *Treasurer*. The oarsmen, with the precision gained from frequent practice, moved the barge smartly to the wharf where it was made fast. Within minutes we were ashore awaiting the opportunity to greet Lord De La Warr who treated us with great ceremony and good will. He personally greeted each of the Indian party and introduced them to Sir Thomas Smythe and the government officials. I had to admit to a sense of pride in the splendid appearance of the Indians. Chief Powhatan could not have sent a more impressive looking group to represent him in England.

I felt a hand on my shoulder. "There you are, John. How good to see you." It was Ralph Hamor.

"You and Pocahontas have been busy I see." He nodded toward Thomas whom Pocahontas had taken from her sister.

"You always were a keen observer, Ralph," I replied. "Tell me. How is your father?"

"He died last year."

"I am sorry to hear that."

"I am convinced that London is not a healthy place. Even Virginia is healthier once you are seasoned. I will be glad to return there."

"That is good news. Good men are needed."

"Thank you. I presume you have had good fortune with your tobacco?"

"We brought two thousand pounds of the best leaf with us on the *Treasurer.*"

"And you had a good crossing?"

"Yes. We lost no one except for the traitor Lembri who was hung when we reached the coast of England."

"He was a strange man. I always felt there was something false about him. But on a more pleasant note, I understand that you and your party are to stay at the Belle Savage Inn."

"The Belle Savage Inn. I have never heard of it. You must be joking." Who would think of sending our Indians to a place with such a name?

"It is rather well known and very close to St. Paul's I too was struck by the name but I am told that the place has been so named for decades. There is no intent to offend."

"Who made the arrangements?"

"Why, the Virginia Company, I'm sure."

I was in no position to object. Since the Company was paying, it was up to them to make the arrangements. This moment of arrival was intended to be a triumph. It should not be spoiled.

At that moment, Pocahontas, who was standing next to Lord De La Warr, spied Ralph Hamor. As she smiled, Ralph moved off to greet her. She turned her attention from several men in order to speak to Ralph. When we had said farewell to him in Virginia we had not known if we would ever see him again.

After what had been an enthusiastic greeting at the Tower wharf the entire group, greeters and greeted, moved off to carriages that took us to rooms that had been engaged by the Virginia Company for a private reception. We were cheered and applauded by the crowds during the short ride with most of the attention given to the Indians. For their part, the Indians seemed to be growing accustomed to their celebrity. Tomocomo waved to the people and the other Indian men followed his example.

At the reception hall we met more people who were investors in the Virginia Company. I was asked to join Lord De La Warr, Sir Thomas Dale, and Pocahontas in a line to receive each of the invited guests. Although it was a less boisterous atmosphere than the Tower wharf there was nevertheless a feeling of excitement in the air. After all, the money of these investors had returned them little over the years and our arrival seemed to signal a new era in the history of the Virginia venture. Sir Thomas Smythe, the principal officer, asked me if I had the report that had been prepared for the King. I told him the report was complete and that I hoped it would meet with his approval. He replied that he would like to see a copy at my earliest convenience and that he was sure it would be the object of great interest.

Finally, the festivities, that included much toasting, drew to a close. We then moved by carriages to the Belle Savage Inn. On the way we were assaulted by the smells from the streets that were little more than open sewers. I thought of Ralph Hamor's remarks about London not being a healthy place. Although the Indians with us could not help but be impressed by the Tower and London Bridge, they likewise could not fail to be repelled by the stench.

The attention of all was soon diverted by our arrival at the

Belle Savage Inn. It was a large and rather antiquated establishment with an arch through which our coaches entered an interior courtyard. In the courtyard there was an impromptu stage. We interrupted the rehearsal of actors who stared at us as we descended and were greeted by the innkeeper.

I was pleasantly surprised by the spacious and clean room provided for Pocahontas and me. The innkeeper informed us that this room was reserved for what he called persons of quality.

Our Indian men shared a room together as did the women. They were crowded but I heard no complaint. That night they were entertained by the theater in the courtyard. No doubt they understood little of the speech but much of the performance involved action that was easy enough to understand.

I could not help but feel that our accommodations were somewhat incongruous for the circumstances. We had ridden that day on a royal barge, been greeted by a titled lord at the Tower of London, and had been honored guests at a reception of the Virginia Company. All of this befitted Pocahontas, the daughter of a king. But now our quarters were in a tavern, open to the public including any patron, no matter how rude, as long as he had coin to pay his way. The situation was an indicator of the economic status of the Virginia Company.

From our first day in London the Virginia Company took every opportunity to acquaint both the leaders of society and the populace at large with Pocahontas and the members of her entourage. They were living proof that there was a land beyond the seas, an exotic land whose people had now become our friends and would help us to exploit its riches. The public was encouraged to think that shares in the Virginia Company would be a good investment.

There was scarcely a day when we were not invited to some luncheon or dinner. Pocahontas and I were invariably invited as well at Tomocomo. We were careful that Tomocomo was not excluded because he had been appointed as Powhatan's representative and a slight to him might be considered a slight to Powhatan. A notable event to which we were invited was a dinner by Dr. King, the Lord Bishop of London, at his Lambeth

Palace. The Lord Bishop showed the utmost courtesy to Pocahontas and appeared to be charmed by her. It was only natural that he should take an interest in the Indian princess who, by her acceptance of Christianity, indicated that the new world was fertile ground for the spread of our religion. For her part, Pocahontas even advanced the concept of a school for Indian children in Virginia where they might be taught by English teachers and learn the principles of Christianity.

It was a different story when the Lord Bishop questioned Tomocomo through an interpreter. That Indian had not been won over to Christianity and had no interest whatsoever in any religion but his own. Tomocomo became almost as great a focus of attention as Pocahontas during his stay in England and his staunch adherence to Okee had a great deal to do with that attention. One Englishman who was particularly drawn to Tomocomo was Samuel Purchas, an erudite clergyman, who was interested in all details of life in Virginia. After many hours of conversation with Tomocomo and marveling at his occult incantations as he called upon Okee, Purchas concluded that the Indian priest could never be swayed from his native gods. Tomocomo himself agreed with this conclusion and told Purchas that he might be more successful winning over the other Indians in Pocahontas' retinue.

Although Pocahontas did not find Tomocomo agreeable, nothing was able to diminish her excitement and enthusiasm during our first months in London. "Do you not find Tomocomo tiresome?" I asked when we returned from the palace of the Lord Bishop.

"He wants everyone to pay attention to him. Sometimes this causes him to be a fool."

"Do you think he hates us?"

She paused to consider. "No, but I do not think he loves us." Then she continued, "You must not let him upset you. Give him attention and he will be happy."

I was silent. She was right of course and I had to remember that someday Tomocomo would return to Powhatan to report on the English and their ways. What Tomocomo saw and felt could conceivably affect our relations with Powhatan.

"Did you ever see such a beautiful building?" She was referring to the Lambeth palace of the Lord Bishop.

"What did you like best about it?"

"I think the light above us from the many candles." She had been impressed by the ornate chandeliers in the dining hall of the palace.

"Did you enjoy your conversation with the Lord Bishop?"

"He is a very kind man. He spoke to me as if I were the Queen."

"He meets many important people and is accustomed to talking with royal persons."

"What is most important is that he is kind. In my father's village, a high priest would wish to frighten you. He would want you to fear him. He would wear a terrible mask and paint to look fearsome."

"Well, you have nothing to fear from the Lord Bishop of London. I think that he is now devoted to the Lady Rebecca."

"Do not make fun of me," she said severely, but then she smiled.

"Have I ever made fun of you? Besides, we must talk now about the lottery to be held tomorrow. It will be held at St. Paul's Cathedral."

"Good. That is not far away."

"True. We can walk there if you like. Sir Thomas Smythe from the company will be there to conduct the drawing on the cathedral steps."

"Drawing?"

"Yes, the drawing means the choosing of a written number from a box. It will match a written number held by someone who paid for this piece of paper. There are prizes of money and also of shares of ownership in the Virginia Company."

"What do you expect of me?"

"The Virginia Company has asked that you and your entire retinue be present. As you know, the people of London are anxious to see the natives of Virginia."

"I must ask Mattachanna. One of the women was sick today but perhaps she can come."

I was not surprised that one of the Indians had fallen sick, given the conditions in London. With the coming of cooler weather, the smoke of a thousand fireplaces hung over Ludgate Hill where the Belle Savage Inn was located. When added to the foul vapors that were trapped under the blanket of smoke it could not have been an environment more alien to the Indians. But they were all young and sturdy so I believed they only needed to become seasoned to the London climate. In this I was wrong; the absence of one of the women from the lottery was just the beginning of the seemingly irreversible illnesses that stretched throughout the autumn and winter ahead.

The lottery drawing was nevertheless a great success. There was excitement in the air and much good natured cheering for the winners of prizes, whether large or small. At the conclusion the Indians consented to dance for the crowd. This was such a success that the spectators crowded in to get close to Pocahontas. Fortunately, we were able to escort her to the carriage of Sir Thomas Smythe in order to return to the Belle Savage.

I was pleased by the interest shown in Pocahontas by Lady De La Warr. Knowing her husband, I was aware that he was a man of great energy and determination. But his wife was every bit his equal, channeling her energies into escorting Pocahontas to functions and preparing her for the events in which she would participate. Pocahontas was often invited to the De La Warr mansion for luncheon or teas. On days when I was not invited I would visit the men called factors in London to whom we made sales of tobacco. They were especially pleased with the leaf I had brought from Virginia on the *Treasurer*. I was told there were literally thousands of tobacco shops now in London and that there was no limit on the amount of tobacco the factors would be willing to buy from me.

It was on one of our visits to Lady De La Warr that Pocahontas was informed she would soon have an audience with the Queen. "I expect that you will receive the invitation today," said Lady De La Warr with obvious pleasure. She and her friends had been lobbying to have Pocahontas presented. A self-satisfied smile played over her features. And why not? This is what persons of high rank seemed to live for, recognition that they and their friends were welcome at the court of King James and Queen Anne. To me this seemed a dubious honor. For one thing, the King lived apart from the Queen and showed more interest in young male courtiers than in her. For another, the royal couple was notorious for making extravagant expenditures that far exceeded the revenues allowed them by Parliament. Nevertheless we had to seek royal favor because of the impact it might have on the fortunes of the Virginia Company.

"We must give a thought to what you will wear," said Lady De La Warr. She herself, like her husband, and indeed her entire household, were expensively attired. From what I saw of her, I do not believe that there was a moment of the day that that lady was not conscious of what she was wearing. But she was helpful and generous and was somehow able to discuss dress and manners without a trace of condescension.

"I would like to wear the clothes I wore for my portrait," said Pocahontas.

"Describe them for me."

"I wore a full skirt, an embroidered tunic with a wide lace collar, and a hat. The picture is finished so you will see it soon."

"It is an engraving," I said, "so many copies will be made."

"We must arrange for a different collar and perhaps a different hat. We don't want people thinking you only have one costume. By the way," said Lady De La Warr, addressing herself to me, "did you like this engraving?"

I hesitated. The artist was Simon van de Passe who made engravings of many highly placed persons. "I must say, the picture is accurate with regard to costume. But I cannot say it is a good likeness of Rebecca. The features are too hard in my opinion."

"He is right," said Pocahontas, "it makes me look too old."

"I am sorry to hear that. We must arrange for a better likeness; perhaps one with your son."

"I would like that."

We then heard a discussion of the rules of protocol at court. Pocahontas listened attentively, as did I. I had no concern about her actions. She was such a self-possessed person she would naturally do the graceful thing in any situation. I was more concerned about myself.

I need not have been. Lady De La Warr said to me, "I must tell you, John, that the invitation to court will only be extended to Lady Rebecca."

I was stunned and could not make a reply. Every Englishman I had met on our return had treated me with respect, particularly because of my marriage to Pocahontas. Why should royalty act differently?

"Why is my husband not to be invited?" asked Pocahontas.

"Because he is a commoner married to royalty."

"Then I will not go either."

"That would be a grave error. Too many people have worked to ensure your invitation. Not appearing would be offensive. I agree that this appears to be strange behavior by our sovereign. But frankly, I must say that our king is a strange man and he is given to doing petty things. This is a great opportunity for you, Lady Rebecca, and you must make the most of it."

Pocahontas was displeased that I would not go to meet Queen Anne but she got over it. On the carriage ride back to the Belle Savage Inn she said, "I know what kings are like. My father is a king and he will do bad things to people for what seems like no reason. But there usually is a reason and it is because something the person did might hurt the king. Sometimes it is a very small thing. We have to remember that a king is different from you or me. He has to think about being king all the time."

My mind was taken off the slight by a visit later in the day from my brother Henry. He had been unable to come to London to welcome us upon our arrival but since then had called on us several times. We had a noisy supper at the Belle Savage in the company of the Indian retinue. They were a source of great interest to Henry and I knew that he would carry many stories about them when he returned to our family home at Heacham.

The invitation of Pocahontas to court arrived the next day. Anticipation of the visit caused great excitement that Pocahontas was able to transmit to her entire entourage. They did not accompany her but assisted in preparations and were present when Lady De La Warr appeared in her coach to escort Pocahontas to the palace. I confess that I was likewise excited. Our access to the Queen could be important to the Virginia Company.

I was anxious to question Pocahontas upon her return.

"Were you admitted directly to see the Queen?" I asked.

"We did not have to wait but we had first to pass through many rooms. There were guards, many guards, and important men that Lady De La Warr knew."

"Do you remember who they were?"

"No. There were too many to remember, but I knew they were important because of the ribbons and jewels that they wore."

"So you were taken to the Queen's reception room?"

"Yes. I did exactly as I was told to do by Lady De La Warr. I must have pleased the Queen because she was very kind to me."

"Were there other ladies?"

"Oh, yes. All of them wearing the most beautiful dresses and wearing the most beautiful jewels. But the Queen had the most beautiful jewels of all. Her hair is the color of gold; no, it is like the sun, almost white."

"And you said she was kind to you?"

"Yes. At first I could hardly understand what she was saying. Then I got used to the way she spoke."

"She was not English at birth. She is from Denmark."

"Well, I was not born English either but we could understand each other. She told me that she had two sons, Henry and Charles, but that Henry had died. I told her that there was a fort named for each of her sons near Kecoughtan."

"Did you tell her about Cape Henry and Cape Charles?"

"She knew about them, but not about the forts. She said we must name something for her daughter Elizabeth."

"Did you meet Elizabeth?"

"No, but she said she would have me meet her the next time I came to court."

"Did she talk about Virginia and the colony there?"

"Some. She said that she had heard I saved the life of Captain John Smith and had brought food to the settlers at Jamestown. That was kind but I do not think she was really very interested in Jamestown. I do think that she was interested in me because she asked me questions about my father and how the Indians lived."

"What did you tell her?"

"I told her about how the women farmed and the men hunted. She laughed and said that her husband hunted all the time but she did not have to farm."

"It sounds as if she enjoys a jest."

"Yes. She and her ladies were always finding a reason to laugh. Is it true that the King hunts all the time?"

"From what I hear, that is his main occupation. I wish that he would spend more time on affairs of state. If he did, perhaps our colony would receive more attention and support."

It was apparent that Pocahontas' visit to court had been a success. She soon received another invitation from the queen as well as invitations to balls and theatrical events. I thought that some of these events were a drain on her energy but she insisted on attending and seemed to enjoy them all.

Not all of the Indians fared as well as Pocahontas. The youngest of the Indian women became seriously ill, without the energy to leave her bed. This caused us a great deal of concern. The Belle Savage Inn was not a quiet place and with all the unmarried women in a single room, it did not seem possible for the young woman to get the rest she needed. When Sir Thomas Smythe learned about her grave illness he insisted that she be brought to his house where she might be better tended. This was done with great tenderness and concern for the sick girl. One of her Indian companions accompanied her to the Smythe household to care for her. She was attended there by the best physicians we were told, but to no avail. On a chilly October morning we were informed that the young Indian woman had died. We sadly attended her funeral the next day at St. Dionis' Church.

∼42∼

The first death in the group of Indians that had accompanied Pocahontas made us aware that they were as vulnerable to ill health when living in England as the first English settlers had been when living in Virginia. Indeed, we had constant reminders when we heard them coughing or when they were too ill to accompany us to events for which we continued to receive invitations. For my part, I told myself that our visit to England was not indefinite and that we would be returning to Virginia where everyone would be freed from the oppressive air of London. Besides, many Londoners coughed and spit throughout the winter months, seemingly without serious effects. While Pocahontas herself was not exempt from occasional coughing, her vitality was not affected. Or so I thought, without realizing that on many occasions it cost her great effort to maintain her energy and interest in our activities.

We continued to have a full schedule. Largely due to the appeal of Pocahontas, we were at the center of the social season and received many visitors and invitations. Probably our most distinguished visitor was Sir Walter Raleigh who called upon us at the Belle Savage Inn. I had long admired this intrepid sailor and adventurer who had established the first colony in Virginia. Although the Roanoke Colony had been unsuccessful it had brought back much information about the land and the native people.

"He does not look well," said Pocahontas after Raleigh had left.

"He has spent more than ten years in the Tower of London as a prisoner. Although treated well, confinement must have been a heavy burden."

"He asked many questions about my father. But I think he was most interested in talking to you about tobacco."

"He has probably done more to spread the use of tobacco in England than any other man. I am very grateful to him for that."

"He has a head of silver but he carries himself like a young warrior."

"There is no question he is a very brave man."

"Do you think we might go to the Tower to visit his friend who is still in prison?"

"That would be the Earl of Northumberland. I see no reason why not."

"I find Sir Walter to be most charming. Even more than you, John."

"I take it as a compliment to even be compared with such a man."

We had been in England for nearly six months and I had never received an invitation to court, unlike Pocahontas who had met the King and was the frequent guest of the Queen. Naturally, this was a great disappointment because I had labored long on my report on the Virginia Colony that I forwarded to the King soon after arriving in London. I had gone to great pains to detail the location of our various settlements, however modest, to show that we had indeed gained a foothold over an area that extended at least one hundred miles up the James River. I had also described the peace that had been achieved after many years of conflict with Powhatan. This peaceful condition I would think to be of great interest to the King and his ministers because it finally removed the great hindrance that existed to successful colonization.

I expected my report of the animals and plants that flourish in Virginia to be of interest to the King. Notwithstanding, the only query that our monarch made was whether a flying squirrel might be provided to him for his private collection of animals. Could it be that the King retained his animus towards tobacco and associated me directly with the development of a plant more readily available to his subjects? Regardless, the King was singularly unsuccessful at inculcating distaste for tobacco in his subjects. Possibly the greatest difference I noticed in London in 1616 and the London that I left in 1609 was the multitude of tobacco shops that had sprung up since then. I thought that our government would have rejoiced in the availability of tobacco from other than Spanish sources.

Nor should our King, being at least outwardly a pious man, have shunned the great opportunity that existed in Virginia for the propagation of the Gospel of Jesus Christ. While the Lord Bishop of London promised support, the silence of the King on this subject was likely a measure of his lack of concern for the Indians to whom I believe we had a Christian duty.

It may be that I did the King injustice; he may have been pursuing these matters with his ministers without further recourse to intelligence that I was able to provide him. But I fear otherwise. I fear that he was too much obsessed with his hunting, his attractive young men, and his intemperate use of alcohol to give much thought to the opportunities open to England in the new world.

A conversation that would have amused had it not been rather pathetic took place between Pocahontas and Tomocomo on the morning after they met the King at a Whitehall reception.

"What did you think of the King?" asked Pocahontas.

"What King? I have not seen a king since Powhatan."

"You were presented to the King last night."

"I have no such memory. I was with you when we spoke to the Queen. She told me that she wanted me to come and dance for her."

"Yes I heard her tell you that. But did you not notice the man beside her?"

"The man with the sad face? His clothes were very dirty. I did not want to touch him."

"He was dirty. But that was the King."

"I do not believe it. Powhatan says I am supposed to speak to the King but I do not want to speak to a man in such dirty clothes."

Tomocomo's experience was not surprising. The King had the reputation for being quite careless of his appearance. Because he believed himself to be beyond criticism, members of his court had given up trying to improve his slovenly appearance. For my part, I was resentful that our sovereign presented such a poor appearance to an uneducated visitor from Virginia that he was unrecognizable as a king. I consoled myself by asking why I should be concerned since the King ignored my report from Virginia.

With the approach of winter, the atmosphere of London grew more oppressive. Another person in Pocahontas' retinue became seriously ill, this time it was one of the young men. Once again, Sir Thomas Smythe offered to have the patient removed to his home but the result was no improvement and the young man died. We attended the funeral service as did all the Indians even though half of them appeared to be too sick to be there. It was a time of sadness.

We might have given in to the spirit of melancholy had it not been for two things. One was the brightness of Pocahontas that never flagged. The other was the arrival of the season of Christmas. Even before Christmas day the churches of London began a chiming that lasted throughout the season. Carolers were everywhere, especially at the Belle Savage Inn and on many nights there were fireworks along the Thames River. There were even more feasts and entertainments than before. Many of them took place at court and I will not attempt to describe them except for one notable event that was the talk of London.

Although the King and the Queen had little in common and did not spend much time in each other's company they both enjoyed balls and masques. This year the masque was to be held on the Twelfth Night of Christmas which was on January 5, 1617. It was rumored that the King had said that no expense would be spared and that the playwright Ben Jonson had been commissioned to write the play that was to be the principal entertainment. Jonson himself had called upon Pocahontas at the Inn, although she was not impressed by his demeanor. As time passed we heard reports of the construction taking place within the royal banqueting hall where the masque would be held.

When it became apparent that Pocahontas and Tomocomo

would be invited to the masque but that I would not, Pocahontas asked Lady De La Warr to intercede on my behalf. This was done and on the day before the event I was informed that I was invited to observe, but not attend, the Twelfth Night Revels. I was to sit in the musicians' gallery along with a few foreign diplomats who were precluded from receiving invitations for diplomatic reasons.

An advantage to sitting in the musicians' galley was that one could observe the entire tableau clearly as well as the dais on which the royal party was seated. I could easily see the King and the Queen. Both were resplendent in clothing that must have been made for the occasion. I was pleased that Pocahontas and Tomocomo were seated close to the King, on his right hand. Because those of us in the gallery were not invited for dinner we had to content ourselves with peering about to see the famous personages in attendance. The diplomats about me were happily noting that neither the French nor the Spanish ambassadors had been invited because of threats of an international incident. The entire evening had an international flavor for me because foreign guests occupied most of the gallery seats and the musicians were from France. Their presence must have added to the cost of the event.

When the guests had finished their dinner, the lights were dimmed in the banqueting hall and our eyes were drawn to the beautiful stage settings. There followed a succession of scenes in which the narrator declaimed the couplets of Ben Jonson while the actors moved about the stage or danced in costumes that were often fantastic. I felt that I had never looked at scenes of such unnatural beauty and only wished that I had been seated next to Pocahontas to see her reaction.

From time to time, members of the audiences were drawn into spectacle. These, I reckoned, were favorites of the King and Queen, who were singled out for their ability to dance and could enter readily into the scene. For relief, there were clowns and, as the play progressed, the scenes became more fantastic. Tomocomo, who was used to apparitions, must have been impressed. At a word from the master of ceremonies the chaos dissolved and was replaced by order. This sudden restoration of harmony was attributed to none other than our monarch, King James. We rose to our feet to applaud the players, the musicians, and Ben Jonson who modestly appeared for a brief recognition.

Although the spectacle was over, the celebration of Twelfth Night continued with much music, dancing and toasting. I was able to make my way unobtrusively from the gallery and the banquet hall. I returned to our lodgings alone, disappointed not to have accompanied Pocahontas but pleased to have at least seen the masque.

~43~

I had never been satisfied with our lodgings at the Belle Savage Inn. Although the rooms were quite adequate in size and were well-furnished and meals were properly prepared and decently served, there was no escaping the fact that we were continually subjected to the noise and bustle of a crowded inn in the very heart of London. Upon some reflection, I concluded that this situation had been created deliberately by the Virginia Company. The company directors wanted us to be on view. Our very presence served as an advertisement for the reality of a viable colony established beyond the seas in a land populated by Indians. It was a situation that I was not inclined to oppose in our first days in London. Soon after, we were caught up in a round of activities and I did not have the opportunity to seek an improvement in the situation.

We had some respite from social activities after the Twelfth Night gala at Whitehall Palace. I then sought out Sir Thomas Smythe and Sir Edwin Sandys, the two most influential leaders of the Virginia Company. I informed them of the need to get our group removed to a location that was more restful. The health of the Indians was at stake. Smythe was agreeable because he was only too aware of the conditions as they existed but he seemed slow to propose a solution. Sandys, on the other hand, saw the need for immediate action and proposed to find better accommodations without delay.

Within a few days we were relocated in Brentford, a village nine miles up the Thames River. All of the Indians, including Pocahontas, were pleased to leave the city. The most noticeable difference to me was in the air; I could see the sun where before there were only dark clouds. I took deep breaths free from acrid

304

smoke and the gutter smells of London. Not only were the streets swept clean but also the crowds that surged through London were absent. Almost as important, at least to the Indians, was the accessibility of a much cleaner stretch of the Thames River. To Pocahontas and Matachanna the open environment afforded the opportunity to take little Thomas out in fresh air where the boy might walk and play without being jostled by the crowds that were always present in London.

The freer atmosphere of the village caused me to think of my home village at Heacham. My mother and brother Edward still lived there and, although we had corresponded, I had not seen them since returning to England. On an impulse I informed Sir Thomas Smythe that I would be away for two weeks and made arrangements for a coach to carry us to Norfolk. There were just the three of us and Matachanna. I did not offer Tomocomo the opportunity to accompany us. By then, I had grown weary of his moods which increasingly were unagreeable.

"Do not trouble yourself, John," said Pocahontas. "He is busy walking about the village and with the priests who continue to seek him out."

It was true that Tomocomo never ceased to be an object of interest to clergymen who wanted to learn about his heathen practices and then convert him if possible. None ever succeeded.

"Besides," she continued, "Matachanna would like to get away from him for a while."

Tomocomo's outlet for his growing discontent with England was to complain to anyone who would listen. I could understand how his patient wife would need a respite from his diatribes.

Heacham, in Norfolk, was even more tranquil than Brentford. I was especially glad to have left Tomocomo behind because the sight of him would have caused a stir among the local people. Even my relatives did not become quite accustomed to Mattachanna during the few days of our stay. Pocahontas, on the other hand, did not differ from them in dress or in language. I believe that both my brother Edward and his wife were quite taken with her and made her feel quite welcome at our family home, Heacham Hall.

"I believe I like Heacham as much as London," said Pocahontas.

"But it is so quiet here."

"Your brother has a fine house and so does your mother." After my father's death when I was a boy my mother had remarried and lived nearby.

"You realize, Pocahontas, that we must soon return to Virginia."

"Why must we go? You have one brother here and one brother in London. You can live in either place."

"Our future is in Virginia. We have land there and I have the position of recorder for the colony. We will probably become wealthy from tobacco."

"You and your brother Henry can become wealthy from tobacco here in England. What does it gain you to be wealthy in Virginia when everything is here in England? I think we should stay here."

"We have been treated as royalty in England it is true. Or at least you have, Pocahontas. But that is only a social recognition. Our true position depends upon what we do. What I do in Virginia can benefit England and us more than what I could do here. That is why we must return."

She was silent but I could tell that she was not convinced. She did not bring up the subject again until after we returned to London.

Upon our return I wasted no time in informing Sir Edwin Sandys that I thought we should be returning soon to Virginia, We had accomplished our purposes in England, insofar as possible. More money had been raised for the Virginia Company including a small amount for a school for Indian children. The King, although giving no money for the school, had agreed with the proposal. The market for tobacco was assured. It was time to return to Virginia to produce tobacco. I found Sir Edwin to be sympathetic and hoped for a sailing in February of 1617.

After all the time that we had spent in England, I was

surprised to hear that none other than Captain John Smith, whom many believed to be the savior of the settlers arriving in Virginia in 1607, desired to come visit Pocahontas. Although he had written a letter to Queen Anne on Pocahontas' behalf he had not troubled to bring himself from the west country of England to visit Pocahontas. It was true that he had been engaged in several sailings to the new world since returning in 1609 and he was actively promoting further explorations. Even so, that did not seem sufficient justification for not visiting Pocahontas to whom he attributed the saving of his life, indeed the life of the entire colony.

"It is up to you, Pocahontas. You do not have to see him if you do want to. He does not enjoy much good will among the leaders of the Virginia Company." I admit I was disturbed by what I considered Smith's cavalier attitude toward Pocahontas. I would not have cared if she refused to see him.

"Of course I will see him. If you believe that I helped the people at Jamestown then how could I refuse to see him? Then I would be showing no better manners than he has."

"You would not want that, would you?"

I could only agree. And so it happened that two of the three major participants in the early days of our colony's history met in the inn at Brentford, England. The third participant, of course, was Powhatan. I wondered how he would have felt about meeting with his enemy, John Smith. Or perhaps he did not consider him his enemy. He had, after all, spared his life; and while Smith was in Virginia he had refrained from war against the colonists. Perhaps Powhatan had mixed feelings about Smith as I did.

I greeted Smith when he arrived to visit. I found him to be smaller of stature than I had expected. He had a strong grip, however, and carried himself like a confident athlete. If he was embarrassed to be calling so late upon Pocahontas there was nothing in his manner that belied it.

"I must congratulate you, Rolfe, on your marriage to Pocahontas."

"Thank you, Captain Smith. I think you will find her quite different from the young girl whom you knew in Virginia."

"Not in spirit, nor in intellect, I am sure. I have always thought of her and referred to her as the nonpareil. There is no one like her."

At that moment Pocahontas opened the door and walked in. Smith stood as if dumbstruck. The adolescent girl he had last seen in Virginia stood now before him in the dress of an English lady. Saying nothing, she extended her hand and he, after a moment's hesitation moved forward to take it. Suddenly she lowered her hand, then raised both hands to her face to cover her features. Obviously quite overcome with emotion, quickly turned on her heels and left the room.

"I seem to have upset her," said Smith.

"For several years she thought that you had died. It was not until we came to England that she learned that you had survived."

After about ten minutes, I excused my self and went to find Pocahontas. She appeared to have dried her tears and had composed herself but was still visibly upset. I asked if I should dismiss Smith but she shook her head, saying in a small voice that she would join us. I then returned to Smith who seemed content to sit and talk with me for several hours, asking me many questions about the state of the Virginia colony. He listened intently to every word about Virginia and I could tell that he felt a passionate attachment to the land. It was unfortunate that his contentious nature had made so many enemies for him and that he would probably never return in the employment of the Virginia Company.

With the passage of time, I felt he was so involved in our conversation that he might have forgotten about Pocahontas.

She had said she would return and she did. She was determined to tell Smith how badly he had treated her by ignoring her presence in England. I almost felt sorry for the man. She reproached him with words that were at once condemning and forgiving.

"You did promise Powhatan what was yours should be his, and he the like to you. You called him father being in his land a stranger."

"For seven years we have heard nothing from you and today you come to us without warning."

"Were you not afraid to come into my father's country and caused fear in him and all his people but me, and now fear that I shall call you father? I tell you then I will call you father, and you shall call me child, and so I will be forever and ever your countryman."

Hearing these words I realized that I never truly knew the depth of feeling that Pocahontas had for John Smith. She must have admired him for there was much to admire, believed there was a bond with him because he seemed to understand her well, grieved for him because she had cause to think him dead, and felt betrayed by him when he paid her no attention in England. She never discussed him further with me but I shared with her, and continue to feel, a sense of hurt for the way she had been treated.

In February it was decided that two vessels would sail for Virginia as soon as the weather permitted. We would accompany Samuel Argall on the *George* while my old friend Ralph Hamor would command the *Treasurer*. Tomocomo and Matachanna would return with us but the remainder of the Indians would stay in England where they would receive education and employment. By February another of the Indian men had become so ill as to require removal to the home of Sir Thomas Smythe.

I was growing increasingly concerned for the health of Pocahontas. I now believe that she attempted to conceal her illness by driving herself beyond her endurance rather than resting when she had the opportunity. Despite the improved air in Brentford, we were subjected to the dreary English winter consisting of cold rain and fog day after day. I felt that the best course of action was to be on our way and I urged Captain Argall to do so. But we could do nothing against unfavorable winds so that it was March before we were finally underway. It was a melancholy departure; Pocahontas did not want to leave England and I was dispirited by the thought that when we sailed for Virginia in 1609 my wife Sarah likewise had not wished to leave England.

There was nothing to raise my spirits during our journey down the Thames River. A drizzle of rain and cold wind that drove the rain down your collar greeted any of us who stepped on deck. Consequently, the passengers abandoned the deck to the crew members required to be there by their duties. We huddled instead in our cabins where, if not warm, at least we might remain dry.

We were underway for perhaps an hour when Mattachanna and I became alarmed by a change in Pocahontas' condition. We thought she was resting comfortably enough when she began an uninterrupted period of coughing. I attempted to give her a draught that might have soothed her throat but she was unable to receive it, so prolonged was her coughing. Her coughing seemed so deep and so severe that it pained us to hear it. It finally ended in a hemorrhage after which the coughing ceased and she slipped into unconsciousness.

Leaving Mattachanna at her side, I went to find Captain Argall. He came immediately and with his usual forthrightness said that we must find her a doctor.

"The next harbor is at the town of Gravesend. We will put in there."

I shuddered at the name of the place. How could anyone stand to live there?

"How long will it take to reach it?" I asked.

"About an hour. I will pull in to the pier so we do not have to lower her into a boat. I will have men standing by with a litter."

It actually required less than an hour for the *George* to dock at Gravesend. We soon had the litter on the pier and sent a man ahead to inquire where we might find an inn or tavern. Fortunately, there was a tavern not far from the foot of the pier and we soon had Pocahontas in what the landlord said was his best room. Shortly after, Pocahontas opened her eyes.

"Are we no longer on the ship?" she asked.

"No, Pocahontas."

"Why?"

"We wanted you to be more comfortable."

She smiled. "You have been a good husband, John Rolfe."

"Do not speak that way, Pocahontas."

"I will speak, and you must listen." She glanced at the other men in the room who silently withdrew,

"I have always loved you, John Rolfe. Since the first day I saw you in Jamestown; and, I say again, that you have been a good husband. But all must die."

"Pocahontas, you cannot die."

"Did you not hear me? All must die. It is enough that our child lives."

I knelt beside her bed, holding her small hand in both of mine. Neither my prayers nor my tears could keep her spirit here on earth.

~44~

So consumed was I by my grief that the events of the next few days are difficult for me to recall. There was a funeral service. It was arranged hurriedly because the *George* had to be on its way. In a dimly lit church named St. George's in the plain little village of Gravesend, the rector conducted the funeral service over the casket of Pocahontas. The Reverend Frankwell promised me that Pocahontas would be buried in the chancel beneath the large paving stones in front of the altar. Although that was an honor accorded to Pocahontas it was of scarce comfort to me.

I found it almost impossible to accept reality: that Pocahontas was gone. She who was so youthful, so energetic and bright had been snuffed out like a candle in an otherwise dark room, leaving me to grope for what was still certain and could be relied upon in my life. Besides our Creator and Savior there seemed little. My small son was sick, no doubt in danger, as was his Indian aunt. Tomocomo had grown so unsympathetic to anything English as to be no comfort. I had never felt close to Samuel Argall and, despite my determination to try to understand him, it was hard for me to trust him.

I was only beginning to realize how much I had grown to depend upon Pocahontas. Her outlook had always been so positive and hopeful and, at the same time, her ideas were pragmatic. She did not, with the possible exception of her expressed desire to remain in England, attempt to unduly influence me. Nevertheless she was ready to advise when asked for an opinion and I now needed sound advice for a pressing problem. That problem was how to care for our son Thomas.

The boy was undeniably ill. What were his chances of

survival during an ocean crossing in early spring? Before the voyage was over we would invariably be on a very limited diet. In the absence of his mother could Matachanna care for him properly or were her physical resources too drained by what was apparently the same illness that had taken Pocahontas? What was the alternative? We were to put into Plymouth before returning to Virginia. Could I arrange to have Thomas sent to my brother Henry? Who would care for him temporarily? Samuel Argall, with characteristic boldness, stepped into this dilemma and offered his advice.

"Don't be a fool, Rolfe. The lad is sick and if we keep him aboard he is likely to get sicker. If we hit rough weather, he will suffer more than we will. It is not as if his mother were here. That woman Matachanna is likely to die herself. Then what will you do? When we get to Plymouth Sir Lewis Stukely can give him a home temporarily until your brother can come down from London. Then when he is old enough to travel, he can come to Virginia."

I had lost Pocahontas. I could hardly bear the idea of voluntarily giving up Thomas, even to my dear brother Henry, for what could be a very long time. But I had to consider the risk of the crossing. Beyond that, I had to ask myself how would I care for the boy after reaching Virginia. There were very few women, if any, that I could employ to be his nurse. But then I wondered what would people think of me if I returned from England after my wife's death and also left my very young son there?

Other people felt the same way that Samuel Argall did. And I believe he approached Sir Lewis Stukely very soon after arrival in Plymouth to urge him to offer me assistance. Whether he did or not, the Admiral was quick to realize that I had a problem and quick to offer me aid. I decided to seek out my friend Ralph Hamor who had preceded us and was waiting at Plymouth with the *Treasurer*. After coming aboard the *George* and seeing the sickly condition of Thomas he also urged me to leave the boy behind.

I suppose that I was fortunate to have friends to advise me, and even more fortunate to have a brother whom I knew would treat Thomas as his own. Nevertheless, it was a sad parting for me when I left Plymouth. How would the lad feel when he realized that not only was his beloved mother gone but also that his father had gone off and left him?

Once underway in April our passage was an easy one. Matachanna improved and in three weeks was restored to health. We were spared most of the incantations of Tomocomo because the weather was not so fearsome as it had been on our previous crossing. We reached Chesapeake Bay in late May in weather so delightful as to give all the passengers a sensation of new life. Shores that had once been foreign now seemed inviting as we passed Point Comfort and sailed up the James River.

At Jamestown we received a hearty welcome that was muted by the news of Pocahontas' death. People remembered the vital appearance of Pocahontas and her retinue when they departed for England the previous year. Our settlers were inured to untimely death but they especially felt the loss of Pocahontas who was a symbol of peace with the Indians. My grief was shared by the entire colony.

George Yeardley had long been waiting the arrival of Captain Argall who would relieve him as acting governor. Yeardley's intent was to take a leave of absence to visit England.

I found myself eager to get to work. Through work I would ward off the loneliness I felt since that awful day in Gravesend when I lost Pocahontas.

My return to Bermuda Hundred was necessarily a sad event. It was as hard for my friends as for me to believe that Pocahontas, only twenty-two years of age, had been struck down by illness while in England. Elizabeth Grave and Mistress Horton were especially kind to me. They had known both Sarah, my first wife, and Pocahontas so they understood the burden of my sadness. I am not sure, however, that they believed that I should have left Thomas in England. It was not something they voiced aloud, at least not in my presence, but I sensed they felt the little boy's place was with his father.

I was also saddened by the loss of my good friend Alexander Whitaker who had drowned in an accident in March of 1617. My thoughts went back to his kindness to Pocahontas and the enthusiasm that he had shown in her education and the grounding of her Christian faith. What a brilliant mind he possessed; I have no doubt that his influence was greater in the conversion of Pocahontas than that of any man, including Sir Thomas Dale.

My land and tobacco had been well cared for by William Sparkes and his men. The plants were well started and I considered the leaves to be of good quality. I looked forward to at least doubling my exports of the previous year. It was the time of year when unwanted growth had to be chopped off so all of us were needed to tend the plants. Although sometimes I felt as though my back were breaking from bending over I was glad to have the work to occupy myself.

There was a large increase in the amount of tobacco grown. Almost every planter it seemed had at least a small amount under cultivation. I would see these plots as I traveled to and from Jamestown. As the secretary of the colony I had business there and would stay with Samuel Argall at the governor's house. George Yeardley had already departed on leave for England while Argall, with his customary self-confidence had settled into his new role as leader of the colony. I could not help noticing how well he lived on the best food available in the company's stores, served by indentured servants.

"We have to do something about Tomocomo, John."

"What has he done?" I asked.

"He had scarcely debarked from the *George* than he began spreading lies about England. Seems he felt he was badly treated and that was an insult to Powhatan because he was his representative. Says the English are dirty and don't give a damn about the Indians. He even thinks that King James should have given him presents."

"I have to say that sounds like Tomocomo."

"I wish we could consult with Powhatan because I am sure all this drivel has reached him. But Powhatan has abdicated and gone to live with the Potomacs. The chief is now his brother Opechancanough."

An invitation was sent to Opechancanough to visit

315

Jamestown, accompanied by as many of his headmen as desired. He accepted and arrived on the appointed day with three of the tribal leaders. Tomocomo was not among them. I was present at the meeting in the governor's house where, after eating and exchanging gifts, we conversed through an interpreter.

"We are sad that Pocahontas has died," said Opechancanough, looking toward me. He spoke with half closed eyelids that indeed gave him a look of sadness, an aspect that was his customary appearance.

"We too are greatly saddened and were sorry to have to send the news to Powhatan," answered Samuel Argall.

"She was his favorite daughter but he was glad that the child lives. Will the child come soon?" Again he looked toward me.

This time I answered. "When he is older and able to make the voyage."

"We are concerned," said Argall "that the death of Pocahontas does not affect the peace."

The reply came without hesitation. "I am still your brother. We want nothing more than peace."

"We are also concerned by the many things that Tomocomo has said about England."

There was no reply. Opechancanough would wait to hear more before he spoke.

"We are told," continued Argall "that he says the English, although many in numbers, are not true friends of the Indians."

There was still no reply coming from Opechancanough.

"Tomocomo seems not to realize that we have the same father, King James. He complains that King James gave him no gift. In fact, King James gave a beautiful piece of pottery to Pocahontas so Tomocomo should not feel badly. Our king does not give many gifts."

At last Opechancanough saw fit to speak. "Tomocomo speaks a lot but we have learned sometimes not to listen. I have known him since he was a small boy and he has always been that way. You should not worry. We know that you are our friends and that King James is a very great king."

I could not help but sigh with relief. The tension went out of the room and the conversation turned to other things, questions about our neighbors the Chickahominys and the quantities of fish that we had caught. Afterwards I thought the conversation had perhaps gone too smoothly. After all, Tomocomo was highly placed and the fact that Opechancanough had not brought him indicated an implacable attitude on the part of Tomocomo. But we had to accept Opechancanough's remarks at face value and so a favorable report on the meeting was sent to London.

I was saddened to hear the news in April of 1618 of Chief Powhatan's death. Although Pocahontas had taken her infant Thomas to visit her father shortly after his birth, I had never met Powhatan. I had been sent by Marshal Dale to negotiate with Powhatan years earlier but, because of the intervention of Opechancanough, was not able to see him. The rule of the Powhatan kingdom devolved upon Opitchapan and Opechancanough, the brothers of Powhatan. Few expected Opitchapan to wield real influence.

The administration of Samuel Argall as governor of the Virginia colony was not a success. Almost from the outset it was noticed how the assets of the colony were expended on his comfort and convenience. This would not have been so bad had it only applied to food. He went further, using the company land and labor to plant crops for his own profit, conducting trade with the Indians for his own account, and even outfitting the *Treasurer* as a privateer to prey on Spanish shipping.

I was in an awkward position. As a senior official of the colony, I was obligated to support Samuel Argall. I even went so far as to defend him and have since regretted doing so. Rather than curtail his excesses, as several people advised him to do he continued and even increased them. The inevitable result was criticism that eventually reached the officers of the company in England. So it happened that in 1618 Samuel Argall was to be replaced as acting governor by no less personage than Lord De La Warr himself. As permanent governor it was his privilege to come to Virginia and take control of the colony. Unfortunately, he was unable to do so. Lord De La Warr sailed from England but died before the completion of the voyage. Thus ended the life of the man who had saved the Virginia colony from extinction in 1610.

Samuel Argall was still in Virginia but he did not remain much longer. He knew that he might be sent to England for trial on the charges against him if someone came from England with the power to arrest him. In April of 1919, just prior to the return of George Yeardley who was once again appointed Governor, Samuel Argall departed Virginia for the last time. He was a man of undoubted ability, who had served the colony well on many occasions, but who did not have the integrity to hold high office.

By contrast with the self-serving ambition of Samuel Argall, one could see in George Yeardley a desire to succeed but not without willingness to serve others. Although I never discussed it with him, I feel sure that he thought that his ability to serve in colonial Virginia would be enhanced if he had a wife to share with him the responsibilities of the higher rank to which he aspired. By the time he returned from England in April of 1619, he had acquired a wife as well as a knighthood and his appointment as governor.

Lady Temperance Flowerdieu Yeardley was a handsome, blue-eyed woman with all the qualities one could desire in a governor's wife. She made the governor's house a social center for the colony where all the settlers might feel comfortable. She took an active interest in the lives of the settlers but was especially kind to me because she had met Pocahontas on several occasions in England and was perceptive enough to appreciate my feeling of loss. Partly to draw me out and partly to increase her knowledge of what was becoming Virginia's most important crop she talked to me at length about tobacco farming – my earliest experiments, the proven methods of growing, and the preparations for shipment. I found her to be quite intelligent and able to share with me the excitement of developing an exotic transplant so well adapted to Virginia.

"I find it stimulating to be at the scene of so many new developments. Do you share this feeling, John?"

"In truth, it was what brought me to Virginia, Lady Temperance. I wanted to be at a place where a man might prosper as much from the exertion he made as from the accident of his birth."

Twenty-two men were elected to the first General Assembly as burgesses. I was pleased to be one of them. The church at Jamestown was chosen as the first meeting place for the General Assembly. For those attending, which consisted of Governor Yeardley, our minister, the Council of State and the twenty-two burgesses, the building proved to be quite spacious. This was a blessing because on the 30th day of July, 1619, Jamestown fairly roasted in the Virginia sun. All of us were dressed in our finest apparel that was generally made from heavy cloth. Adding to this burden was the custom of wearing hats to meetings of this type where hats were only removed when the wearer was recognized to speak from the floor. The tolling of the church bell informed anyone in Jamestown who might have been unaware that an important occasion was about to take place.

Governor Yeardley entered in his most splendid attire to open the meeting. My old friend Richard Bucke rose to ask for God's blessing on the Assembly. I could not help thinking how steadfast he had been throughout the vicissitudes occurring since he left England ten years earlier. He was a man whose character was enhanced by adversity rather than being diminished. He was now witnessing before God to our emergence from authoritarian rule to representative government.

The first work of the General Assembly was to determine a framework of laws that would be enacted for the governance of the colony and the laws that would regulate the distribution of land. Committees were appointed that adjourned to other buildings where they could work without disturbing each other. The opportunity to move offered the delegates some relief from the sweltering heat. Later in the day they reconvened to act on the measures that the committees recommended. At that time the Assembly also considered the question of representation for Martin's Hundred.

The difficulty was caused by the unwillingness of Captain John Martin to accept any infringement on his personal right to govern the people on the land that he held by patent called Martin's Hundred. It was illogical to recognize the two burgesses who had been elected from Martin's Hundred if the laws enacted by the General Assembly would not apply there.

In an effort to resolve the dilemma, Governor Yeardley questioned Captain Martin on the floor of the Assembly. "Captain Martin, will you allow yourself and the people on your land to be governed by the laws passed by the General Assembly?"

Captain Martin rose and faced the Governor. After a lengthy pause he replied, "No sir, I will not. I will, however, rule my people justly."

Although some men in the Assembly were surprised by this response, I was not. Captain Martin had been consistent in his effort to rule his plantation like a feudal lord. It disturbed me that the personal freedom we had striven for in Virginia could be curbed by men like him who obviously favored a ruling aristocracy. I was thankful when the Assembly voted not to seat the delegates from Martin's Hundred and was pleased when Captain Martin was required to leave the Assembly.

Among the many actions taken by the Assembly was a petition to the Virginia Company to change the name of Kecoughtan, one of the principal boroughs. As explained by their delegate William Capps, the name Kecoughtan was derived from the Indian village that had previously occupied the site. Many of the settlers considered it an inappropriate name and asked that the name be changed to Elizabeth City. The new name was to honor Elizabeth, the daughter of King James and Queen Anne. While I knew that the new name would please the Queen, I found many of the Indian names to be attractive and hoped that we would not remove all of them from use.

The Assembly also took action to fix the price of best quality tobacco at three﹒shillings for the pound. The rapid increase in the quantity of Virginia grown tobacco was already having an effect on its price. Even so, a farmer could produce five times as much value from his labor growing tobacco compared with other crops.

The Assembly adjourned on August 4th after what others may have considered a short session. In retrospect, a great deal had been accomplished. To continue while suffering the extreme summer temperatures would have been unproductive. As it was, one delegate died, a victim of heat prostration.

Although I was the guest of Governor Yeardley during the session of the General Assembly I spent several evenings in the home of Lieutenant William Pierce, who had sailed for Virginia in 1609 aboard the *Blessing*. He and I were planning to cultivate a large acreage at Mulberry Island on land that I felt well suited for tobacco growing. During these evenings with William Pierce, I became reacquainted with his daughter Jane who had been a child when she first came to Jamestown. Jane had grown to be an attractive young woman and I found that I looked forward to visits to the Pierce household for the opportunity to talk to her.

Although my cultivated land at Bermuda Hundred was prospering and I had acquired even more land on the south side of the James River, I determined to establish a residence on the land at Mulberry Island. For one reason, I was saddened by the memories that engulfed me at Bermuda Hundred. Pocahontas and I had made our home there, it was the birthplace of our son Thomas who was now far away in England, and I felt deprived of their presence every time I entered the house at Bermuda Hundred. It also was sensible for me to have a residence nearer Jamestown where I had duties to perform as secretary for the colony and as a member of the Governor's Council. After seeking the advice of my friend Richard Bucke who urged me to make a fresh start, I decided to build at Mulberry Island.

When I started my house I had not admitted to myself that another reason I had for relocating was to be nearer Jane Pierce. She was, after all, almost twelve years younger than I and I had no thought that she and I might ever marry. But, as I saw her more frequently and came to appreciate her many good qualities, I realized how fortunate I would be if she would become my wife. This possibility of marriage may have occurred to her also because she readily consented to my proposal and we were married by Richard Bucke, with the blessing of her parents, in the autumn of 1619.

The land at Mulberry Island proved excellent for the cultivation of tobacco. The clearing of trees did not prove difficult because much of the area we chose to cultivate was like meadow. The slopes were gentle and there was, of course, easy access to the river for shipping our crop. It is difficult to describe the rapid growth of tobacco cultivation in the Virginia colony. Over 50,000 pounds were shipped to England in 1619 and there was continued expression of concern that too much tobacco was being grown to the exclusion of other crops.

While it might be easy to argue in the council chamber about the merits of controlling tobacco production, there was not much argument on the farms and homesteads. Our chief inducement was the availability of credit that a successful tobacco farmer received from his crop. London merchants were dispatching ships to Virginia loaded with manufactures, including fine cloths, furniture, clocks, and tools that we might purchase.

Indeed, my wife Jane and I furnished a good portion of our new home in this way. Virginia was now more than a producer of crops; it was a market.

Our population grew in pace with the economy. Investors who paid the passage of indentured persons were rewarded with fifty acres of land for each passage paid. My friend Ralph Hamor had brought sixteen such persons with him, including his brother Thomas, when he returned to Virginia. There was even a ship that put into Point Comfort with twenty Africans who were later sold as indentured servants in Jamestown. The arrival of the Africans was of interest, particularly since many of the settlers had never seen an African. This interest was small, however, compared with that occasioned by the arrival of one hundred unmarried women in Virginia.

Two ships, the *Jonathan* and the *London Merchant* arrived bringing the young women who were seeking husbands in the new world. Because some of them were joining sweethearts who were already in Virginia, the arrival was especially joyous and an occasion of much waving and calling out as the ships put in at Jamestown. Governor and Mrs. Yeardley made a great effort to ease the way of the future brides and received all of them at the Governor's house. After being welcomed, they were then assigned to families that took them into their homes in Jamestown and the other settlements. Jane and I sponsored Martha Mason who had come from Norfolk and I gave her in marriage two months later at the church in Jamestown.

Our own marriage was blessed in 1620 with the birth of a daughter Elizabeth. She in turn has been blessed with good health and, as we near the end of 1621, she is walking about the house with firm footsteps, speaking her first words with the encouragement of her fond parents. My thoughts go often to Thomas in England who is now six years old. From the letters received from his uncle Henry, he is growing into a sturdy lad. It is my hope that he will be able to join me soon in Virginia.

Sad to say, my own health has deteriorated greatly during the past year. In the summer of 1621 I contracted a persistent fever that continued unabated until the autumn with the arrival of cooler weather. The fever left me greatly diminished in weight and strength. Scarcely a night passed that I did not awake shivering with chills that no physician was able to banish either with bleeding or any physic. With these harbingers of my mortality pressing upon me I found it prudent to prepare a last will and testament this spring that provided for my family. By that will I leave to my son Thomas four hundred acres of land south of the James River near Hog Island. To my wife Jane and daughter Elizabeth I have left my interest in the 1,700 acres on Mulberry Island whose ownership I share with her father. All other property, including cattle is to be divided equally between my three heirs.

With the return of warm weather I find the fever has returned that has done so much to sap my strength. While I am still able to do so I rise for a few hours daily in order to direct the work of the men in my employ. Fortunately, we are having another good growing season and as I look out over my acres I praise God for the increase he has given us.

I shall close this chapter filled with thanks for the blessings afforded me in this life. Both my fortunes and the fortunes of this English speaking colony in Virginia are on the rise.

Everywhere I look about me I see high hopes and expectations for the future. I realize nevertheless that this may be the final season in my life, that I may have run my course, and that I must entrust my hope to my Lord and Savior. God grant that I may recover to live out my years in this great country we call Virginia. If I should not recover, I thank our God for his manifold blessings and join the countless host who praise his name forever.

Jamestown, Virginia

October 12, 1622

Master Thomas Rolfe
London, England

Dear Thomas:

Your stepmother, Jane Pierce Rolfe, asked me to read the enclosed letter from your father, along with the relation of events accompanying it, for the purpose of verifying its completeness. There has been much upheaval here in Virginia that has caused a delay in sending these documents to you. An uprising of the Indians under Opechancanough in March of this year interrupted the continuity of our lives in great measure. Over three hundred colonists are reckoned to have been killed and many documents have been lost. Fortunately, your stepmother and stepsister had moved to Jamestown which was not attacked. My brother and I were not so fortunate, our plantation was attacked and some property lost but we defended ourselves successfully.

When your father died in January, I lost my closest friend and confidant in Virginia. Reading his relation of events has brought back memories of times we shared and I am confident that this is a complete and true relation. In reading his story, I regret that I was responsible for publishing his letter to Marshal Dale that caused your father some embarrassment. This was due to the reader's perception that John Rolfe was marrying Pocahontas more out of a wish to save her soul than because he loved her. I must say that your father advanced that perception in order to win over Marshal Dale. In fact, I will attest that John Rolfe loved her unreservedly. She was irresistible, not only to him, but also to all of us who met her. We were all glad to be in her presence, even at Sunday catechism on a cold winter evening in remotest Virginia.

Your father's account describes his development of Virginia tobacco, the crop that has made this colony a financial success. I cannot express the enjoyment, I should say triumph, that he and I shared when we together smoked the first tobacco that he was able to raise using seed from the Indies. It was so unlike the native product as not to be comparable. I can think of no moment in my experience in the new world that I enjoyed more than his bringing forth that golden leaf here in Virginia.

I trust that your Uncle Henry shall keep these pages for you until you are able to read and understand them for yourself. When you do I hope that you will realize that it was the marriage of your parents, John Rolfe and Pocahontas, that began an interval of peace, from 1614 until 1622, during which time the Virginia colony became firmly established. For this, we in Virginia will forever be indebted to them.

I could not conclude these comments of praise for John Rolfe's contributions to the peace and prosperity of Virginia without mentioning his love of the freedom and opportunity that Virginia offered him. He truly appreciated the possibilities to be of service and the rewards of great effort that are available to any man fortunate enough to come to Virginia. Having said all this, I hope that you will appreciate the opportunity that awaits you here and will choose to live your life in Virginia. I look forward to greeting you when you come to receive your inheritance.

Your humble servant,

Ralph Hamor
Member,
The Governor's Council

~PARTIAL LIST OF CHARACTERS~

CAPTAIN SAMUEL ARGALL - Replaced Captain Christopher Newport as Admiral of Virginia, became Governor of the Virginia Colony

REVEREND WILLIAM BUCKE - Passenger aboard the *Seaventure,* minister at Jamestown, married John Rolfe and Pocahontas

SIR THOMAS DALE - Governor and Marshal of Virginia, campaigned against Powhatan and expanded the Virginia Colony to Henrico

LORD DE LA WARR - Appointed Governor for life of the Virginia Colony; his arrival resuscitated the settlers at Jamestown

SIR THOMAS GATES - Governor upon arrival of the *Seaventure* in Virginia, later brought significant reinforcements to the Virginia Colony

RALPH HAMOR - Passenger aboard the *Seaventure,* later Secretary of the Colony, friend of John Rolfe

DIEGO DE MOLINA - Leader of Spanish group seeking information about the Virginia Colony; was captured and detained in Jamestown

CHRISTOPHER NEWPORT - Admiral of Virginia who brought the first colonists to Jamestown and was captain of the *Seaventure*

OPECHANCANOUGH - Brother of Powhatan who exercised considerable influence in Powhatan's chiefdom

CAPTAIN GEORGE PERCY - Acting President of the Virginia Colony at arrival of the *Seaventure*, later Acting Governor

POCAHONTAS - Favorite daughter of Powhatan; also known as Matoaka and later as Lady Rebecca.

POWHATAN - Paramount Indian chief of the Tidewater Virginia area; his power had reached its zenith at the time of the arrival of the English

THOMAS ROLFE - Infant son of Rolfe and Pocahontas, accompanied them to England but did not return to Virginia until he had reached manhood

SIR GEORGE SOMERS - Admiral of the fleet which included the *Seaventure*, guided the colonists through their shipwreck and safe completion of their voyage to Virginia

WILLIAM STRACHEY - Passenger aboard the *Seaventure*, later Secretary of the Virginia Colony

TOMOCOMO - Brother-in-law of Pocahontas, sent by Powhatan to accompany Pocahontas to England

REVEREND ALEXANDER WHITAKER – Minister at Henrico, influenced education of Pocahontas, later at Bermuda Hundred

About the Author

James H. Tormey is a graduate of West Point and Princeton University. His career as military and civil engineer included an assignment as the Norfolk Army District Engineer in Virginia where he was intrigued by the exploits of early settlers in mapping the waters of Chesapeake Bay. Place names in tidewater Virginia still reflect the names of these settlers as well as the native American tribes who were a part of Chief Powhatan's empire.

He lives in Hampton, Virginia, where the original Virginia colonists stopped en route to Jamestown in 1607. His interest in early Virginia history led him to write a musical play about the first settlers and Pocahontas. More recently, he has served with a group of citizens who raised money to construct a museum devoted to the history of Hampton.

He and his wife Ann have two sons who live in Williamsburg and Yorktown.

Printed in the United States
80095LV00005B/24

9 780931 761355